To the memory of my Grandfather, Billy Clynes, a Durham soldier who fought and survived the Great War, to be the source of so many enthralling stories.

Paul Doherty was born in Middlesbrough. He studied History at Liverpool and Oxford Universities and obtained a doctorate for his thesis on Edward II and Queen Isabella. Paul is now headmaster of a school in north-east London, and has been awarded an OBE for his services to education. He lives with his family in Essex. Paul's first novel, THE DEATH OF A KING, was published in 1985. Since then he has gone on to write over one hundred books, covering a wealth of historical periods from Ancient Egypt to the Middle Ages and beyond.

To find out more, visit www.paulcdoherty.com

Praise for Paul Doherty's historical novels:

'Teems with colour, energy and spills' *Time Out*

'Deliciously suspenseful, gorgeously written and atmospheric' *Historical Novels Review*

'Supremely evocative, scrupulously researched'
Publishers Weekly

'An opulent banquet to satisfy the most murderous appetite' *Northern Echo*

'Extensive and penetrating research coupled with a strong plot and bold characterisation. Loads of adventure and a dazzling evocation of the past'
Herald Sun, Melbourne

By Paul Doherty

Novels

The Death of a King
Prince Drakulya
The Lord Count Drakulya
The Fate of Princes
Dove Amongst the Hawks
The Masked Man
The Rose Demon
The Haunting
The Soul Slayer
The Plague Lord
The Love Knot
Of Love and War
The Loving Cup
The Last of Days
Roseblood

Non-fiction

The Mysterious Death of Tutankhamun
Isabella and the Strange Death of Edward II
Alexander the Great, The Death of a God
The Great Crown Jewels Robbery of 1303
The Secret Life of Elizabeth I
The Death of the Red King

Series

Hugh Corbett Medieval Mysteries
Sorrowful Mysteries of Brother Athelstan
Sir Roger Shallot Tudor Mysteries
Kathryn Swinbrooke Series
Nicholas Segalla Series
Mysteries of Alexander the Great
The Templar Mysteries
Matthew Jankyn Series
Alexander the Great Mysteries
Canterbury Tales of Murder and Mystery
The Egyptian Mysteries
Mahu (The Akhenaten-Trilogy)
Mathilde of Westminster Series
Political Intrigue in Ancient Rome Series

ROSEBLOOD

PAUL DOHERTY

headline

First published in 2014 by
HEADLINE PUBLISHING GROUP

First published in paperback in 2014 by
HEADLINE PUBLISHING GROUP

1

Cataloguing in Publication Data is available from the British Library

ISBN 978 0 7553 9598 9

Typeset in Sabon LT Std by Palimpsest Book Production Limited,
Falkirk, Stirlingshire

Printed and bound in Great Britain by
Clays Ltd, St Ives plc

HEADLINE PUBLISHING GROUP
An Hachette UK Company
338 Euston Road
London NW1 3BH

www.headline.co.uk
www.hachette.co.uk

Historical Note

The reign of King Edward III of England (1327–77) sowed a dragon seed that came to bloody fruition generations later. At first, everything seemed fair and prosperous. Through his mother Isabella, Edward could exercise a claim to the throne of France; he ruthlessly pursued this, and so began that long season of strife known as the Hundred Years War. Edward's wife, Philippa, presented her husband with a gaggle of healthy sons. However, the eldest boy, the famous Black Prince, died before his father, leaving his ten-year-old son Richard as the English heir apparent.

When he acceded to power, Richard II proved to be autocratic and despotic, which led to an escalating crisis with his great lords, in particular his uncle, John of Gaunt. In 1399, John of Gaunt's son, Henry of Lancaster, deposed Richard and imprisoned him in Pontefract Castle, where he died. Henry succeeded to the throne as the fourth king of that name, claiming descent from Edward III through his father. The only problem was that the House of York also had a claim to the throne, through Gaunt's elder brother, Lionel, Duke of Clarence.

The House of Lancaster, however, crushed opposition at home, whilst Henry united the country in an all-out war against France, which reached its climax in his son's outstanding victory at Agincourt in October 1415.

Henry V died in 1422, to be succeeded by his nine-month-old son, Henry VI. As he developed, it became clear that the young prince was not of the same calibre as his father and grandfather. Henry VI was pious, a recluse, a man of peace rather than war. At times he experienced what were referred to as fits of madness, a mental condition he inherited from his mother, Katherine of Valois.

The war in France now proved to be a disaster that only increased unrest at home. The House of York, under its leader Richard, openly demanded control of the Council and the kingdom when Henry VI was judged incapable of ruling. Secretly, Richard of York, supported by his Neville allies, hungered for the crown, emphasising his rights both in fact and in law.

Henry VI's position was defended not so much by himself as by his charismatic and energetic young wife, Margaret of Anjou. The kingdom became divided. Margaret depended upon a faction of nobility, men like William de la Pole, Duke of Suffolk, but even more on her husband's cousins, the Beauforts, John and Edmund, first and second dukes of Somerset. The Beauforts claimed descent from Edward III through John of Gaunt and his mistress, Katherine Swynford; the Beaufort faction remained passionately devoted to the House of Lancaster.

By 1450, with defeat in France and growing unrest at home, the kingdom was slipping towards civil war . . .

Prologue

London, 22 May 1450

London was burning. The rebels had stormed the gatehouse on London Bridge, killing the redoubtable Captain of the Tower of London, Matthew Gough, before retreating to fire the suburbs and brighten the smoke-filled night sky with shooting flames of sinister red. Corpses lay piled on the approaches to the bridge, whilst the Thames, as it gushed towards the sea, shooting past the city docks and wharves, carried its own grisly harvest of cadavers, severed heads and shattered limbs. In the city churches, frightened congregations crouched before the soaring carved rood screens as their priests chanted the solemn words of the sequence from the requiem mass: 'Oh day of wrath, oh day of mourning, now take heed the Prophet's warning, heaven and earth in ashes burning.' No one dared leave the candle-flamed darkness. The aisles and transepts were crammed with the dying and the wounded. Women and children wailed piteously, their cries rising above the feverish ranting of those slipping into death. Everyone accepted that disaster had befallen the city.

The preachers were correct. The Four Horsemen of the Apocalypse had swept out of Kent, with Lord Death, on his pale horse, no less a person than Jack Cade, an Irishman and former soldier. Cade also rejoiced in the name of Jack Amend-All, and sometimes Mortimer, to show his kinship with the allies of the Duke of York. A man of blood, this self-proclaimed Captain of Kent was many things to many people. He had served in the retinue of Sir Thomas Dacre of Suffolk until forced to abjure the realm for killing a pregnant woman. He'd fled to France and fought against the English when they lost at Formigny and had to surrender Normandy. He later assumed the name of Lylner, married the daughter of a squire and posed for a while as a physician. Yet mischief does what mischief is. The Devil always comes into his own, and Cade certainly came into his. Lord Jack, as his henchmen called him, was Satan's own evil envoy, Hell's mist-strewn messenger. He was a sign of the times, the season of murder, theft and rapine.

An eerie, sinister figure, Cade first prowled the roads of Kent and Essex. Sometimes he called himself King of the Faerie Realm and preached hotly against the powers-that-be. On occasion, he would slip into the city. Rumour had it that he'd murdered two Hanse merchants from their enclosure at the Steelyard, who were found floating face down in the Thames. Others claimed he used to beg around St Paul's graveyard when he lived in Pie Powder Alley just off the Crutched Friars. He had even tried to trade musty velvet in a stinking dark shop; when this failed, he sold face washes of hog's gristle mixed with oil of cloves, to remove flushes from the face and prevent pimples from erupting. The lotions did more harm than good, so Cade turned to pimp and pander.

Nobody perceived Cade as a danger to the Crown until he allegedly received secret monies and the support of a cohort of mysterious French mercenaries whose livery was a dark red coat and a badge depicting a flying crow against a light blue field. Ragged mercenaries were flocking to England, but this cohort was special, well financed and armed. They called themselves LeCorbeil, and were reputed to be master bowmen, very skilled with the arbalests hanging by leather cords from their saddle horns. LeCorbeil were seen here and there, but mostly in the wastelands of Essex, north of London, lurking on the fringes of the dense sprawling forest of Epping. No one dared accost them. Rumour claimed they were here to support the Duke of York, and what could local levies do against such well-armed, professional mercenaries?

Nevertheless, Cade and LeCorbeil were not the root of the present evil; merely the offshoots of a deeper malignancy. The chroniclers in the monasteries and abbeys sat at their lamp-shrouded desks and described the true cause of the growing chaos: the King. They pricked the point of how Henry V, of not so blessed memory, that great punisher of the French, had died, his bowels turned to a filthy fluid amongst the marshes of Meaux, screaming into the darkness, 'No, no, my lot lies with the Lord Jesus.' Those present around the royal deathbed believed that the myriads Henry had slaughtered in northern France must have assembled to greet him on either side of that broad thoroughfare sweeping down into Hell.

Henry left a baby son, christened with the same name, born of tainted Valois stock; his mother was Queen Katherine, daughter of the mad Charles VI of France, who believed he was fashioned out of glass. Henry VI grew and matured, more sinned against than sinning, a holy man, living proof of the words of scripture: 'That the children of this world are more astute in dealing with their own kind than the children of the light.' Certainly a child of the light, who sat closer to the angels than many, Henry could not deal with the great warlords who snarled around him, though his beautiful, hot-tempered wife-queen, Margaret of Anjou, certainly could. Their marriage was one of milk and wine. Margaret was passionate in her pursuit and defence of her rights and those of her husband and family. She gathered to herself three great lords: William de la Pole, Duke of Suffolk; John Beaufort, Duke of Somerset; and the latter's brother Edmund. This precious trinity served as a living shield for Margaret, her husband and the entire House of Lancaster against the fervent ambitions of Richard Plantagenet, Duke of York, who believed himself to be the King's heir if Henry died without male issue. York also secretly considered that he had a better claim to the throne: the House of Lancaster only descended from the third son of Edward III, whilst the

House of York claimed descent from the second son, Lionel of Clarence.

The Year of Our Lord 1450 swept all of England's troubles to full bursting, and the putrid mess of failure, frustration, defeat and incompetence seeped out to taint the entire kingdom. When John Beaufort lost Normandy, the archers who'd proudly garrisoned the great castles and towns of northern France were shipped home humiliated, miserable and poor. Bishop Moleyns was sent by the Exchequer to meet these returning soldiers and pacify them. He took with him their long-overdue wages, but the archers thought the good bishop had not brought enough. They fell on Moleyns and cruelly murdered him. Worse came, swift and hard like the charge of a warhorse. The English were defeated at Formigny, and all of France except Calais was lost. The Commons at Westminster turned in fury on Suffolk and Somerset, determined to kill both. Dark souls steeped in malice plotted to seize the two dukes and sever their heads on Tower Hill.

Queen Margaret, who loved the Duke of Suffolk to distraction, urged him to flee abroad. On 30 April 1450, Suffolk, in disguise, embarked at Ipswich, but his flight was discovered by Richard of York. The French mercenary troop LeCorbeil suddenly appeared outside Dover. They hired a pirate cog, *The Nicholas of the Tower*, to stand off Dover Head and wait. Suffolk's ship was intercepted, and Queen Margaret's good duke resigned himself to death. A witch had prophesied that he would die at the Tower. Suffolk had always thought the allusion was to London's great fortress, but when he learnt the name of the ship bearing down on his, he lost all will to fight. He was arrested and taken aboard the cog, and after a brutal court-martial was thrust into the vessel's bumboat and made to kneel before a block. LeCorbeil gave a rusty sword to one of the pirates, who took the duke's head with a dozen hacking strokes. Suffolk's corpse was then left on the sands beneath Dover Castle, his severed head impaled on a pole, beside it the corpse of a crow.

LeCorbeil were not finished. Once Suffolk's grisly execution was known, rumours spread throughout the Kentish villages that the Sheriff of Kent and his father-in-law, Lord Saye, Treasurer of England, both Lancastrians body and soul and favourites of the Queen, were plotting revenge. They maintained that Kentish folk were responsible for Suffolk's murder and so should face devastation by fire and sword. According to a report coursing swiftly as a breeze through the shire, both Saye and the sheriff had sworn that Kent would be reduced to nothing more than a royal deer park. Alarmed by such vicious rumours, the country people of Kent flocked to the shire's May Day celebrations, which rapidly changed into commissions of array when all men capable of bearing arms were assembled. A deep fear descended. The black banners of anarchy were hoisted. Shouts of 'Harrow! Harrow!' echoed across the mustering grounds as the hue and cry was raised against so-called traitors 'intent on murdering the common people'.

It was at these May Day celebrations that Cade, taking the name of Mortimer, emerged, with the support of LeCorbeil, that mysterious company of French mercenaries. He and his army swept through Kent, camping at Blackheath and publishing their grievances. The rebel army denounced the King's advisers who had persuaded the royal mind against true lords such as the Duke of York, as well as against the King's faithful commons. They proclaimed how false councillors had lost royal land. How the King's merchants were greatly despoiled on both land and sea, and how the French were now raiding the southern coasts of England. They spread their message by proclamation and charter.

Armed bands from Surrey, Suffolk and Essex marched to join them under great flapping standards of red and black. In London, Queen Margaret mustered royal troops and sent them south against the rebels. Cade immediately withdrew to Sevenoaks. The royal vanguard under the two Stafford brothers hastily pursued him, intent on bringing the rebels to battle and utterly destroying them. Instead they clattered into an ambush, and both leaders and a host of their retinue were cruelly slaughtered. The rebels poured back into London. They forced the Constable of the Tower to hand over Lord Saye, who was immediately arraigned at the Guildhall and charged with treason.

The following morning, at eleven of the clock, Cade, along with some of LeCorbeil and others of his retinue, rode into the city. The self-proclaimed Great Captain, clad in a blue gown of velvet with sable furs, a straw hat on his head and a naked sword in his hand, ordered Saye to be dragged from the Guildhall and taken to the Standard in Cheapside. He was not even allowed to finish his confession to a priest before his hair was grabbed and his head severed and placed on a pole. Afterwards, his blood-soaked trunk was stripped, tied by the legs to the rear of a horse and dragged around the city, the poled head carried before it. Now and again the macabre procession would pause so that Saye's severed head could kiss that of his son-in-law, the Sheriff of Kent, whom the Essex bands had also caught and executed.

Such blasphemous desecration provoked opposition to Cade. On the night following Saye's murder, the mayor and certain aldermen decided to resist. Once Cade had withdrawn to Southwark, the city council fortified London Bridge. Fierce, resolute street fighting took place. Old grudges and grievances were settled. Householders opened their doors to find corpses dangling from shop signs and the eaves of their gabled homes. Murder prowled the streets; revenge, hatred and curdling resentment followed in its retinue. Long-buried blood feuds, their tangled roots deeply embedded, came to full poisonous flower.

Edmund Roseblood recognised that as he knelt on the filthy shale left by the retreating river tide. He moved on his knees, the small, sharp stones biting into his flesh. Hands tied behind his back, he stared up at the ripe summer moon and the glorious flowers of heaven. He wondered how his brother, Simon, and the rest of the family would be dealing with the malice of Cade, LeCorbeil and others of that coven. He himself had been tricked and betrayed. Guilt about the past and a desire to begin again now held him fast, and the hunter's snare could not be broken. Edmund Roseblood was about to die.

They had promised to be swift. He gazed at the three sinister figures before him, cowled and visored; their eyes, hard and cold, reflected their hate-filled souls and marble hearts. They had invoked a blood feud that was almost fifteen years old, ignoring his pleas of innocence. According to them, he had been at LeCorbeil when that French town was put to fire and sword. Others had paid; now, they claimed, so must he. They had provided a priest, some wretched hedge-parson shivering with terror, to shrive him before he died.

'You have one request, one favour.' LeCorbeil's voice was harsh.

Edmund stared at that sombre figure who had trapped him with such sweet promises. LeCorbeil was the name of a village, of a hideous massacre, and of a group of vengeance seekers. Each who sought revenge took on the LeCorbeil name in waging their blood feud. Edmund could only distinguish the leader of the coven by the snow-white coif beneath the deep hood. He closed his eyes and breathed in. Simon would avenge him; Simon always did, in his own time and in a place of his own choosing.

'You have one last boon, a final favour,' LeCorbeil repeated. 'More than you gave my people.'

'I am innocent.'

'No one is innocent. Well?'

Edmund indicated with his head. 'Untie my hands. Where can I go? To whom can I flee?'

LeCorbeil whispered an order. One of his company approached, boots crunching on the shale. Edmund felt the knife sawing at the bonds about his wrists. He shook these free, drawing himself up. He made sure his shirt collar was clear of his neck and caught a sob in his throat. Eleanor had sewn that collar. She had been there when he had put this shirt on.

'I'll stretch out my hands,' he shouted over his shoulder. 'Do it then.'

Edmund closed his eyes and summoned up Eleanor's sweet face, so perfectly formed: the arching brows, the lustrous grey eyes, the full lips he'd kissed so merrily. Yet Eleanor was the reason he was here. She had persuaded him to try and escape from the past, as well as from his own brother. Now all that was gone . . .

'May you walk the rest of your life in peace and friendship.' he whispered. 'May your path stretch long and straight before you. May the sun always be on your back. May you drink the cup of life in all its richness. May you see the length of days, and when your day is done, the shadows lengthen and the hush descends, come out to meet me as I will always wait for you.'

Edmund opened his eyes and stretched out his hands, and LeCorbeil's great two-handed sword severed his head in one clean cut.

Amadeus Sevigny

London, April 1455

Smithfield was in gloriously hideous turmoil. Executions always drew the crowds, especially when the sun burnt strong and a swift breeze wafted away some of the more pungent odours. The beggars had assembled in all their tawdry glory, with their lank bellies, hemp-like hair, hammer heads, beetle brows and bottled noses, their cheeks festooned with warts and carbuncles, their jagged teeth turning yellow or black. One of these ancient beauties, Pannikin, who styled himself a story-teller, perched on an overturned barrel to report the wondrous news from Oxford. According to Pannikin, a monster had been born with only one hand, one leg and no nose, with one eye in the centre of its forehead and its two ears sprouting from the nape of its neck. The crowd laughed this to scorn, as Pannikin was regarded as a born liar, twice as fit for Hell as any Southwark rogue.

A more enterprising character, Lazarus, named

because of the multitude of black spots that mottled his shrivelled face, was closely studying the clerk who stood next to the barber's stool under the sprawling ancient elm tree formerly used for hangings. A court clerk, Lazarus decided, scrutinising his intended victim's expensive dark robes and snowy-white cambric shirt, yet he had the shorn head, shaven face and harsh look of a soldier. Lazarus noted the war belt strapped around the clerk's slim waist, as well as the clinking silver spurs on his high-heeled Castilian riding boots. The scavenger's real quarry, however, was the bulging coin purse hanging by cords from that belt. Lazarus, a skilled foist and nip, drew his needle-thin dagger and edged closer.

The barber was shaving the head of a greasy kill-calf, a butcher from the Newgate shambles who had shuffled into Smithfield to walk among the cattle pens as well as see the condemned dancing in the air. Deep in his cups, he lashed out with his bloody fingers against the strings of false teeth the barber had tied to a overhanging branch that danced and clattered close to the flesher's face. Nearby, a Friar of the Sack thundered against the evils of drink, especially the London beers known as Mad-Dog, Angel's Food, Dragon's Milk and Merry-go-Dance. Unlike the hapless Pannikin, the friar had drawn a good audience, eager to be diverted in their wait for the execution carts. They stood and listened as he pointed out the many drunks staggering across the great open expanse before St Bartholomew's church, dismissing them as 'tosspots, swill bowls, drunken swine who'll end their day sleeping, snorting in their vomit, more fit for the dunghill than the house'. His makeshift congregation loved that. They would recall such rich language and use it themselves when they caroused to the chimes of midnight in some Cheapside tavern. The barber, however, roared for silence when his customer began to curse the friar, threatening to slice the butcher's nose and hang it alongside the dangling teeth.

A quiet did descend, even the dust billowing away, as a funeral cortège appeared on its way to St Andrew Undershaft. Sir Richard Workin, knight and merchant tailor, recently departed, was being escorted to his requiem mass with torches, tapers, pennants and glorious banners all festooned with the insignia of his guild and carried by squires clothed in black worsted livery and blood-red hoods. A priest, garbed in a black and gold chasuble, preceded the coffin, carrying a cross. Beside him walked two altar boys, one carrying a lofty beeswax candle whilst the other lustily swung a thurible, which incensed the air with the most fragrant smoke. Every so often the procession would pause so that one of the livery men could bawl out, 'Rest be to his ashes. He tailored well and served God and his guild.' As if in answer, a distant church bell began to toll.

Once the mourners were gone, the tumult across Smithfield broke out even more stridently. Lazarus seized his opportunity. He scuttled closer to his prey, who turned, deep-set eyes watchful. Lazarus prided himself on both his patter and his skill. He held his cutter very close to his side as he began his beggar's chant.

'For the love of God . . .' His left hand, all scabbed and wrinkled, went out to distract his prey. 'Look at me, Lord, with merciful eye, so lamed by a cankerous worm that gnaws the flesh from my bones—' He stopped abruptly as the clerk brought up his cleverly concealed Italian stiletto with its long, wicked-looking blade and sharp dagger point. He pressed its serrated edge against Lazarus's neck.

'Sir,' the clerk's voice was soft, 'I recognise you. You are Lazarus, leader of a pack of scavengers who prowl Queenhithe ward. You are known for your thievery and your brutality. You see, sir, I have been there and watched you.' He pressed on the dagger. 'Because I am Amadeus Sevigny, nephew of Sir Philip Malpas, sheriff of this city. A former schoolman of Balliol Hall in Oxford, serjeant of law, trained by the Crown and now principal clerk in the secret chancery of Richard, Duke of York. I am here to watch the execution of one gang of malefactors and go hunting for another. You, sir, have a knife in your right hand. You intend me harm. I have introduced myself, so when you enter Hell, you can inform Lord Satan who sent you there.'

Lazarus lunged, but he was too slow. Sevigny's dagger opened the beggar's throat in one swipe, and the blood spurted out like juice from a split ripe plum. Sevigny took a step closer, watching the soul light die in Lazarus's eyes. He caught the beggar as he slumped to his knees, and laid him gently on the mud-strewn cobbles. The sight of blood drew in the crowd. A woman screamed. Someone shouted, 'Harrow!' even as Sevigny rose to his feet, hands extended, one holding his own knife, the other that of the dying man.

'Self-defence!' he cried. 'I am a clerk, tonsured and protected by Holy Mother Church, henchman of his Grace the Duke of York.' He pointed down at Lazarus, still jerking slightly in his death throes. 'This man attempted murder.'

'I was witness to that.' A group of serjeants, all wearing the red and white livery of the city, now pushed their way through. Their leader, Skulkin, a burly, pig-faced man, grasped the thick leather belt attached to the collar of a great war mastiff; its huge jaws were tightly muzzled, though the fury raging in its red-brown eyes was frightening enough. 'I witnessed that,' the chief bailiff repeated, his words being chorused by his companions.

No one objected. Those sharp-eyed and keen-witted enough glimpsed the chancery ring on Sevigny's left hand, as well as his silver-gilt-embossed sword in its embroidered scabbard. The crowd drifted away. Black-robed members of the Fraternity of the Hanged moved in to place Lazarus's corpse on a stretcher and take it to the waiting paradise cart for burial in some poor man's lot. Sevigny went back to studying the thronging crowd. He lifted a gloved hand, beckoning the chief bailiff closer.

'I cannot see our quarry,' he murmured, 'but he must come here. Sir Philip is sure of that.'

'And the scavenger?'

'Lazarus?' Sevigny wiped the blade of his dagger on

Skulkin's sleeve. 'He may have intended to kill me, or just rob me. I have recently arrived here, Master Skulkin. My reputation is not yet known.' He grinned boyishly. 'Though it is time it was. Lazarus was a help in that. He drew a dagger and crept up on me. You, Master Skulkin, were sent to guard me. Next time,' Sevigny leaned down and patted the mastiff on its huge bony head, 'next time it may be *your* throat. Now tell your comrades to keep strict watch. Four of the gang are to be executed as traitors; however, their leader Candlemas and two of his henchmen escaped.'

'And the Lord Sheriff thinks they will come here to watch their comrades being turned off?'

'Sir Philip does think that, and I tend to agree,' Sevigny retorted, standing on tiptoe, eyes on the great wooden scaffold on its dais. The fires in the braziers either side of the soaring four-branched gallows were now being blown fiercer by a blacksmith with his bellows. 'They will come,' Sevigny declared. 'Felons always do, as a last courtesy to their comrades. Most of the gangs of London are represented here.'

'But they have not been seen in the city, whilst Simon Roseblood would not dare shelter them.'

'Oh they are in the city all right!' Sevigny laughed softly, staring across the shoal of people thronging the spacious marketplace. 'Oh yes, they are here, Skulkin.' The clerk tapped his boot on the hard-packed earth. 'I suspect they are very close. Perhaps even beneath us. Stay vigilant. Candlemas will come like a thief in the night.'

'How will we recognise him?'

'Look for three Friars of the Sack who go cowled, faces down, hands in the sleeves of their gowns.'

'Master Sevigny?'

'I know. Such friars are common at executions, but these three will be different. They will not seem as interested as they should be in the people around them.'

Sevigny fell silent and stared around. Lazarus's corpse had now been removed. The noise of the marketplace had grown to a true babel of clamour, shouts and screams. Somewhere horns blew and bagpipes shrilled as malefactors were led to the great stocks, thews and pillories on the far side of Smithfield. Traders and hucksters bawled out the sale of spiced bread, custard suckets and portingales. There were shouts about spices and salt from Worcester being available, along with pepper mills, hot oatcakes, brooms, the latest mousetraps as well as the best protection against fleas. Vendors offered stopples for garderobes in order to keep the feet warm whilst sitting on the jakes. These raucous boasts and invitations rang above the lowing of cattle and the bloodcurdling scream of hogs being driven down to the slaughter pens.

Sevigny, a mailed clerk who had stood in the shield wall of York's forces in France, carefully studied the shifting currents among the crowd. He noted the various colours and watched any individual who caught his curiosity: the black-robed monk with his shaven pate blistering in the sun; the juggler with his pet monkey sitting on his shoulder; the moon man in his cheap glittering finery; archers, sweaty in their leather jerkins, on leave from the Tower. He wondered what his own escort, Bowman Bardolph, would be doing. Perhaps he should have brought him here. He dismissed the thought. Bardolph was a taciturn, morose Dalesman who seemed to resent even being with him. Sevigny chewed the corner of his lip. And Argentine, Giles Argentine, that elusive former royal physician? Would he dare venture out into a place like this? No, too dangerous, Sevigny concluded.

Abruptly a trumpet blast stilled all clamour and movement. A further shrill clarion call caught everyone's attention. On the far side of Smithfield, close to the thoroughfare leading up to Cock Lane, Greyfriars and the towering Mass of St Paul's, city banners and pennants were fluttering in the breeze. Horsemen appeared. Serjeants in their polished brigandines; archers with glistening sallets on their heads, longbows slung across their backs. Immediately on the high gallows stage, the towering cressets, iron baskets crammed with logs, coals, pitch and tar, were set alight. The executioners, garbed in black leather, their faces hidden behind devils' masks with projecting silver horns, climbed their ladders to stand beneath the gallows. The crowd glimpsed these and the cry went up.

'The condemned are here! Hats off, heads bare!'

Sevigny pushed his way through the throng, almost oblivious to the hurdy-gurdy around him: the fiddlers, the tumblers, the painted dwarves who bawled how they had the horse of knowledge and a learned pig in a makeshift booth nearby. Other grotesques appeared before him: the stone-eater, the fire-swallower, the self-proclaimed magicians in black gowns spangled with gold. All these were now being ignored as a more macabre masque was about to unfold. Sevigny kept his eyes on the scaffold. Escorted by the bailiffs, their great war mastiff Caradoc padding like fury incarnate, he reached the cordon of soldiers. The undersheriffs in their long gowns were already forming a ring around the execution biers, leather sledges, each carrying a bound prisoner, naked except for a loincloth, pulled by sturdy plough horses, their hogged manes festooned with ribbon.

People were shouting and screaming. The executioner's assistants scrambled down like imps from Hell to assist. The prisoners, groaning and crying after their long and brutal haul along the sharpened cobbles, covered in hideous bruises, were released from their hurdles, pushed up the scaffold steps and forced to face the people. A herald, garbed in a glorious tabard boasting the city arms, proclaimed them to be outlaws and traitors. He described how they had attacked a comitatus taking silver to the Tower mint and feloniously killed a royal serjeant. How they must have been suborned by the Devil to commit such horrid treason and so were deserving of death. He cleared his throat before continuing to describe how the condemned would be half hanged, their bodies sliced open and their entrails and hearts plucked out to be burnt before their eyes, after which their heads would be severed and their bodies quartered, then boiled and tarred so that they could decorate the gates of the city.

The herald's powerful voice pealed out over the shouting and crying, the lamentations, the songs of mourning and the psalms for the dead. Beside Sevigny, a ballad monger bawled out his doggerel verse:

> Think sinners on your sins all seven,
> Think how merry it is in heaven.
> So pray to God and with him stay
> So he will forgive you on Domesday.

The prisoners were more concerned about the executioners now painting blue lines on their naked white bodies where they intended to make the cuts. Nooses were lowered and placed around necks, ladders brought. Fire and smoke billowed. The shouting rose to a roar. Jongleurs chanted about the day of desolation. The prisoners began to scream as the ropes were roughly hauled up by the sweaty executioners. Bodies danced, legs kicked, feet fluttering for the ground.

Sevigny did not watch; he never could. It reminded him of his own swift, brutal brush with death's dark cloak on that lonely moonlit road in Normandy. Even now, years later, he could recall the Jacquerie, the rebel French peasants, milling about him, the noose tight about his throat, hands bound behind his back, his horse moving perilously beneath him, the rope tightening. His breath had choked until those goose-quilled arrow shafts came whipping out of the darkness . . .

He opened his eyes, trying to ignore the hideous choking sound coming from the scaffold above him. The air reeked of blood, fire and iron. Plumes of dark smoke eddied. Sevigny recalled a grotesque vision of Hell on a church wall outside Formigny. 'Stop, stop!' he whispered to himself. He tried to concentrate on the crowd. More shrill screams from the scaffold as the condemned had their bodies split open.

'Jesu miserere!' a woman shouted. A Franciscan began to recite the absolution. Horses neighed and reared at the stench of fresh blood. The city archers guarding the scaffold plucked at their bowstrings. People shoved and pushed; a few turned away to vomit.

Sevigny stared around and glimpsed three friars, cowls pulled forward to shield their faces, dressed in mud-coloured robes, sandals on their feet, hands hidden in their sleeves. He and his bailiffs started forward. A relic seller, bearing scraps of parchment that had allegedly touched the True Cross, was pushed aside. The man screeched. One of the hooded figures raised his head, his cowl sliding back to reveal the fiery red hair and thin, candle-white face that gave Candlemas his nickname. He stared at Skulkin and Sevigny, then plucked the sleeves of this companions and all three turned and fled, even as the first of the condemned screamed his last.

Sevigny burst into a run, followed by the bailiffs, knocking aside everyone in their path. They pursued Candlemas and his coven up the slight hill, the Compter on one side, Cock Lane on the other. The mouth of this notorious alleyway was packed with prostitutes, faces painted under fire-red wigs, bodies garbed in garish gowns. They hooted and hurled all kinds of obscenities at the fleeing felons. Candlemas and his two companions turned down a runnel, a stinking narrow alleyway, a black tunnel that twisted beneath the decaying houses leaning over either side. At the sound of pursuit, windows were shut, shutters pulled fast and doors slammed.

At the bottom of the alleyway stood a tavern; the peeling sign above a narrow doorway proclaimed it to be the Key to Heaven. The fugitives disappeared inside. Sevigny, following, kicked the door open and entered the dingy low-beamed taproom. Rush lights gleamed on overturned barrels. An oil lamp, slung on a wall hook, glittered through the gloom. Shadows jerked and vermin scuttled through the mush of filthy reeds on the floor.

'Where?' Sevigny walked across to the common table squeezed between stacks of barrels.

'Where what?' replied the lean-faced tapster.

'Hang him!' Sevigny stepped back. 'Put a rope over the rafters and hang him for being caught red-handed sheltering fleeing traitors. Hang him!' he repeated, pointing to one of the rafters.

Skulkin hastily found a rope; one end was sifted over a blackened beam, the onions and hams dangling there knocked aside. A noose was slipped around the hapless tapster's neck as he struggled, fighting the bailiffs who hoisted him on to one of the barrels. Skulkin kicked this away, and for a few heartbeats the man danced in the air. Then Sevigny sliced the rope with his sword and the fallen tapster, face all red and sweaty, eyes popping, gestured at a door across the tavern.

'There,' he gasped. 'I will take you.'

Skulkin hustled him to his feet. They went through the cellar door, down stone steps. The floor below was sloppy with wine and ale seeping from barrels and casks. A filthy cobwebbed path ran between these; at the far end stood a huge rounded vat. The sweating, gasping tapster pulled this aside to reveal a darkened tunnel. Even from where he stood, Sevigny could hear the clatter of those he pursued.

'Release Caradoc!'

Skulkin obeyed. The mastiff's muzzle was removed, the leash untied and Caradoc darted like a demon into the darkness. Sevigny and the others followed, carrying fluttering lamps, pausing to light the sconce torches fixed into wall crevices. The tunnel was narrow, its ceiling just above their heads, and the walls either side glistened with damp mould. An offensive stench caught mouth, nose and throat. One of the bailiffs murmured that it was an old sewer built by the ancients, a truly macabre place. Now and again they would pass mounds of bones glistening white like snow, tangled skeletons that rattled as the horde of rats nesting there fled from the light.

The gasps and groans of Sevigny's escort were abruptly silenced by a deep bell-like bellowing.

'Caradoc's trapped them,' Skulkin explained.

As if in answer, further chilling growls echoed, followed by hideous screams. The bailiffs hastened on, a mob of men in the dim flickering light. Sevigny followed cautiously. He and his uncle, Sir Philip Malpas, had discussed Candlemas's apparent disappearance from the city. The sheriff's lurchers, the two bounty hunters Cosmas and Damian, had informed him about these tunnels that ran under Smithfield and led directly to the Great Sanctuary in St Paul's graveyard; they were the refuge of outlaws and wolfsheads, who could claim ancient privileges against officers of the law. Candlemas and his two companions must have thought they were safe down here, but Caradoc had neatly trapped them, forcing them like fleeing sheep into an enclave. The only protection they carried was torches and knives. Caradoc now lay crouched before them, ready to spring at any aggressive move by his quarry. One of the three had apparently tried to resist and been ferociously savaged, his belly ripped open. The wounded felon lay in a brimming pool of blood, groaning and pleading.

'Well, my friends.' Sevigny stepped into the torchlight. 'Master Candlemas, former priest, is it not? You're well known for your disguise as a Friar of the Sack. I did wonder whether you would let members of your coven die alone. You couldn't resist the challenge, could you? And these two must be your accomplices. Devil-Drawer, a failed painter, and Cross-Biter, one of London's finest pimps and panders. All three of you have a bounty on your head. Silence!' he shouted at Devil-Drawer; the wounded felon was now screaming in agony. 'All three of you are wanted dead or alive, and you can't claim sanctuary. Oh, for the love of silence.'

Sevigny drew his dagger, bent over Devil-Drawer and swiftly sliced the wounded man's throat from ear to ear. Devil-Drawer kicked and gargled, choking on his own blood until he fell silent.

'As I was saying . . .' Sevigny stared at the remaining two terrified felons. 'You can join your friends on the scaffold, or I could let Caradoc rip you to shreds. Or . . .' He paused.

'Or what?' Candlemas took a step forward, only to halt as this terrifying clerk raised his dagger.

'You could turn King's Approver and win yourself a pardon. Obtain some money and cross the Narrow Seas for ever.'

'And whom do we accuse?'

'Why,' Sevigny smiled, 'Master Simon Roseblood!'

Simon Roseblood

London, April 1455

Simon Roseblood, vintner, taverner and alderman of Queenhithe ward on the north bank of the Thames, rose from the great throne-like chair in the sacristy of his parish church of All Hallows. Roseblood had many titles. He had sealed indentures with the city council to manage, control and direct all the scavengers, rakers and gongmen in each of the city wards. His enemies called him Duke of the Cesspool and Lord of the Bum-Pit. They claimed that his family escutcheon should be a huge blue-arsed fly feeding on a turd. Naturally they dared not say that to his face. Simon Roseblood was a London lord, one with fingers in many pies, a man who filled his goblet at numerous fountains. Now he stopped in front of the great sacristy table and stared at his own reflection in the highly polished piece of metal that served as a mirror.

'Recognise yourself, Roseblood?' he murmured.

He stood for a while studying the lean lined face,

the skin all shaven, the silver-threaded black hair combed back over his broad forehead, the slightly slanted green eyes, the stubborn mouth and chin. He patted the quilted russet jerkin and checked the points on his bottle-green hose. He fastened his sword belt and swung the pure dark blue woollen cloak about his shoulders. Then he eased off the soft buskins and, hopping from foot to foot, quietly cursing, put on his boots and straightened up.

The rest of the parish council had left. The day was drawing on. Soon the Vespers bell would toll and the beacon fires proclaiming the curfew would flare into life at the top of the church tower, to be answered by other beacons in steeples throughout the city. Roseblood stared around the sacristy, checking that all was well. The massive aumbry for storing vestments in all the varieties of liturgical colours had been clasped shut. The solid carved parish chest was firmly locked; Roseblood, as church warden and wine bearer, carried one of only three keys to it. Everything was in order: the polished card table, the caskets and coffers, the brilliantly hued triptych on one wall, a huge replica of the San Damiano Cross on the other. Roseblood quietly translated the Latin inscription on the polished oak tablet beneath the crucifix. 'Sacred to the memory of John Beaufort, first Duke of Somerset, Captain General of the King's forces in France . . . All gone,' he murmured to himself.

He left the sacristy and wandered into the darkened sanctuary. He scrutinised the high altar with its heavy bejewelled velvet frontal; the polished oak chair and quilted stools for the celebrant and his assistants; the altar crucifix of gold and ivory flanked by two tall candlesticks of precious metal holding the purest beeswax candles. At each corner of the altar rose an oaken column, highly decorated, with a transverse beam above; along this stood silver-gilt statues of Christ, the Virgin Mary and Roseblood's patron, Simon Peter. From the beam hung a rich tapestry, embroidered with gold and silver thread, portraying the Marriage at Cana. His gaze was caught by the dazzle of light from the stained-glass windows high in the sanctuary wall depicting scenes from the life of St Peter: fishing on the Sea of Galilee and confronting the warlock Simon Magus among them.

Roseblood flinched at an unexpected sound further down the darkened nave. The doors, except for the corpse door, should be locked. Eleanor would be praying in her anchorhold, the Swan's-Nest, a converted chapel in the northern transept. Of course Ignacio, Roseblood's deaf-mute henchman, that subtle shadow of a man, would be watching from the darkness; these were dangerously fraught times. Roseblood tapped his dagger hilt. He had heard the rumours. How those two miscreants Candlemas and Cross-Biter had been taken and hidden away. How Malpas, that conniving sheriff, had promised them a pardon if they turned King's Approver. Roseblood's spy had given him dire warnings about what was being planned. How the sheriff had been joined by his kinsman Amadeus Sevigny, York's man, a mailed clerk with a reputation for being a ruthless blood-seeker.

Roseblood breathed in as he prayed for protection. He left the sanctuary, going under the exquisitely sculpted oaken rood screen. At the bottom of the sanctuary steps he genuflected towards the glowing red sanctuary light in its mother-of-pearl glass case hanging on the end of a silver chain next to the richly jewelled pyx under its silken canopy. He turned as the corpse door in the far transept opened. A figure stood against the light, a fearsome spectre, his cloak fanning out like the wings of a bat.

'Who are you?' Roseblood caught his breath. Something about this stranger frightened him, as if he exuded a miasma of fear.

'Amadeus Sevigny. Clerk and henchman of His Grace, Richard, Duke of York, special envoy to Sir Philip Malpas, sheriff of London, now his adviser on certain, how shall I say, delicate issues.' Sevigny approached and extended a hand. Roseblood did not grasp it; he just raised his own as if in greeting and let it drop.

'As you wish,' Sevigny murmured. He jabbed a finger, 'You sir, must be Master Simon Roseblood, alderman.' He waved a hand. 'Et cetera, et cetera. And you have just signalled to your constant shadow, the deaf-mute Ignacio, not to do anything foolish, which makes me think that both of you are wise men.' He paused as the corpse door opened and a small, fat-faced man waddled into the nave. 'This,' Sevigny didn't even turn, 'is Walter Ramler, city official and personal scribe to Sir Philip Malpas.'

'I know who he is,' Roseblood retorted. He was wary of Sevigny. A raven, he concluded, darkly garbed, be it his boots, hose, padded doublet or cloak; the only relief was the collar and cuffs of the white cambric shirt beneath. Sevigny's face was saturnine, sallow and lean, his black hair closely cropped. He was tall, slender and wiry. A handsome man, though his full lips seemed ready to sneer and those clever eyes eager to mock.

'Ignacio is here, Master Roseblood?'

'Very close.'

'Italian, is he not?'

'Castilian. Captured as a child by the Moors, trained as a Janissary. Rescued by me when—'

'The late but not so lamented Duke of Somerset's war cog intercepted a galley near the Pillars of Hercules, close to the entrance to the Middle Seas. He was chained, was he not? The galley was capsizing; you were on its fighting platform. You could not bear to see a chained man drown.'

'He pleaded with his eyes,' Roseblood answered. 'You seem to know a great deal about me.'

'Oh, I do, I do.' Sevigny peeled off his leather gloves.

'And your business?'

'In a while, Master Roseblood, though I suspect you already suspect why I am here, which makes us all highly suspicious. Oh, by the way, I must inform you: like your good self and Master Ignacio, I know the sign language you learnt from the Carthusians, that unspoken tongue they use during their Magnum Silentium, the Great Silence.' Sevigny was now so close, Roseblood could smell the clerk's fragrant perfume whilst also noting the healed scars on that clever face.

'A good cook, Ignacio.' Sevigny raised his eyebrows. 'Or so I understand. He buys well. He can tell an ancient hen or pheasant by its sunken eyes or the stink of its beak. A clean cook, who insists the spit be regularly scrubbed with sand and water. His speciality is a chine of beef or a fresh young capon—'

'Master Sevigny, why are you here?'

'The Chantry Chapel of the Doom? The place where your late departed brother—'

'Murdered brother!'

'Where your late brother lies buried.' Sevigny spread his hands. 'I would like to pay my respects.'

Roseblood stared at this sinister clerk, then led him into the darkness. He paused and stared down the nave, glimpsing a shadow deeper than the rest close to the baptismal font. Ignacio was watching. Roseblood nodded at Ramler, the scribe, and led Sevigny towards the side chapel that had been transformed into a chantry dedicated to his dead brother's memory. Here, behind the ornately sculpted gleaming oak screen, with its carved bosses and geometric shapes, mass was offered for the repose of the soul of Edmund Roseblood, a daily occurrence just before the Angelus bell tolled.

Roseblood pushed open the heavy elm-wood door. The chapel inside was an island of peace and light, the air fragrant with the perfume of beeswax and incense. Immediately facing them was a table tomb surmounted by a carved life-size replica of the dead man in his guild robes. The Purbeck marble sepulchre was positioned just beneath a round rose window, which caught the light so that a vivid array of blues, reds, greens and golds bathed the square chapel in its own special glory. To the right of the entrance stood the altar, now covered in a silver-fringed purple mantle; above it hung a stark black crucifix, and two prie-dieux stood before the dais. On the far wall, a gorgeously painted fresco proclaimed the exploits of John Beaufort, first Duke of Somerset. In the corner, to the left of the altar, stood a replica of the statue of Our Lady of Walsingham, beneath its plinth a polished bronze stand for candles and tapers.

'Truly exquisite. Truly exquisite,' Sevigny breathed. He knelt beside the tomb, which bore statues of four carved mourners, cowled and cloaked, along its side. The shoulders of each statue bore the Beaufort arms, very similar to those of the King except for the black bar sinister, the sign of illegitimacy, which cut diagonally across. After a while, he rose and peered at the doves of the dawn carved on each corner of the tomb, whispering:

> My heart is ready, oh God.
> My heart is ready.
> To sing your praises, I will sing your praises.
> Awake my soul,
> Awake harp and lyre
> I will awake the dawn!

He turned and smiled brilliantly at Roseblood. 'Like you, Simon, I was educated by the Benedictines, though at Fountains Abbey on the beautiful moorlands of Yorkshire. You have been there?' Roseblood shook his head. 'No, no, of course not, you are from the West Country, yes? Glastonbury, beneath the soaring tor, a place of mystery.'

'You slew Lazarus, one of my principal scavengers!'

'I am the clerk of Richard, Duke of York. Lazarus drew against me, so I killed him.'

'And Candlemas?'

'In a short while, Master Simon. For the moment . . .' Sevigny fished into his purse, drew out two coins and put these into the poor box, a small iron chest screwed to the wall beneath the statue of the Virgin. He then lit two tapers and smiled at Roseblood. 'For your brother! Let us also say the requiem.'

Roseblood joined him in the prayer. He now recognised the subtle soul of this adversary, a veritable smiler who kept a dagger close beneath his cloak. He also wondered why Ramler, the sheriff's scribe, still stood waiting patiently in the nave. Sevigny crossed himself and studied the wall fresco depicting Beaufort's exploits in France.

'Very good, very accurate.' He pointed to a part of the painting that showed the duke, holding a staff and dressed in pilgrim's garb, being helped into a small boat by a sturdy shipman. 'Just like Suffolk was,' Sevigny whispered. 'You know, Master Simon, when he was caught off Dover and beheaded.' He turned abruptly.

'What truly happened to your brother? He too was a great friend of Beaufort.'

'He was murdered.' Roseblood retorted, hand falling to his dagger. 'My brother was seized and slain when Cade's men invaded the city. I truly don't know why or by whom. When we found his corpse and severed head, we also found a dead crow pinned to a pole.' He paused. 'The Norman French for crow is *corbeil*. A cohort of French mercenaries now in England, serving in your master's retinue, enjoy the same name.'

'There was also a town in Normandy called LeCorbeil where a hideous massacre took place. I just wonder sometimes whether this is all connected, like beads on a string.'

'Perhaps you know more than I do,' Simon said quietly, 'about these hirelings.'

'Many people,' Sevigny glanced away, 'pretend to act on behalf of my master Richard of York. The same could be said for Beaufort and his coven.'

'I was born on Beaufort's estates in the West Country,' Simon replied. 'I entered his household. I became his henchman by sealed indentures. I swore to be his man body and soul, in peace and war. I served him in France, where my brother and I witnessed the aftermath of the massacre at LeCorbeil.'

'You also won numerous ransoms to build your fortune.'

'As did many.'

'You saw Joan of Arc, the Maid of Orleans, burnt in Rouen?'

'I was a stripling at the time.'

'Then you came home to build your empire in London, strongly supported by Beaufort. I mean, until his mysterious death. Suicide?' Sevigny cocked his head to one side. 'You must know the rumour? How John Beaufort, first Duke of Somerset, was recalled in disgrace from France and replaced by Richard of York. Some people say he could not accept the humiliation and took his own life.' Sevigny paused. 'They also say that a dead crow was found near his corpse, just like your brother's.'

'I believe Beaufort could have been murdered.'

'Of course you would.' Sevigny nodded. 'You would believe the best of him, wouldn't you, as I do of York. I was the only son of doting parents.' Sevigny's face abruptly changed; just for a fleeting moment, a deep sadness softened his hard expression. 'They held manor and meadow from the Duke of York. During the early, tumultuous days of Beaufort's regency, the manor was attacked; my parents were murdered. York took me into his household. He hunted down my parents' murderers and hanged them before Micklegate Bar in York. He also educated me at Fountains Abbey, then the halls of Oxford. So we have a great deal in common, Master Roseblood: both loyal servants to our lords.'

'Put not your trust in princes,' Eleanor's voice thrilled from the Swan's-Nest, 'nor your confidence in the war chariots of Egypt, nor the swift horses of Assyria. Blessed be the Lord God of Israel who prepares my arms for battle and trains my hands for war . . .'

'My good sister-in-law, Eleanor,' Simon murmured. 'She heard your words. This church has a strange echo.'

'Ah yes, the recluse, the anchorite. Why is she so?'

'Master Sevigny, that is her business, not yours, and I am very busy. I have listened to you long enough. Why are you here?'

'They say you are a dangerous man, Simon,' Sevigny answered blithely. 'A taverner, a vintner, an alderman, but also lord of the dunghill and the latrine. The knight of the night soil. You control the scavengers who swarm through the filthy alleys of London. They clean the guts, filth and bloody rubbish of the shambles. They pile the dirt of the city into muck hills and middens.'

'And?' Roseblood demanded.

'You have spies in every ward, Master Simon. Your minions of the mollocks collect the gossip, spread the rumours and fan the flames. Your adherents jostle, mix and crackle with the rest of the mob.'

Sevigny wiped the sweat from his upper lip. Simon smiled to himself; this clerk might claim to know a great deal about him, but he did not understand him. Never once had Sevigny managed to provoke him. The clerk turned away. Simon was sure he was trying to compose himself.

'Master Sevigny, I am waiting.' Simon deliberately kept his voice light. 'We have danced and curtseyed, flattered and threatened. Now, your business or I walk away.'

Sevigny opened the door to the chantry chapel. 'Master Walter!' he shouted. The scribe hurried out of the shadows, head down, one hand held high. 'Serve it!'

The scribe thrust a warrant, folded and sealed, into Simon's hand.

'Master Simon Roseblood,' Sevigny declared, 'you stand accused of treason, robbery, murder and other heinous felonies. You are summoned by lawful writ to present yourself at the Guildhall in two days' time, before the market bell sounds, when a true bill of indictment will be laid against you.' Sevigny let the legal terms roll off his tongue. 'A jury will assemble and you will be indicted to appear before a special commission of oyer and terminer sitting in the same Guildhall. For the moment,' he lazily waved a hand, 'you are free. However, at your first meeting at the Guildhall, heavy recognisances will be demanded of you.'

Sevigny pushed Ramler out of the chapel. Roseblood followed them to the corpse door, trying to curb his anger.

'Sevigny?' he called.

The clerk turned.

'Listen well. Tell you and yours that this is *à l'outrance*, *usque ad mortem*, to the death.'

Sevigny sketched a bow, fingers on the hilt of his sword, and left the church. Simon closed the door and leaned against it, the parchment still in his hands. He crumpled it into a ball, put it into his purse and walked back into the chantry chapel. 'To the death,' he whispered. Fury surged within him. He had been baited, taunted and threatened here at the very heart of his life.

He glimpsed a shadow shift to his right, and Ignacio moved into the pool of light. The Castilian was thin and angular, eyes worried in his dark-lined face, hands tapping the war belt around his waist. Roseblood winked at him and made a sign: 'Peace and goodness.' Ignacio relaxed, his fingers flickering and fluttering as he described what he'd seen and felt. Roseblood sensed the Castilian's profound anxiety. Amadeus Sevigny was truly dangerous, and they were involved in a fight to the death. Using signs, he told Ignacio all he had learnt, both from the clerk and from his own spy in the sheriff's household: Candlemas and Cross-Biter had turned King's Approver; they would probably indict him, serve as witnesses against him, so they must die. Ignacio's reply was swift and brutal: they would!

Roseblood watched him leave. Ignacio would certainly take care of it. Candlemas and Cross-Biter might think they were safe in the Shadows of Purgatory, a special house put aside for important prisoners, which stood along an alleyway off Cheapside. Ignacio would prove them wrong.

As Roseblood crossed the nave, walking down to the anchorite's cell, his gaze was caught by a wall painting, *The Torments of Hell*, a compelling vision of the damned. A horde of demons, hairy, humpbacked creatures with swollen bellies and bulging calves and buttocks, prowling a blighted wasteland. Trying to clear his mind of Sevigny's threats, he crouched to study the various colours, noting how the demons, half human, half animal, were in constant conflict with the golden-haloed, sword-wielding angels.

'What are you, Simon Roseblood, angel or demon?' Eleanor the anchorite could glimpse him through the squint gap of her cell.

'A mere man,' Roseblood replied, walking towards the Swan's-Nest. 'A very tired, rather worried one. My sleep is disturbed by demons and my waking hours by those who hate me.'

'Then come and be shriven.'

Roseblood approached the anchorhold. This had once been another side chapel, but he had persuaded the parish priest, Father Benedict, to remove the wooden trellis screen and replace it with a heavy stone wall containing both a squint and a narrow door under a black Hospitaller cross. Now the door opened and Eleanor ushered him into the Swan's-Nest. Sunlight poured through the large window high in the wall, its shutters pulled fully back.

Eleanor smiled at him, her beautiful ivory-pale face framed by a starched white wimple beneath the brown veil of a nun of St Clare. She ushered him to the only chair, while she sat on a stool close to his knees. Embarrassed, as he always was by this woman whom he loved, had loved and would love beyond all telling, Roseblood stared round as if seeing the simple contents of the cell for the first time. A cot bed stood beneath the window, next to it a table that also served as a desk. A diptych depicting the Five Wounds of Christ and the Seven Sorrows of Mary hung on the wall alongside a coloured cloth proclaiming the Jesus Prayer beneath the Franciscan Tauist symbol. He shuffled his feet on the coarse rope matting and stared at the lectern, which bore a book of hours containing the divine office.

'You are agitated, Simon. I heard most of what that clerk said – the echoes of this church carry long and clear – although I did not catch his name.'

'Amadeus Sevigny, Yorkist clerk, a nephew of my enemy Malpas.' This time Simon held Eleanor's grey-eyed gaze. He noticed her long lashes, the finely etched brows, the lips still red even without any carmine. He thought she looked tired and wan, yet this was a face that plagued his dreams and left a soreness of heart that could not be soothed. He curbed his agitation. He had lost this woman to his brother, and, after Edmund had been murdered, to God.

Unnerved and most uncomfortable with such a feeling, he rose and went across to study a painting of the Resurrection of the Dead that decorated the plaster above the squint. It was unlike anything he had ever seen before. The dead were rising from their long sleep as if from a good night in bed. Some came to life yawning and stretching; a few immediately sprang up to eternal life. Others were slugabeds, so lazy that angels armed with crowbars levered their coffined lids and gently roused them into eternal wakefulness.

'Is it serious?' Eleanor abruptly asked. 'Don't hide from me, Simon.'

Roseblood looked over his shoulder. 'York will invade. Civil war is imminent.'

'And the King?'

'Poor Henry, long-jawed, bewildered, his dark eyes full of sadness, cowers like a bird in its cage when the cat is around. York's badge, the fetterlock, and his insignia, the white rose, are appearing all over the city, on the great crosses at Cheapside and St Paul's; even on the doors of Beaufort's quarters at Greyfriars.'

'And you, Simon, why are you being threatened?' She laughed softly. 'Of course I know, but why now?'

'I am Beaufort's man. I control the babewyns and the gargoyles of London, the scavengers, muckrakers and gong men in every ward. I can spread rumour and collect gossip. I speak for the King, his Queen and the Beauforts on the city council. My spacious tavern can host special guests. I can bring in and dispatch whomever I want. If Beaufort wishes to send someone abroad, I can arrange it. If he or the Queen want to receive some secret envoy, their wish is my command. If a street fight begins, I can whistle up my hoard of rifflers and ruffians. York and his henchmen, Malpas and Sevigny, would love to destroy that.'

'But why now? Why has Sevigny appeared? Surely this is connected to my Edmund's death. The same deadly game?'

'I think so.' Simon breathed in the heavy fragrance from the herb pots arranged around the chamber. 'Yes, the same deadly game: who will control London? Five years ago, Cade occupied the city. He slaughtered many of the King's party in an attempt to win it. In the end, he failed. Now Malpas is attempting the same before York marches, and has brought Sevigny in to assist. They will use the law, or in this case, Candlemas.'

'I recall his name. I have heard rumours about the attack. What happened?'

'Oh, Candlemas and his coven failed to steal silver being escorted to the Tower mint.' Simon grinned. 'They didn't realise that there was no silver to rob; just sacks of old iron castings. No, no,' he waved a hand, 'I cannot tell you the full story. Four of the robbers were taken and tried before the justices at the Guildhall. Malpas had no choice. They had killed a royal serjeant, so they were sentenced to death for treason. Sevigny used the executions to see if Candlemas would appear. The fool did not disappoint him. He and two other rogues took refuge in the sanctuary of St Paul's. On execution day, they stupidly left this and used a secret tunnel, an ancient sewer that runs close to Smithfield. They were captured and offered pardons as King's Approvers. They must testify that I was the moving spirit behind the robbery.'

'Were you?'

Simon just smiled. Despite his sea of troubles, he was quietly revelling in the subtle trickery he had played.

'Simon, I remember Candlemas: a defrocked priest, a roaring boy with flame-coloured hair and a raucous mouth. Would he have the wit to plan such a robbery? Surely someone else . . .' Eleanor paused in a fit of coughing, then abruptly gripped her stomach.

Simon walked over to her and stared down at the

face he loved. The skin was taut, her eyes slightly starting; she was biting her lip as if in pain. He studied her carefully. Father Benedict had mentioned that she had asked for physic, medicines for her stomach. She glanced away, both hands nursing her belly.

'Eleanor, are you well?'

'I fast too much, too often.' she confessed. 'That is all.' She rested a hand on his arm, 'If you were not involved in this robbery, how do you know so much?'

Simon just winked at her.

'Simon!' she added warningly.

'Everything can be bought, Eleanor.'

'No, Simon.' She half smiled, relaxing as the pain in her belly faded. 'Not everything. Now,' she added briskly, 'our good sheriff will use Candlemas to indict you. Why didn't they offer the same pardon to those executed?'

'Somebody had to die for that robbery. Four of the gang were caught. What could Malpas do? The city would expect it. More importantly, they wanted to terrorise Candlemas and his companions, which they certainly have.'

Eleanor swiftly crossed herself. Roseblood wished he could stretch out his hand and cup her beautiful face, push back that hood and wimple to see her gorgeous black hair, though this would now be shorn and crimped. He also wondered, not for the first time, at this recluse's absorption with the affairs of the city.

'Eleanor?' He touched her gently on her cheek. 'Eleanor, why this? Why the flight from the world? Why not petition the bishop to be released from your vows? You know how I feel.'

'Simon, how many years is it since your wife died?'

'A good number of years.'

'Do you still miss her?'

'Of course,' he lied. 'Every day I speak her name and say the requiem.' Eleanor's grey eyes held his. You know I am lying, Simon thought. I did love Rohesia, but not as much, God forgive me, as I love you. 'Why, Eleanor?' he repeated. 'This has nothing to do with Rohesia. Why have you locked yourself away?'

'Atonement, reparation.'

'For what? What did you do? You loved Edmund.'

'Passionately. One heart, one soul, one mind, one body, breath for breath, life for life.'

Roseblood kept his face impassive, yet the very essence of his being surged at those passionate words.

'So why?'

Eleanor glanced away. Simon turned, blinking furiously, staring at the two magnificent swans Eleanor had painted either side of the narrow door: beautiful, heavenly white, with their fluffed feathers and arching necks. Eleanor had always loved these birds. She used to beg Edmund to take her out on the great tavern barge, *The Glastonbury*, to feed them or just stare at their exquisite beauty. All around the chamber were other reminders of the anchorite's fascination with swans, be it an incense holder or a hand-painted jug displaying the mythical Knights of the Swan. Little wonder parishioners referred to the anchorhold as the Swan's-Nest.

'Why did he leave?' Roseblood asked, as he had so many times. 'The night Cade's men stormed through the city, Edmund left the tavern. We had it secure, fortified like any castle under siege. I'd summoned a legion of rifflers, yet Edmund slipped out. Why?'

Eleanor just stared dully back, as if the very life had drained from her.

'Why, Eleanor?'

'I don't know,' she muttered. 'He talked of men called LeCorbeil, Cade's men . . .' Her voice trailed away.

'I know of LeCorbeil,' Roseblood sighed. 'God knows what Edmund had to do with them!'

Eleanor simply sat threading beads through her fingers. Roseblood marvelled at the change in her. She had been Eleanor Philpot when he first met her ten years ago, around the anniversary of his wife's death. He had never thought any woman could catch his eye and heart so swiftly. She was the vivacious daughter of a failing, sickly London merchant who had lost his wealth due to sea monsters – Breton pirates in the northern seas. Simon had been deeply smitten, but so had Edmund, and Eleanor only had eyes for him.

'Simon, this sea of troubles?'

'Like any brother and sister, we'll face it out.' He paused.

'Simon?'

'Nothing, nothing.' Roseblood fell silent; then, 'I cannot walk away Eleanor, they will not let me. Out there,' he pointed at the door, 'are a multitude of empty bellies, not to mention my own kith and kin who depend on me. In the end, the life that I have is the life that I lead, and the life that I lead is the life that has been thrust on me.' That was the real difference between him and Edmund.

'And your children, how are they? I see them at mass; they talk to me, though I am never sure if they are just telling me the things I want to hear.'

'Raphael is a pillar of strength; a serjeant at law, he has returned to help me in the tavern. He looks after all my business, which eases the humours of both mind and body. Gabriel is now a novice in the Franciscan order at Greyfriars under Prior Aelred.'

'Edmund had a special regard for Gabriel. He saw him as the son he always wanted.'

Simon just shrugged.

'And Katherine?'

'As lovely as ever, though her right leg still pains her sometimes. She is just about her eighteenth summer, keen and sharp-witted. Others think she is slightly fey. She has read too much about Arthur and the romances of Avalon. I am sure,' Simon laughed sharply, 'that Katherine expects Galahad of the Grail to ride into the tavern courtyard. She is constantly retreating to what she calls her greensward bower in the orchard.'

'And the Fraternity of the Doom?' Eleanor smiled knowingly. 'I know that they pray for Edmund's soul. That in his name they do good work along the Thames, combing its waters for those who have drowned, bringing their corpses back to Greyfriars for Christian burial.'

Simon crouched beside her. 'Of course you know, sister,' he teased, 'as you know how the Fraternity also meets the wine cogs from Bordeaux, taking and selling their claret without paying custom. But . . .'

He paused at a tumult from the other side of the church. He left the anchorhold and hurried to the men tangling on the threshold of the corpse door. Through the poor light he recognised the thickset figure and harsh features of the parish priest; beside him Benedict's curate and keeper of the Chapel of the Doom, Father Roger, thin as a beanpole, his blond hair cropped. The two priests were trying to drag into the church a man whose chest and belly were a soggy, gleaming mass of blood, his face half hidden by a cowl. They clutched him tightly, at the same time striving to drive off the city bailiffs, who held on to the wounded man's legs, attempting to drag him back.

'Desist!' Father Benedict bellowed. '*Hic est locus terribilis.*' He intoned the official sanctuary greeting. '*Haec est porta Caeli et domus Dei*. This is indeed a terrible place, the gate of Heaven and the house of God. This man, like Joab of old, claims sanctuary according to the tenets of Holy Mother Church. You shall be excommunicated.'

The bailiffs, led by Skulkin, would not be cowed. 'He has not reached the horns of the high altar,' the chief bailiff bellowed. The fugitive was now screaming in pain, kicking his legs as the priests pulled him in.

'One more step.' Roseblood, sword and dagger drawn, stepped round the priests, the blades of his weapons darting dangerously close to Skulkin and his companions. 'One more step,' he repeated, 'and you will die, whilst I will be hosted by Holy Mother Church as the champion of her liberties.' He sheathed his dagger, dug into his purse and drew out a few coins, which he threw over the bailiffs' heads. 'For your pains. Withdraw your men. Wet your throats or,' he smiled, 'you can have them sliced.'

Skulkin and his men retreated. Roseblood helped the priests with the wounded fugitive, now jerking in and out of consciousness, his belly wound spluttering blood. They laid him on the cold paving stones of the nave and Roseblood pulled back the man's cowl. His heart skipped a beat. Bolt-Head! He recognised that bony face, the head shaved as smooth as a pigeon's. Whatever his baptismal name, the wounded man had acquired his title from his protruding skull, used in many a street fight.

'You recognise him?' Father Roger whispered.

'Bolt-Head is a raker from Cripplegate ward, often seen in the company of Candlemas. He has been lying hidden for some days.'

The wounded man abruptly stirred. Arching in pain, he stared bulbous-eyed up at Roseblood.

'Master Simon,' he gasped, 'thanks be to God. I was coming here when Skulkin's men recognised me. I thought I was safe. I stopped . . .'

Roseblood leaned down; the smell of ale was rich on Bolt-Head's blood-bubbling breath.

'You stopped at some alehouse, where you would

stand out like a friar amongst nuns! Come, let's lift him into the sanctuary.'

They carried him up into the recess for fugitives. Father Benedict fetched some wine from the sacristy. Roseblood coaxed the wounded man to drink.

'A physician?' Father Roger murmured.

'Not for me,' Bolt-Head murmured. 'I know belly wounds. The knife ripped deep and harsh; soon it will get worse.'

Roseblood pulled back the man's tattered jerkin to reveal a savage black-red rent across the stomach. He shook his head.

'Absolution?' Father Benedict, nervous as ever, pulled a set of Ave beads through his fingers. 'He must be absolved.'

'Not yet, Father.' Bolt-Head gagged at the pain. 'Just you and me, master, for a while.'

The priests withdrew. Outside, the agitation and tumult had subsided. Simon knew that Ignacio had left, speeding like a lurcher to take care of certain matters, but others of his guard would be assembling.

'What is it?' Simon knelt down, his face almost touching that of the dying man.

'Master, I went into hiding. You know I had to. I told you what I knew. Rumours milled about how there was no silver. How Candlemas and his company were either killed or taken up. People now smell trickery.' He clutched Simon's hand. 'Master, who was behind that robbery? Who persuaded Candlemas?' He coughed on his blood. 'Was the silver replaced with sacks of rubbish? They are saying that Candlemas is going to blame you for the robbery.'

'Hush now,' Simon soothed.

'I feel so cold,' the dying man groaned. 'So very cold. I had to come. I am your sworn man, aren't I?'

'You are a comrade,' Simon assured him, 'but why did you creep out of hiding now?'

'Strange tales are told. Candlemas has turned King's Approver.' Bolt-Head shivered; the bloody froth between his lips had thickened. 'They – I don't know who; perhaps your enemies at the Guildhall – are sending all kinds of rumours to run like ferrets in a warren.' He gasped noisily. 'Last night, in the Palm of Jerusalem, three Essex wolfsheads – you might know them, Blackshanks, Gull-Groper and Scalding-Boy – announced that they would be taking over all the raking and scavenging in Cripplegate ward. They would hold an indenture from the city council.' He coughed blood and gratefully sipped at the wine, only to jerk at another searing jab of pain that convulsed his entire body. 'That is all I have to tell you, master. They say you will be indicted.' His eyes pleaded with Roseblood. 'Do what you have to do. Jesu miserere! Master, are men like us redeemed?'

'We are sinners,' Simon was already distracted by Bolt-Head's news, 'and we do what we are good at: sinning.'

He called across, and Father Benedict hurried to shrive the dying man. Simon withdrew until the priest had finished, making the sign of the cross in the air above Bolt-Head, who now lay against the sanctuary cushion coughing and spluttering.

'Do what you have to,' Father Benedict whispered to Simon as he passed. 'There is nothing we can do. You know that. According to the law of sanctuary, not even medicine can be brought in.'

Simon crossed himself and knelt beside Bolt-Head, whose face was now as white as snow, mouth gaping in pain.

'Please,' the fugitive opened his eyes, 'the mercy cut.'

Simon drew his misericord dagger and gently put his hand behind the dying man's head. 'Look at me, old friend.' Bolt-Head did so, and Simon expertly drew the dagger across his throat, holding his comrade as he jerked and trembled. Once he was still, he withdrew his arm and knelt for a while reciting the requiem, trying to recall all those other comrades he'd sent into the dark; the friends lying gashed and wounded in the war-ravished fields of Normandy.

'Simon.' Father Benedict touched his shoulder, 'Go now. Roger and I will dress the corpse. I will sing the requiem mass tomorrow and bury him in God's Acre with a fine cross and a posy of spring flowers on the grave.'

Simon cleaned his dagger, shook Benedict's hand, nodded at Father Roger and walked out through the corpse door. A beautiful evening; the sun was still strong and the market horn had yet to bray. The cemetery, God's Acre, stretched down to its red-brick curtain wall and massive oaken lychgate. The crowd had thinned.

A few city bailiffs, watched by Roseblood's men, still lounged in the long grass around the stone tombs and wooden crosses. The wild roses and other late spring flowers had bloomed rich and full to incense the air with their perfume. As he walked along the path to stand in the shadow of the lychgate, his mind was elsewhere, swirling and turning like a lurcher hunting a hare. A sea of troubles was boiling up. York would soon march south, and what could Simon do except defend himself?

The sounds and smells of the ward wafted towards him. A market beadle – Simon couldn't recall his name – was ringing a bell, his shrivelled face all furious, his hooked nose cutting the air. He bawled a proclamation 'Against rotten mutton, beef that is turnip-fed, lean measly pork from hogs glutted on city muck. Against all meats charred and sweaty and thrice roasted.' Simon recalled the delicious dishes served at his own tavern. A group of courtiers passed in their ridiculously padded jerkins, multicoloured hose and hats of the same florid design. Clean-shaven, they allowed their hair to fall down almost to cover their eyes and to lie ringleted and curled on their shoulders. All of them were armed.

'You are the dangerous ones,' Simon whispered, 'the city bully boys. When the black banner is raised, you'll be there to rob and rape.' He closed his eyes and murmured a prayer. If he fell from power, those same deadly fops would swagger into the Roseblood tavern to take what they wanted. The same could be said of many who flowed by the lychgate. The peasants pushing their barrows, merchants strolling arm in arm, storytellers full of eerie tales about elves and fairies, changelings and witches. Prior Aelred claimed that the city mob remained hidden, concealed behind ten thousand masks; in truth, it was a beast in waiting. Cade's invasion had proven that.

'Master Simon Roseblood!' He glanced up. A dust haze had risen, stirred by the iron wheels of heavy carts. A line of strumpets, Venus's children, went by dancing and stamping their feet, garish wigs askew, low-slung bodices open to reveal all. The dust cloud shifted to reveal a gallant in padded doublet, black hose and costly riding boots. He had long dark hair, his face hidden by a silver satyr's mask, which he held elegantly in place with one gauntleted hand, the other resting on the stabbing dirk thrust into an embroidered scabbard. 'Master Roseblood?' The figure stepped closer. Simon glimpsed the insignia on the left shoulder of the blood-red jerkin: a crow in full flight against a blue field. 'My name is LeCorbeil—'

Roseblood started forward. 'My brother!' he protested. 'My brother mentioned you the night he died. You meddle in our affairs, a constant refrain—'

'Monsieur, I beg you. Your men are some distance away, whilst I . . .' LeCorbeil gestured at the crossbowmen, three in number, now standing behind him. 'I believe,' he continued, his melodious voice tinged with a French accent, 'that the time is opportune for me to introduce myself yet again.'

'Yet again? We have met before?'

'Oh yes, many years ago.'

'You are York's creature?' Simon demanded.

'Monseigneur of York has his part to play in this, but so do you, Master Roseblood.'

'Why?'

'Don't you remember, Englishman? You should, for I am LeCorbeil, come for vengeance!' And the mysterious figure, protected by his henchmen, disappeared into the noisy jostling crowd.

Katherine Roseblood

London, April 1455

'And we shall all go to Avalon, kiss the Holy Thorn and peer into the golden Eternal West.' Katherine, daughter of Simon Roseblood and Rohesia, now departed, whispered her mythical incantation as she gingerly climbed the massive ancient oak. The tree stood in the furthest corner of the great garden of the orchard that lay to the west of the magnificent Roseblood, a three-storey tavern built of gleaming honey-coloured Cotswold stone. The sloping roofs of the tavern, which Katherine glimpsed as she climbed, were tiled with gleaming slates, its chimney stacks firmly constructed to withstand the gales that swept along the nearby Thames.

The Roseblood was a monument to English victories in France and the vast profits accrued from them. The old timber and plaster tavern had been torn down, and Master Simon had hired the finest artisans, stonemasons, carpenters, plumbers and tilers. He had imported stone by road and river from Cotswold quarries, paying his bills from the treasures and ransoms he had collected fighting in France under the Beaufort banner. The tavern, built in squares, could equal any stately manor house. Its northern arched gatehouse opened up on to the city; its southern to that stretch of lonely riverside carpeted by grass, briar, bramble and sandy shale that swept down to the busy port of Queenhithe.

The Roseblood imitated the great courtyards of France. The Great Cloister, as the central square enclosure was called, did not contain stableyard, washroom, bakery or slaughterhouse like other taverns. Instead it was modelled on the enclosure of an abbey: a rich grassy garth in the middle, with flower beds along its four sides. In the centre of the cloister garth rose an elegant fountain carved in the shape of a kingfisher standing over a deep bowl of water where lily pads bobbed, reeds thrust up long, lovely and lush and small golden fish darted. Each corner of the garth contained a shady arbour with turfed seats and stone benches. The air was constantly sweet with the perfume of plants and flowers: holly and ivy for Christmas; yew and hazel to be carried as palms during Holy Week; birch boughs for Easter, sweet woodruff for chaplets and garlands at Corpus Christi and white lilies and red roses for the Great Lady days. The bailey – the working courtyard with stables, well, smithy, bakehouse and other storerooms – lay to the east of the Great Cloister, connected by an arched gateway. On the west, a similar gate led into the tavern's various gardens and orchards; a true paradise, with stew ponds, dovecotes and even a small warren.

Katherine, garbed in a russet smock, stout boots on her feet, pushed herself further up the oak tree to what she and her brothers always called Merlin's Nest, her greensward bower, a great tangle of ancient branches that provided a canopied platform. Years ago her brothers used to join her, but Gabriel was now a novice with the Franciscans, while Raphael was a serjeant at law and her redoubtable father's principal henchman. She stopped and turned to her mythical companion, Melisaunde.

'No one comes here, you know. This,' she gestured towards the gardens, 'is our Avalon. Here Galahad will come bearing the Grail and Morgan le Fay to spin her web of dreams.' She stared out over the gardens, with their turf-topped stone seats, their fruit trees, herbers and flower plots, the patchwork of paths across the lawn. 'They claim that I am fey,' she murmured, 'but Avalon is definitely here.'

Katherine smiled. She knew she was imprisoned in the past. Father had been raised on the Glastonbury estates, and had crammed her mind with stories of the great abbey where Arthur and Guinevere had slept; the Holy Thorn planted by Joseph of Arimathea; the ghostly knights; and the whereabouts of the Grail and the Crystal Cave where Merlin rested until he came again. In the principal tavern refectory her father had nailed swords to the wall above the inscribed names of their owners, Arthur's knights: Lancelot, Galahad,

Gawain, Bors and all the others. Tapestries in the elegantly furnished solar, the Camelot Chamber, proclaimed the story of the Green Knight and the Lady of the Lake. In the centre of that chamber stood a huge round table, modelled on the original kept at Winchester, with silver arrows painted on it proclaiming the titles and positions of Arthur and his glorious chivalry.

'But when will Mordred come?' Katherine whispered. 'Mordred, Melisaunde, Morgan le Fay's death-bearing son? Will he come and shatter Avalon? Is this our time of sunset? Will Father take his special sword, Excalibur, from its carved chest?'

Undoubtedly, she reflected, the shadows were stretching closer and deeper. Five years ago, around her thirteenth summer, the terrors had sprung out of the darkness: Cade's minions milling about the tavern, only driven off by a host of spears and clusters of notched bows. Nights of fire and horror. A time of chaos and sorrow, when Uncle Edmund had slipped away. They'd eventually brought his body back in an arrow chest, his severed head resting against his blood-soaked trunk. Father Benedict and his curate Father Roger, who according to Malkin, master of the taproom, were closer than man and wife – though God knows what he meant by that – had tended to the corpse. The two priests, who had served in Father's retinue in France, had sewn the head back on, and cleaned and waxed the corpse for burial in its elm-wood casket, but even then Aunt Eleanor could not bring herself to look. Mad with grief, she had withdrawn to All Hallows and remained there ever since. Why? What had Uncle Edmund intended by slipping out that summer evening? Who was he to meet? Katherine, who had honed the skill of eavesdropping, had heard the name LeCorbeil mentioned, but who or what they were remained a tangled mystery.

'Mordred's time has certainly come, Melisaunde,' Katherine whispered, half listening to the cooing from the dovecote, which was answered by the heart-thrilling song of a thrush hidden in a hedgerow. 'Father is concerned. Rumour has it that he could be indicted.' She wished her mother was here, and swiftly crossed herself. Father had intimated that tonight he would convoke a consilium juratorum, a council of sworn men. She would be part of that. Father had insisted on it, overruling her taciturn brother Raphael. They would meet in the Camelot Chamber, gathering round Arthur's table. Raphael would be present; Ignacio too, with his soul-dead eyes, long fingers fluttering as he and her father talked their silent speech.

Gabriel never came. He would meet Raphael when his elder brother brought in the wine smuggled from cogs in the river – barrels and tuns unstamped by the keepers of the custom – along with corpses culled from the water. Sometimes her father would go on such nightly expeditions. Under cover of dark, as the barrels and corpses were unloaded on to the friary carts, he would hurry ahead to Greyfriars to secretly meet the Lancastrian lords, Stafford of Buckingham and, above all, Edmund Beaufort, second Duke of Somerset. Such meetings were necessary. Beaufort could no longer move openly in the city, so strong was York's growing grip. Moreover, rumours that Queen Margaret's son was Beaufort's, not the King's, had caught the attention of the songsters, balladeers and minstrels, though none would dare proclaim such scandal in the Roseblood.

Others would also attend tonight's consilium juratorum, including the two priests. 'I hope, Melisaunde,' whispered Katherine, flicking at the scraps of bark on her smock, 'that Father Roger has stopped crying. He went to Colchester recently to bury his poor mother, and since his return he has not been the same. But there again, that's what I love about the Roseblood. Like Avalon, all is shrouded in mystery and intrigue.'

She fell silent as she heard servants pass by to collect herbs – mint, parsley and sorrel – for the kitchens and buttery. Once they'd gone, she returned to her musing. Father swirled like some knight clothed in a magical mist confronting his enemies, be it on the city council or along the filthy maze of Queenhithe's alleyways. Strangers came and went in the dead of night. Courier pigeons were dispatched, messages attached in thin copper sheaths. The grotesques of London, her father's gangs organised into their various companies, slid in and out of the tavern with a host of others who looked to Simon Roseblood for sustenance and protection: relic sellers, pardoners, tinkers and traders, moon people and mummers, quacks and conjurors, pimps and prostitutes, beggars and rifflers. He greeted all these with open hands. No one who begged for a platter of food or a black jack of ale was ever turned away.

Other visitors remained mysterious, such as a present guest, Master Reginald Bray, who professed to be on pilgrimage to the house of St Thomas of Becket's parents in Cheapside. Perhaps he was, though Katherine had noticed how he was most observant about all that happened in the tavern. Even more mysterious was the small, rather plump lady who had visited the tavern all hooded and visored at least once a fortnight over the last few months, arriving just before the Vespers bell on Friday. She was always given the Medlar, a spacious bedchamber on the second storey overlooking the Great Cloister, and would move straight up the private staircase, clinging to the balustrade. No less a person than the trusty Ignacio would escort her and take care of the little baggage she brought.

Curious, Katherine had set up close vigil on this enigmatic lady, who was visited by various young men in their padded jerkins and tight-fitting hose, hair all coiffed, jewellery glinting at throat, chest and wrist. Ignacio would always bring up a jug of white wine, together with some sweet subtlety such as marchpane, prunes and syrup, or succade of lemon peels. The mysterious woman would leave long after dark, and Katherine had heard the squeals and cries of lovemaking from the chamber; very similar to those she heard whilst hiding in the Great Tithe barn, when she was forced to witness one of the grooms tumble a maid in a flash of white flesh and threshing legs on the straw below. 'I asked Father, only once, who our mysterious woman was, Melisaunde. He just grasped me by the shoulder, tapped me on the nose, called me his little squirrel, and told me to be careful of the circling hawks. Now what could that mean?'

A blackbird darted from the arboured trellis below in a flurry of wings, to be joined by the gang of sparrows that frequented the flower beds around the carp pond. Katherine tensed: the oak tree was not yet in full bloom and did not offer a thick green canopy as in midsummer. Somebody was approaching.

'Mistress Katherine! Mistress Katherine, you are needed. Both taproom and refectory are busy. Come, there's a minstrel fresh from Outremer, or so he says.' Dorcas, the leading chambermaid, had a trumpet-like voice that belied her size. 'Mistress Katherine, you are to come.'

'Mistress Katherine and her boon companion Melisaunde are to stay!' Katherine whispered back fiercely.

She waited until Dorcas had gone, then clambered down. She crouched, peering around, but the gardens and the orchard slept under the strong April sun. She picked up the walking stick, her crutch and her help, as she mocked it, but her faithful companion to favour the slight weakness in her right leg that had dogged her since childhood. She moved swiftly and silently past the trellises and the herbers rich with periwinkle, sage, soapwort and betony. She skirted the small orchards, which provided apples and pears, cherries and plums, the air blessed with their mouth-watering flavours. The sun was still strong. Butterflies, flickering like darts of light, flitted over the garden, and the summer's first bees competed with the growing chatter of crickets in the long grass. From the city, the tolling of bells summoned the faithful to pray.

Katherine ignored all this, aiming like an arrow for the small postern gate in the south wall, which led down to the riverside. Only once did she pause, at the high-bricked enclosure that her father called the Hortus Mortis, the Garden of Death, a special herb plot tended only by Ignacio. This macabre garden contained deadly shrubs: the soft spiky pods and shiny brown seeds of castor, friar's cowl; the white bell-shaped flowers of mandrake; yellowish hartshorn: purple-spotted hemlock and others. Katherine and her brothers had been warned ever since they were knee-high to a cricket never to enter that herber or have anything to do with it. Raphael once asked why the herbs were grown. Father had replied that such plants could also be medicinal.

Katherine hastened by. She reached the postern gate, pulled back the three bolts and stepped out on to the scrubland that stretched down to the man-made inlet, wharves and quayside of Queenhithe. She loved coming here. The Roseblood stood on an ancient hill that swept down to the Thames. Katherine had a favourite place – she called it the Eyrie – from where she could stare out over the river and watch the great cogs of war, the full-bellied merchant craft of the Hanse, the sculls of Flanders, the woads of Picardy and the whelk boats of Essex, as well as a horde of other barges, wherries and skiffs. Sometimes, on a very clear day, she could hear the sailors singing their hymn of praise to the Virgin Mary, the 'Ave, Maris Stella'; all except the Greeks, who were allowed to sing their Kyrie.

A flash of colour caught Katherine's eye. She turned and briefly glimpsed a flaxen-haired woman with a red mantle around her shoulders. 'Calista!' she breathed.

Calista was a street girl, a prostitute, who'd often drift into the Roseblood to ogle and entice would-be customers. Now she was threading through a copse, walking arm in arm with a tall man, cowled and garbed like a friar. A priest? Katherine wondered. But she could see no more. They had turned down a trackway skirting the trees that cut between the copse and some crumbling boat sheds.

Katherine walked slowly towards the ancient ruins halfway down the hill, lost in thought about what she had just glimpsed. She recalled the taproom gossip about whores disappearing along the alleyways and runnels of the ward. Father didn't believe that anything had happened to them; he claimed that such ladies of the night moved around the city to escape the sharp gaze and greedy fingers of the bailiffs. She entered the crumbling ruins. Monkshood, one of Father's henchmen, a former clerk, believed that the Eyrie had once been an ancient lighthouse built by the Caesars, or even the Trojans. Resting on her walking cane, Katherine peered through the broken masonry back up the hill at the jutting curtain wall of the Roseblood. She heard a sound, but ignored it.

Is this your bower
Oh lady of the Tower?

The couplet came soft and mocking. Katherine whirled round, raising her walking cane. A man now blocked the ruined entrance, cloak falling to his knees. Katherine glimpsed his shadowy face and white teeth, the gleam of silver on his chest and fingers. He seemed to fill the ruined tower with his presence.

'Who are you, sir, to creep up on a maiden like that?'

The stranger stepped closer, rearranging his cloak and war belt. He was clean-shaven, the black hair on his head shorn close, his sallow face redeemed by sharp green eyes and a mocking mouth. He was dressed in a black leather sleeveless jerkin; the linen shirt underneath was clean and embroidered at cuff and neck, and a small silver medallion engraved with the fetterlock of York hung round his neck, a chancery ring on the little finger of his left hand. A man of power, Katherine swiftly concluded; she was fascinated by that clever, saturnine face.

'What do you want?' The words came blurting out even as the stranger stretched across and gently eased the walking cane from her fingers.

'Mistress Katherine, is it not?' The voice was soft and melodious. 'Daughter of Master Simon Roseblood, now summoned to appear before the sheriff's court before the market bell tomorrow?' He bowed. 'I am Amadeus Sevigny, principal clerk in the secret chancery of Richard Plantagenet, Duke of York.' His eyes crinkled as she stared. 'Perhaps you have heard your worthy father mention my name?' He took her by the hand and courteously kissed the tips of her fingers. 'My apologies, mistress, I did not mean to startle you. Like you, I was simply wondering how remarkable it is what you discover and see. I am sure I glimpsed one of the priests from All Hallows, all hooded and cloaked, in the company of a common whore. Would one of your priests be steeped in such sin?'

Katherine frowned. 'You are Mordred!' she exclaimed without thinking. 'You have come to Avalon. You mean us no good!'

The clerk stared blankly at her, then threw his head back and roared with laughter, so loud it echoed around that ruined tower. Katherine blushed as Amadeus turned away, one hand to his side. When he turned back, tears were glistening in his eyes. He touched her on the arm. She just glared at him, which sent him into further peals of laughter. He sat down on a plinth, wiping his eyes, trying to compose himself.

'Oh for the love of God!' she snapped. 'It was no jest or witty sally!'

'No, no, it wasn't,' he agreed, mopping his cheeks with the back of a gloved hand. 'Yet you look so serious. Believe me, mistress, I have been called many things in my life, but never Mordred, Arthur's great enemy and the destroyer of Camelot.' The humour drained from his face and he rose to his feet. 'Mistress Katherine, my apologies. I came to study Avalon, not to destroy it. I have walked the entire length of the Roseblood.' He waved down towards the quayside. 'I have been down to study the tavern barge, *The Excalibur*. It is very impressive: stout, deep-bellied, six-oared, with a canopied stern. I understand that the Fraternity of the Doom use it to collect the dead. Others whisper how it smuggles in wine.'

'Many people are liars,' Katherine retorted, but she could not stop the flush returning. This stranger so deeply unsettled her, she was relieved when Dorcas, standing on top of the hill, shouted her name.

'Mistress Katherine, I had best let you leave.' He swooped down, lifted her hand and gently kissed her fingers again. 'It was an honour and a privilege.' He escorted her to the entrance and returned her walking cane. 'I bid you God speed.'

Katherine fled the ruined tower, banging the stick on the ground. When she joined Dorcas, she blamed her obvious fluster on the steep climb. She half listened to the maid, who could chatter without pausing for breath: how Master Roseblood seemed very distracted, how the taproom was busy and hadn't Katherine heard her shouting?

They passed through the Great Cloister. The refectories, as her father grandly described the eating chambers, were positioned on either side of the gateway. Here, each table was cleverly closeted so that customers could dine and talk in peace. The principal taproom and buttery, fronting the city, seethed with noise and bustle. The drinking chamber was spacious and high-ceilinged, its tiled floor regularly brushed and swilled with clean water; no rushes were ever strewn there. Hams, cheeses, flitches of bacon and dried fruit hung in white string nets from the rafters, well away from vermin, their tangy smell mingling with the sweet odours from the wine tuns and beer barrels, not to mention the fragrance from the hog roast turning on its spit under the mantled hearth. Some of the shutters and horn-covered windows had been removed to provide more air. The noise was clamorous as tradesmen, beggars and scavengers crowded into the popular tavern.

Katherine's father, protected by Ignacio, stood near the common board. He glimpsed Katherine and raised a hand in acknowledgement, indicating with his head that she should help the scullions and slatterns hurrying about with brimming pots, tankards and black jacks. Servants scurried in from the kitchen courtyard bearing platters and bowls of stewed capon, mutton and lemon, aloes of beef, strips of venison all hot and sauced in chopped vegetables and tangy spices. Shreds of crispy pork were being cut from the spit turned by the buttery boy, whilst the tavern baker managed the ovens either side of the hearth, where fresh bread was being baked.

Katherine donned the offered apron. She bundled her rich auburn hair under a kitchen bonnet and helped where she could, only pausing to peck at her father's cheek, kiss Ignacio roundly on the lips and wave at Raphael, who, his square face all worried, bustled in with a ledger. As she moved around, she listened to the conversation. The great taproom was the meeting place of the Guild of Scavengers, the Fraternity of the Doom, the Brotherhood of the Babewyns and the Coven of the Gargoyles, all inhabitants of the decaying tenements and crumbling garrets along the narrow runnels of Queenhithe and beyond. Katherine glimpsed Master Reginald Bray, seated in the corner all by himself, a bowl of pottage before him. This self-styled pilgrim looked serene and smiling, but his unblinking stare carefully took in all around him. He caught her eye, scratched his mop of blond hair and raised a beringed white hand in greeting.

She moved across the taproom and into the calm buttery chamber, where the greyheads of the ward gathered. Wherever she went, be it the Great Cloister garth or the kitchen courtyard, Katherine caught the tension and fraught mood of the day. The summons issued against her father was now common knowledge. York's threat was real: he wanted to be regent and remove the fey-witted King. She also heard fresh comment about the disappearance of prostitutes, and recalled glimpsing Calista with the man dressed as a monk whom Sevigny had thought to be one of the priests from All Hallows.

The very thought of the clerk made Katherine pause: those mocking eyes, the laughing mouth, the way he found her so amusing. He was Mordred, however, the black knight about to enter the lists of Camelot and challenge the world of Avalon. So lost was she in her thoughts that Katherine almost dropped the jug she was carrying when a voice boomed out.

'I am the rider of the Pale Horse and all hell follows in my retinue.' The speaker stood in the sun-filled entrance to the taproom, cloak thrown back, sword and dagger drawn. He was tall, with shaggy hair and beard, his jerkin and hose stained and tattered, cheap jewellery decorating his fingers and wrists. He walked into the tavern followed by two others similarly attired. The raucous noise subsided as customers drew away. A relic seller hastily grabbed his tray of special stones from the rock of Moses and tried to leave, only to be pushed back. A juggler, his pet monkey on his shoulder, a ferret in the crook of his arm, fell off his stool and crawled under the table.

Katherine watched the three rifflers swagger further into the taproom. According to whispers around her, these wolfsheads were Blackshanks, Gull-Groper and Scalding-Boy. Her father, Ignacio behind him, left the common board and went over to confront the new arrivals. Katherine was surprised at how calm and measured he seemed, for he had a temper second to none.

'Good day, sir.' Simon bowed. 'Welcome to this tavern. I—'

'The Dominus of the Dunghill,' Blackshanks, the leader, interrupted rudely. 'I know you, Master Roseblood, and you know me, as you do my two friends, Gull-Groper,' he turned mockingly, 'and Master Scalding-Boy. We have just come from Cripplegate ward.' Blackshanks's voice grew stronger. 'I quoted from the Book of the Apocalypse. Ever since my days as a scholar I have loved that verse. It signifies the end of things.' He poked Simon in the chest with the point of his sword. 'And you, sir, are certainly at the end of things. Candlemas and Cross-Biter will indict you, then it will be Newgate for Master Roseblood.'

'You have everything planned!' Raphael pushed his way through, hand resting on the hilt of his dagger. 'You have us judged, condemned and hanged.'

'As the cock, so the chick,' jeered Scalding-Boy, his scorched face ugly.

'You are all wanted men yourselves,' Raphael retorted. The usually quiet-faced lawyer was now flushed with anger. 'Are you not,' he declared, 'wanted by the sheriffs of Essex and Hertford for various crimes and felonies?'

'Misunderstandings!' Blackshanks lifted the point of his sword. 'Sir Philip Malpas,' the felon turned to the left and right so that all could hear him, 'is about to issue pardons. In the meantime, Cripplegate is without its scavengers because you, Master Roseblood, led them into a failed and bloody robbery. Accordingly,' Blackshanks brought his sword back to rest the blade against his shoulder, 'my two learned colleagues and my good self will take over all their duties, as we might well do here too.'

'A former cleric, now a collector of shit!' Raphael jeered.

Blackshanks moved threateningly; his two companions brought up their swords and daggers. Katherine caught a glimpse of polished steel, the fresh leather war belts all three wolfsheads wore. She knew that these had either been recently purchased or were fresh from the armoury of her father's enemies at the Guildhall. The three men had been sent here to proclaim her father's imminent downfall; to weaken, even shatter the patronage he exercised. Her father, however, remained unperturbed. He stepped back, spreading his hands.

'My friends, you are welcome.'

Blackshanks's shoulders drooped in disappointment. He glanced in surprise at his two companions.

'You are most welcome,' Roseblood insisted. 'Some wine, some food, but not here, yes? Let us meet in the great tithe barn, where we can talk in private and reach some form of agreement. Ignacio, fetch what our guests want.'

Katherine hurried from the taproom. She had heard about her father's meetings in the barn, a place where he dispensed justice. She ran through the Great Cloister and into the kitchen bailey. Toadflax, one of her father's leading scavengers, a captain of the cohort, stood on guard outside the barn. He stared bleary-eyed at Katherine, who lifted her finger to her lips as a sign of silence and fluttered her eyelids. Toadflax would do what she asked. Katherine had turned many a blind eye to the free pots of ale he quietly supped, not to mention his cogged dice, which her father regularly seized and destroyed.

She slipped through the half-open door into the dappled, sweet-smelling light of the barn, all warm and close. Her mind was a-tumble with lines from the poems about Arthur and the appearance of the Knight from the Red Lands, as well as snatches from the sequence of the mass for the dead. 'See what fear man's bosom rendeth.' The sombre line echoed through her head, followed by: 'When from Heaven the judge descendeth.' She thanked God her leg was not troubling her as she climbed the ladder into the hayloft and hid behind the bales, holding her breath.

The sound of voices grew louder. The barn door opened and her father, accompanied by Raphael and Ignacio, carrying a tray bearing a jug and three goblets, came in. Whilst Ignacio served the goblets, Raphael positioned two heavy lantern horns. Blackshanks and his companions stood slurping the wine, unaware of the danger closing in like a hawk. There was movement, her father crossing to the left, Ignacio to the right. Raphael had slipped behind the three wolfsheads. Katherine could feel her heart beating, her jaw tightly clenched.

'Well?' Blackshanks bellowed, taking another gulp of claret. 'What do you have to say?'

'Never drink wine with your enemies.'

'What do you mean?'

'Well, if you are holding a goblet . . .'

Blackshanks dropped his cup, but it was too late. Her father's sword came hissing out of its scabbard, and in a glittering arc of steel he severed Blackshanks's head. At the same time, Gull-Groper was dealt with by one swift cut from Ignacio, while Scalding-Boy, still grasping his goblet in shocked surprise, never even saw Raphael's sword as it whipped through the air.

Katherine froze to the spot. She could only stare at the severed trunks, the spouting blood, heads rolling away as the bodies collapsed. She closed her eyes, but all she saw was Sevigny's brooding face.

Raphael Roseblood

London, April 1455

Raphael Roseblood crossed himself and gazed around the beautifully furnished solar. The Camelot Chamber was exquisitely decorated, and its carved mantled hearth, with a woodwose in the middle and a Robin Goodfellow face on either side, housed a merrily spitting fire. The flames crackled the pine-scented logs and illuminated the gorgeous arras that adorned the pink-plastered walls above the polished oak wainscoting. The floor had a tiled mosaic replicating what the master mason had seen in an ancient Roman villa along the Great North Road: a brilliant depiction of leaping dolphins above cream-crested blue waves. The chamber was dominated by the splendid round table furnished with high-backed chairs cushioned in purple and red stuffing. In the centre of the table rose the gold-encrusted replica of the ship that took Arthur into the Eternal West. Simon Roseblood always met his council of sworn men here. Tonight the conclave was most serious in the face of the threats gathering against him.

Raphael stared hard at his father: his black and silver hair was combed back to reveal his leathery face, and those clever eyes looked deeply troubled, whilst the resolute chin and mouth betrayed some of the tension he must be feeling. Father Benedict, sitting on Simon Roseblood's left, claimed that his patron's face was one well lived in. Raphael wondered what plots and counter-plots his father's teeming brain was sifting. Ignacio, Monkshood, Wormwood and the other principal henchmen were present; all had served with his father under Beaufort's banner in France. Raphael smiled to himself. The only persons here who had not served in such an array were himself and his sister Katherine, who, hair decorously hidden under a veil, now sat nervously on her chair. Raphael had objected to her presence, rejecting her as being a woman of tender years, but his father had been adamant.

'Blood is blood,' he'd muttered. 'If mine flows, so will hers. She deserves to be one of us. Mark my words, Raphael. Katherine is a better man than many we know.'

His sister seemed lost in her own thoughts. Raphael suspected she had been in the tithe barn earlier that evening. Indeed, he was sure he'd glimpsed her white face between the bales in the hay loft. She had probably witnessed her first executions. Raphael had grown used to them, slaying men who threatened him and his family. For a brief moment he fought a surge of anger at his younger brother, Gabriel, safely closeted away in holy seclusion at Greyfriars. He breathed out; but that was Gabriel! The two of them often laughed at the names given to them, their mother insisting that her sons be named after God's great archangels.

Raphael sat back in his chair, relaxing against the softness of the cushion. Ignacio lit more candles and Monkshood served white wine and marchpane. Raphael wondered how he would make reparation to God for the man he'd killed that day: either by creeping to the cross on Fridays or through a rigorous fast on holy days. Sometimes he would reveal the burden of his guilt to the priests, but they just echoed the words of their patron: 'The life that we have is the life that we lead.'

'In praise of the Blessed Peter, God's own fisherman!' Simon Roseblood tapped the table with his hand and took a generous sip, his first of the evening, from the jewel-encrusted Glastonbury goblet. 'The business before us now . . .'

He paused and stared at Raphael, who nodded. All was in order. Men stood on guard outside, the doors were sealed, the windows of thick mullion glass had no gaps or slits for traitorous eavesdroppers. The chamber fell silent, all eyes on Simon Roseblood, the only movement the shifting shadow of flickering candle flame.

'The day of the great slaughter is imminent,' Simon intoned. 'The fortresses will fall.' Raphael watched his father; he had never seen him so tense. 'York will move south,' Simon's voice had fallen to a whisper, 'and the days of Cade will return. That is why we are facing this sea of troubles. Now you are all sworn men, so I shall reveal to you my most secret thoughts.' He paused again. 'Candlemas and his coven, without my authority, were involved in that raid on the silver bullion intended for the royal mint. I can now tell you, as I learned from my own spy at the Guildhall, that the robbery was plotted by no less a person than Sir Philip Malpas, our noble lord sheriff. I learnt a few more details from Bolt-Head, God rest him, before he went into hiding.' Simon stilled the gasps and exclamations. 'York needs silver to pay his troops. Malpas intended to enrich York and of course weaken the King and my lord Beaufort.

'Now you all know Candlemas: loud-mouthed, insubordinate, with no real loyalty to me. Malpas easily turned him, but the second part of our good sheriff's plot was then to betray that stupid moon man to a bloody death. A few of Candlemas's coven would be pardoned, but this is what Malpas truly revelled in: they would indict me as responsible for the robbery. Somehow or other, a little of the stolen silver would be found in this tavern. I thwarted their plot. My lord of Beaufort was alerted and the silver was replaced with rusty filings not worth a penny. Malpas and Sevigny, who had just arrived in the city, were furious. Four of Candlemas's gang were apprehended and executed. The city would expect that. This was to terrify the rest: it would only be a matter of time before they were captured and the second part of the sheriff's plot could go ahead. I would be indicted and Beaufort would lose a most powerful ally in this city. Tomorrow, Candlemas and Cross-Biter will be used to testify against me.'

'And they will do that?' Raphael exclaimed.

'We shall see, we shall see.' His father smiled.

'And Blackshanks's coven?' asked the Fisher-King, captain of *The Excalibur* barge.

'Monkshood,' Simon gestured at his grizzled Captain of the Damned, 'tell them what you have done.'

'Their corpses lie in arrow chests.' Monkshood grated. 'Their heads stand poled just inside the gateway below. We have taken them to every tavern in the ward, a clear proclamation of Master Roseblood's power.'

'Can we justify what we have done?' Raphael asked.

'My son,' Simon lifted his goblet in toast, 'and you the lawyer?' As he spoke, his fingers translated the words for Ignacio. 'First, Blackshanks and the others were outlaws; they'd received no royal pardon. Second, they drew their weapons and publicly threatened me, an alderman of this city. Third, they intended to usurp the power of the council at the Guildhall.' He pulled a face. 'Blackshanks was arrogant, deep in his cups. He moved too swiftly. He brought about his own death and that of his companions. I will claim self-defence. Any justice of oyer and terminer, not to mention those of the King's Bench, would agree.'

Raphael nodded in agreement. Who would plead for three wolfsheads, proclaimed *ut legati* – beyond the law – in the surrounding shires?

'They had their uses.' Simon murmured, provoking laughter.

Raphael glanced at Katherine, who sat white-faced, staring at the arras on the far wall. He had accompanied

Ignacio, Toadflax and Monkshood through the ward, each bearing a severed head on a pole. They had stopped at alehouses, drinking booths and taverns as well as the lychgates of churches and chapels. The message was clear. Here were three wolfsheads, taken red-handed, weapons drawn against Alderman Roseblood; for this they had been brutally and swiftly executed, a warning to everyone to wait and see if Roseblood's power had been truly weakened.

'What other business?' Simon gestured at Raphael.

'Candlemas?'

'His candle may have blown out,' Simon joked. 'Now listen,' he continued. 'Tomorrow we will surprise our noble sheriff with a pageant he'll never forget.' He drew himself up and described what would happen the following morning, his plans provoking laughter and further discussion.

Raphael tapped the table. 'There is the question of the whores. In the last fortnight, three have disappeared as swift as smoke on a clear day. Now whispers claim that Calista has not been seen. She was supposed to join her sisters here before moving on to the Three Cranes, where the King's sailors are mustering.'

Katherine suddenly stirred. She spoke carefully. 'I was out near the lighthouse ruins this afternoon. I thought I saw Calista. She was with someone.' She put a finger to her lips. 'I could not say. I mean, it may not even have been her . . .'

Her voice trailed off as she darted a glance at Father Benedict. The parish priest, however, seemed lost in his own thoughts, and Raphael realised that Father Roger was not present: still grieving over the death of his mother? he wondered.

'Anything else?' Simon asked.

The Camelot Chamber remained silent. This was not the first time whores had disappeared. Raphael remembered other occasions: how his father had once told him that some men had to be violent to a woman to seek their pleasure. He recalled a line from the Psalms about demons prowling the other side of darkness. For all its beauty, the Roseblood tavern was a battlefield. Shadow armies moved. Ghostly warriors, troublesome spirits armoured in hate and seething malice, envy and jealousy against his father, ran swift like some filthy surging sewer, whilst Roseblood's constant allegiance to the Beauforts posed a steely threat to York both in the city and beyond. Once again Raphael felt a stab of resentment towards his brother.

'LeCorbeil.' Simon's voice was hard. 'I have been threatened by LeCorbeil.' He swiftly described what had happened near the lychgate of All Hallows. Raphael could see how agitated Ignacio, Monkshood and Father Benedict became. He spoke without thinking.

'They say that during Cade's rebellion, Uncle Edmund left the Roseblood to meet this LeCorbeil. Why?'

'He went to his death,' Simon admitted. 'Edmund and I served Beaufort, first Duke of Somerset, in France. We fought well. I took many ransoms.' He waved around the solar. 'That is obvious. Then the tide of war turned against us. We burnt the Maid of Orleans, Joan of Arc, in the marketplace at Rouen. Many, including myself, believed that we became cursed. We murdered a saint who had ordered us to go home in our ships or she would send us back in our coffins. Joan's martyrdom certainly brought this about. English rule collapsed. Commissioners of array found it difficult to levy men here in London and in the shires both north and south of the Trent, so the prisons were emptied, be it Newgate or Windsor Castle.'

'Les Écorcheurs!' Father Benedict exclaimed abruptly, drawing himself up. 'Les Écorcheurs!' he repeated. 'The Flayers.'

'Les Écorcheurs,' Simon agreed. 'The scum of our prisons – rufflers and rifflers, cut-throats, murderers, rapists and worse – were dispatched by ship to Normandy. No rules of war for them. They raped, plundered and engaged in the cruellest methods of killing another human being. They particularly liked to flay their victims, peel their skin from their bodies as you would take off a tunic. No one was safe, be it man, woman, child or priest.' He shook his head. 'Beaufort hired companies, but he could not dictate what they did.'

'LeCorbeil?' Raphael insisted.

'A town in Normandy. Edmund and I visited it after the Écorcheurs had been there: a true slaughterhouse. The wells and streams were choked with naked lacerated corpses. Cadavers hung from steeples, market crosses, gable ends and shop signs. The place stank like an open sewer. Plumes of black smoke billowed down narrow streets, their cobbles glistening red. We had no part in this, but I suspect we were blamed. Some survivors of the massacre – we do not know or cannot even imagine who they are – have sworn vengeance against the English, and Beaufort in particular. LeCorbeil is more than one person, and whoever they may be, they are generously financed and warmly supported by the French Crown. They are a veritable will-o'-the-wisp, a shape-shifter, a dark strider.'

'What do they want with you?'

Simon paused to collect his thoughts. 'To answer your question bluntly, I do not really know. LeCorbeil were certainly involved in Cade's uprising. They had a hand in the seizure and execution of William de la Pole, the Duke of Suffolk, and they slaughtered other Beaufort adherents, both here and elsewhere. Somehow – and only God and his angels know the truth – LeCorbeil enticed Edmund away from the security and safety of this tavern and struck off his head.' He rubbed his brow. 'John Beaufort, first Duke of Somerset, was another of their victims. Gossips claim that he took his own life, distraught at being stripped of his command in France.' He tapped both hands against the tabletop. 'I do not think so. Shortly before his death, our good duke, sheltering in his castle, was visited by a Gascon minstrel, a very handsome, charming young man.'

'LeCorbeil?' Raphael asked.

'Certainly. One thing is constant. Beside the corpses of my brother, de la Pole, Beaufort and others, a dead crow was left. The message is clear: LeCorbeil hold us personally responsible for the massacre.'

'But why?' Monkshood demanded. 'Beaufort didn't hire the Écorcheurs.'

'The company who ravaged LeCorbeil,' Simon replied, 'had links with Beaufort. It was led by a mercenary captain – I forget his name – who had acquired a reputation for ferocious cruelty.'

'But you were not responsible,' Raphael said. 'Surely? And nor was Beaufort.'

'I have racked my brain,' Simon confessed. 'Edmund and I visited the town on Beaufort's orders; that company was under his command. We were as shocked as anyone. I can't recall seeing any survivors, yet now LeCorbeil appears to summon up a cohort of mercenaries to wreak its revenge.'

'Which gives them a path into England,' said Raphael. 'All the great lords are hiring mercenaries, French, Spanish, German and the rest.'

'I suspect that LeCorbeil . . .' Simon paused, 'yes I am sure of it, have sealed indentures with the Duke of York; they will also carry letters of marque from him, a sure defence against any sheriff or royal bailiff courageous enough to confront well-armed mercenaries. My mystery, the one that has haunted me for five years, is how they were able to entice a shrewd, seasoned soldier like Edmund to his death.'

'So they are here to assist York?' Father Benedict asked.

'Oh, LeCorbeil hate the Beauforts, but they also hate the English. I have learnt a little about them. They are here to agitate, to stir up violence, to set York against

Lancaster like two fighting cocks locked in a struggle to the death. They will weaken the English Crown so that this realm never again threatens the kingdom of France. Little wonder they are well financed by the secret chancery in Paris while being given free rein to pursue their own blood feud.'

Simon sipped from his goblet. 'Heart speaks to heart,' he continued. 'As I have said, the day of the great slaughter is imminent. York will march. Our enemies will lay siege, either to convert us to their cause – which would cast us as Judases, never to be trusted – or,' he shifted his goblet, 'to destroy us completely. They have to. I control the scavengers, rakers and refuse collectors in every ward. I can dispatch rumour swifter than a pigeon, whilst a thousand eyes and ears watch and listen for me.' He gestured round. 'The Roseblood stands on the river. We can send or receive whoever and whatever we want. Our enemies cannot, will not tolerate this; hence our summons to the Guildhall tomorrow.'

'But Candlemas and Cross-Biter,' Raphael warned, 'will take the oath.'

'If they are there.'

'And if they are?' Raphael insisted, curbing the panic pains in his already nervous belly.

'I will challenge them to trial by combat, as is my right. Now, business as normal. *The Excalibur* awaits.'

'What about Sevigny?' Father Benedict asked. He waited as Simon translated the question for Ignacio, followed by the henchman's reply.

'He will strike whenever he can and we shall certainly strike back.'

'And the stranger?' Katherine spoke up. 'Master Reginald Bray? He sits in our tavern like a sparrow on a branch watching everything.'

'He will reveal his hand soon enough.' Simon chewed his lip. 'I cannot decide whether he is friend or foe. But come, *The Glory of Gascony* is making its way up the Thames. The Fraternity of the Doomed must be ready. I shall go with you this evening. Prior Aelred at Greyfriars wants to speak to me.'

A short while later, Raphael, heavily cloaked and hooded, joined the rest leaving by the water gate, making their way past the old Roman ruin down to the quayside. He rubbed his stomach. It was a brilliant evening; indeed, too bright. The stars were clear and full, while the moon hung like a thick silver disc. Nevertheless, the day had been warm and a river mist was gathering, a grey mass of weaving wisps that seemed to gather in the middle of the river before spreading. Some concealment would be possible. Seven other figures slid through the dark either side of him: his father, Ignacio, Monkshood and four of their captains. They paused at the old lighthouse where Pennywort and Loosestrife kept their nightly watch. The two beggars, sheltered by the ruins and warmed by a bed of crackling charcoal, told them strange tales about shuttered lanterns flickering close by the Roseblood and fire arrows being loosed against the sky, though what these betokened remained a mystery. Raphael was concerned, though his father believed both beggars had gulped too many black jacks of strong ale.

They whispered farewell and moved on down to where the Fisher-King and his barge *The Excalibur* were ready to cast off. Lantern horns glowed either side of the prow and a powerful stern light flared against the darkness. The six oarsmen took their places; Raphael and the rest squatted in the canopied stern. The order was given and *The Excalibur* eased away on the swell, a tilt boat towed securely behind it. The tide was running strong, the breeze light; only the river mist was a reminder of how treacherous the Thames could be. Raphael stared up at the midnight sky and wondered if it was pregnant with fresh terrors for the new day. The lights of the Guildhall would burn low tonight as Malpas and Sevigny plotted their strategy. He forced himself to relax, to concentrate on what was happening.

The barge headed downriver, aiming for the great reed banks. Along the wharves and quaysides bonfires flared, torches spluttered, sounds and cries echoed strangely. The air was rich with the tang of the river and its added swirl of odours: thick mud, burning pitch tar, salted herring and the ever-clinging smell of fish sauce. The barge passed scaffolds and gibbets where river pirates hung; their corpses, left for three turns of the tide, turned slightly on the swell.

The Fraternity of the Doom now became involved in their great work of charity, searching for corpses swept by the tide into the thick forest of reed and water sedge. They found two: an old man clothed in a threadbare tunic floating face down, the body bobbing out as if to greet them and beg to be plucked out; the second, on the edge of the reed beds, a flaxen-haired woman, a red shawl spreading out like a cloud around her. They bundled the old man's corpse into the barge, then turned the woman over. In the dancing light her face was truly gruesome, a mask of horror, twisted and discoloured. The rough twine round her throat had strangled her as tight as any chicken, according to Cat's-Head, the principal rower. Raphael took one look and agreed with the rest that this was Calista, who had recently disappeared.

The Excalibur nosed for a while amongst the reeds and then turned, its grisly cargo lying sheeted on the floor, and rowed out to midstream, going down to where the cogs, carracks and ships of many kinds and nations rode at anchor. They passed Broken Wharfe and Trygge Lane, heading towards the grim dark mass of Baynard Castle. Raphael and Ignacio studied the shadowy outlines of various ships: the glittering sterns of Venetian carracks, the big-bellied cogs from Lubeck.

'There!' Raphael pointed to the darkness. 'The Sanctus sign.' He watched as a shuttered lantern flashed the words of the mass: 'Holy, holy, holy.' He murmured a prayer. The light flashed again and he recited along with it, finishing with 'Hosanna.' The rhythm of his speech was identical to the flashes from the lantern horn.

'It's safe, pull in,' he ordered. The barge did so.

Raphael tried to ignore the corpses hidden under their rough sacking, to forget the horrid anguish on Calista's face, her throat all tight.

'Raphael!' his father hissed. Raphael shook himself free of his dire reverie and left the canopied stern to ensure that the tilt boat remained secure. As they closed in on *The Glory of Gascony*, its master Jean Betoun whispered greetings over the taffrail. Simon responded, and the finest claret from the fertile vineyards of Saint-Emilion, outside Bordeaux, was swiftly lowered down into both barge and tilt boat. Good-natured insults were exchanged between the crews. At last, just before they left the deep-bellied cog, Betoun leaned over the gap where the rail had been removed.

'For what it's worth,' he hissed through the darkness, 'rumour has it that French war galleys are mustering off Boulogne. Thank God you are not living in the Cinque Ports.'

Raphael acknowledged this. He wanted to be away. The tide was turning, the barge rising and falling against the hull of the wine ship. He was also anxious, and Betoun's warning did little to soothe him. He recalled those two beggars sheltering in the ancient ruin, chattering about lanterns gleaming and fire arrows red against the sky. Why so close to the Roseblood? He tried to raise the matter with Simon, but his father was more phlegmatic, checking the tuns and barrels, though Betoun was a man of honour, innocent of any trickery.

'Father, we should go,' Raphael insisted. 'Those strange lights, the fire arrows! God knows what mischief the council are up to; there might even be war barges on the river.'

Simon simply grunted, pressing his seal against the last two barrels being loaded on to the barge. Raphael waited impatiently. Only twice before had they been forced to pitch their cargo into the Thames; he didn't want a third time.

At last they pulled away. The oarsmen, cowled against the cold river mist, leaned over their oars, quietly chanting the verses of some song as they ploughed the now choppy river, heading towards the quayside close to Greyfriars, a lonely wharf used solely by the Franciscans. As they drew alongside, lay brothers appeared out of the murk, whispering 'Alleluia!' This was followed by subdued laughter as the good brothers lifted the wine on to the waiting carts. It would be taken to the friary cellars, decanted into barrels from the Roseblood, and then quietly carted to the tavern. The tuns would be given back to *The Glory of Gascony* when it next docked. Consequently no custom official would find a barrel of Bordeaux unstamped in the cellars of either Greyfriars or the Roseblood. The smuggling was much suspected but never proved. Raphael, who kept the ledgers, reckoned they would make heavy profits, especially during this present sea war with France. The money paid to Betoun and Prior Aelred was proving to be a most lucrative investment.

When they entered the cold, incense-smelling precincts of Greyfriars, however, the bony-faced prior seemed agitated. He greeted his midnight guests in his parlour, served them spiced posset and explained how Brother Gabriel was on a journey to Canterbury so could not meet his family, whilst Beaufort and his retinue had moved to the Tower. Every so often he would pause as a lay brother hurried in to whisper in his ear. Eventually Aelred put his goblet down and took Simon and Raphael down to the friary's icy, whitewashed vaulted death house. The corpse of the old man they had plucked from the river had been washed, blessed and rolled in a linen shroud emblazoned with a black cross. Calista, however, was sprawled on a corpse table. Her clothes had been removed and placed on the floor, and a linen scrap covered her privy parts. When the infirmarian removed this, Raphael glanced away, pushing the pomander provided against both mouth and nose. He could not control his stomach and fled the death house to vomit in the yard.

His father eventually came out to join him. 'From what I understand,' Simon declared, one hand on his son's shoulder, 'whoever did that strangled her first with a rough cord. He then took a knife and mutilated her Venus parts, God assoile her. I've paid Aelred to sing three requiems. He'll sheet her and bury the corpse honourably in the poor man's lot. What you saw, Raphael, keep to yourself. Rumour and gossip fly swifter than sparrows along the streets of our ward. There is enough turmoil and tumult. Now come, I understand we have a visitor.'

'In a while.' Raphael could still feel his stomach lurching. He turned his face to the cold breeze. What he'd seen deeply repelled him. He felt a sickness of both heart and soul, a cloying weariness that killed all joy. He recalled meeting Calista one May's eve; how they'd fumbled, kissed and laughed in those ruins overlooking the Thames.

'Sweet Jesus, have mercy on her,' he prayed. Who could have done that? When had these disappearances started? Who was the first? He closed his eyes. Surely it was Damana, about a month ago? But why then? Who had emerged in the ward during that time? Sevigny? LeCorbeil? He opened his eyes. Then there was that innocent-looking pilgrim, the one Katherine called a sparrow, with his sharp eyes and benign smile.

'Raphael!' He glanced to his right. A shadow moved. Confused, his mind riven by what he'd just seen, and tired after the river journey, Raphael was sluggish. 'Raphael!' the voice hissed. 'A message for your father. We are both the slave and the master of what we were, what we are, what we've done and what we do. We watch and wait. Our day is fast approaching. Vengeance will be ours . . .'

The voice was so mocking, Raphael leapt to his feet, the fury curdling within him coursing like a fire. He flung himself in the direction of the voice, so swift he caught the edge of a cloak. He stumbled, but steadied himself, drawing both sword and dagger. He lunged and gasped in pleasure as his blades caught steel, their scraping clash ringing like a bell across the deserted courtyard. He lunged again, using every trick Ignacio had taught him, dagger constant, sword blade whirling, turning slightly sideways as he attempted to drive his opponent across to where torchlight flared against the blackness. He drew a deep breath. He had caught and engaged his opponent, but his adversary was equally swift and skilful. He concentrated on the slither of steel swirling before him.

Shouts of, 'Out! Out! Out! Harrow! Harrow!' showed that the alarm had been raised at this clash of weaponry. Doors were flung open. Raphael could hear his father shouting, yet he fought on, driving his opponent back. They reached a runnel, a narrow gap between the friary buildings, and his adversary was gone. Raphael crouched to catch his breath, aware of the sweat drenching his skin; his father, Prior Aelred and others gathered round. Swords were being drawn; the sound of footsteps echoed.

'Who was it?' Aelred demanded.

'I glimpsed a fleeting shadow, a night-tripping demon, but now he has gone.' Raphael tried to control the sickness in his belly even as his father crouched to face him. 'I am not strong enough for this,' he whispered.

'Nonsense,' his father retorted. 'You would have killed him. You attacked him like any good knight. Who was it? Sevigny? What did he say?'

Raphael told him.

'LeCorbeil!' Simon retorted. 'He is spinning his web. God knows what, but your speed surprised him. He will be more careful in the future. Now come.' He got up. 'The hour is late. Soon the good brothers will sing Matins, but we have a visitor.'

Raphael followed his father and Prior Aelred back into the maze of friary buildings. They were ushered into a comfortable chamber, where the pilgrim Reginald Bray sat, smiling benevolently as always. Raphael and his father took stools before the table. Prior Aelred gestured at wine, bread and cheese. Raphael filled the goblets and broke up the manchet loaf and hardened cheese. Once finished, he offered these to their visitor, who courteously refused.

'I understand,' Bray's voice was deep and throaty, 'that you have had quite a stirring evening. An intruder, yes?'

'So I believe,' Raphael snapped.

'LeCorbeil!' Bray replied. 'It must have been him. And you, Raphael, truly surprised him. But enough.' He sipped at his goblet. 'Master Simon, you are Beaufort's henchman. I am new to his service, being indentured to the Lady Margaret; she is the thirteen-year-old daughter of your former master, John Beaufort, First Duke of Somerset. Margaret is a young woman with the pale, smooth face of a maid and eyes a thousand years old. So,' Bray gathered his cloak about him, 'I am not here to discuss the disappearance of whores, the smuggling of the best wine from Bordeaux or the perjured testimony of Candlemas.' He smiled. 'I am confident, one way or the other, that you will meet that challenge. I speak on the logical premise that you will.'

He paused and stretched across to grasp Simon's arm. 'Raphael, your father is a survivor; he is also a man whom my mistress and the Beaufort lords trust with their very lives.' He removed his hand. 'Indeed, Master Simon Roseblood is more Beaufort than the Beauforts.' He produced a sealed document from the folds of his robe. 'This is from the Lady Margaret, so that you know I am to be trusted.'

Simon broke the red blob of wax, moved the candlestick closer, then passed the document to Raphael. The contents were stark and simple. Written undoubtedly by the Lady Margaret herself, the letter introduced Reginald Bray, her 'trusty and well-beloved clerk', to Simon Roseblood, 'close friend and henchman' of her late beloved father, the good duke. It went on to describe how Bray wore her signet ring on the little finger of his right hand – Raphael glanced quickly at this – whilst around his neck hung a medal of St Maurice, her dead father's patron saint. Raphael could see that the letter had not been opened and resealed, so the description given was in full accord with what he now saw.

'Very good.' He handed the document back. 'So you are whom you claim to be. A rare enough event in this vale of tears.'

'Amadeus Sevigny?' Simon asked.

'A mailed clerk. York trusts him as my mistress does you, though Sevigny is not liked by the duke's wife, Dame Cecily, the so-called Rose of Raby.'

'Why not?'

'We'll come to that; I have my suspicions. However, let me assure you, Sevigny is cunning and skilled. He played a hand in Jack Cade's revolt.'

'My brother was—'

'I have heard about that, though Sevigny would not be involved. He is too cunning to start a blood feud. Plotting politics is his skill. The destruction of York's enemies by process of law, hence Candlemas turning King's Approver. Our noble sheriff, Malpas, is too ignorant for such a ploy; he lacks both the courage and the wit. Sevigny wants to block you and,' Bray squinted through the gloom, 'more dangerous for us, subvert your allegiance.'

'Never!'

'War is coming, Raphael. Men will assemble with the commissioners of array, wearing York's livery with Lancaster's beneath. The lords, the merchants and even the clergy will change sides as fast as a rat scuttles. Men will be bought, body and soul.'

Simon snorted with laughter and grasped Raphael's arm. 'We are as one on this.'

'Good.' Bray looked serenely at Raphael.

'My father speaks for me.'

'Ever the lawyer,' Bray grinned. 'Which is what I am as well. Now, LeCorbeil. He has undoubtedly spied on you. He followed you into this friary to frighten you as well as to create the illusion that he can come and go as he wishes, threaten, menace, but never be held to account. Your ferocious response will give him food for thought. I understand that in the tourney at the Inns Court you won a reputation for such swordplay.'

Raphael shrugged, slightly embarrassed at the praise. 'Now, LeCorbeil, what do you know of him?'

Simon summarised what he had said in the Camelot

Chamber at the Roseblood. When he had finished, Bray nodded in agreement.

'LeCorbeil's leader is undoubtedly a man of great wit and sharp mind. He is a mummer, a shape-shifter, appearing here and there.' Bray held up a warning finger. 'He leads a group just as skilled and highly organised. They are masters of the crossbow—'

'But there are many such,' Raphael interrupted.

'No, no. Listen,' his father declared. 'I have heard of this. Master Reginald, I suspect what you are going to say.'

'In the last great conflicts in France,' Bray continued, 'when the English lords went on chevauchée or laid siege to castles, the number of English captains killed was quite significant. Reports came in of master bowmen who singled out the English commander and, when given the opportunity, loosed a killing bolt.'

Raphael made to interrupt again, but his father seized his wrist. 'Listen, Raphael, in battle, what are you frightened of?'

'Why, the enemy!'

'Of course. You turn, strike, shield and sword moving up and down, but these master bowmen don't.'

'It requires great courage,' Bray declared. 'They ignore what is happening around them and concentrate solely on their intended victim. Now such a bowman can be protected, but this must be done subtly, otherwise you will attract the attention of your enemy. The master bowman waits. The English lord, either mounted or on foot, is surrounded by his henchmen. He is fully armoured, his visor down. Sooner or later he must raise that visor, even for a short while, to breathe more freely, to cool his face, and that is all the master bowman needs. The bolt is loosed, the commander killed, banners fall, chaos ensues.' Bray pulled a face. 'We believe LeCorbeil are responsible, individually or as a group, for such killings. They have snatched the lives of a great number of English commanders in France.'

'But here in England, both York and Lancaster remain their enemy?' Raphael asked.

'Now,' Bray sighed, 'we come to LeCorbeil's other undoubted challenge. They provoke agitation, which is what happened in Kent and Essex during Cade's uprising. More importantly, when this city decided to resist, its military commander, Matthew Gough, Captain of the Tower, together with John Sutton, a leading alderman, rallied to defend London Bridge. LeCorbeil were undoubtedly there. Gough, Sutton and others were killed by this.'

Bray opened his wallet and took out a squat red-feathered crossbow bolt. Raphael studied it. A lethal shot, the goose flight starched and firm at the end of its elm-wood stem, whilst its jagged steel point could easily crack a man's skull or shatter the bones of his face to a bloody mess.

'That's their weapon of war. So, LeCorbeil are here,' Bray continued briskly, 'to stir and agitate as well as wage their own blood feud against the Beauforts. The only solution we have is to kill them all.'

Bray's doom-like words rang like a funeral bell.

Raphael stared across at a crucifix nailed to the wall. A triptych to its right proclaimed scenes from the Passion of Christ. Did Jesus's sufferings, Raphael wondered, have any relevance to himself, his father, his family? They had no choice but to swim in a filthy sweep of politics, perjury and perdition. Even this chamber, sanctified by decades of prayer, fasting, study and soul-searching, was being used to describe bloody murder, vengeance and treason.

'Am I . . . are we,' Simon asked, 'responsible for LeCorbeil's destruction?'

'Yes and no,' Bray replied. 'But first, we must destroy someone else.' He clasped his hands, fingers laced. 'Beaufort, York and LeCorbeil share one thing in common: they fish in very troubled waters. Have you ever heard of Giles Argentine?'

'A doctor,' Simon murmured, 'one who used to be much in demand by the great and the good: a royal physician, a member of the King's household. He studied at Salerno and even amongst the Moors in Spain. Beaufort sometimes talked about Argentine, a man who loves wealth and intrigue.'

'Too true,' Bray agreed. 'But now Argentine has disappeared from court because of his love of mischief.'

Bray poured some more wine, then rose. He opened and closed the door before walking around the parlour ensuring that all the shutters on the outside of the windows were firmly sealed. At last he returned to his chair.

'Now you know,' he hunched forward, his voice just

above a whisper, 'how Richard of York alleges that our present King Henry's son and heir is actually the illegitimate offspring of Queen Margaret of Anjou and the great love of her life, Edmund Beaufort, recently promoted to Duke of Somerset after the death of his brother John, the first duke. God and his angels know the truth,' Bray added. 'Queen Margaret certainly shows enough passion for her favourite, being guided by his every word.'

'And the truth?' Raphael demanded. Bray just looked away.

'Argentine,' he replied, measuring his words, 'claims to know the truth, having been present at the royal birth as well as being personal physician to our noble King, with all his failings, both physical and mental. Argentine claims to hold certain documents regarding these.'

'Is he implying,' Raphael asked, 'that the King is impotent?'

'I cannot, shall not answer that.' Bray refused to meet his eye. 'The problem is that York wishes to seize this learned physician and all his documents.'

'Naturally!' Simon declared.

'Ah, but there is more. You see, York himself has secrets, and these may be the source of the antipathy between York's wife and his henchman, Sevigny. Argentine was also hired by York; he was present at the birth of the duke's eldest son, Edward. Gossipmongers whisper that Edward is not York's but the result of an infatuation by his duchess for an English archer in the garrison at Rouen. So, you can understand: the Queen and the Beaufort lords need to silence Argentine and use whatever secrets he holds about York against the duke, who in turn also wishes to seize Argentine.'

Bray raised his eyebrows. 'Finally there is LeCorbeil and their French masters, who have learnt all about this. They are also hunting Argentine, and you can see why. For over a hundred years, English monarchs have claimed the crown of France by descent from Isabella, once Queen of England. You can imagine how the French now watch the pot of bubbling intrigue here in England. When Richard II was deposed in 1399, the crown went to the House of Lancaster, both the royal line and its illegitimate offshoot, namely the Beauforts. York maintains that he has a better claim. Now there is this foolish physician with his scandalous stories about how the heirs of both York and Lancaster have no claim to anything, be it their own dukedoms or the crown of England.'

'Or of France?'

'Oh yes, Raphael. How the masters of secrets in the palaces of the Louvre and Fontainebleau would love to proclaim that abroad. They would make a mockery of us all over Europe.'

'So LeCorbeil has also joined the hunt?' Raphael laughed abruptly. 'Little wonder Argentine has disappeared. Whom will he turn to?'

'Logically the French. He will be safer, more honoured, greatly rewarded and protected. York and Lancaster would probably seize his manuscripts and cut his throat.'

'Where is he hiding, do you know?'

'In the house of lepers, St Giles Hospital, near Tyburn stream, close to the great scaffold. We have done our searches. I certainly have; my task whilst lodged at the Roseblood. St Giles is the logical choice for a man like Argentine.'

'Nonsense!' Raphael exclaimed.

'True!' his father declared. 'Leprosy is a living death. It can only be contracted by eating the same food, drinking the same water as lepers, and above all by constant and close touch with them.' He smiled grimly. 'An excellent place to hide; even if people suspected, they would remain wary. Most people flee at the very thought. I suspect Argentine has bribed the master of the hospital, whoever that is, to be given a private cell, his own clothes and fresh food. He is a physician; he will know exactly what to do to resist the contagion.' Simon winked at Raphael. 'I have travelled to Outremer. I have also had many dealings with lepers, usually former soldiers.'

'Master Simon,' Bray smiled, 'you are certainly correct on one thing. The master of the hospital is Joachim Brotherton.'

'Who?'

'To many just a name, but I have also learnt he is close kin to Argentine and a great lover of silver.' Bray held up a hand, up as if taking an oath. 'I know he's there. He must be, and we must deal with him.'

'Ah.' Simon's voice faltered at the way Bray was studying him. 'You want me to enter St Giles?'

Bray nodded his agreement, then, stooping down,

picked up a chancery bag. He shook out its contents: a scroll, documents sealed with coloured wax, and a heavy purse.

'Simon, the Beauforts ask you this as a great boon to themselves and your dead beloved master Duke John. You are a man of great subtlety and subterfuge. You are also deeply acquainted with all aspects of this city. You control many of the counterfeit men, who can replicate the most repellent diseases, infections and other morbid conditions. You have also served in Outremer and know a great deal about leprosy. We want you to enter St Giles, find Argentine, kill him if necessary and seize all his documents.'

'Why now?'

'Because Sevigny and LeCorbeil are also hunting him. It's only a matter of time before one or both of them find him, to our great loss.'

Bray paused at the tolling of a bell, followed shortly afterwards by the swell of voices from the choir chanting the opening lines of a psalm: 'Blessed be the Lord God of Israel who throws horse and rider into the great deep.'

'Aye, blessed is he indeed,' Raphael whispered. He glanced at his father, who just shrugged and raised his eyes heavenwards.

'Soon York will move,' Bray hurried on. 'The Queen and Beaufort will have no choice but to confront him. We will all be part of that. We must strike before this city slips into chaos, which is what Argentine and LeCorbeil will be waiting for.'

'You suspect that LeCorbeil know where Argentine is?'

'Oh yes, but their problem is moving him undetected. We do not have anyone in St Giles, though watchers remain beyond its walls. You will pose as Brother Simon, a hospitaller, a lay brother from Rhodes. You are suffering from leprosy in its second stage; these documents prove this. They also carry recommendations for your acceptance by St Giles. More importantly, the bag of gold and silver will open all doors without any trouble.'

'And the duchess's dislike of Sevigny?' Raphael asked. 'It's because of this secret scandal?'

'From the little we have learnt,' Bray shifted, 'Duchess Cecily has always resented Sevigny for being too close to her husband and the master of many of his secrets.'

'And will LeCorbeil and Sevigny work as allies on this—'

'Oh no,' his father interrupted. 'This goes beyond York; true, Master Reginald?'

Bray nodded. Simon sat, head down, feet tapping the floor.

'I accept.' He waved at Raphael to keep silent. 'I accept for many reasons, but I pray I meet LeCorbeil.' He scooped up the documents and the purse.

'Master Simon,' Bray gestured around, 'our world is about to be turned upside down. One final thing. If matters go against us, we will need your tavern, your assistance in fleeing the power of York.'

Amadeus Sevigny

London, April 1455

Amadeus Sevigny stepped around the splintered door. He gazed in utter disbelief even as he shouted at Skulkin and Walter Ramler to stay outside. He stared down the narrow, windowless corridor in the Shadows of Purgatory, a city house used to shelter those who had secret business with council officials, then glanced back into the bedchamber at the two corpses sprawled there: Candlemas and Cross-Biter, two King's Approvers.

'Now you have gone to a higher court,' Sevigny whispered. 'But who dispatched you there, who served the demand for your souls and how they did it is a great mystery.'

He stared round the secure chamber, wrinkling his nose at the fetid stench from the jakes pot, then crossed to the window. He loosened the clasps, pulled back the shutters and tried the iron bars embedded deep in the concrete sill. They held firm. He moved to the corpses, which both lay stretched out, daggers not far from their hands, and knelt to scrutinise them. The cadavers were hardened, eyes staring glassily in that last startled gaze as their souls fled into the darkness. Both men had died in pain, mouths gaping, their unshaven faces a horrid pallor. Sevigny sniffed their mouths and knelt for a while, thinking. Then he crossed himself, got to his feet and carefully inspected the wine flagon and cups. He could detect no taint, either there or on the food platters; not a trace of the malignant odour that, even hours after it was administered, would seep from poisoned food and wine. Perplexed, he ransacked the stinking, shabby chamber. He could find nothing out of the ordinary.

'Walter, Skulkin?' He called both men into the chamber. 'Look around,' he invited them. 'This chamber was secure.' He pointed back to the heavy door. 'No one came in here until I did this morning, yes?'

'Yes.' Skulkin retorted, his heavy face all flushed. 'Last night they were given wine, a platter of bread, fruit, cheeses and meat.'

'Who served them that?'

'I did,' squeaked Ramler, the scribe. 'Master, you came here yesterday evening . . .'

'I know that,' Sevigny replied drily. 'What I want to establish is what happened after I left.'

'Both Candlemas and Cross-Biter were in good health,' gabbled Ramler. 'Skulkin and I brought up the food and wine.'

Sevigny raised a hand for silence. He went and knelt near the corpses.

'Unloved in life, ugly in death,' he whispered. The chapped, unshaven grey face of Cross-Biter was heavily pitted with the pox, whilst Candlemas's skin, now even paler in the pallor of death, seemed tight and taut. 'Fetch a physician to scrutinise the corpses,' he ordered. 'Have them removed to the death chamber at the Guildhall.' Once again he sniffed at the mouths of both corpses but could detect nothing except the very rich odour of claret. He rose, went across to the table and scrutinised both the food remnants and the last dregs of wine in the large jug.

'Master?' Ramler now came up close beside Sevigny, beckoning at Skulkin to follow. 'Last night – and Skulkin will verify this – I brought up both food and wine. Candlemas, as you know, was very suspicious and wary. He was terrified that Roseblood would strike.'

Sevigny grunted his agreement.

'Master, he didn't trust any of us either.'

Sevigny noticed how the scrivener was highly nervous; his pert, rather pretty face was sheened with sweat. Ramler was a fussy little man, but kinsman Malpas trusted him implicitly. Sevigny glanced at the rugged, burly Skulkin, again a man deeply trusted by the sheriff.

'I did my best,' the scrivener's words came in a rush, 'didn't I, Skulkin? I drank some of the wine.'

'A good half-goblet,' Skulkin agreed. 'As did I. Candlemas insisted that we eat and drink a little of everything we brought. We did so, then bade them good night. The door was bolted and barred on the outside.' He walked over, pushing it back on its stout leather hinges. 'My men and I were on guard at the foot of the stairs; no one went up. This door was not opened until you came just before the Jesus bell.'

Sevigny gestured at the wine and food. 'Have these taken into the Guildhall cellars. Leave them there until the Angelus bell, then go down and search for dead rats. If there is poison, you'll find them. I will be in the church of St Mary-le-Bow. Master Walter, report back to Sheriff Malpas, tell him the obvious: Roseblood's indictment cannot go ahead.'

Both men hastened to obey. Sevigny went down the stairs and collected his war belt and cloak from one of the bailiffs, who, when asked, faithfully repeated what Skulkin and Ramler had described. Sevigny shook his head in disbelief, left the house and walked down Cheapside. It was a beautiful fresh spring morning; a golden sun in the deep blue sky. Already the city was busy with tinkers, traders and merchants eager to seize the hour and make a profit. The gong carts were out, piled high with the stinking, steaming ordure of the previous day. Rakers and scavengers walked beside each cart, all hooded and masked. Sevigny glanced at these and wondered if the rumours sweeping the Guildhall were true. How Roseblood had brutally executed three men who had allegedly tried to usurp his authority over the scavengers in Cripplegate. He walked along the great thoroughfare and turned right, entering the empty cavernous porch of St Mary-le-Bow.

In the beautifully carved lady chapel, Sevigny sat on the stool he'd plucked from the sanctuary and stared up at the face of the statue of the Virgin. He loved this church, and no better than now. The early-morning sunlight poured like God's grace through the painted glass windows, driving away the ghostly shadows and filling the nave with glowing colours. The air remained rich with the fragrances left after the Jesus mass. Incense and candle smoke curled and mingled.

Sevigny rose and put a coin in the alms box riveted to the floor. He lit three tapers, placing them gently on the spigot; one for each of his parents and the third for himself. Then he knelt on the blue and gold prie-dieu, crossed himself and recited the requiem followed by an Ave Maria. Afterwards he went back to sit on the stool, aware of the church quietening as the last worshippers left, the side chapels emptied and the sacristans finished their tasks on the high altar. The statue of the Virgin, carved by some master craftsman, had the most exquisitely serene face, which always conjured up visions of his own mother. Distant gold-tinged memories of sweet eyes and the gentlest touch before his world turned black as night and the forces of Hell consumed that lonely manor house high on the Yorkshire moors. Demons with smoky faces, hanging corpses . . .

Sevigny blinked, crossed himself swiftly and glanced away. He felt deeply uneasy. Kinsman Malpas, sheriff of this city, was a royal officer but was secretly working for York and would not flinch at murder or perjury to get his way. Simon Roseblood was supposed to be Sevigny's enemy, yet he liked the man; something about him struck a chord of friendship. Undoubtedly Roseblood was dangerous, yet the alderman taverner was devoted to his family and seemed to easily win and keep the allegiance and friendship of others. A gang leader, but a very generous one, who looked after not only his rifflers but also those who simply couldn't cope with the harshness of life. Sevigny had kept the tavern under close scrutiny. He had questioned rigorously and listened attentively. The community of the Roseblood and its parish church of All Hallows seemed pleasant enough.

Sevigny grinned to himself. That certainly included Simon's daughter, Katherine. In truth, he found it difficult to forget her: the tangled auburn hair framing that fierce ivory-white face, the determined lips, those beautiful light green eyes. '*Femina ferrea*,' he whispered to himself. Truly a woman of iron, and yet a beautiful damsel with a talent no other woman possessed, at least as far as Sevigny was concerned. She made him laugh, smile and relax. Lovely of face and fair of form undoubtedly, yet Mistress Katherine was also funny: the way she drew herself up, her dramatic confrontation with him followed by the swift allegation that he was Mordred come to Avalon. He would have loved her to stay, to tease her mercilessly and demand to know, if he was Mordred, then who was she? Katherine Roseblood was a dreamer, and one with no deceit, nothing contrived, none of the false smiles and self-serving simpering of so many court ladies. Try as he might to ignore her, she remained fresh in his mind's eye. Sevigny prided himself on being alone, at peace with his own presence. This was different. He missed

Katherine and wanted to meet her again, sooner rather than later.

Sevigny peeled off his black leather gauntlets and undid his sword belt. He also recalled those strange sights around the Roseblood, that whore with the flaming hair walking so close to a priest, friar or monk. Was it one of the priests from All Hallows? He was intrigued. He had heard the rumours, and Skulkin had informed him about the whores disappearing in Queenhithe ward. He shrugged; that was not his business.

He idly wondered how his servant, Bardolph the bowman, was faring at the Golden Harp, a rather dingy tavern along an alleyway off Bread Street. York's household had ordered Bardolph to be Sevigny's henchman on his journey south. In the main, Sevigny had avoided the surly, taciturn Dalesman, a former archer in Warwick's retinue, a hard-bitten veteran who, by his own admission, had little time for the great lords. Bardolph had kept his own counsel as they journeyed south along that ancient Roman road. By the time they reached London, Sevigny's patience had worn thin. He had brusquely instructed Bardolph to stay at the tavern, tend the horses, guard the baggage and be ready to hasten north if there was any news.

The clerk rose and walked slowly down the northern transept. He paused to examine a wall painting depicting the Angel of the Blood, the Herald of the Antichrist appearing with the host of smoky-faced demons above the leaping, soul-burning fires of Hell. 'Judgement time,' Sevigny whispered. 'Yes, judgement time is close.' The

House of Lancaster had been weighed in the balance and found wanting. York would assert his claim. Sevigny had been sent to London to prepare for this. York had taken him into his secret chamber, its one lozenge-shaped window bright with sunlight. The floor was of red tile; bare white plaster-covered walls at least a foot thick. The chamber lay at the heart of Middleham Castle, the centre of York's power. No door-lurker could approach, no spy overhear the conversation of this great duke, direct descendant of Edward III, who dreamed deep dreams of seizing the crown and establishing his own dynasty. Shadows leapt like troubled ghosts around that ill-lit privy chamber as York described his secret commission to a clerk he trusted with his life.

'Go to London, Amadeus.' His long, wind-bitten face pressed close, blue popping eyes unblinking, blond moustache and beard streaked with grey. He leaned so close Sevigny could smell the oil of roses the duke loved to soak himself in. 'Make yourself known to our friends in the city, especially kinsman Malpas. Obstruct the likes of Roseblood. Bring him down or turn him to our cause. Make whatever mischief you can against our enemies. Seek out LeCorbeil. Watch him and his coven for the malicious sprites they are. If necessary, we will use him, but he is no friend of ours or the crown that is mine by right. Find the malignant Argentine. Undoubtedly both LeCorbeil and the Beauforts will be hunting him too.'

York paused, playing with his signet ring boasting the Yorkist colours of blue and murrey. 'Argentine distils rumour about my lovely wife.' Sevigny caught a tinge of sarcasm in the duke's voice. 'Kill him for the malicious gossip he is. Seize his manuscripts. Discover what you can about the power of our enemy in London.' York always refused to name the King; instead he would refer to the 'bastard Beauforts', and their ally Queen Margaret as 'the Jezebel of Anjou'.

'Above all, Amadeus, seek out the sorcerer, the warlock, Ravenspur. Ask him to cast my horoscope and that of my line. He gave me good advice before.' York pushed a bulging coin purse into his clerk's hand. 'Use this as you think fit.'

Sevigny recalled that conversation, as he did the duchess's beautiful, spiteful face as he left York's chamber. He'd stepped aside for her on the narrow, gloomy spiral staircase. She and her ladies passed in an exquisite aura of perfume, lace, silk and taffeta. Duchess Cecily, however, paused just for a breath, her lovely heart-shaped face all sharp and predatory, those rose lips curled back in a rictus of hate. For once she had let the mask slip. Sevigny would never forget that look. She recognised what he knew, and for that alone she would take his head. He could not continue in the face of such rancour. He recalled his teacher, Eadmer the Rhetorician at Fountains Abbey. 'Be logical in all you do, Amadeus. Follow Aristotle. Think good thoughts. Do good acts. Anger and hate are swift horses to Hell.'

Sevigny glanced up at the elaborately carved rood screen that separated the nave from the chancel. In the centre rose a crucifix flanked either side by life-size statues of the Virgin and St John. Beside these, he noted with amusement, were similar statues of the leading merchants of Cheapside when the rood screen was first erected. His smile faded. Duchess Cecily! She resented him knowing her family scandals. She was also the one who encouraged the duke to consult warlocks and sorcerers such as Ravenspur, though Sevigny constantly warned him to desist. The dark arts were a true menace; their practitioners met in stinking charnel houses and gloomy haunted cemeteries to make the midnight sacrifice. If the duke was discovered, accusations of witchcraft and even treason could be levelled, and he would have to face both the wrath of the Crown and the full power of the Church. The fate of Joanna of Navarre, widow of Henry IV, as well as that of the present King's uncle, Humphrey, Duke of Gloucester, showed that nobility was no defence against judgement. York, however, remained insistent, whispering how Ravenspur had exciting news for him that could only be communicated by word of mouth.

Thankfully, Ravenspur would have to seek Sevigny out here in London, so all he had to do was wait. Other problems would not. LeCorbeil, that elusive French threat, could be anywhere. London thronged with Bretons, Burgundians, Gascons, Picards and other French mercenaries, all seeking to seal indentures with the great lords as the bubbling cauldron of bloody politics came to full boil and spilled over into war. LeCorbeil would have to show himself, if he ever did. At the same time, Sevigny's secret hunt for the malicious physician Giles Argentine depended on two sinister creatures, Cosmas and Damian, bounty-hunters, lurchers in human flesh, the very best according to kinsman Malpas. Both had simply been given Argentine's name and description, nothing more, before disappearing into the tangled, murky maze of London's streets, snouting for their quarry, while Sevigny remained busy on other matters, collecting information about royal troops in London, the strength of the garrison at the Tower, the number of men being summoned to Blackheath, which war cogs were moored in the Thames and how many of Beaufort's allies, such as Stafford of Buckingham, were whistling up their liveried retainers. Finally, there was Candlemas.

Sevigny walked across to the life-sized statue of St Christopher, slightly bowed, carrying the Christ Child on his back. The sculptured face of the saint was strained, eyes bulging, mouth gaping under the weight of the burden he carried. Sevigny recalled the legend: how a plea to St Christopher would fend off sudden and violent death that day. Leaning forward, he pressed his lips against the carved stone and whispered his prayer, crossing himself before returning to the problem of Candlemas.

'The dead felon organised the robbery, secretly encouraged by Malpas on behalf of York.' Sevigny paused in his whispering to himself, a common practice ever since childhood. He listened sharply, but the church still lay silent. From outside rose the clanging of market bells and the faint shouts of street-sellers, proclaiming:

'Fresh milk!' 'The purest water from St Mary Grace's!' 'What else do ye lack?' He peered around the church; votive candles flickered before statues but all else remained quiet. Man's business with God was done; now it was Mammon's turn.

'Candlemas,' Sevigny whispered to the statue of St Christopher, 'was a fool, easily duped. The attack was expected; they had only opened one bag full of rusty scraps before Candlemas and his gang were beaten off. Frustrated, Malpas sprang the second part of his trap. Four of Candlemas's coven were seized and, to satisfy justice, executed. Candlemas and his two henchmen fled into hiding. Cosmas and Damian informed me about the underground passage. I killed one of the fugitives and seized the other two, who promptly turned King's Approver. Malpas and I wanted them to indict Roseblood. Placed in a secure room, bolted and locked on the outside, they were served food and wine that to all appearances seemed untainted.'

Sevigny paused at the sound of a door opening and closing. He walked deeper into the nave. Three Franciscan nuns in heavy blue-edged veils and earth-coloured robes had entered St Mary's, moving across to a chantry chapel. Sevigny shrugged and walked back, deep in reflection on what he'd seen, heard and felt in that death chamber. According to all the evidence, Candlemas and Cross-Biter had been safely locked in. Ramler had departed, whilst Skulkin and his coterie remained on guard. Sevigny had arrived just before dawn; the room was still secure, but he had found

Candlemas sprawled dead on the floor near the table stool he'd been sitting on. Cross-Biter lay a little further in, with his head towards the door. The two victims had died violently, faces grotesquely twisted; both men had drawn their daggers, but against what? Was it suicide? Sevigny shook his head. Poison? Yet Ramler and Skulkin had tasted everything and Candlemas had been vigilant against such a threat. So how it had been done?

'Look for the common factor, Amadeus.' The advice of Eadmer sounded like a bell down the memory of years. Malpas's plan to steal the silver had been betrayed. Candlemas was spared to give evidence against Roseblood and he had been betrayed. What was the common factor here? Sevigny sat back on the stool and searched for an answer. In his mind he listed all the people involved in Malpas's plot. He scrutinised each name until a solution occurred. As he sprang to his feet, he heard a soft slurry of movement along the transept. Who could that be? The Franciscan minoresses?

Sevigny's mouth went dry. He quietly cursed his own mistake: those nuns had neither genuflected towards the pyx nor bothered to bless themselves from the holy water stoup. He had half drawn his sword from its sheath when the assassins, now free of their disguise, faces all blackened, slipped out of the shadows. Armed with sword and dagger, they moved silent and soft like deadly wraiths, fanning out, weapons jabbing the air. Former soldiers, Sevigny judged, now turned professional assassins. All three closed, blades whirling. Sevigny stood swaying, sword held in both hands, slightly low so as not to tire easily. He soon had the measure of his three assailants and easily blocked their thrusts, his blade slicing the air between them in an arc of shimmering, twirling steel. He held his ground, then abruptly lunged, jabbing his sword point against the assailant to his right, drawing it back in a savage cut along the left side of the attacker's neck. The man staggered , screaming in pain. Sevigny had turned on the other two when a door crashed open further down the church.

'Master Sevigny, Master Sevigny! You must see this!' Skulkin's voice echoed harshly. Ramler repeated the cry. Both assailants lunged together desperate to strike.

'Aidez-moi! Aidez-moi!' Sevigny shouted the alarm so often heard along London's streets. Skulkin's heavy footsteps rang out. Sevigny's two opponents abruptly broke off, fleeing silently back into the gloom. Sevigny stood, sword down, catching his breath.

'Master Sevigny!' Skulkin, followed by Ramler, hastened towards him. Sevigny ignored them. He collected his war belt and went to crouch by the dying assassin.

'Help me!' The man spluttered blood. 'For sweet God's sake . . .'

'You are dying,' Sevigny remarked. 'You need to be shriven.'

'A priest.' The man's desperate eyes pleaded. 'For mercy's sake.'

'Shall I cut his throat?' Skulkin, kneeling on the other side, drew his misericord dagger.

'A priest! My eternal soul!'

'Damned to Hell!' Skulkin snarled, resting the tip of his dagger against the man's quivering throat.

'Mercy,' Sevigny gently touched the man's face, 'has a price. Who sent you?'

'A stranger. He met us in a tavern, the Inglenook in Southwark. Two silver pieces,' the man gasped, body arching in pain, blood frothing between chapped lips. 'Two pieces for hiring, two more when we were done. We were to bring your seals and war belt as proof.'

'Who?'

'For pity's sake,' the man pleaded.

'I can hear Lord Satan's emissaries,' Sevigny responded. 'Dark and menacing. They gather rattling their chains. So who?'

'On my soul, a stranger, hooded and masked; a soldier, I think. He spoke with a strange accent, that's all I know. Please?' The man's fingers scrabbled at Sevigny's wrist.

'Master?'

'Skulkin, fetch a priest. He will probably demand that our fallen friend be taken out to God's Acre.' Sevigny crossed himself and bowed in the direction of St Christopher's statue. 'This shrine is already polluted and will need to be reconsecrated. Tell the priest to shrive him.' Sevigny tightened his war belt about his waist whilst Skulkin went deftly through the man's paltry possessions. 'Give the priest a coin; keep whatever else you find, including his weapons.' He kicked a dagger away and stared down at the man lost in his last painful agony.

'Then what?' Skulkin asked.

'Send him to God. Master Ramler, what do you want to show me?'

'You'd best see for yourself.' Ramler looked pale and peaky. Sevigny noticed his long eyelashes, and a smear of red on his left cheek.

'Sealing wax stain,' Ramler murmured, following Sevigny's gaze. The clerk went to brush it off, but the scribe hastily stepped back, nervously pawing at the mark before beckoning Sevigny.

'Sir, you must see this. Roseblood—'

'Soon.' Sevigny raised a hand and looked back at the dying man still jerking against the paving stones. Skulkin had hurried out to search for a priest. Sevigny wondered whether Roseblood was responsible for the attack, but was that his way? Or was it LeCorbeil, that French will-o'-the-wisp who seemed to dabble in all kinds of mischief? If so, why? Was it because they were both hunting Argentine? Skulkin would have to take care of all of this; explain to the priest how a royal clerk had been attacked during his oraisons by city assassins. Sevigny recalled the dying man's story of being hired by someone with a strange accent, but that would have to wait.

He followed Ramler out through the corpse door. They crossed the cemetery, which lay quiet under the strengthening sun. Even the birds seemed to have fled from the ancient yew trees, their drooping branches shading the battered crosses and moss-covered houses of the dead. As he approached the majestic lychgate,

Sevigny could hear the shouts and cries that heralded some unexpected tumult along the great thoroughfare of Cheapside. He left the cemetery, following Ramler down a needle-thin alleyway and into the great trading area of London.

Despite the relatively early hour, the markets were thronged; a shifting sea of colour, a shoal of people shoving and jostling their way down the broad concourse: merchants and their wives in their costly embroidered robes, as well as soil-stained peasants pushing their handbarrows piled high with produce. Bells chimed and clanged. Traders shouted prices. Dogs barked and yelped. Children being taken to the church schools darted like sparrows amongst the stalls. Sevigny surveyed the milling crowd. He wondered if the two assassins who had escaped, faces now cleaned, weapons concealed, were mingling with the throng, searching for a fresh opportunity.

The source of the clamour came from the direction of the soaring Tun, the main water conduit of London, with its black-barred prison cage on top packed with the nightwalkers, whores, drunks and other curfew-breakers from the night before. The massive, elaborately sculptured conduit now swarmed with Londoners drawn by the procession assembling there. Sevigny narrowed his eyes and pinched his nostrils. The spring breeze carried the reek of the fleshers' stalls further up Cheapside, close to the ugly, brooding mass of Newgate prison. The odours mingled with the scent of sweat, leather and horses, as well as the stench from a mass of unwashed bodies. The dusty fug cleared and he could clearly glimpse the colourful banners and brilliant sheen of a group gathered on the steps of the Tun. He made out the blue and white standards and pennants of Lancaster, as well as the gorgeous livery of the Vintners' guild. He also glimpsed three long poles with severed heads on the ends, like small black balls against the bright colour behind them.

Sevigny left his vantage point and vigorously pushed his way through the crowd. Other spectators scuttled out of the way of this harsh-featured mailed clerk in his black leather jerkin prigged with gold and silver thread, the war belt strapped around his waist holding a long sword and a stabbing dirk in their brocaded scabbards. Such a man was to be feared and avoided. The palliards, beggars, cunning men and their doxies, who could mark a possible victim from head to toe in the twinkling of an eye, soon recognised the clerk. News of Sevigny's swift and brutal execution of Lazarus, as well as his seizure of Candlemas's gang, had swept the dingy alehouses and dismal taverns. His name, reputation and appearance had been swiftly posted by word of mouth. No one impeded him.

The clerk reached the foot of the steps and stared up at Simon Roseblood, resplendent in his gorgeous alderman's robes. On his right, Raphael was also richly garbed in hose, tunic, soft boots and ermine-lined cloak. On his left, a sight that made Sevigny catch his breath. Katherine stood attired like a great court lady in an exquisite sky-blue dress powdered in gold and silver and trimmed at neck and cuff with the costliest lace from Bruges. Her beautiful auburn hair lay hidden under a thick gauze veil, and a jewelled cross on a silver chain circled her swan-like neck. Her lovely face had been painted to emphasise her lustrous eyes and delicate mouth. She looked slightly amused, her snow-white hands, shimmering with rings, resting against a gold-brocaded stomacher.

In front of Roseblood and his family, on the lower steps, stood Ignacio and other minions whom Sevigny recognised from the tavern. These were all dressed in their master's livery and well armed with swords, daggers and maces. On the bottom step, three members of the Fraternity of the Doomed, garbed completely in black, grasped the long poles bearing the severed heads of Blackshanks and his two companions. Neatly shaven at the neck, these gruesome trophies had been as skilfully pickled and tarred as any of those decorating the parapet along the gatehouse on London Bridge.

On either side of the great Tun stood carts laden with barrels of ale as well as wicker baskets heaped with fresh bread, fruit and dried meats, which servants from the tavern were now preparing to distribute to any citizen who asked. Roseblood and his family, however, just stood there like figures in one of those glorious pageants the city would organise to welcome the return of a conquering king. Sevigny quietly marvelled at the sheer effrontery of the taverner, who seemed to be waiting for other leading citizens and officials to gather and witness the unfolding of this elaborately staged masque.

Hand on sword, the clerk edged closer. Roseblood caught his eye and nodded; Raphael glowered down at him. Katherine's smile, however, widened as if she and Sevigny were fellow conspirators, and try as he might, he could not resist smiling back. Roseblood saw this and took it as a sign to begin. He gestured, and three of his retainers flourishing trumpets came round and stopped just before Sevigny. The clerk stepped back as the trumpets brayed commanding silence. Once they had finished, Roseblood raised his hands.

'Fellow citizens!' His powerful voice carried clear as any clarion. 'Fellow citizens of this great city, I come before you as your alderman, a member of your council, a true subject of His Grace our saintly and well-beloved King. I, who have worked so hard and striven earnestly for this city, have been feloniously threatened and attacked by these malefactors.' Roseblood flourished a hand at the three impaled heads. 'Mark my words, these are not fellow citizens but aliens, foreigners to this great city and, what is more, wolfsheads from the wilds of Essex. These felons had the temerity to trespass on my dwelling, to threaten, menace and subvert the King's peace and that of this city.'

Roseblood's words were greeted with growls and shouts of approval, though Sevigny noticed that some just stood silently staring up at this audacious alderman.

'In the presence of a host of witnesses, now here before you,' Roseblood continued, 'these wretches dared to draw weapons on me, your alderman, in direct contravention of this city's ordnances. If they can do that in my home, what protection does an ordinary citizen have?' The taverner had hit his mark, his words being greeted with roars of approval and shouts of 'Harrow! Harrow!' the usual proclamation when the hue and cry was raised. Roseblood again lifted his hands.

'Fellow citizens, I swear by God, the Virgin and all the angels and saints, especially my patron, Fisherman Peter, that I shall now proceed to the Guildhall, where I will meet my accusers. Mark my words, however: God will strike them down as he did Agag and the Amalekites.'

Roseblood paused to nod at the clear calls of approval. Sevigny stared at Katherine, who grinned impishly back. Sevigny was sure that she and the rest of her family knew about Candlemas and Cross-Biter being long gone to God. He raised one hand in salute before returning to Roseblood, who was now thoroughly enjoying himself.

'In the meantime,' that cunning vintner continued, 'let me share my hope in God's justice as well as that of the King by welcoming you, my fellow citizens, to a celebration fitting for such vindication. Moreover,' Roseblood stilled the growing cheer as the crowd stared hungrily at the heaped carts, 'such hospitality will also be available at my tavern, where true and loyal subjects of our King and this glorious city may raise their tankards and chorus "Alleluia!" in the cause of right.'

Without further ado, Roseblood turned to his trumpeters, and the entire procession, horns and clarions ringing out, standards and pennants fluttering, moved down the conduit steps and along the broad thoroughfare, winding past the stalls, shops and stately mansions of Cheapside to the imposing gateway leading into the great bailey of the Guildhall. Sevigny followed behind. At the gatehouse, a line of Sheriff Malpas's archers and men-at-arms allowed the Roseblood household through but pressed back the accompanying crowd. The throng had now turned into a mob, growing increasingly unruly as the midnight folk of the city, sensing mischief and with a sharp eye to easy pickings, swarmed through. Sevigny was recognised and also permitted through. He hurried to join Malpas, dressed in half-armour, waiting on the steps beneath the soaring statues of Justice, Faith and Wisdom and blocking the entrance to the principal court of the Guildhall. Behind him stood men-at-arms and, on either side, members of the council hostile to Beaufort, as well as two judges of oyer and terminer in their scarlet robes and caps all fringed with the purest lambswool.

Roseblood turned, gesturing at his entourage to stand peaceful before walking forward to confront Malpas. The exchange was swift and rancorous. Roseblood immediately demanded that the witnesses justifying his summons be produced. Malpas, his leathery brown face twisted in anger, gauntleted fingers fluttering about his grey hair, moustache and beard, shrugged and retorted that there was no case as both witnesses had mysteriously died during the night. Of course this was posed as a true mystery, but everyone knew that Candlemas and Cross-Biter had been cunningly slain and that Simon Roseblood was probably responsible. Malpas openly hinted at this. Roseblood, swift as an arrow, declared how God had vindicated him and punished two liars and oath-breakers. Wasn't this, Malpas retorted, pointing at the severed heads, a crime? Roseblood seized the opportunity to repeat everything he had said at the conduit. All three of his victims were beyond the law, proclaimed as wolfsheads by the sheriff of Essex and to be slain on sight.

'Indeed,' he proclaimed, turning so that his voice filled the spacious cobbled bailey, 'I understand that a reward, a bounty, is posted on their heads. Accordingly, Sir Philip, I now claim that reward. I will also submit a schedule of costs and expenses to the city treasury.' He paused. 'So, gentle friends,' the mockery in his voice was obvious, 'rejoice with me that such malice has been frustrated. God's will has been done. All assembled here whose precious time has been wasted are invited to my tavern for an evening of delicious food, good ale and the finest wine ever shipped from Bordeaux. The celebrations will begin in five days. I look forward to seeing you all.' And with this dramatic proclamation, a flourish of trumpets and the heavy beat of a tambour, Roseblood and his brilliantly attired retinue turned to leave the Guildhall precincts.

At any other time, in any other place, Sevigny would have burst out laughing, but one look at the sheriff's face, mottled with anger, discouraged this. Moreover, he was trying to catch Katherine's gaze, but that young lady was acting her part, all cold and severe like Susanna from the Scriptures after she had been vindicated by the prophet Daniel. Sevigny sighed with disappointment and, eyes narrowed, lips puckered, watched the Rosebloods leave. Once the gates closed behind them, Malpas bowed curtly to the justices, mumbled what might be taken as an apology and stormed back up the steps, gesturing at Sevigny to follow him.

A short while later, Sevigny, Ramler and Skulkin joined Malpas in his dark-wood exchequer chamber with its hard-tiled floor. The pink plaster above the panelling was covered with smoke-tinged tapestries depicting the exploits of King Brutus and the legends of Gog and Magog. For a while, Malpas just sat, face in hands. At last he lifted his head, groaned loudly, tore off his sheriff's collar and threw it on the chancery desk.

'My lord of York must be informed. I'll send a courier. Amadeus, you . . . I . . . we . . .' Malpas sighed noisily. 'We thought we could trap Roseblood with the law. We have failed to do that. His pageant will be relayed all over the city. I received your message about Candlemas and Cross-Biter. Roseblood is claiming both deaths as an act of God. We know he gave God more than a helping hand! Not that it really matters now, but how was it done?'

Sevigny turned on his stool and stared at Skulkin and Ramler by the door.

'The dregs of both food and wine,' the scribe stammered, 'were left for the rats that teem in the cellars below. The vermin remained unharmed. Skulkin's men have kept me informed.'

'And the physician?'

'Took his coin, pronounced the obvious – that both of them were dead – then listed the chief symptoms: faces liverish, bellies swollen—'

'Poison?' Malpas demanded.

'Poison, some deadly contagion, a breakdown of the humours, fear or even an act of God,' Ramler gabbled. 'He concluded, like the physician he is, that he truly couldn't say.'

Malpas raised a hand, gesturing that Ramler and Skulkin withdraw.

'A major reversal?' Sevigny demanded once the door closed. 'Is it really, kinsman? If those two miscreants had lived, Roseblood would have produced a host of witnesses to reject their story. I admit, I underestimated our noble taverner.' He rose; he had his own ideas about those two mysterious murders, but he needed evidence to test his hypothesis.

'True,' Malpas snapped. 'Roseblood would have produced witnesses, evidence even; challenged both men to trial by combat. Still, an indictment would have hurt and hindered our noble taverner. As it is, he has made a fool of me and the office I hold.'

'Why the hatred?' Sevigny asked. 'I mean, we know what star each of us follows.'

'It is not the stars we follow now,' the sheriff murmured, 'but those we followed in our green and salad days when Roseblood and I were young, allies, even friends.' He drew a deep breath. 'But the past is sealed.' He pointed at Sevigny. 'Try and discover how those men were murdered. For the rest, you are busy on York's other affairs in this city?'

Sevigny agreed.

'Then know this.' Malpas leaned across the table. 'It will be common knowledge soon enough. The King and Beaufort have called a great council at Leicester to discuss certain matters.'

'But York has not been invited,' Sevigny declared. 'Nor have any of his allies such as Neville of Warwick or Howard of Norfolk.'

'York,' Malpas replied, 'has moved to Ludlow in Shropshire to be near his allies along the Welsh border. He can march within the day, if he and his do not receive a writ of summons for Leicester.' The sheriff looked under finely shaven eyebrows at this enigmatic, close-souled clerk who kept his own counsel. 'And the physician, Argentine?' he demanded.

'I cannot say, kinsman, except York wishes to have him. Yet he remains most elusive.'

'Why does he hide?'

'I don't know,' Sevigny lied. 'But when I find him, I shall certainly ask him that.'

'And the attack on you at St Mary-le-Bow? One of Skulkin's bailiffs informed me about it.'

'God knows!' Sevigny shrugged. 'Outlaws, Beaufort, Roseblood . . .' He walked towards the door. 'We live in dangerous times, kinsman.'

'Amadeus?'

The clerk turned.

'Be careful whom you trust.'

Sevigny left the room. He walked down the stairs, nodded at Skulkin and Ramler and crossed the great bailey to stand just within the shadow of the Guildhall gatehouse. Once again the clerk quietly marvelled at Roseblood's sheer effrontery. Sir Philip was correct: the damage to the sheriff's pride and reputation was devastating. Roseblood's warning not to meddle in his affairs was clear and stark, though Sevigny was determined not to forget Katherine, a most remarkable young woman. She was definitely a dreamer who lived deep within her own soul and viewed the rest of the world with detached amusement. She reminded him of the Children of the Sun, or so they called themselves, young men and women who tramped the highways and byways of France owing allegiance to no one, proclaiming how everyone was equal before God, that owning property was a sin and that all goods, especially those of Holy Mother Church, should be held in common. Katherine Roseblood had said nothing about that, yet her attitude and her absorption with Camelot reminded him sharply of the fairy-like innocence of those wanderers.

He opened his wallet and brought out the crude medal one of these young women had given him, an act of kindness to an English foreigner. He turned it so it would catch the light, tracing his finger around the three-stemmed fleur-de-lis resting on the back of the Agnus Dei. Other Frenchmen were not so tolerant. Sevigny had heard about the massacre at LeCorbeil. York had informed him about those mysterious mercenaries, supported by the masters of secrets at the Louvre in Paris, intent on stirring up as much unrest in England as possible whilst at the same time pursuing their own blood feud against the Beauforts, whom they held responsible for the slaughter in their home town. The details of all this were vague. Sometimes Sevigny thought LeCorbeil was an individual; at other times a group or the title of the leader of that coven. York was certainly playing a very dangerous game. Apparently he had reached some sort of understanding to use LeCorbeil against Beaufort as he had during Cade's revolt. In the end, though, LeCorbeil was a beast that could well devour the hand that fed it. York should be extremely prudent.

Sevigny put the medal away. He recalled Roseblood's invitation and wondered whether he should join the celebrations. Perhaps he should collect his great warhorse Leonardo, and ride into the tavern yard as Mordred come to Camelot! He turned as his name was called. A Guildhall retainer hurried across and pushed a thin square of parchment into his hands.

'This was delivered whilst you were closeted with Sir Philip.'

Sevigny thanked the man, broke the crisp red seal and unfolded the expensive parchment. The handwriting was as neat and cursive as that of a chancery clerk; a note from those two eerie bounty-hunters Cosmas and Damian informing him that they would be present in the Holy Lamb of God in Cheapside any time after the Angelus bell sounded. It was just about that time, so Sevigny, one hand on his sword hilt, strolled out of the shadow of the Guildhall and across the broad thoroughfare, surveying the various colourful tavern signs – the Holy Ghost, the Bishop's Head, the Brazen Serpent, the Goshawk in the Sun – till he glimpsed the Holy Lamb further down.

He had to fight his way through the colourful, smelly throng, shouldering and jostling past traders, tinkers and the garishly garbed whores with their fire-red wigs all askew. He kept a sharp eye out for the nip and the foist. A counterfeit crank, a rogue dressed in filthy rags, his face daubed with blood from the fleshers' stalls, fell grovelling at his booted feet. This sham was sucking on a piece of soap to give the impression of a frothing mouth. Sevigny kicked him aside and then kicked him again for good measure. Other members of the cranking crew saw this and kept their distance.

He paused to allow the Fraternity of the Hanged, all gowned in deep funereal purple, to process down Cheapside behind a cart with a banner bearing a red cross stretched across the corpses of those cut down from the gibbets at Tyburn. The solemn words of the death psalm echoed above the noise and chatter of the market and the clanging of the Angelus bell. As he watched them go, he wondered who would see to the burial of Candlemas and Cross-Biter. He must remember that. If his memory served him right, both corpses would be buried in quicklime as soon as possible and be swiftly corrupted.

He reached the Holy Lamb and entered its spacious taproom, which smelled sweetly of smoked ham, crushed onion and strong ale. The rushes on the floor, sprinkled with fresh herbs, were glossy green and supple. The two bounty-hunters were seated in the garden beyond, closeted together in a rose-covered arbour, tankards of ale on the table before them.

'The ideal place for a meeting,' Sevigny remarked, sitting down opposite them. Both nodded in unison and Sevigny quietly marvelled at this sinister pair; twins, they looked alike except that Cosmas had his left eye socket sewn up, Damian his right. They wore the same clay-coloured robes bound round the middle with a rough cord, stout sandals on their bare feet. Each had a silver ring dangling from his right ear lobe; their faces were small, round as a pebble, rather womanish. According to Sheriff Malpas, both men had served as spies in the Byzantine army. They had been captured by the Ottoman Turks, blinded in one eye, castrated and pegged out in the desert. A hermit had, by God's favour, rescued them and nursed them back to health. Born of English stock, they had returned to London under their adopted names, Cosmas and Damian, after two Greek physicians martyred for their faith. Once in the city, this precious pair had acquired a reputation second to none for being the most skilled of searchers.

'God knows how they do it,' Malpas had growled. 'They dress like mendicants yet they have amassed gold and silver from many rewards and bounties. Perhaps that is their secret: no one truly fears them, since they are overlooked, or rejected as grotesques, nothing more.'

'What have you discovered?' Sevigny took two thick

pieces of silver from his purse and laid them on the table.

'Giles Argentine.' Cosmas leaned forward even as Damian did, his voice trilling like that of a young boy. 'A physician with secrets, yes?'

Sevigny nodded. He had told them little about the scandals Argentine cherished.

'A true busy bee,' Cosmas whispered. 'Stories about this, tales about that. Well, he has disappeared like mist on a summer morning. Now, he will not hide in the shires, where strangers are soon noted. We suspect he is not far from London. However, no hospice, abbey, monastery or convent shelters him. Again people chatter, especially the guest masters.'

'So,' Damian took up the story, 'we did our own searches. We sat, thought and discussed, didn't we, brother? We reached the conclusion that the best place to hide is where no one will go, a leper house, a lazar hospital, especially one where your kinsman is the master. That brings us to our own leper hospital at St Giles, only a walk away from the gallows, a large house, a sprawling hospital for men and women. Argentine could hide there, well protected by his powerful kinsman Master Joachim Brotherton.' Damian smiled; he had the strong white teeth of a dog. 'Now, Master Sevigny, my brother and I have served in Outremer; we have seen leprosy in all its horror. We will not, cannot go in there.'

'But I can?' Sevigny pushed the silver coins over. 'These are still yours.'

'Amadeus,' Cosmas murmured, 'you are a powerful clerk. I am sure my lord sheriff would grant you powers of search . . .'

Nodding his head in agreement, Sevigny turned and asked a slattern to bring three black jacks of ale. Once these were served, the clerk sat sipping his, staring at these two grotesques with their falsely benign smiles.

'And LeCorbeil?' he demanded.

'Strange, strange and stranger still,' both chorused together, then paused as a travelling juggler with a weasel in the crook of his arm and a monkey wearing a bell cap perched on his shoulder came into the garden. He sat down on a turf seat, where he was joined by a teller of tales garbed in a patchwork of colours. The new arrivals were drunk and garrulous, showing each other tricks and sleights of hand. Cosmas indicated them with his head. 'Trickery and shadow,' he declared.

'What do you mean?'

'LeCorbeil is many things: a town in Normandy, the place of a hideous massacre; the name of a Frenchman who hates the English Crown, and Beaufort in particular; as well as a group of mercenaries skilled in the crossbow.'

'How many?'

'To quote the Gospels, their name is legion.'

'And where do they shelter?'

'Here, there and everywhere. At the moment, a deserted village deep in the Essex countryside. More than that we cannot say, except,' Damian abruptly pushed across another square of parchment, 'after we leave, read that. We take our task seriously. We also wish to impress. We like to know our customers, so we have kept you and yours under strict watch. We heard about the attack on you at St Mary's.' He gestured at the parchment. 'You have been honourable, you have paid us and shown us courtesy.' He pulled a face. 'You might find that of great interest. Now . . .' They made to rise.

'No, wait!' Sevigny put the piece of parchment into his wallet and asked the slattern to bring inkhorn, quill and a scrap of vellum. He scribbled for a while and handed the memorandum to the two searchers. 'Watch them,' he said, tapping the table. 'Follow them for a day or two, discover what you can, then let me know.'

Damian read Sevigny's message, glanced at his brother and raised his hand in agreement. Then both hunters rose, bowed and slipped out through a narrow wicket gate into the alleyway beyond.

When they had gone, Sevigny opened the parchment he had been given and read the precise chancery script. He felt a shiver of coldness followed by a spurt of fiery anger. He sat clenching his hands in rage as he fought the hideous red mist that had plagued his soul since childhood, disembodied voices echoing through his mind shrieking battle cries.

'Sir! Sir!'

Sevigny opened his eyes. The white-faced slattern was gaping fearfully at him. He realised he had drawn his dagger and was holding it up, blade out, his other hand on his sword hilt.

'Sir?'

'I am sorry.' Sevigny let the knife clatter on to the table and took out a coin. Leaning over, he pressed it into the girl's bony hand. Then he drew a deep breath, rose, sheathed his dagger and left the tavern.

Sevigny was blind and deaf to the noisy crowds as he walked back to the Golden Harp, where he and Bardolph were staying. Once there, he calmed himself by going into the stables to stroke the glossy black coat of Leonardo, his great destrier. He leaned against the horse's warm flank, letting the horse nuzzle at his hand, soothing his soul. He patted Leonardo, kissed him on the muzzle, rubbing between the horse's ears and whispering endearments. At last he was ready. He crossed to the taproom. Bardolph was drinking in a candlelit corner; the tallow flame illuminated the archer's unshaven face, his drooping eyes and the bitter twist to his mouth. Sevigny moved a stool close to the barrel table and drew his dagger. Bardolph started in surprise. Sevigny leaned closer, pressing the dagger tip against the man's slightly swollen belly.

'It is dark in here,' he murmured. 'No one can see. Even if they could, I am a royal clerk. I'll draw your dagger and push it into your hand as you die. I'll claim it was self-defence.' He watched the fear flare in Bardolph's eyes. 'Just a push.'

'What is this . . . why? Bardolph's fear could not hide his realisation of a trap being sprung.

'The Inglenook in Southwark.' Sevigny pressed on the dagger. 'You went there, I know you did. Two associates of mine followed you. You met three wolfsheads, former soldiers. You hired them to murder me. I killed one of them. Before he died, this assassin confessed that he'd been hired by a man with a strange accent. You hale from the Yorkshire dales. Your burr would sound like a foreign language to a Londoner. Don't lie; more importantly, don't waste my time.'

Bardolph blinked and wetted his lips. 'You think I'm sullen,' he replied. 'And so I am. Why not? I am a bowman, one of the best. A master archer, not an assassin.'

'Who ordered you to have me killed?'

'You know full well,' the archer whispered. 'The duchess hates you. She fiercely resents your influence in her husband's affairs. Perhaps you know more about his business than you should. I was given a choice: either you died in London or I would not return to her service or that of the duke.'

'Do you know what secrets the duchess suspects I hold?' Sevigny tried to keep his voice steady as he realised that the fabric of his life was tearing, crumbling here in this tawdry tavern corner.

'No, master, but like others, I have heard certain whispers about her. I used to think they were tittle-tattle; perhaps they're not.' Bardolph picked up his tankard even as his hand stole to the long Welsh stabbing dirk sheathed in his belt.

'Don't!' Sevigny warned. 'I'd be much swifter. Drink with two hands.'

'You can kill me,' Bardolph grasped the tankard with

both hands, 'God knows I deserve it, yet I tell you this. The duchess wants to be rid of you. If I do not succeed, you will be sent on some embassy to the far reaches of the earth and you will not be coming back.' He lifted the tankard in toast. 'I don't want to die unshriven.'

'You are not going to die.' Sevigny let the dagger droop. 'You cannot go back to the duchess, but I do not want your blood on my hands.' He gestured with his head. 'Go, Bardolph. Take passage abroad. They need good English bowmen, be it in Hainault, Flanders or the cities along the Rhine. However,' he sheathed the dagger, 'if we meet again, I shall certainly kill you.'

Bardolph stared in disbelief and swallowed hard. Sevigny gazed back. He was tired of killing, and for some strange reason he could not forget Katherine Roseblood's beautiful face, so vibrant with merriment, life and the good things of an innocent soul. She would not like these filthy doings in the deepest shadows.

'Go, go!' He gestured with his fingers. Bardolph got slowly to his feet and extended a hand, but let it fall when Sevigny did not respond. He pushed past the clerk, then abruptly clasped him on the shoulder and leaned down.

'I asked the duchess what would happen if I failed. She replied that there would be other men and fresh occasions. My gift to you, remember that, clerk.' And he was gone.

Sevigny sat for a while. He felt trapped in the deepest darkness. Demons prowled and the only sound was their gasping breath and the rasp of steel being drawn.

York was a good lord. Sevigny had sealed indentures with him, done fealty, though he had never sworn the oath of allegiance. Strangely enough, York had never asked for that. Had he always known that one day he might have to abandon Sevigny to the murderous whims of his beautiful duchess? The Rose of Raby had wrapped herself around the duke, body and soul. Sevigny had heard the whispers of how skilled and versatile she was in bed, creating a kingdom where she was lord and York her humble servant. He ignored the pressing feeling of despair, though he accepted in his heart that he and York were finished.

'I will see this through,' he murmured to himself, 'and I will be gone. But what then?'

As a member of York's household, Sevigny received robes, supplies and monies every quarter, but that did not concern him. He had inherited money from his parents' estates and had secreted it away with bankers in London, York and Lincoln. Would he engage with another lord's household? He was registered as a royal clerk in the King's chancery.

Sevigny shook his head and rose to his feet. The future would have to wait. Cosmas and Damian were now busy on their errand. And Argentine? The searchers were correct: he would have to invoke the authority of the sheriff. Ravenspur was a different matter. Nevertheless, he would finish that task as well, keep faith with York even if the duke did not keep faith with him. Whatever happened, he would return to report on his mission. Afterwards he would put as much distance between himself and the malevolent duchess as possible.

The next morning, after a night's sleep plagued by ghosts from the past, Sevigny rose, shaved and washed. He put on fresh robes and visited the taverns near New Temple where the lawyers gathered, Hell's Inn and Heaven's Hope. The two hostelries stood only a few paces apart and were the favourite gathering places for lawyers and judges before the courts sat at Westminster. They provided a rich source of gossip, lawyers being party to the devices and plans of the great warlords.

He soon learnt that Malpas was correct. Beaufort and the Queen intended to call a great assembly at Leicester without York or his allies being present. Secretly the Crown was issuing writs for troops to be raised in every shire north of London so that when they left the city, Beaufort and Queen Margaret would be escorted to Leicester by an army. York of course suspected this and had sent urgent messages to his northern allies begging them to raise their forces and hurry them south. The narrow-eyed lawyers in their costly robes, bulging chancery bags on the floor between their feet, were eager to cap each other's rumours. Sevigny learnt the truth: the parliament at Leicester was only a cat's paw to mass troops and strike at York.

He left the taverns and walked across to the ancient church of St Alphege. He was about to enter through the Devil's door when his name was called. He turned.

Shadows emerged from the billowing mist blown in from the river.

'Master Sevigny, you must come with us. Ravenspur awaits you.' The speaker was wrapped in cloak and mantle. Sevigny glimpsed a young, shaven face, one hand held up in a gesture of peace, the other offering a scroll of parchment, a request from Ravenspur courteously asking Sevigny to join the escort provided. Sevigny nodded his agreement and six other strangers similarly attired came out of the murk, their leader whispering how they would escort the clerk back to the Golden Harp.

On his return to the tavern, Sevigny collected a few possessions, saddled Leonardo and followed his mysterious escort out into the mist-filled streets. The sun had risen but the mist was stubbornly thick, cloaking his view and dulling all sound. Candle and lantern horn shimmered a dirty yellow. Images swam out of the murk: the chapped, wounded faces of beggars, the round smoothness of curious urchins, the white, skeletal features of some hooded friar. They crossed London Bridge and journeyed down past the majestic stone walls and soaring turrets of the Tower, lit by fiery brands and flaming braziers. Eventually they reached the Mile End Road, heading for Bow Bridge and the marshes that separated London from the wild Essex countryside.

It was an eerie journey. Sevigny's escort remained as cloaked and cowled as a group of black monks; only the occasional glint of weapons or the clatter of scabbards betrayed who they really were, a group of mercenaries, one of the many now journeying through England.

Sevigny listened to their chatter, usually French, though in a patois he could not understand. He wondered if they were Brabantines, as each rider carried a powerful crossbow looped over his saddle horn. On one occasion he witnessed their skill when they surprised a flock of pheasants that broke from the thick undergrowth, their harsh calls shattering the silence of the countryside. Immediately, three of the escort unhitched their crossbows, swinging them up, each loosing a bolt to bring down a bird in a splutter of feathers and blood. The carcasses were collected, heads shorn off and the bodies hung for a short while from a tree branch until the blood drained out. Once they were cleaned, they were tossed into a sack and the journey continued.

Sevigny watched and changed his mind, curbing the excitement in his belly. He grew certain that these were no ordinary mercenaries. He glimpsed an insignia on a dark red quilted jerkin: a crow, wings extended, against a light blue field. LeCorbeil! He was sure that he was now surrounded by those mysterious French mercenaries who came and went like shadows in the night. They were well armed and horsed, and with the kingdom slipping into war, few would dare challenge them. Even if they did, they probably carried some form of documentation, forged or genuine, that would allow them safe passage. If these men were LeCorbeil – and Sevigny became convinced that they were – then Ravenspur was not only a warlock but their leader. York had not informed him about that.

He tried to draw them into conversation, but the

only one who replied was Bertrand, their leader, a handsome young man with a smooth Italianate face, dark eyes and a blunt manner. He assured the clerk that he was in no danger, that he would be treated with every respect, but conceded nothing else. Sevigny could only ride on. The cavalcade kept well away from villages and hamlets such as Leighton and Wodeford. They eventually entered the dark greenness of Epping Forest, where the trees thinned though the brooding stillness of that ancient woodland still hung heavy. The mist had lifted slightly but the sky was now blocked with heavy grey clouds.

The journey reminded Sevigny of boyhood rides across the harsh Yorkshire moors, going on pilgrimage with his parents to the Carthusian house at Mount Grace or the great abbey of St Hilda at Whitby. He reflected on where such days had led, before his mind drifted back to Katherine Roseblood staring at him so coquettishly from the steps of the Tun. He also plotted how he would break in to the leper house at St Giles, whilst he hoped that Cosmas and Damian would be able to offer help in solving the mysterious deaths of Candlemas and Cross-Biter. Sevigny felt personally insulted by these; the two men had perished in his care, so he was determined to resolve the mystery. He wondered again about Katherine, and decided to visit the Roseblood on the night of the great celebration, a welcome relief against the menacing shadow of Duchess Cecily and this sombre journey.

Shouts and cries roused him from his reverie. He

glanced around. They had entered a deserted village, its buildings much decayed, almost hidden by the coarse undergrowth thrusting up around them. An ancient well, its wall cracked and crumbling, stood at a weed-choked crossroads under the shadow of a three-branched gibbet. Wisps of hempen rope still twirled from its rusty hooks. It was one of those ghostly, deserted hamlets through which the Great Pestilence had swept over a hundred years ago, extinguishing all life as swiftly and surely as snuffing out a candle. Rotting signs, dangling from rusty chains, moved in a macabre creaking melody. Empty windows gazed sightlessly out above crumbling doorways and entrances. Garden fences and palisades, benches and horse troughs lay topsy-turvy, their decaying wood snagged by creeping grass and trailing bramble. An oppressive, baleful silence closed about them, as if ghosts and spectres swirled full of resentment at being disturbed.

Above a clump of trees Sevigny glimpsed a decaying square church tower. Bertrand lifted a hand and pointed in its direction. They made their way up the potholed trackway, through a gap in the cemetery wall and into the wild heathland that had once served as God's Acre, most of its tombstones and crosses now hidden from view. The yew trees planted there had grown untended, their heavy branches hanging down to create small chambers of shadows. The cavalcade approached the main door of the church, which had been recently mended; this opened, and a man dressed as if for the hunt came out on to the steps. He wore long riding boots, and bottle-green jerkin and hose under a heavy military cloak clasped at the throat. In appearance he reminded Sevigny of Sheriff Malpas, with his silver hair and beard that only emphasised dark weathered features. When he came closer, Sevigny was struck by his eyes: a light grey with a hard, piercing stare. He offered his hand, gaze unflinching. Sevigny leaned down, clasped this, then dismounted.

'I am Ravenspur. You are most welcome, Amadeus.' Ravenspur gestured at the escort. 'Have no worries. Your splendid horse – Leonardo, isn't it? – will be well looked after, as will you. You shall be given good food and a safe guide back to the London road.' He grinned, his eye teeth white and sharp like the fangs of a hunting dog. 'Now come.'

He led Sevigny into the dark church. Sevigny tried to identify the man's accent. French? Or was that pretence, a ploy to hide his true identity? His clothing was dull and sober but of the costliest wool, while on his wrist a silver bracelet glinted, jewelled rings shimmering on his fingers. The door shut behind them. Sevigny stared around. The church was ancient, with a long nave like a manor hall, with wooden rafter beams and stout drum pillars down each side. Cresset torches flickered along the narrow, shadow-filled transepts. A line of braziers glowed in the centre of the church, providing both heat and light. Wall paintings had been whitewashed over. Crucifixes, statues, rood screen, lectern and pulpit had been removed. Only the square stone high altar at the far end of the chancel remained.

Two thick red candles glowed there, haloes of light in the murk that hung heavy as any mist despite the light piercing the arrow-slit windows high in the walls either side.

Ravenspur beckoned Sevigny to the table and chairs where the rood screen had once stood. The warlock sat, fingers steepled, staring gently, even sadly at Sevigny. The clerk swiftly recalled how York considered this sorcerer, who now looked as pious as any country parson, a most powerful necromancer. York believed that Ravenspur was responsible for the mysterious death of the King's uncle, Humphrey, Duke of Gloucester, whilst under house arrest at St Edmundsbury. A shocking, sudden death that had never been resolved.

'You must wonder about the journey.' Ravenspur smiled. 'The mummery at being brought to a deserted church in a long-forgotten village peopled by ghosts.'

'And my escort?' Sevigny demanded. 'They are LeCorbeil? You are their leader?'

'Acolytes, disciples,' Ravenspur replied evasively.

Sevigny stared down the nave. He would leave that for the time being. 'So why here? Why this, as you say, like some mummer's masque?'

'You know my answer, Amadeus: you are York's principal chancery clerk.' Ravenspur played with the bracelet around his wrist. 'Even though you are fiercely resented by the lovely but deadly duchess, a true witch. Anyway,' he continued briskly, 'you are in London and you are probably being watched. However, you are well protected; I am not. I cannot meet you there. I do not want Beaufort's bully boys bursting through the door with warrants for our arrest.' He pulled a face. 'I don't want to suffer the same death as Bolingbroke. You've heard of him, the former Dominican? Hanged, drawn and quartered in St Paul's churchyard for witchcraft? So that is why you have been brought here. The duke trusts me. I prophesied the death of Suffolk, as I did the King's malady of the mind.'

'And now?'

'And now, my friend, you will eat, drink and relax.'

Ravenspur left, closing the door behind him. Sevigny rose and walked around the deserted church. Images and memories drifted through his mind. Katherine Roseblood; the duchess; Candlemas and Cross-Biter sprawled dead in that chamber; Argentine, cowled and masked, hiding amongst a hideous horde of lepers; and now this. He smiled cynically at Ravenspur's boasting. Humphrey, Duke of Gloucester, might have died mysteriously, but he had ruined his health through drinking and dissipation. King Henry's mind had also turned, but he had inherited such a weakness through his mother from Charles VI of France, who never washed because he believed he was made of painted glass.

And now? Ravenspur might be a charlatan, but Sevigny recognised a truly dangerous one. God only knew what power he had acquired. The Devil's troop constantly prowled through the twilight, along that eternal frontier between the seen and the unseen. Would the Lord Satan cross to help the likes of Ravenspur? Or was it all trickery? Was he playing such games now?

Sevigny paused in his pacing. The church had grown remarkably cold. Sounds echoed eerily, as if sandalled feet slithered. Shadows darted around the pools of light. He startled at a sound above him, a fluttering, as if some bird had been shut in amongst the rafters, yet he could detect nothing. Dark and light flittered. He walked to the altar and stared down at its harsh stone surface. In the juddering glow of the red candles he thought he could detect bloodstains, but when he peered closer, these seemed to fade. He went for his sword as a faint chattering echoed from the gloomy transept. He drew his weapon and walked across, but the cold stone gallery lay desolate. He felt his heart quicken and his mouth grow dry. Above him, something scrabbled at the thick horn covering a window, as if desperate to get in or out.

Sevigny crossed to the door and opened it; he stood on the crumbling steps, staring out across the sea of gorse and bramble. All lay quiet. On the breeze he caught the sound of indistinct shouting and laughter, and smelled the mouth-watering fragrance of roasted meat. He sheathed his sword and went back into the church. A short while later, Ravenspur, accompanied by one of his acolytes, brought in a tray of food: freshly roasted pheasant, soft fruit bread, a flagon of wine and two cups. He served the food and filled the goblets, then gestured at his guest to begin. When the acolyte had left, Sevigny blessed himself and leaned across.

'My apologies,' he smiled. 'Do not take offence.' He swiftly changed his platter and goblet with those of

Ravenspur. The warlock laughed merrily, his strange eyes crinkling.

'I heard about the mysterious deaths of Candlemas and his companion. Do you believe they were poisoned?'

'Possibly.' Sevigny ate and drank in silence. He was still intrigued by the way Ravenspur had spoken. He was certain he had caught a slight tinge of a French accent. He also recalled his strange escort, their skill with the crossbow, and this sparked memories of defenders being killed by crossbow bolts on London Bridge during Cade's rebellion, whilst a similar fate had befallen certain English captains in France. He had asked Ravenspur about LeCorbeil and not truly been answered. He was determined to resolve the matter.

He finished the meal and Ravenspur cleared the table, then moved the candle spigot into the centre, softly chanting to himself in a tongue Sevigny could not understand. The warlock closed his eyes.

'You have heard that the King, his she-wolf wife and her lover Beaufort are to move to Leicester?'

Sevigny grunted in agreement.

'Advise my lord of York to accept no peace offers but to attack savagely; he must not delay. Let him unleash his fierce war dog, Neville of Warwick.' Ravenspur opened his eyes and smiled, as if savouring the thought of York's most impetuous war captain being loosed against the court party. 'Tell my noble duke that crowns will decorate his head.' He blinked and flinched, as if he'd glimpsed something he didn't like. 'Yes,' he repeated, 'tell York that a crown will decorate his head as well as those of three of his sons.'

'That cannot be!'

'It shall be,' Ravenspur continued remorselessly, 'but each crown will be different. The greatest danger to York will come from within. Tell him his grandchildren shall inherit the crown.' He paused, rubbed his face with his hands and glanced up. 'York's peril stems from fair faces – as does yours, Amadeus – rather than the cut and slash of battle swords.' He leaned back, his face drained, as if he had delivered some long discourse in the schools. 'You can stay,' he murmured.

Sevigny recalled his soul-chilling walk around this neglected chapel. 'It's still daylight,' he replied. 'If a guide could take me back to the London road, I will be in the shadow of the Tower by nightfall.'

'Very well, as you wish.' Ravenspur's eyes were half closed. 'Advise my lord of York that help will come when he attacks. What happened to the greyhounds can happen to Beaufort and his coven.' He straightened up and leaned across the table. 'You should go, but walk carefully, clerk, draw your dagger and keep your back to the wall.'

'I guard it well enough, even against those who delve in mystery and hide behind charades.' Sevigny jabbed a finger. 'You are LeCorbeil, are you not? You are their captain. You lead a coven of French mercenaries dedicated to the destruction of Beaufort as well as the weakening of the English Crown. I asked you that before; I do so again!'

'Your master the duke does not tell you everything, Amadeus. Yes, I am – we are – LeCorbeil, and what is that? A living, pulsing memory and we are its incarnation. We are LeCorbeil. We exist for vengeance.' Ravenspur rose to his feet. 'I am surprised the good duke did not inform you more closely, but there again, I am pleased we remain a mystery. Now I must be gone, and so should you.'

Sevigny left without further incident. A two-man escort guided him to the old Roman road south to London before disappearing back into the misty twilight. He joined a group of well-armed pilgrims making their way to pray in Becket's chapel on London Bridge before travelling on to venerate the Black Virgin at Willesden. Once back in the city, he returned to the Golden Harp, where Minehost informed him that Bardolph had sold his own mount, settled his bill and left saying he would take ship from Queenhithe.

Sevigny found everything else in order. He spent the next days writing memoranda on what he had recently learned, concealing all this in his own cipher based on the Greek alphabet. Once he had finished writing, he found his mind clear to concentrate on the problems confronting him as well as the logical conclusions to be reached. He repacked his chancery satchel and strolled out to have Leonardo carefully examined by a horse leech who also acted as the tavern smithy. Afterwards he visited the bathhouses in Southwark, followed by a visit to a barber, who trimmed his hair and closely shaved his face whilst chattering about how hale and hearty Sevigny seemed for a man approaching his thirtieth summer. Sevigny grinned to himself and wondered if Katherine Roseblood would find him old. He fully intended to join the celebrations at the tavern in Queenhithe planned for that Friday evening, becoming even more determined when Cosmas and Damian slipped into the tavern to reveal what they had discovered.

'About Argentine,' Cosmas hissed in the secrecy of Sevigny's chamber. 'It is as we already suspected. We are certain that Joachim, master of the leper hospital at St Giles, is sheltering his kinsman. More than that we cannot say, and we shall certainly do no more. Now, as regards the other matter . . .' He leaned closer, whispering what they had witnessed. Both searchers, when questioned by a disbelieving Sevigny, carefully repeated what they had seen. When they had finished, they pocketed payment and left Sevigny to reflect. Eventually the clerk snatched up a quill and scribbled furiously, constructing a logical argument that resolved the mysterious deaths of Candlemas and Cross-Biter. Once completed, he rewarded himself with a deep bowl of claret, which would ensure a good night's sleep before he went to visit the Roseblood.

The following evening, just as the bells pealed the end of market trading, Amadeus Sevigny, garbed in his best robes, a jacket of the purest lambswool dyed a deep murrey over a lace-edged cambric shirt, hose of a similar texture pushed into Cordovan riding boots, cloak draped about his shoulders, war belt strapped around him, his leather buckle and scabbard gleaming, rode his night-black destrier into the busy bailey yard of the Roseblood. He was pleased that Katherine was there to witness his arrival. He dismounted and gave the reins to an ostler, who, harelip blurring his words, declared that he was Mousehole and he would take care of the warhorse.

'As we will of you.' Simon Roseblood, dressed in the same splendid alderman's robes he'd worn during his triumphal march down Cheapside, came forward to grasp Sevigny's hand. Raphael hung back, his solemn face all cynical. Katherine, however – and Sevigny felt a deep rush of joy – beamed like the lady moon. She looked magnificent in a bottle-green dress tied high at the neck with a gold cord, a silver medallion cincture around her narrow waist, soft black buskins peeping from beneath white petticoats that hung just below the hem of her dress. She had arranged her hair to hang in tresses under a white muslin veil held in place by a red-gold circlet.

'Well met, Guinevere,' Sevigny murmured. He grasped her hands, gloved in the softest doeskin, as they exchanged the kiss of peace, closing his eyes momentarily and breathing in her lovely fragrance. She gently pushed him away.

'Welcome, sir . . . and are you,' her eyes fluttered, 'the mysterious knight on some mysterious errand?'

The laughter she caused broke the strained attitude of her father and brother. Simon gently took Sevigny by the elbow and asked him if he was on sheriff's business, or indeed anyone else's. Sevigny, with mock solemnity, swore that he was here only to glimpse the fair Katherine. Roseblood grinned, shrugged, said that he had other guests and handed him over to what he called 'the close security' of his daughter. Katherine, as if she had known Sevigny for years, slipped a hand in his and led him through the glories of the tavern.

The clerk was truly astonished at the sheer wealth of the place, eloquent testimony to the popular belief that Simon Roseblood had fingers in many pies. That evening the taverner was certainly determined on creating a splendid display of his generosity and patronage. Other aldermen had been invited, along with officials from the Exchequer, the Chancery, the King's Bench and the Common Pleas. Officers from the Tower garrison mingled with archdeacons, abbots and friars. Roseblood had also summoned all those who served him: the legion of scavengers, babewyns and gargoyles. All the grotesques of London's underworld had assembled. The Tribe of Fools wandered cow-eyed, straw hats pulled down low. The Brethren of the Blade mingled with swaggering sword boys, hucksters and traders, tinkers and turnkeys, foists and nips, the colourful throng from their sanctuary on the Thames at the Old Manor in Cold Harbour. They rejoiced in names such as Rats-Tail and Twice-Hung Henry; the latter, according to Katherine, had been hanged at least twice, only to dig his way out of a scaffold grave and reappear in the city. These parishioners of the Devil's chapel jostled and taunted the ladies of the night, the wicked wenches, the wantons, the satin sisters and their pimps the Devil's disciples. They had all arrived in their tawdry glory, cheap jewellery glittering, a vivacious, bustling throng whom Roseblood entertained most royally.

A maypole had been set up in the Great Cloister, as well as a huge spit above a roaring fire to roast an entire hog basted with oil and all kinds of delicious herbs. The tavern ovens offered a constant supply of fresh bread. Trestle tables set up in the taprooms and refectory groaned under platters, tranchers, dishes and bowls filled with steaming vegetables and meats. Cooks and scullions laboured under the lashing tongue of Wormwood, who shouted, 'Cut that mallard!' 'Unbrace those two coneys!' 'Split that venison!' Wormwood had the voice of a crane, though Katherine described it as the shriek of a stabbed goose. Strips of pork, salad and boiled egg, pastries of fallow deer, red salted herring and mince sausages were offered. Ignacio and a group of burly henchmen wandered everywhere imposing order as well as recruiting some of the guests to act as servitors. Musicians offered the melodies of gitern, shawm, rebec and citole. Minstrels sang about magical woods with purple-crested apple trees, leafy oaks, beautiful copper trees and hazels with yellow clustered nuts. A porcupine had been brought in a cage from the Tower for people to marvel at. White-winged swans waddled in from the river, whilst a Hainault giant juggled a Castilian dwarf on his shoulders.

Katherine, very proud of both the tavern and her father, fussed and cosseted Sevigny. The clerk felt like some hero being led through a strange but exotic underworld of remarkable sights, smells and sounds. Music and laughter merged with snatches of talk and the greedy clatter of eating and drinking. Katherine showed him the various taprooms, storehouses, refectories, butteries and kitchens. Remembering what Cosmas and Damian had told him, Sevigny asked to visit some of the chambers and was led up to the polished galleries. Simon's henchmen patrolled here, ever vigilant against the legion of light-fingered brethren who had swarmed in for their master's feast day. Katherine, chattering like a sparrow, led him on. Sevigny, sharp-eyed, noted the narrow postern door to the right of the main entrance and judged it to be ideal for what Cosmas and Damian had described.

'You seem distracted.' Katherine stopped to face him squarely.

'Only by your beauty.' Sevigny leaned down to kiss her, but she stepped back.

'I am no tavern wench!' she teased.

'No, you are the lady without pity. Perhaps,' he let go of her hand and gestured around, 'we should go and sit where we first met and chatter to the moon.'

Katherine looked at him, her face all serious, then she smiled and, leaning forward, brushed his lips with hers.

They left the tavern by the rear gate, going down to the old Roman lighthouse, where torches and braziers had been lit against the cold sleep of the night. Darkness had descended and a thick river mist was creeping across the wild heathland. Sevigny, holding Katherine's hand, felt as if he had never been so elated, so happy. She walked carefree beside him, asking questions about where he had been born, at which hall he had been educated in Oxford. He answered as best he could, describing the Yorkshire moors over which blue-eyed hawks floated, fields and meadows rich with every kind of harvest. He talked of rushing streams stocked with fish, of sleek brown round-faced otters gambolling along the banks. How as a boy he would collect watercress to eat and cut blackthorn for toy weapons.

They entered the ruins and sat on a plinth. Katherine begged him to tell her a story about the wilds of Yorkshire. Sevigny talked about a great-jawed monster with a sharp snout that lurked deep in the most ancient forest. Katherine sat, hand tightening, as he described this horror of nature, baleful and hungry, sloping through the undergrowth . . .

The clerk abruptly paused. He rose to his feet, letting go of Katherine's hand, and stared out over the heathland. A sense of danger, of hidden threat, pressed close, that haunting feeling he had experienced in France when an ambush was about to be sprung. He breathed in deeply and slowly. Something was wrong! He caught the reek and stench of smoke and flame through the gathering mist. Further along the riverbank, fires glowed. He turned, eyes and ears all alert, and for just a heartbeat, he was certain of it, he heard the clash and clatter of battle, of voices screaming in agony.

'What is it?' Katherine had caught his alarm.

Sevigny grasped her hand, staring across the mist-hung river. Lights bobbed and fluttered; there were so many of them! The mist parted like a veil and he glimpsed the long, rakish ships low in the water. Each bore a lantern and most of these were being swiftly extinguished. Sevigny had seen the like before, off Calais and Boulogne: French galleys, sea wolves crewed by the most ruthless and skilled mercenaries France could muster. He recalled how, when keeping the Roseblood under close watch, he'd glimpsed lanterns glowing, fire arrows searing the night sky. Now he knew the reason: this attack had been planned and plotted. The galleys had been plundering along the Thames, and the Roseblood was their next quarry.

'Amadeus!' Despite the emerging danger, Sevigny thrilled at Katherine's use of his first name.

'Galleys!' he exclaimed. 'French galleys! They will moor close by . . .' Ignoring her protests and questions, he almost dragged her from the ruins. They raced up the hill into the tavern gardens, across these into the Great Cloister. Sevigny demanded a hunting horn from a sleepy-eyed groom and, standing on the rim of the well, gave three long, strident blasts. The feasting and revelry was already drawing to an end. Bellies full of food and good cheer, many guests had taken to dozing on benches and stools or stretching out on straw beds in the barns and stables. Sevigny blew another blast.

'In God's name!' Simon Roseblood bustled through.

'Galleys!' Sevigny shouted at him. 'French galleys

along the Thames! By the time you recite a rosary, their crews will be climbing your tavern walls.'

Roseblood dragged him off the rim of the well.

'Believe me,' Sevigny insisted. 'Either believe me or die along with everyone else here!'

Roseblood stared at him, then pushed him away. The taverner rubbed his face, holding a hand up for silence. Sevigny's declaration had already roused many of the guests. Some, including the clergy, were immediately intent on leaving. Others stayed. Simon stood for a brief while staring down at the cobbles.

'Clear the tavern,' Sevigny advised. 'Women and children should go. Secure the gates and blockade them. Open your barbican, arm everybody who stays. The French will attack direct from the river and move to outflank you by circling the tavern. Man the walls but keep a force here to reinforce any gap or weakness.'

Roseblood lifted his head, stared at Sevigny and nodded. The taverner's panic and shocked surprise soon subsided, and he became as forceful as any seasoned castellan. Women, children, the aged and the infirm were swiftly moved to the security of All Hallows church. Katherine wanted to stay, but her father was most insistent that she go. The stone storehouse that served as the ward's barbican was opened. Weapons, jerkins and helmets were swiftly distributed. The tavern gates were locked, barred and blocked with carts and barrows. Precious items were hurriedly taken down to the secret strongroom in the cellar. All the time watchers along the parapet wall stared into the mist-filled darkness.

The galleys were now visible, their captains still unaware that their intended victims knew how close the wolf had crept to the sheepfold. Boiling water and bubbling oil prepared for cooking or cleaning were moved to the parapets, along with dishes of glowing charcoal. The makeshift garrison of the Roseblood swiftly armed itself. Beggars and rakers stood side by side with scavengers, traders, soldiers from the Tower and two city aldermen. Most of these had seen service against the French; none had any illusions about what would happen if the Roseblood fell and French corsairs swarmed through the streets of Queenhithe. Messages had already been dispatched seeking reinforcements, though Sevigny knew it would take some time for these to be mustered.

The clerk, still elated after his meeting with Katherine, almost relished the prospect of battle. He held a swift meeting in the principal taproom with Roseblood, Raphael and Ignacio. They agreed that all would man the parapets to counter what would be the first and very savage assault. After a while, Sevigny and Raphael would fall back to command a schiltrom of kite-shielded foot protected by a few archers. This would deal with a breakthrough by the French or staunch any gap in the tavern defences.

Sevigny watched Simon and Ignacio talk their strange sign language. The taverner was now sober, thoughtful. Sevigny recognised Ignacio for what he was: a killer like himself; a warrior who gloried in battle. He could sense the Castilian's anticipation. Sevigny himself had experienced that before, along the battle lines in France, a thirst for bloodletting.

The defenders, garbed in a variety of armour, bascinets, brigadines, sallets, mail shirts and other battle harness, were swiftly organised. Yellow war bows were strung, quivers crammed with yard-long shafts, their feathered flights dyed grass green or blood red. Mousehole, a cooking pot on his head, burst in to breathlessly announce how the French had landed further downriver.

'They have avoided the main quayside at Queenhithe,' Sevigny declared. 'They do not want to raise the alarm too soon. The Roseblood is their main quarry.'

The meeting broke up. Sevigny followed the rest out to the southern wall of the tavern. The steps to the parapet were steep, the actual ledge rather narrow. The defenders knelt or crouched behind the top of the curtain wall. The darkness had deepened. Sevigny glanced up at the cloud-shrouded sky. The attackers had chosen their hour well; the night was now moonless, the stars well hidden. He peered over the crenellations into the blackness, staring until he glimpsed what Mousehole had seen: shapes sloping up from the river. No sound, no light, nothing but a creeping terror drawing closer and closer. Abruptly he got to his feet, holding a torch.

'Stay silent!' he hissed. Ignoring the whispered protests, he took a deep breath and began to sing a raucous tavern song, shouting out the doggerel lines about a tavern maid tricked by a friar. At the same time, he staggered about waving the torch, creating the illusion that he was a toper serenading the night. In truth he kept himself calm and composed. The rest of his companions now realised that he was falsely telling those dark-shrouded crawlers that the alarm had not been raised. Sevigny staggered against the wall, then huddled down. He gripped the tight twine handle of his war bow, stood up and began to sing again, keeping the weapon hidden. Every so often he would interpolate a whispered instruction.

'Ten yards!' he murmured hoarsely. 'Eight yards! Six yards and closing fast!'

He kept this up until the figures below grew quite distinct, then he abruptly screamed 'Now!' just as the first scaling ladder crashed against the wall. The defenders immediately rose, bows braced, arrows notched. 'Loose!' Sevigny shouted.

The arrows whistled through the darkness, as boiling oil, scalding water and pots of fire were hurled against the enemy. The blackness beneath the walls erupted into flame, the roaring shoots of fire illuminating the mass of men swarming below. The corsairs were taken completely by surprise as this hellish rain of fire and goose-quilled shower of steel enveloped them. Screams and yells of agony shattered the night, to be answered by oaths, shouts and battle cries. Again and again the night air was riven by the whoosh of arrows and the angry whirring of crossbow bolts. Occasionally a defender staggered away as the French archers strove to cover their comrades desperately trying to climb the ladders; these were pushed away by poles with a

Y-shaped blade. The windswept fire raging along the south wall shifted, and Sevigny glimpsed a stiffened scarlet pennant emblazoned with a yellow beaked crow in full flight. LeCorbeil!

Simon tugged at his arm. 'They are breaking away,' he shouted. 'They will try elsewhere.' Sevigny agreed. Simon sounded his war horn, three sharp blasts, and the two of them left the parapet, hurrying down to the Great Cloister. Here Sevigny donned a bascinet, slipped his arm through the straps of a kite-shaped shield and drew his sword. Raphael was beside him; neither he nor his father had objected to Sevigny's authority. The mailed clerk had proven to be a skilled veteran.

Others gathered around, panting and sweating, hardly sparing a glance at the wounded being carried on make-shift stretchers into the tithe barn. Sevigny stilled his own breathing, curbing the excitement. Now it would come, the climax of battle. The tavern garrison could not hold every line of its defences. The corsairs would scale a wall, probably into the garden, and the hand-to-hand fight would ensue: heart against heart, sword on sword, the clatter of dagger against shield.

He thought of Katherine, slender and lovely, her hair brightly braided, lips warmly smiling, eyes all merry. Even as the red mist gathered, he recognised that she was his heart's love. Souls would be smudged out tonight by gashes and rents through which their blood would pour, but Sevigny was determined to survive because of Katherine, a woman he had just met. He would be her hawk prince. He would swoop to kill her enemies and those of her father. In truth, he shouldn't even be here defending York's enemies, but where else could he go? The ties that bound him to the duke were fraying fast. He had met Ravenspur and LeCorbeil, and no intimation had been given about this ferocious assault. The die was cast. Malpas would hear of this. Sevigny did not care. His world had abruptly changed. Roseblood's enemies were now his.

'The garden!' Mousehole burst into the cloisters. 'They have breached the walls!'

Sevigny rapped out orders: his retinue, about three dozen men, closed, locked their shields, swords out. The schiltrom moved through the arched entrance into the sweet-smelling night air, pushing by the flower borders, trellis arbours and herb plots. Sevigny peered over his shield and breathed a prayer as the enemy, torches in one hand, axes or swords in the other, stormed out of the darkness, their hooded faces full of the murderous fury of battle. Cries of 'St Denis! Mountjoie!' were greeted by those of 'St George! St George!'

Sevigny's world shrank to the heart-chilling clash of steel. He became locked in the packed confusion, the slaughter, the bloodletting, the sheer soul-numbing terror of battle. At first there were pricks of fear, until the blood-red mist engulfed him. He was butchering foes on every side, men with desperate, fierce faces, mouths snarling, eyes murderous, yet all he could see was his parents' manor house roaring with flames and his father and mother hanging from the branches of that elm tree that overlooked the flower-covered grotto of the Virgin. He believed that if he could reach them, if he could only break through this sea of swords, all would be well. He sensed he was too late, as he was always too late; the house was fire-devoured, his parents dead, but he could still wreak vengeance.

Sevigny began to chant. He dropped his shield, holding his great sword with two hands. This now became part of him, a cruel scythe to cull and kill. He was in the vineyard of the great slaughter, blood oozing like wine between his trampling feet. He was in a field where the sunlight hurtled before him, a blurring flash of flame drawing him on. He could hear the howling of a wolf pack and the piercing shriek of the battle raven. Pelting blows rained down on him, but he blocked them, moving forward into the meadows of the dead until he could go no further. Great weights hung on his arms; something held him fast around the waist.

'Master Sevigny, Master Sevigny, in God's name!'

The clerk shook his head and stared around. He was in the tavern orchard, his sword blade deep in the trunk of a tree. Raphael gripped one arm and a bloody-faced Wormwood the other. Simon stood behind him, pulling him away. Sevigny grasped his sword hilt, freed the blade and thrust the point into the ground. He sank down, sweat-soaked, his skin chilling swiftly under the night breeze. Shouts and cries carried the groans of the wounded.

'They've gone!' Simon knelt before him. 'Master Sevigny, they've fled. Look.' The taverner pointed through the darkness at men-at-arms wearing the red and white city livery. 'Relief came sooner than we thought. In God's name, man, are you well? I have heard of the battle rage but never seen it.' He gestured across the garden. 'Shattered, they are! Men shorn and slaughtered like pigs on fleshing day. They fled from you!'

Sevigny let his hands fall away from his sword. He slumped to the ground, turning on his side, knees coming up as the shock of battle faded.

'Leave me,' he whispered hoarsely. 'It will pass.'

'Nonsense!' Simon grabbed him by the arm; Raphael and Ignacio helped. Sevigny did not resist. A cold trembling had begun.

'Some wine,' he muttered, 'and bread. My belly . . .'

He was dragged across the garden. Turf seats, trellises, benches and fences lay overturned. Herb plots and flower beds were trampled down. Strewn across all these were the remains of the butchery of battle: puddles of blood, patches of gore, scraps of armour, splintered weapons. Corpses lay huddled like sleepers; here and there a hacked limb or a severed head. The English wounded had already been moved. Simon explained how the French had taken their injured. The few who had been left had been given a mercy cut before being gibbeted along the riverbank.

Sevigny was taken to a trestle set up in the main taproom. He stripped off his armour and carefully checked his war belt and weapons. Wine and food were brought, and he became aware of the bustle of the tavern. He asked after Katherine, and was told that she would not return until her father believed it was safe. He grunted his agreement, wolfed down the wine and food and promptly fell asleep.

Sevigny left the tavern early the next morning. He had visited the garderobe, bathed his hands and face in a tub of clear water and broken his fast at the common table in the taproom. Simon's henchmen were busy combing the bailey, garden, orchard and heathland beyond for any wounded or scraps of plunder, be it a mailed shirt or a sword. Voices carried, shouts echoed.

He visited his horse in the stables, then concentrated on what he must do. He would complete the task York had entrusted him with before making a decision about his future. He just wanted to be free, to get away from the Roseblood, despite the allure of Katherine, so that he could think, reflect, plan and plot. Mousehole assured him that Leonardo would be safe and well. Sevigny paid him to take the destrier back to the Golden Harp, then left the tavern.

He found the mist-filled streets of Queenhithe eerily silent. The previous night's events had frightened even the whores and beggars back to their dungeon-like lairs. Men-at-arms patrolled. Archers wearing Beaufort's livery stood at the mouths of alleyways; horsemen clattered by. Some of the main streets still had chains drawn across them. At one crossroads a movable scaffold bore the corpses of those summarily tried and executed for using the confusion to attempt pillage and housebreaking. Sevigny was stopped, but once he produced his warrants and seals he was allowed to pass on.

He could still smell the stench of battle and the reek of slaughter. The clash of steel and the hiss of arrows remained as faint echoes in his mind, whilst his arms, legs and wrists ached painfully. He paused as the bells tolled to announce the Jesus mass. Finding himself outside St Nicholas Olave, he went up the main steps. Above the arched doorway sat four stone angels each wearing a hat. In one hand they carried a sword, and in the other a flambeau. The carvings reminded Sevigny of the enemy he'd battled the previous evening.

He pushed open the door and went inside. Taper flame shimmered in the darkness. Through the door of the heavy rood screen he glimpsed the high altar and the sanctuary lamp glowing on guard next to the brilliantly jewelled pyx box. Voices prayed from a chantry chapel along one of the transepts. Morning mass was being celebrated, but Sevigny found he could not answer the sacring bell summoning the faithful. He could not take the Eucharist after the hideous blood-spilling of the previous evening. He glanced to his right at a wall painting depicting Christ with snow-white hair, flame-coloured eyebrows, moustache and beard: the Saviour in Judgement. He felt the guilt well within him. He shifted his glance to an angel with auburn hair, her lovely face all merry, and thought of Katherine. He shook his head at these distractions, resting against a pillar as he collected his thoughts and plotted the logic of what he intended . . .

* * *

A short while later, Sevigny rapped on the door of the narrow two-storey house in Soap Lane. Ramler the scribe, eyes heavy with sleep, opened the door and stepped back in alarm as Sevigny knocked him inside, slamming the door shut behind him.

'You are not a soldier, Master Ramler,' Sevigny warned, 'so please do not act the part.' He pushed the scribe, dressed only in a bed tunic, down the needle-thin passageway into what must be a chancery chamber, and made him sit on a stool whilst he brought another, positioning himself so close their knees nearly touched.

'What is this?' Ramler stammered. 'I heard about the affray at Queenhithe. I am to attend on Sir Philip. He is—'

'Shut up!' Sevigny hissed. 'Shut up and listen. True, you are Sheriff Malpas's scribe, but you are also Roseblood's spy and indeed his assassin.'

'I—'

'Hush now,' Sevigny soothed. 'Sir Philip is York's man. His master wanted that silver intended for the Tower mint. Malpas suborned Candlemas and his coven to steal it, enrich his master and humiliate Beaufort and the Queen. The second part of the plot was to lay the blame for all of this on Roseblood, Beaufort's principal ally in the city, who was to be arrested and accused of a whole string of crimes. Roseblood might be brought down or at least seriously impeded. I was to play a part in this. Candlemas would be arrested and secretly offered a pardon if he turned King's Approver.' Sevigny pointed at the scribe. 'You, however, informed Roseblood about all of this. The silver was replaced with scraps of rubbish and Candlemas depicted as a fool. Sir Philip was furious. Four of Candlemas's coven were executed as a warning. I was used to hunt the rest of the gang down. Candlemas was then held to his bargain.

'No, no.' Sevigny leaned over and pressed a finger against Ramler's lips. The scribe's face was now ghostly white, eyes brimming with fear, lower lip trembling, one hand clawing at his crotch. 'Go and relieve yourself.' Sevigny nodded towards the door. 'You are terrified. Don't be stupid and try to escape, or I will kill you out of hand and take your head to the Guildhall.'

Ramler jumped to his feet and scuttled out. Sevigny went into the small buttery. He filled two goblets with wine and brought them back. Ramler returned, a night robe around his shoulders, and Sevigny ordered him to sit down.

'Have you ever been to Venice, Master Ramler?' he began. 'No? Ah well, if you are arrested, tried and condemned by the Secret Ones, they give you an abrin seed to swallow. If you survive, God has vindicated you. If you die, then the Secret Ones have been justified. Of course, abrin is deadly poisonous. If the Secret Ones want to spare you, you will be ordered not to chew the seed so that it passes through you out into the privy, its shell intact. If they want you dead, you will be forced to chew it and, of course, deadly juices are released into both mouth and stomach. Death follows swiftly.'

'I know nothing of abrin.'

'Of course you don't. However, Master Roseblood

and his henchman Ignacio know a great deal about both abrin and other poisons. In fact, Roseblood's garden contains a special poison plot, a bed of deadly juices such as belladonna, known to others as deadly nightshade, the Devil's herb or banewort.' Sevigny lifted a goblet from the floor and pressed it into Ramler's hand. 'Don't worry.' He grinned. 'Nothing is tainted. I know a little about poisons. I was educated at Fountains Abbey, where one of the brothers was a keen herbalist. Belladonna can grow to about five feet high, with spreading branches. Its leaves always grow in pairs, one slightly longer than the other. The flower is a deep violet; its fruit are dark, shiny berries with a purple juice, very like claret. However, all parts of that herb are most deadly.'

'What are you implying? Skulkin and I tasted the wine.'

'Of course there are other poisons; for example, arsenic, red or white. It is imported from the east; some people claim it's an aphrodisiac.'

'I tasted the wine,' Ramler moaned.

'Of course you did, but you poisoned it afterwards. Remember what happened. You brought the wine up; Skulkin accompanied you. Candlemas and Cross-Biter are all agitated and suspicious. You fill both goblets. You and Skulkin taste the wine; your two victims are satisfied. They now concentrate on you tasting the food. You act the solicitous clerk. Just after you have tasted the wine, you draw out, probably from the cuff of your jerkin, poisoned pellets. You drop these into the goblets as you stretch your fingers across the rims of the cups.'

'That would have been seen.'

'No, the goblets were deep pewter bowls, the wine a dark purple. You were moving them about on the table. Your victims did not even suspect. Claret is heavy; the pellets soon dissolved. You leave Candlemas and Cross-Biter, securing the door behind you. Your victims are nervous, thirsty; they drink swiftly, filling the goblets with more wine.'

'No poison was found in the cups.'

'Of course not! They were drained, along with any dregs left in the jug. Roseblood expected this. Every time they drank and refilled those goblets, any trace of poison, whatever it was, was removed by the wine. Come, Master Ramler, don't act the innocent. Surgeons pour wine to clean wounds. Some of them even say their knives and hooks should also be washed in it. Scullions use coarse wine to scrape dishes. Now the poison probably acted within the hour, cup after cup being downed. The early symptoms would be dismissed as some ill humour of the belly, until the pains began to spread. Belladonna in its deadly stage is most swift.'

'But the physician—'

'Master Ramler, the physician you hired probably couldn't tell the difference between a cadaver and a living being! You hired the worst for that reason.' Sevigny pulled a face. 'We could have him seized and questioned, if he is sober enough. Your physician looked at both corpses and pronounced them dead, though he couldn't provide a solid reason. He took his fee and left. And what use re-examining them? I'm sure that as sheriff's scribe, you have already used your authority to have Candlemas and Cross-Biter buried in the thickest quicklime, where their corpses will soon corrupt. Yes?'

Ramler, his pale face all fearful, just stared back.

'So strange.' Sevigny sipped at his wine and put the goblet down. He had to be careful; exhaustion from the night before was making itself felt. 'Strange,' he repeated, 'that you have never asked why you should be blamed. Why should Master Ramler, scribe to the sheriff of this city, murder two men at the behest of the taverner Simon Roseblood?' Ramler made to rise from his stool. He was gibbering silently to himself, head shaking, face all distracted. Sevigny gently pushed him back. 'Roseblood got to know your secrets. He blackmailed you.'

'What do you mean?' the scribe spluttered.

'You are a strange man, Ramler. I have heard of your type. The proof of what I say lies hidden in your bedchamber.' Sevigny paused. 'In appearance you are a man, but deep within your soul you wish to be a woman, to be used as one, yes?'

Ramler could only gaze back in stricken terror.

'You like to dress as a woman, to have congress as a woman. Roseblood discovered your ruling passion, an easy enough task. He controls the whisperers and the eavesdroppers, the prostitutes and the pimps, the men who like other men.' Sevigny waved a hand. 'And so and so on. He offered you a chamber at the Roseblood where you could act out your dreams with some young man hired for the occasion. You entered his tavern and left it as a woman through a postern door. My searchers, Cosmas and Damian, watched you and marvelled at what they discovered. No one would ever suspect. Of course if the city council discover your secret . . . well, you have probably attended such trials: you would burn as a sodomite at Smithfield.'

Ramler put his face in his hands and began to sob. Sevigny felt a strange compassion for this little man trapped in the cage of his body, forced to live a life he hated.

'Ever since I was a boy,' the scribe took his hands away from his face, lifted the wine goblet and drained it, 'I have been ghosted by what I secretly wish to be.' He sighed and put the goblet down. 'You are correct. I lived a haunted life until Roseblood discovered my secret. He offered to protect me, and at the same time let me be what I am. He even recruited the young men; none of them knew who I was. You once saw the remains of paint on my face.' He sniffed. 'When I entered the Roseblood, I became another being. I was happy. I could be what I wanted.' He stared at the floor.

'And what does it really matter?' He glanced up. 'All the filthy politics of the great ones, with their puffed-up ambitions, their retinues of treachery, murder and perjury.' He half smiled. 'Of course Roseblood had a price. I betrayed the sheriff, though in truth that wasn't hard. Malpas is a cruel taskmaster. He would have me burned as swiftly as he blinked. I told Roseblood about the plot to seize the silver. I kept him informed about Candlemas and Cross-Biter, and I took care of them. It wasn't difficult.' He lifted a hand. 'I had a small purse here under my wrist; Ignacio provided the poison. They were so distracted they never even saw me. It was so very, very simple.' He blinked. 'They must have known they were dying. They were violent men, so they drew their daggers as if death could be driven off . . .'

Ramler's voice trailed away; he was now more composed, as if preparing himself for the inevitable. Sevigny rose, drew his sword and rested its blade on the scribe's unresisting shoulder.

'Sheriff Malpas would have you torn apart.'

'A swift cut would be a mercy.' Ramler held his gaze. 'Afterwards, go to my chamber. Please remove and destroy what you find there. I don't want my memory mocked. Mine will be just another death during a murderous time.'

Sevigny grasped his sword hilt with two hands, staring at this pathetic clerk even as memories of the previous night's slaughter crowded his mind. And before it? Walking with Katherine in the gathering dusk, holding her hand, teasing her, feeling his heart sing. He lifted the sword.

'Just a prayer . . .' Ramler swallowed hard.

'Hush now,' Sevigny replied. 'I will not kill you.'

The scribe glanced up in astonishment.

'Pack what you must, destroy what you have to,' Sevigny urged. 'Go to the Roseblood, tell Master Simon exactly what has happened. He will help. Take ship to some port far from London, for as the angels are my witness, if I meet you here again, I will have to kill you.'

'And Sir Philip?'

'He'll be confronted with another mystery: why should his faithful scribe abruptly disappear? I tell you this, Master Ramler, it would have only been a matter of time before our noble sheriff began to suspect. You are ruled by your passions. My two searchers discovered it, so be warned.'

Sevigny lifted his sword in mock salute, sheathed it and left the house, going immediately to a tavern, the Silver Griffin, to break his fast and resist the wave of exhaustion lapping his soul. He sat in a window embrasure staring out over the late spring garden. Sparrows hopped around the conical beehives, the air broken by the cooing and fluttering from the nearby dovecote. He wondered if he should leave London, ride through the spring countryside to Ludlow or wherever York had set up his standard. The attempt to indict Roseblood had failed, but at least Sevigny had removed a spy from York's camp. He also had considerable information about the troops and armaments the Queen and Beaufort had assembled at the Tower and elsewhere.

He paused in his reflection to thank the servant who brought the morning ale and fresh bread, before returning to his brooding, eating and drinking absent-mindedly. The loneliness of the tavern garden brought back memories of his meeting with Ravenspur and LeCorbeil. He was certain he had seen the same mercenaries during the attack on the Roseblood. That would be logical. LeCorbeil supported York, and by doing so deepened the crisis around the English Crown.

As for Ravenspur's prophecies, York would be pleased, even though they were baffling. And the reference to the greyhounds? Sevigny recalled the various escutcheons of the English commanders. Surely the greyhound was the insignia of the Talbots of Shrewsbury, and hadn't both father and son been killed in the last futile battle of the English at Castillon some two years earlier? However, that was a matter for York. One further task remained – Giles Argentine – and after that? Sevigny plucked at the crumbs on the platter. Two women now dominated his life: the beautiful, malevolent duchess who wanted him dead, and the daughter of the man who was supposed to be his enemy. Sevigny knew he could never forget Katherine's beautiful face; even the sword storm of the previous evening had not stifled the glorious glow of her eyes. He pulled himself up. He would not leave London yet; he could not forsake that lovely face. 'Even if I had the wings of an eagle,' he whispered, 'and flew to the edge of the dawn, you would be there . . .'

Simon Roseblood

London, May 1455

'So, we have met before I leave.' Simon Roseblood gazed around the gleaming oaken table in the Camelot Chamber. All had gathered: Katherine and Raphael, Ignacio and Wormwood, Father Benedict and the most recent arrival, Reginald Bray. 'Master Clerk,' Simon pointed at Beaufort's messenger, 'you missed the excitement, our visitors from France!'

'Were you their main quarry?' Bray retorted.

'I have spent some time,' Simon declared, 'searching for an answer. The galleys made landings along the south coast. They later entered the estuary, attacking communities along the north bank of the Thames. But yes, we seem to have been the principal target for the corsairs. Now everybody chatters as if they are experts on war. They talk about strange lights being seen, fire arrows glimpsed, as if someone, perhaps LeCorbeil, was determined to mark our tavern and the riverside beyond.' He pulled a face. 'Such rumours are correct.

The corsairs must have sent scouts, spies, and we know LeCorbeil are in London. If they had destroyed us,' he chose his words carefully, 'Beaufort would have lost a powerful ally.' He paused, deep in thought, before continuing. 'And LeCorbeil, whatever the mystery behind them, would have wreaked a hideous vengeance for what they believe Beaufort did against them in France.'

Simon gestured for the rest to break their fast. He wished to gather his thoughts. He rose and walked to the mullioned glass window, gazing out into the darkness. The French had escaped before the admiral of the coast north of the Thames could muster his fighting cogs. The dead of both sides had been buried in All Hallows. Simon glanced over his shoulder; his companions were now eating and drinking, except for Father Benedict. Simon noticed how pale and drawn the priest looked. Benedict had taken a mace during the attack and shattered a few heads, scrupulous about following canon law, which stipulated that a cleric could not use sword or dagger. Was the parish priest recovering from the attack, or was something else bothering him and his curate, who always looked so agitated? Father Roger was withdrawing more and more into himself, often in his cups.

Simon shifted his gaze. Raphael was deep in conversation with Katherine. Simon whistled under his breath as he recalled Sevigny's battle madness. A strange man, he mused. Sevigny looked and dressed like a priest, but he was certainly a warrior and also a troubadour deeply smitten by Katherine, as she was by him. Simon grudgingly conceded that he had underestimated Sevigny. He and Ignacio had plotted the mysterious deaths of Candlemas and Cross-Biter, a ploy to baffle Malpas so that he could never lay their deaths at his door. Sevigny had outwitted them. He had concentrated on the possibility of a traitor and spy on the sheriff's own council, tested his theory and so uncovered Ramler's scandalous secret, as Roseblood and Ignacio had done so many months ago. Ramler had been surprisingly cooperative, dominated as he conceded by his hidden sins. He had cheerfully agreed to betray his master in return for safe lodgings and protection. Sevigny had brought that to an end. Malpas might soon find out, but . . . Simon grinned to himself. Ramler had been sent packing on a grain ship. Cornwall might be lonely, but it was the best Simon could offer and certainly not as dangerous for the scribe as Cheapside would be. The taverner was surprised by Sevigny's clemency. Was that the effect of Katherine, or something else?

'Raphael?' He turned. 'You say Sevigny was attacked in St Mary-le-Bow?'

'So rumour has it. He killed one assailant; the other two escaped. I made careful enquiries. That was not us, was it?'

Simon shook his head and turned back to the window. Ramler had certainly told him something interesting. How Sevigny might be York's man, body and soul, but Duchess Cecily fiercely resented her husband's faithful clerk.

'Will you welcome him back, Father?' Simon turned. Katherine was staring beseechingly at him.

'He is always welcome here,' he replied, leaning down to kiss her brow. 'I assure you,' he smiled, 'you could do a lot worse than win the heart of a royal clerk.'

He was tempted to continue the teasing, but Reginald Bray, still garbed in his travelling cloak, picked up a knife and chimed it against a decanter. The Camelot Chamber fell silent. Simon returned to his seat at the head of the table.

'Time is passing,' he began. 'I must go with Master Reginald. I have described to you the present dangers and possible outcomes. My absence, and the reasons for it, will remain secret. Raphael knows what I have to do. He will be in charge whilst I am away. He will make sure that all signs of the recent attack are removed and will use our friends and allies amongst the river folk to keep sharp guard against any fresh assault. After I leave, Ignacio will return.' He used his fingers to translate what he had said for his henchman.

Once finished, Simon clasped hands and kissed Katherine on the brow. A short while later, he, Ignacio and Master Reginald Bray slipped out of the Roseblood along the narrow lanes leading down to the riverside. It was a cold evening; the rain had ceased, but a snapping breeze wafted the mist along the runnels. Simon pulled his cowl forward to hide his face, though he and his party kept their swords and daggers clear to frighten off the hooded shades lurking in alcoves and filth-strewn corners. Ignacio carried a torch, its busy flame creating a moving pool of light.

They passed painted whores of every description and variety, hurrying down to the quayside to satisfy the lusts of the sailors from the royal cogs gathering in the shabby quayside alehouses. Two blowsy slatterns shuffled by holding between them some young coxcomb, so drunk he could hardly stand. Simon glimpsed Milwort, a stumbling shadow of a beggar, carrying as usual his tattered leather sack containing the dried severed head of an Ottoman Turk, or so he boasted. Simon wondered about the beggar, who claimed to have fought in the armies of the east and taken the head of a Turkish champion. Occasionally Milwort would change his story and describe the salted head as that of Herod the Great, plundered from his tomb in the valley of Gehenna outside Jerusalem. Simon realised he was about to enter the make-believe world of men like Milwort. He would become one of those floating, repulsive figures with a strange story and even more loathsome diseases.

They passed the gibbet on the corner of Thames Street and hurried down arrow-thin alleyways to Quicksilver Manor, the home of the Alchemist. They pushed open the wicket gate, went along the garden path and pulled at the bell under its gleaming iron coping. A taciturn manservant welcomed them through the battered metal-studded door and led them along a maze of gloomy passageways and up rickety stairs. They stopped at a door; the servant pulled back the oxhide covering and rapped the iron carving of a satyr. The door flew back and Simon and his two companions were ushered into the most luxurious chamber. Turkey rugs dyed a deep scarlet covered the coloured tiled floor; black wooden panelling shimmered against the walls; a fire crackled vigorously in the mantled hearth, whilst candlelight dazzled the eye with its golden glow.

A man sitting in a throne-like chair beside the fire rose and shuffled towards them, hands extended. His face was almost hidden by long iron-grey hair and a shaggy beard and moustache. He was dressed in a blue robe dusted with silver moons, whilst his fingers and wrists boasted gleaming precious stones. He embraced Simon in a gust of spices and rich red wine. They exchanged the kiss of peace and Simon introduced Master Reginald.

'The Alchemist,' declared the taverner as the two clasped hands. 'Called so because he can change any man or woman into something completely different. He will transform me into a leper so loathsome even my own children would not recognise me.'

'True.' The Alchemist's deep, rough voice held all the power and music of a professional preacher. 'I can change base metals into gold and, on rare occasions, gold into dross.' He gestured to his visitors to sit on cushioned stools before the fire. 'I received your letter, as you must have received mine, Simon. I can do what you want.'

The Alchemist served them deep-bowled goblets of the finest wine as he chattered about all the gossip in the city: Simon's triumphant procession to the Guildhall; the murder of the whores in Queenhithe, the attack by French corsairs, as well as the looming rift between the Beauforts and York. 'All grist to the mill.' He grabbed his goblet, sinking back into the cushions of his oaken chair. 'People will need my help to change their appearance lest they lose their heads.' He never asked Bray what his business was. Simon had given him every assurance about his companion, so the Alchemist cheerfully talked about his own experiences disguising important citizens of London as well as courtiers who had to flee. Simon half listened. The Alchemist was a veritable prince amongst the villains of the city, highly revered by the trugs, tumblers, wapping-morts and counterfeits, all those skilled in disguise. Never once had he been indicted nor seen the inside of a prison.

At last the Alchemist ceased his chatter and turned to the business in hand. 'So you want to become a leper, Master Simon, and enter the lazar house at St Giles?' He narrowed his eyes, 'Joachim Brotherton is the master there, and . . .' He paused.

'And?' Simon asked.

'Strange stories,' the Alchemist replied. 'Even stranger,' he grinned, 'that you wish to enter a leper colony. It can be done, however. Let us begin.' He turned to Master Bray. 'You should leave with Ignacio now that you know what I can do.'

Simon lapsed into sign language, fingers twisting swiftly, watching Ignacio's lips move as he silently repeated what he was learning. When he stopped, the mute nodded in agreement and they embraced, exchanging the kiss of peace. Simon shook Bray's hand and waited whilst the Alchemist ushered his two companions out of the chamber and down the stairs.

On his return, the Alchemist busied himself in a small chamber off the main solar. Simon opened the chancery bag that he had placed next to his feet and took out the documents and purse Bray had given him. 'You will assume a new identity,' Bray had insisted in the secrecy of the Roseblood. 'You will become Simon Meopham from Norwich, a hospitaller lay brother who has seen service in Outremer. You have been there, haven't you, yes?' He hadn't even waited for Simon's answer, thrusting documents into his hands. 'These are letters of accreditation, memoranda of testimony, a physician's verdict and, above all,' he flicked the heavy purse, 'enough silver to pay for a year's lodgings and a little more. Master Joachim will accept you. The letters you carry are genuine; both the mayor and master at Norwich are like you, *viri jurati*, sworn men, Beaufort's retainers body and soul. Money and power turn every lock. Remember, Simon, the Beauforts will never ever forget this, but you must be successful. Argentine must be silenced for good and his journal and any other documents seized.'

'Are you ready?' The Alchemist stood in the doorway of his chancery office. 'You must come with me.'

Simon followed him out of the solar, down the stone-flagged corridor and into a stark cellar of a room, its whitewashed walls completely bare except for a crucifix with a sprig of green wound around it. There were a few sticks of furniture and a narrow garderobe in the corner. In the centre of that bleak chamber stood a throne-like chair similar to the one in the Alchemist's solar. Above this hung a Catherine wheel, lowered so that its concentric rims crammed with candles bathed the chair in light.

'I would prefer open windows,' the Alchemist ushered Simon into the seat, 'but that always attracts the curious. Now,' he pulled up a stool to face Simon, 'my friend, I am going to hurt you. If you are a leper, your flesh is corrupt, its texture changed; your eyes become rounded and thinly lidded. There is a strange sparkle in your gaze. Your nose is shrivelled, your voice hoarse, your nails grow rough and coarse. Fingers become crooked, your breath reeks like a midden heap, your skin is so fleshy fat that water will roll off it as it does off an oiled hide. No hair, no moustache or beard, your eyebrows mere marks. So,' he pushed his face closer, 'are you ready for the journey to the dark side of the night? You will approach the very doors of hell. You will meet the key-jangling janitors of the shadowlands where bad men bustle no more and a profound silence reigns. When you walk abroad, windows become shuttered, street doors slam closed, birdsong dies; even the dogs and cats will avoid you.'

'I have been warned and advised.' Simon held the Alchemist's gaze. 'Red and brown nodules will appear on my face, upper body, fingers and hands. A leper's face thickens so his features are similar to those of a cat. Ulcers appear, the limbs stiffen and the pits of my body will reek like those of a male goat on heat. The letters from Norwich claim that I am in the first stages of the disease.'

'Good.' The Alchemist breathed. 'So you know. You will wear thick woollen gloves and stockings of the same texture. I will supply these, as I will the face mask, tunic, sandals and the grey-hooded cloak with its red cross.'

'Ignacio will bring you payment.'

The Alchemist waved his hand as if that was of little importance.

'And you have been closely instructed on how to protect yourself at St Giles?' he asked.

'Take no food or drink touched by a leper. Avoid their fetid breath and any of their body fluids. That will be easy. I am a wealthy guest. I will be given quarters similar to those of a Carthusian monk. I can eat—'

'The only real danger,' the Alchemist broke in, 'would be a scrupulous study of your body by a trained, very skilled physician. However, knowing what I do of Master Joachim, that will not happen.' He rose to his feet. 'Simon, why are you really going?'

'I am a sworn man.' Simon shrugged. 'What I am, the Beauforts made me. There are other reasons, but every man has his secrets.'

'God rewards such loyalty.' The Alchemist rubbed his hands. 'Now we begin. You will become a leper, a revolting disease that has no cure.' He tapped his head.

'You must adopt the attitude that you are joining the living dead from which there is no respite or pardon. So, let the alchemy begin.'

Over the next four days, Simon experienced a harrowing of the soul. The Alchemist shaved all the hair from his body, deliberately cutting the skin to draw blood. Simon was covered with a thick, oozing fat, its reek making his stomach turn; his teeth were blackened with a special juice, his eyelids clipped, his flesh rubbed with a paste made from iron rust and unslaked lime. Tinctures of ratsbane provoked great blisters. He was not allowed out of the cell. The Alchemist tried to distract him by describing how he had prepared all the great counterfeit men of the city. Small yellow, brown and red buboes appeared on Simon's hands and face. The Alchemist trained him on how to walk and speak and instructed him to practise this throughout the day. The pain and soreness robbed Simon of sleep and rest, although the Alchemist was very pleased.

'You must assume the look of a man,' he advised, 'in whom the silver cord has snapped, the golden lamp broken, the pitcher shattered. Your life is darkness and the shadows threaten to engulf you completely. Your coffin lies ready and the mourners await.'

Simon was left to reflect on such sombre thoughts, but other memories and images came drifting back. He thought of his wife Rohesia, buried beneath the cold slabs of All Hallows, and his secret love for Eleanor. Why had she cut herself off so suddenly? Did she fear him? Was it guilt over the death of his brother? Eleanor had sent him a message after the attack by the corsairs saying how she wished to see him. He had not replied. Regrettably, that would have to wait until this present business was finished. Once it was, Simon was determined to confront Eleanor and demand that she speak the truth about the night Edmund had so foolishly left the tavern. He wanted to discover if LeCorbeil truly had had a hand in his murder, and how that malevolence, rooted in some hideous massacre in France years ago, had provoked such hatred as to claim Edmund's life and carry out the brutal, bloody attack on the Roseblood.

The pain and cruel discomfort of his disguise deepened, forcing Simon to pace his cell during the death watches of the night. He had no choice but to reflect on his life and the dangers pressing in on him from every side. He must do something about the hideous murders of those whores. Prostitutes, strumpets and streetwalkers came and went; sometimes they were spirited aboard ships for the flesh markets of France, Flanders or even further afield. But these gruesome murders? Simon, tired and weary, racked his memory. Similar outrages had taken place many years ago in Dowgate; a tailor, that was it, had been responsible. Moonstruck and of hellish soul, he had inflicted various forms of cruelty on whores and tavern maids to satisfy his own deep hatred against all women. Eventually the murderer had been caught and strangled at Smithfield, but had the demon that possessed him returned to haunt some other soul?

The Alchemist eventually took notice of how weary and dispirited his patient had become and began to feed him rich claret laced with a mild opiate. Even then Simon found it difficult to sleep, and would lie listening to the mysterious comings and goings at Quicksilver Manor. The Alchemist was certainly a busy man, responsible for dispatching along the alleyways and runnels of London a veritable legion of piteous-looking beggars whose suppurating sores and weeping wounds opened the purse strings of the charitable. Simon knew that the counterfeit men could earn in a week what a labourer or soldier would be paid over two years. The Alchemist always took a percentage. God help the cunning man who reneged! The Alchemist's host of enforcers would ensure that all future wounds were real and lasting.

Simon was kept hidden away. Three days after his treatment began, Ignacio paid a secret visit. The henchman's surprise immediately told Simon how the Alchemist's preparations had transformed him into some loathsome victim of leprosy. In fact he forgot the pain, laughing at Ignacio's haunting, muted questions. Fingers moving swiftly, Simon assured his henchman that it was all mummer's play. He then sat quietly as Ignacio reported on life and business at the Roseblood. Raphael had cleared all signs of the French attack, whilst trade was prospering due to the arrival of more war cogs at Queenhithe. Apparently the Queen and Beaufort were stripping Calais of its garrison, as well as moving ships and troops from the defence of the Cinque Ports. A great mustering was to take place at Blackheath. The royal commissioners of array were even offering pardons to prisoners in the Fleet, Newgate and Marshalsea. York was ready to strike. Handbills proclaiming the justice of the duke's cause had been posted on the cross at St Paul's churchyard and the Standard in Cheapside. The lords of the soil were choosing their sides, and some of London's leading citizens had already slipped away to York's camp. Sheriff Malpas was busy summoning up as much support for his master as he could, though his failure in the matter of the Tower silver and his humiliation over Candlemas had cost him dearly. Proclamations had also been issued to determine the whereabouts of Master Ramler, but that had only deepened public amusement at the sheriff's expense.

Another whore, Florence of the Four Corners, had been murdered; her mutilated corpse had been crammed into a filthy laystall on Snakes Lane, close to the river. No one could say who had killed her, though according to rumour, she had been hurrying to meet a customer somewhere in Queenhithe on the evening she disappeared. Simon could only cross himself, murmur the requiem and ask about Sevigny. Ignacio smiled. The clerk had visited the Roseblood for a black jack of ale. He'd sat supping his drink in a corner before leaving as swiftly and silently as he had arrived. Mistress Katherine had been informed, and appeared very cross that she had not been there. Indeed, Dorcas openly declared how the girl seemed either moonstruck or love-smitten, spending hours in the orchard or alone in her chamber.

Simon smiled thinly at that before Ignacio went on to give more details about the attack on Sevigny at St Mary-le-Bow. Some claimed it was the work of friends of the late Candlemas, but, Ignacio added, Candlemas had no friends. His next item of news was more interesting. How Sevigny's archer companion Bardolph had disappeared from the Golden Harp and was last seen securing passage on a cog bound for Hainault. Simon wondered if there was some link between Bardolph's sudden departure abroad and that attack on Sevigny. From the little Ignacio had told him, the archer was from York's camp, a hard-bitten veteran. Was Ramler correct? Did Sevigny enjoy the duke's favour, but not his duchess's? Had she and Bardolph had a hand in that mysterious attack at St Mary-le-Bow? Perhaps he could entice Sevigny into an honest conversation. The clerk had been dispatched to London to destroy Roseblood or even to subvert his allegiance. Could he be turned? Had he become so alienated from the duchess that he was looking for a new master? Times were changing, and so were loyalties, though that too would have to wait until Simon had dealt with Argentine. If Bray was correct, York too was hunting for this mysterious physician. Was that another task secretly entrusted to Sevigny?

Simon rubbed his face and concentrated on the matters in hand. He gave Ignacio instructions as to how Raphael was to visit his brother Gabriel at Greyfriars to ensure all was well. Ignacio and others must also mount a keen watch over the Roseblood, and alert the scavengers, babewyns and gargoyles and the Fraternity of the Doomed to discover anything they could about the murdered whores. The Alchemist joined them. Simon fell silent. He did not want this master of charades to know all his business. They agreed that Simon would be ready in two days. The taverner insisted that when he left Quicksilver Manor after the bells rang for Lauds, Ignacio would follow discreetly to ensure that no mishap occurred.

The morning in question broke dry after a night's drizzling rain. Simon, who felt pain and soreness from head to toe, shuffled out of the postern door of Quicksilver Manor, up a covered alleyway and on to the main thoroughfare. He was cloaked and cowled in the regulation light grey with a white mask covering his face. On his feet were stout marching sandals, in his right hand an iron-tipped stave. Over his shoulder bulky leather panniers fastened with straps carried all his worldly goods. He paused and, with his left hand, freed the wooden clapper from his cord belt. He had perfected a shuffling, shambling gait, and as he moved forward, he hoarsely murmured his lament: 'Vanity of vanities, says the preacher, and all is vanity. The sun rises, the sun sets. What was will be again, for there is nothing new under the sun . . .'

Rattling the wooden clapper, Simon made his way up Cheapside. Ignacio, hooded and masked, stood in a nearby doorway. Simon shook the wooden clapper in recognition and passed on. The morning was cold. The streets were not yet busy. Heavy-eyed, yawning apprentices opened shopfronts. Streetwalkers and whores found soliciting beyond Cock Lane were herded down to the great cage on the Tun. A songster tried to recite a poem, only to be scoffed at by a group of beadles, whilst the prisoners they guarded mockingly imitated him. A shabby preacher was describing a vision he'd received: how devils gathered in the steeples of London churches, so wicked had the city become. All these fell silent as Simon made his clattering approach. People swiftly turned their backs, terrified lest they be infected by his breath. A few shouted curses. The cook shop and pie stall owners stopped their chants offering strips of bacon or a farthing's worth of sausage. Even the deep-dissembling rogues with cozening tongues and sinister eyes slipped back into their narrow bolt-holes. The alley creepers and wall sliders searching for quarry retreated into the shadows. Street cries faded. The tinkers and smiths, their hammers beating tubs and pots, paused to cross themselves.

Simon was now walking up the centre of Cheapside. Despite his raw discomfort, he secretly smiled at the contrast between what was happening now and his last triumphant procession along this same thoroughfare. He passed the closed gates of the Guildhall, where the city archers on guard pulled up the folds of their mantles to cover nose and mouth, and reached the great fleshing market. Cows, pigs, geese and birds of every kind were being slaughtered; here the misty haze became tinged with spraying blood, whilst the cobbles beneath were soaked in scarlet juice and slimy globules of entrails and other offal. He skirted the stalls, hurrying past the forbidding mass of Newgate. The executioners, garbed in black with yellow face masks, offered him a ride to a swifter death at Tyburn. Simon ignored them, trudging along the gibbet road, past the Last Bowl, where the execution carts always paused so that the condemned could be given a stoup of ale by the Fraternity of the Hanged before being turned off the great scaffold, which rose like a bleak monster through the morning mist. He glimpsed the long execution ladder, the hanging nooses and the scavenger birds clustered on the cadavers left to dangle above the yawning execution pit.

At the double-gated entrance to St Giles, he pulled on the chain that hung from its coping carved in the shape of a grinning skull. A lay brother, dressed like a Carmelite in a cream-coloured robe with a brown mantle over it, invited him into the visitors' parlour, a bleak lime-washed chamber where he was told to sit on a bench just inside the door. A short while later, Master Joachim, his shaven face all oiled, blond hair cut in the neatest of tonsures, swept into the room. The master was dressed like the lay brother, though his robes were of pure wool, whilst his gloves were of the costliest deerskin and studded with miniature pearls. He was prim and pert, with a smug face and eyes constantly flickering. Simon took an instant dislike to him, as he did to Brother Gervaise, the prior, who boasted the protruding features of a mastiff. Simon suspected that Gervaise was the master's bully boy. The third person present was a nonentity; silver-haired, with a narrow, dusty face, Brother Gratian was the lazar house scribe and clerk.

At the prior's request, Simon took off his face mask. Joachim studied him, and sniffed noisily.

'There is no cure for leprosy, short of a miracle. Mercury and viper's flesh do more harm than good. Whilst I,' the master smiled falsely, 'search for the true remedy.' He let this enigmatic remark hang in the air as he took and studied the letters of accreditation and recommendation.

Joachim and his two companions seemed to have little interest in Simon, and indeed, why should they? Leprosy was a living death. St Giles was no more than a sanctified tavern where people came to die, the only difference being that some of the residents would end their days in one of the very comfortable cells named after a benefactor; Simon was given 'The Mortimer', on the east side of the cloister garth, a two-storey cell set in its own garden plot, comprising a monastery in miniature, with sleeping chamber, chancery and prayer cell. The less affluent were housed in the great dormitory, where they were provided with a curtained bed, a table, stool and small coffer.

Brother Gratian pushed across a small book, its parchment leaves sewn tightly together; this was the Regula, or Rule of St Giles. He pattered through its contents, describing the daily routine from Matins and Lauds to

Compline after sunset. He explained that St Giles possessed a refectory, kitchens, a water house to draw on underground streams and an inner court where the granary, kitchens, stables and storerooms were situated. He gave details of how food and all the necessities would be served. He spoke in a monotone; the only time he and the other two showed any interest was when Simon opened his purse and counted out the silver to cover his first year. An indenture was drawn up, signed and sliced as if it was the prime goose at a Christmas feast. Wine suddenly appeared. Goblets were filled, toasts exchanged, then both wine and silver abruptly vanished. Simon now had the measure of Joachim and his coterie: they were no better than Minehost in some Southwark alehouse.

Once the meeting was over, Simon was given a tour of the men's side of the sprawling lazar house, its gardens, fields and courtyards. Eventually, as the bells tolled for the noonday mass, he was taken to the Mortimer cell, a carving on the door proclaiming that noble family's insignia. He was quite surprised at his comfortable quarters, which fronted the great cloister garth. The door contained a hatch through which food could be delivered. There was an entry passageway and a small hall that served as kitchen, buttery and dining place. Next to this was a narrow chancery office and, on the second floor, a bedchamber and oratory. The windows were glazed with diamond-shaped quarters of plain glass. A door in the hall led out to a small garden, with a patch of grass bordered by ill-tended flowers and herb beds.

Simon made himself at home as best he could. Gervaise instructed him on what he could and couldn't do, naming a high price for attempting to alleviate the infection, the cost being incurred by buying a red adder with a white womb whose venom had been drained off, tail and head removed and the remaining flesh soaked in moss. Simon recalled what the Alchemist had told him and remained silent in the face of such an offer. All he wanted to do was merge swiftly and silently into the daily life of the lazar hospital. Time was precious. Reginald Bray had given him a week. Moreover, the Alchemist had warned how the painted sores, imitation buboes, shorn hair and powder rubbed into Simon's skin were only a disguise; without constant attention, they would begin to fail and fade.

Simon kept himself hooded and masked, stockings on his legs, gloves on his hands. He took food from the kitchens, simple fare: lentil stew, a mix of onions and almonds thickened with crusts soaked in white wine. He attended Divine Office when he could, though this proved to be a macabre event. Master Joachim, Prior Gervaise and other officials stood in the carved stalls of the lazar church, the patients in the choir benches either side of the chancel. A ghastly sight, as if ghouls had gathered to chant the psalms. Masks and gloves were removed and the full horror of the malignant disease was plain to see in the light of candle and taper: suppurating eyes in rotting faces, where nose, lips, eyelids and ears looked as if they had been gnawed by some rabid animal. Hands too weak for anything clung to the wooden rails. Mouths and tongues, horribly disfigured, tried to voice praise to God. The inmates would shuffle into church, leaning on sticks, canes and staves. The thick incense smoke and the sweetness of beeswax could not hide the rank, fetid smell of their corrupting bodies.

Simon found attendance in the refectory even more distasteful. Eventually he decided to eat only in his cell, though he would use all common occasions and public ceremonies to study and scrutinise. He suspected that Master Joachim would keep his errant kinsman in comfortable lodgings hidden well away from any searcher. He carefully studied the thirty or so inmates who lived in the cells around the cloister garth, but quickly concluded that none of these truly sick men could be a healthy physician in disguise. He wondered if Argentine was hiding in the master's household or with the lay brothers, who had their own dormitory and buttery, but he could not detect any such subterfuge.

Simon took to wandering the precincts, or at least the male quarters of the great lazar house. He chatted to servants and was most generous in slipping these a few coins, but failed to detect any conspiracy to conceal. Indeed, by the end of the third day of his stay, he was more concerned by the heavy, oppressive atmosphere of St Giles: walking, breathing and eating amongst the living dead. He had wandered battlefields in France searching for the bodies of wounded or slain comrades.

He had sifted amongst shattered flesh, chunks of limbs, the slimy entrails of horse and rider mixed together. He had seen faces smashed, heads staved in, arms, legs, hands and feet severed by slicing steel. St Giles was more heinous; a fog-bound Purgatory hanging between Heaven and Hell. The sun shone down on cornices, ledges and fretted stonework. Light shimmered in stained glass or on the surface of carp ponds and fountain bowls. Gardens lush with flower beds and rich herb plots exuded heavy scents. Birdsong rang through the massy greenery of the orchards. Nevertheless, the brooding shadows of sickness and death clustered heavy and close.

As Simon walked, searching and probing, often distracted by some cleverly carved statue in its niche, he would meet the living dead in all their blood-chilling horror, shuffling along a path, arising ghostlike from a bench, or slipping through the dappled light of the church. His sense of danger deepened. Contagion corrupted the very air and he had to be most prudent where he washed, ate or defecated. He desperately wanted to find his quarry and be clear of all this. He also became aware of a new danger, of being carefully watched, kept under close scrutiny. As a newcomer this might be expected, but had someone seen through his disguise? At first he suspected the master, but Joachim, after their first meeting, never approached, and nor did Gervaise or any of the other officers.

On his fifth day at St Giles, Simon was roused from a noonday sleep by the sound of shouts and cries. He hobbled out of his cell and his heart sank. Across the cloister garth stood Amadeus Sevigny, surrounded by city bailiffs. All these were hooded and visored, gloves on their hands as protection against any poisonous miasma. Sevigny, however, stood bare-headed and open-faced, hands on his hips as he surveyed the cloisters. Simon retreated into the shadows and watched as York's clerk divided his men into groups. A thorough search began, continuing for most of the afternoon.

Simon's prayer that Sevigny would not be the one who visited him was answered. Skulkin crossed the cloister garth and immediately went into the cell next to Simon's. Afterwards, he walked into Simon's chamber, stared around, glanced at him, then promptly left. Simon breathed his relief. Skulkin would follow orders, but not too closely. Sevigny, however, was thorough, inspecting the dormitories, refectories and infirmary as well as the private quarters of the master and prior. Simon drew quiet comfort from that. Sevigny was searching for Argentine. York would love to silence that elusive physician, and if a powerful clerk could not find him, then perhaps Argentine was not hiding in St Giles at all, and his own mission was fruitless. He wondered about the French. LeCorbeil would be eager to seize Argentine. They might also conclude that St Giles was an ideal hiding place, or did they know that already? York and Lancaster wanted Argentine dead. LeCorbeil would very much like him alive and well. Did they know that he was here, and were simply biding their time? If so, their problem would be how to smuggle

Argentine out of the hospital and through London to some lonely port or harbour and a waiting French ship.

By the time the bell rang for Vespers, Sevigny had finished his search with nothing to show for it. Ostensibly, or so the whispers ran, the clerk had been searching for outlaws who had attacked and murdered a Genoese merchant and thrown his naked corpse into the nearby Fleet river. Many found this difficult to believe, but after Sevigny left empty-handed, the hospital returned to its normal routine.

Simon decided not to attend Vespers or Compline. Instead he sat at his cell window, watching the shadows lengthen. He felt uncomfortable after Sevigny's search and still could not shrug off the chilling feeling of being followed and watched. He picked at his food on a pewter platter and wondered if his stay here was no more useful than hunting moonbeams. The bells tolled again. Darkness edged the window and the breeze turned cool. Simon's eyes grew heavy, but he wakened at a rattle on his door. When he opened it, a hooded, gowned figure crept out of the shadows of the cloister alley.

'For the love of God, Simon Roseblood,' the stranger hissed, 'let me in and let us speak.'

Simon gasped in consternation at being recognised so openly. He stared quickly around the cloisters and almost pulled the shrouded figure into his cell. Once inside, the stranger pushed back his cowl and removed his mask to reveal a face ravaged by leprosy. Dark blotchy tumours the size of walnuts disfigured his features; his eyelids were shrunken, his nostrils and lips chapped and cut by the disease; wisps of hair hung from a balding, blotchy pate and scabrous cheeks. The man sat down on a stool, small bright eyes glistening with mucus. Roseblood just stared back, wondering who this could be. A stranger, yet one who knew him well enough to see through his mask and disguise. The man lifted a claw-like hand, the fingers wreathed in wet rags.

'Leprosy.' The voice was strangely powerful, the hoarse whisper carrying across the cell. 'Leprosy,' he repeated, 'is the firstborn of Death. I have studied you, Simon Roseblood. I can see through your pretence.'

'Who are you?' Simon drew the dagger concealed beneath his cloak.

'No need to threaten,' came the reply. 'I am, I was Thomas Holand, routier, mercenary, a sinner twice, thrice, four times bound for Hell as any of them.' The stranger leaned forward. 'Once a drinking, swiving, lecherous captain of mercenaries in the Beaufort company; one of those cohorts that terrorised Normandy along with the likes of Glasdale. Remember him? The Maid of Orleans threatened to send him to Hell or to England.' He paused. 'My throat is dry as sand. Please.'

He took the goblet tied to the leather belt beneath his cloak and stretched it out so Simon could fill it with sweet white wine. Holand drank greedily, his ulcerated tongue lapping at the cup. He lifted his head.

'Fourteen years ago, Master Roseblood, on Lady's Day, I was captured by Brabantines serving in the Dauphin's army. Ah yes, you remember? I was carrying messages that I successfully burnt in my campfire, so they thought they would use the same fire to loosen my tongue. They—'

'Stripped you naked, pegged you out on the ground, fastened a hollow pipe against your side and put a hungry rat down it,' Simon declared. 'I remember it well. Of course! Thomas Holand!'

'They put the rat down.' Holand leaned across and clasped Simon's gloved hand. 'I could feel its cold, hard snout and the first skim of its teeth against my skin. God save me, and he did.'

Simon took up the story. 'I remember they were so taken with their cruel amusement that we were upon them like hawks.'

'You kicked the pipe away and speared the rat with your dagger.' Holand pointed at Simon. 'Despite the mail coif, I remember that face, those eyes. I always have. You could age to be a hundred and be as rotting as me, and I would still single you out as I do now.'

Simon picked up the dagger and pulled his stool closer. Holand held his bandaged hands up in a gesture of peace.

'I mean no harm. No one else knows. At first I thought you were simply a new patient, until I stared into your face. Then I began to watch you. Your movements are a little too swift at times, but above all, you made one real mistake.'

'Which is?'

'Your eyes mark you out, so bright with curiosity.' Holand cackled with laughter. 'Like those of a child amongst old men. Oh do not worry. Others will never learn your secret. Why should they? People see what they want to see. No one would expect any but the most diseased to be closeted here, a healthy body amongst those of the living dead.' Holand coughed on his laughter and greedily slurped the wine. 'And why should I betray you? You who once saved me? No, friend, I am here to advise, to help if I can, and to beg a favour.'

'What favour?'

'To secure my release from here as swiftly as possible.'

'You are not cured.'

'Of course not. I am for the burial pit, but not here. I don't want to be hurried to my grave by Master Joachim and his coven.' Holand stretched out a hand. 'And you should be careful of that as well. As you grow ill and become weaker, you are moved to the infirmary; well, at least those who have wealth.'

'And?' Simon had already noticed that two inmates in the cells around the cloisters had been moved since his arrival.

'Master Joachim and Prior Gervaise love gold and silver. Rumour says they hurry the wealthy to their graves. All the dead man's possessions are then rifled and a great deal stolen. Heirs and relatives are in no position to object. Very few want to enter here and handle goods, even precious ones, held so long by an infected person. Moreover, Joachim and the rest prepare their bills containing all sorts of spurious expenses.'

'So why hurry them into the dark?'

'To catch their victims unawares. Leprosy is a creeping disease. It can be a long time before you feel its final fatal embrace. The dying can summon their defendants and friends.' Holand's voice trailed off. 'Master Joachim puts a stop to that. Once in the infirmary, death follows swiftly.' He grimaced. 'They also whisper how Joachim dreams of discovering a cure. How he experiments on the dying with oils, salves and potions.'

Simon recalled Joachim's enigmatic words when they first met. Did the master use the dying to see if he could fashion a cure?

Holand shuffled his feet. 'So, Master Roseblood, why are you here? How can I help? You search for something or someone, as did that mailed clerk earlier today.'

Simon pulled back his cowl and sat staring at the floor. He fully recalled Holand, even as he realised how little he was aware of how much his own life had touched others for good or ill. He crossed himself. Now was not the time for speculation. He made a decision. He would trust the man. He pulled his stool up closer, as if he was a penitent confessing his sins. He whispered about himself, his family and his determination to find Argentine for his Beaufort masters. He was surprised how agitated Holand became when he mentioned LeCorbeil.

Once he had finished, Holand demanded more wine. He took a sip, staggered to his feet, opened the cell door and went out to ensure all was quiet before returning. Hands trembling, he put the cup on the floor beside him.

'Perhaps I can help you with Argentine,' he murmured. 'More importantly, friend, I lie at the heart of a great terror that confronts both of us.' Simon stared in disbelief. 'LeCorbeil!' Holand hurried on. 'I know the truth; I was there. You know how it was in Normandy before the great defeats at Castillon and Formigny. English free companies prowled northern France. This was about fifteen years ago, a different lifetime. I was part of it, a member of a company called the Beauforts, allegedly patronised by that great family. In truth, we were the scum of Hell. We rode under the black banner of anarchy, led by a professional killer, Gaultier.' He paused, as if listening to the faint sounds of the lazar house. 'Gaultier was a damned, doomed sinner who feared neither God nor man. He owed nominal allegiance to the Beauforts, but in fact he worshipped Satan and all his horde. Beaufort could not control him or our hellish troop.

'Anyway,' Holand continued, now lost in his bitter memories, 'on the eve of the Feast of John the Baptist, we stumbled upon LeCorbeil, a sleepy, prosperous village deep in a wooded valley east of Provins. It was untouched by the furies of war. We soon changed that. Indeed, we annihilated the place. We rode in just before dusk. We looted a small chateau nearby and discovered that its cellar was crammed with fine wines, barrels of brandy and other liqueurs. We drank until we were sottish. God forgive us all. Every woman, young or old, was violated, raped repeatedly then gutted like a pig from crotch to throat.'

'Did you . . .'

'You will not believe me, but no, I did not. I would like to say that I refused. Instead, I lay like a drunken hog, although I awoke later to see the aftermath.'

'As did I,' Simon declared. 'I told you about LeCorbeil and my brother.' He cleared his throat. 'The Beauforts heard about the outrage, and dispatched me and Edmund to see for ourselves. We arrived after the massacre. We saw the corpses of women hanging upside down from gibbets, trees, door lintels, shop signs; anything that would bear a corpse. The well in the marketplace was crammed with bloody cadavers, hacked, hanged or burnt. We were there briefly, a place of nightmare. We turned our horses and fled. Naturally the Beauforts were furious, but the war was over, the English were in retreat. Beaufort could do nothing about it and I forgot it. I later heard about Gaultier, or at least his name and reputation. He disappeared, didn't he?'

'Oh yes.' Holand's ruined lips curled back in a grin. 'Two years afterwards, he was found in the Bois de Vincennes – or at least what was left of him. He had been captured, tortured and torn apart by four horses. His mangled remains dangled from a tree branch alongside his head and the corpse of a dead crow.'

'And, as I have said, my brother Edmund also paid with his life.'

'And you?' Holand asked.

'Oh, they threaten me.' Simon quickly described his mysterious visitor outside All Hallows and the recent corsair attack on the Roseblood.

'LeCorbeil,' Holand agreed. 'And do not think there is only one. Like the demon in the Gospels, their name is legion because they are many. Let me explain.' He took a deep drink. 'After LeCorbeil, the Beaufort company dissolved like snow under the sun. A deep sense of shame rankled even in our sin-stained souls, whilst Lord Beaufort's displeasure meant no patronage, no wages. The indentures we had signed – and these later proved to be our damnation – were rescinded. I drifted into the Street of Swords, that long, murderous alleyway that stretches from London to the end of the world.' He stretched out his hands. 'These were trained for sword and dagger, club and shield, bow and arrow. I sold my skills abroad for the highest price. I fought for Genoa, Rome and Naples. Eventually I arrived in Constantinople and became an auxiliary in the Varangian guard. This was just before that great city was encircled and besieged by the Turks.

'Now, in my travel along the Street of Swords, I had encountered strange tales about former comrades who had served under the black banner. I learnt about Gaultier's fate and that of others: Vecheron of Hainault, Blaisgale of York and Simon the Fleming.' Holand waved a bandaged hand. 'All barbarously slaughtered, the corpse of a crow left beside their butchered remains. I thought that was merely the fortunes of war.' He paused in a fit of coughing. 'Until Constantinople fell. I had served as an archer,' he shrugged, 'as did others from every nation under the sun. I was befriended by three Frenchmen who had slipped into the city. They claimed to be Gascons who had fought in the retinue of the Duke of Suffolk.'

'LeCorbeil?' Simon queried, rubbing his arms against the chill that had gripped him. Was it the cold of the evening or the presence of some ghost or demon from his own blood-soaked past?

'Listen, friend. Constantinople fell to the Turks in torrents of blood. The city became a flesher's yard. We mercenaries, however, fought our way out. The Janissaries and Sipahis were only too willing to give us safe passage, more intent on sacking the city. The Frenchmen took me under their wing. We had all taken part in the looting and seized treasure; we hoped to take ship across the Middle Sea to Naples or Marseilles. We reached Izmir in Asia Minor, the old city of Ephesus, where we decided to stay for a while. One night I joined my French comrades for a drinking bout in a wine booth. My life changed. I drank deep on uncut wine and the opiates soaked in it. When I awoke, I was in a cell black as night. I was served food and drink. I was taken out to wash. Never once did my gaolers speak. They were cowled and masked. From the start, I was aware of a foul stench from their bodies.'

'Lepers?'

'Yes. I was left there for months unsuspecting. I'd eaten infected food, drunk tainted water, bathed in tubs they had used, defecated in their garderobes. Of course the contagion struck me. The first signs were dryness of the skin, a perpetual itchiness, the eruption of boils, a sickness that coursed through my body from head to toe. I was in a leper colony, a prisoner in a stockaded encampment outside the city. I had been fully immersed in all its filth, but I only became aware of this when the disease struck.

'After six months, the French returned. They took me out to a desert oasis, where they had prepared a repast, an eerie, sinister experience. Can you imagine it, my friend? A light blue sky with date palms rising against it, lush green grass sprouting high around a spring-fed pool, blankets stretched across the ground, on them bowls of fruit and bread, a jug of wine and pewter beakers. I cursed and blasphemed, but I was already beginning to rot, my ankles were manacled and of course they were well armed. They made me eat and explained as a matter of mocking courtesy why they had condemned me to a living death.'

Holand held out his cup. Simon, fascinated by his tale, filled it, glancing swiftly at the narrow shuttered window. Daylight had disappeared. Darkness had truly fallen and the ghosts were gathering.

'My captors sat taunting me for a while.' Holand continued drinking noisily. 'The desert sun set in a blaze of fire, bathing everything in changing colours. Buzzards floated above us and the call of night creatures welcomed the dark. Only then did they take my soul back to LeCorbeil on that summer's evening locked away in its cool green wooded fastness.'

'They had survived?' Simon asked.

'Listen, listen! The parish church of LeCorbeil was St Sulpice. Of course, it was ransacked, desecrated and pillaged. However, that particular evening was the vigil before the Feast of the Baptist. The parish priest of St Sulpice was a young cleric who had graduated from the University of Paris. He was a man dedicated to the beauties of plainchant, a Breton called Etienne Rupsnevar, an expert in the Missa Cantata – the sung mass. On that particular evening, Rupsnevar had assembled the male choir of his church to sing the psalms. Most of these were boys, adolescents.'

Holand paused to clean the scum frothing on his chapped lips with a rag. Simon felt the chill of fear grip him more tightly. He almost anticipated what Holand was going to tell him.

'When we attacked, Rupsnevar was given early warning. He hastily locked and barred the church. He then extinguished all the candles, gathered the precious vessels and ushered his choir down into the great crypt. Once below, he fortified the door and led the choir along a secret passageway that ran beneath the church and cemetery to an ancient ruined chapel deeper in the forest. They sheltered there, praying that all would be well.' Holand sighed deeply. 'Of course it wasn't. When they emerged, they saw the nightmare we had created.'

'How many?' Simon asked.

'Oh, about forty, between the ages of eleven and twenty at the time of the massacre.'

Holand paused again. On the breeze echoed the bell-like growling of the mastiffs that patrolled the far grounds of the lazar house. Simon idly wondered why such dogs were kept and loosed after dark. To deter intruders? But who would want to break into a leper hospital? To prevent escape? But why should any leper want to do that? Where would they go? The poor creatures could scarce climb steps, never mind scale a wall. Unless of course Holand was correct and Master Joachim and his disciples were amassing a treasure hoard that had to be protected. Or was it something else? Simon quietly promised himself that when all this danger, the tumult caused by York, receded, he and his gangs would bring St Giles under closer scrutiny.

'The survivors of the massacre,' Holand resumed, 'took the collective name of their village, LeCorbeil. Rupsnevar turned his own name round to become Ravenspur. He gave up the priesthood, the Cross of Christ and the belief in a loving God. He organised his young men into a fighting troop. They fortified the old church. Ravenspur sold the precious plate and used the wealth to arm and train those young men into a vengeful warband. They became skilled in combat, above all the crossbow; marksmen, master bowmen. Others joined them, men with similar grudges against the English, villagers who had been working in the fields and hid during the massacre. They soon established a fearsome reputation. God help any Englishman who fell into their hands.'

'And no one objected? The local bishop? Seigneurs?'

Holand laughed, a strange, craking sound. 'For the love of God, friend, this was Normandy after the Maid. Anyone who killed the tail-wearing goddams, as they called us English, was regarded as sent by heaven.

LeCorbeil were generously patronised and supported. True, Ravenspur was a warlock, wizard or sorcerer, but this was the age of Jeanne d'Arc and Gilles de Rais; who could distinguish whether he was sent by God or Satan? The local clergy, including the Inquisition, looked the other way. The fame of LeCorbeil spread. Ravenspur was invited to Paris and Rheims to confer with the King and his secret chancery. Money, arms, livery, purveyance, horses and harnesses all came their way. They were given an open mandate. Whatever they did, they did for the King and the realm of France. Accordingly, all seneschals, bailiffs and other royal officers were ordered to provide them with every sustenance. They became the Riders of the Night, the Sons of the Dark. According to popular legend, they dwelt in the wilderness of dragons. They spread their net wider, acting as spies and provocateurs. When the English left France, they followed. They had a hand in the mysterious death of John Beaufort, first Duke of Somerset. He allegedly took his own life, but the corpse of a crow was found next to his bed. They were present when William de La Pole, Duke of Suffolk, was killed on Dover sands, and they left their mark there too. Cade's rebellion was supported and encouraged by LeCorbeil.'

'What else?' Simon asked, mouth dry, as he tried to recollect the brief visit he and Edmund had made to the village of LeCorbeil.

'Oh, these French wraiths of vengeance, these dark riders, are always in for the kill. Do you remember the battle of Castillon, and England's defeat? Talbot of

Shrewsbury, together with his son, rode out to inspect the enemy's position. Both were brought down by crossbowmen, bolts to the head and heart.'

Simon murmured his agreement.

'LeCorbeil,' Holand continued throatily, 'are committed to damaging English power, either through direct attack or by stirring one faction up against another. York against Lancaster, Percy against Neville, lord against peasant; but they have a special hatred for the Beauforts and their power.'

'And they have hunted down all who took part in that massacre?'

'Yes, quite easily done. During the English retreat from France, chancery chests were taken, indentures, letters and other documents seized. When they captured Gaultier, they also ransacked his muniment chest. They seized all the agreements he'd signed with mercenaries. Every single man in that troop has been hunted down and executed.'

'But my brother Edmund and I took no part . . .'

'Didn't you? We are all guilty, Roseblood. All those who were involved in the great chevauchées across Normandy, plundering and pillaging.'

'But why were Edmund and myself singled out? Others fought for Beaufort.'

'You said you were sent by the Beauforts to view the aftermath?'

'Yes.'

'And what happened?'

Simon closed his eyes. The ghosts were returning.

Edmund in particular had been shocked at what he had seen at LeCorbeil and elsewhere. He had returned home a changed man. Simon recalled how his brother and his own younger son, Gabriel, would sit for hours in the gardens and orchards discussing what they enigmatically described to him as 'the way of the world'. Had Edmund's experience in France caused some form of inner conversion, a popular religious theme, according to Father Benedict, of the *devotio moderna* coming out of Flanders and the Low Countries? Had Edmund influenced Gabriel to enter the Franciscan order and live in a world radically different to that of the Roseblood?

'Friend, I asked you a question.'

Both men started at the ghostly hooting of the old owl that sheltered in the massive oaks on the other side of the church, a grim reminder of where they were, a leper house full of secrets, traps and dangers. Simon rubbed his eyes and stared into the darkness. In truth, he'd tried to forget LeCorbeil, even when that mysterious visitor confronted him outside All Hallows. Now, though, he concentrated. He recalled riding into the village, its cobbled marketplace glittering with rivulets of blood, corpses choking the well. The creak of signs where more corpses dangled. He rocked backwards and forwards on the stool. A demon-filled place, but there had been something . . .

A young boy! That was it! A child, certainly no older than ten years. He was dressed in the stained surplice of a choirboy, and now Simon knew why. The boy was one of those who'd hidden. He'd been sent out to see who they were. He didn't draw close, but stayed in a shadowy corner, ready to flee. He acted all innocent, asking their names, where they had come from and who had sent them. Edmund had been only too eager to help. The boy had then disappeared, leaving them in that gruesome marketplace. They too had fled, unable to cope with the horror around them.

Simon rubbed his face. 'The man who threatened me outside the lychgate of All Hallows,' he murmured. 'He said we'd met before. He was that choirboy from LeCorbeil.' He closed his eyes for a brief moment. 'I have learnt a lot,' he whispered. 'But that will have to wait. You want my help?'

'And I will give you mine in return.'

Holand moved restlessly. Simon caught the rank odour from his companion's rotting body and polluted robes. He glanced away, vowing silently to be free of all this as soon as possible.

'You are looking for Argentine in the wrong place.'

Simon turned back in surprise.

'You seek him amongst the men,' Holand chuckled, 'but of course he will be hiding amongst the women.' Simon gasped in astonishment. St Giles was a sprawling establishment, with the men living like monks and the women as nuns in a convent. 'Easy enough,' Holand continued. 'The women's precincts on the other side of the church are similar to this. the inmates all wear the garb of a Franciscan minoress: brown gown and capuchon with a linen wimple shrouding the face. Most of them wear gloves and a veil. It would be easy for a man to dwell in disguise, sheltered and hidden in their cloisters.'

'But how can I enter?'

'Promise me, when this is all over,' Holand pointed at Simon, 'that you will help me to move to the leper house at Harbledown.'

'I promise. I will get you out of here.'

'Then listen. We must begin tonight. Keep wearing your hood, gloves and face veil, as if the contagion is biting deeper, but secretly remove the false boils, tumours and buboes. Cleanse your skin, let your hair begin to grow again. Tomorrow I will bring you the gown and hood of a lay brother; there are many of them here. They move between the precincts, involved in a myriad of tasks.' Holand paused, fighting for breath. 'Pretend to be doing the most disgusting tasks, such as cleaning the latrines. Get into the women's precinct. You may find something suspicious. Master Joachim will protect his kinsman and yet keep him comfortable. I suspect that Argentine, disguised as a female inmate, lodges in the women's cloisters. Now I must go.'

Simon rose to his feet, nodding his agreement. They clasped hands and Holand left, flitting like a shadow along the moon-washed cloister alley. Simon watched him go. He was about to turn back when he felt a chill of apprehension similar to that experienced during his soldiering days. He glanced across the garth. A shadow shifted out of the light thrown by a torch. He stared again, but it was gone. He returned to his cell, locking the door before going up to lie on his bed, staring into the darkness. He heard the tolling of the infirmary bell proclaiming that some poor soul had died, and recalled Holand's macabre tale about the master helping his patients into the dark. The tolling was immediately answered by that ominous barking of the war dogs, those huge mastiffs that Simon had glimpsed, muzzled and strapped, being taken by their keepers to their kennels. Why did Joachim need these? Even the Roseblood lacked such protection. He wondered how matters were at the tavern and breathed a Pater and three Aves for all those he loved, both living and dead. He thought about Katherine and Sevigny. Would the clerk be moved to express his regard for her? He smiled at the problems that would incur.

Eventually he drifted into sleep, waking in the early hours as the church bells tolled for Divine Office. He rose and began his preparations. He did not shave as he frequently did, but used the lavarium and the great pitcher of water to remove what he could of the Alchemist's disguise, including the swathe of bandage around his right foot, which made him hobble. He felt better as his skin, still pocked with real cuts and bruises, was cleaned and the tight bandages around his fingers, wrists and elbows removed. Afterwards, he dressed in the grey lazar robe of the hospital and put the mask back on, but decided to stay in his cell, only leaving when he had to, reverting to the shuffling gait he'd learnt so well. He also opened the heavy panniers he had brought and took out his weapons: a hand-held arblest, a leather case of barbed bolts and a Welsh stabbing dirk.

On the evening following their meeting, Holand brought a lay brother's robe, a linen gauze face mask, and a pair of the thick dark blue mittens and stockings worn by those who cared for the lepers. The next morning, suitably disguised, Simon mingled with the other servitors. He easily left the male quarters of the lazar hospital, crossing to the other side of the church and into the women's precinct. Its organisation was similar to the men's, though it was easier for the female inmates to hide behind the robe, wimple and face mask of a nun. A sombre, lonely place with that same brooding sense of decay and imminent death. Simon concluded that if Argentine was hiding here, he would be in deep disguise, closeted in one of the cells around the garth.

Simon pretended to be moving rubbish; he even managed to secure a wheelbarrow, which he pushed around acting all busy. His efforts were soon rewarded. He noticed one cell at the far end of the row on the north side of the cloisters; its door had been recently strengthened with metal studs and a new latch, whilst to the right hung a brass bell. No one approached this cell; whoever was inside received their food and drink through the hatch. Just before Vespers, Simon, pretending to clear twigs and dead leaves from a flower bed, noticed Joachim slip along the cloisters, knock on the door and disappear inside. He rose hastily, and, using the crowds now milling towards the church, returned to his own cell. He was confident in his disguise. No one would dream of volunteering to work amongst lepers, and in his hood and mask, he was just another grey shape moving around the hospital. He decided that tomorrow he would strike at that cell, and if he was wrong, then he'd failed and would confess as much to Bray. Whatever the outcome, he must be out of here, away from this filthy contagion and its sense of unknown watching malevolence.

He slept poorly that night, and was roused in the early hours by a commotion in the cloisters. He dressed hastily, putting on his stockings and gloves before going out. A deep shifting fog flowed around the pillars and dulled the flames of torches and lanterns. A crowd of hooded, visored inmates clustered around a door further down; Simon realised it was Holand's. He hurried along, pushing through the crowd into the rank-smelling chamber. Two lay brothers were already moving the corpse from the cot bed to a stretcher. Holand's head lolled back, his eyes bulbous and staring. From the snatches of mumbled conversation, Simon gathered that he had died in his sleep. His flaking face was purple-hued, as if his breath had been swiftly choked off.

Simon gazed around, and froze in horror at the sight of the dead crow hanging by its shrivelled neck from a shelf above the bed. LeCorbeil had struck. The rest would dismiss the bird's corpse as some deviation of Holand's distorted mind. Simon knew the truth. He hastily withdrew and returned to his own preparations. He cleared his cell, packed the panniers and changed into the robes of a lay brother. He waited for a while until the hubbub outside died down, then left, slipping through the mist-filled cloisters to the common refectory, where he broke his fast on honey bread and a black jack of ale. Holand, he reasoned, had been summarily executed by those malevolent ghosts that had haunted his life. LeCorbeil were here at St Giles, probably keeping Argentine under careful watch until he could be safely spirited down to one of the city quaysides and aboard a French ship. During their stay here, they must have recognised Holand and decided he had lived long enough. But were they simply settling an old score, or had they discovered that Holand was involved in this subterfuge?

Simon recalled that flitting shadow and smiled grimly. Holand had wanted to leave. He was openly suspicious of Master Joachim. There must be some connection between Joachim and LeCorbeil: those French assassins had not only settled their grievance but removed a possible threat to Argentine, whom they must regard as a great prize. Perhaps LeCorbeil were not yet suspicious of Simon himself; maybe he was just regarded as Holand's confidant, but he would not wait to find out.

He finished breaking his fast and left the refectory, walking purposefully as if on some errand. No one even glanced at him. Once he had reached the women's precinct, he paused in a mist-filled corner of the cloisters. He waited for the passageway to clear, then slipped down towards the door, knocking gently and gabbling in French how he carried urgent messages from the master. The shutter across the grille opened and shut. Bolts were drawn and the door swung open. Simon took out the primed hand-held arbalest and stepped inside, knocking the veiled figure back into the chamber before slamming the door shut behind him. He dared not turn and draw the bolts; his quarry had recovered from the shock and would have lunged at him but for the arbalest held close to his face.

'Remove your hood, wimple and mask,' Simon ordered. The brown-garbed figure hesitated. Simon pushed the arbalest closer; the quarrel in its notch had a jagged, barbed point. Hood, wimple and mask were quickly removed and Simon stared into the man's narrow, mean face, eyes gleaming furiously, tongue wetting lips dry with fear.

'Giles Argentine,' he murmured. 'Physician extraordinary. The keeper of royal secrets.' He peered at Argentine's pale face. 'No leprosy. Your skin is as smooth and unblemished as a child's.' He gestured around the warm, opulent chamber. 'All the comforts of court, yes? Your secret known only to you and your kinsman, both cheeks of the same filthy arse.'

'Who are you?' Argentine clutched the back of a chair to steady himself, eyes desperate for escape. 'Who are you?' he repeated. 'How did you discover—'

'Hush!' Simon replied. 'Silence is the beginning of wisdom. One thing only will spare your life. Lie or obstruct me and I will kill you. Then I will ransack this chamber.'

'What do you want?'

'Your confession, your chronicle, your account of the births of certain children, be it those of the King or the Duke of York.' Simon smiled at Argentine's consternation, 'I have come to collect that.'

'Who are you?'

'Shut up!' Simon ordered. 'The document?' Argentine looked as if he was about to refuse, but with Simon closely following, he moved across to a small coffer. He removed a key from a chain around his neck and, hands shaking, opened the coffer and drew out a calfskin ledger. Simon took this and forced Argentine to sit on a chair with his hands on his lap. He pushed the tip of the crossbow bolt against the physician's brow.

'Any movement,' he warned, 'and my finger will slip. Open the ledger, and hold it as if you are an acolyte bearing the book of the Gospels in mass.'

Argentine did so, hands trembling. He undid the binding cord and turned the ledger so that Simon could leaf through the cream-coloured vellum pages. Pressing gently on the arbalest, Simon read a few entries and quietly whistled.

'By all the angels, Master Argentine, you weave a tale of deep deceit.' Simon felt the physician stir. 'No.' He stepped back, snatching the ledger. 'You have copies?'

Argentine's spiteful eyes glittered, lips twisted in fury as he realised he was about to lose his pot of gold.

'There is no copy.'

'Just to be sure . . .' Simon, watching the physician carefully, pulled the coffer closer and threw down his own pannier beside it. 'I am sure you keep everything in the same casket in case you have to flee.' He pushed the crossbow closer. 'Empty it. Put everything in the saddlebag.'

Argentine reluctantly obeyed, this time staring at the door. A bell tolled. Simon tensed. The pannier was full. The bell kept tolling. Footsteps echoed from outside and the door crashed open. Master Joachim and Prior Gervaise swept into the chamber. Argentine sprang forward. Simon's finger slipped and the barbed bolt whirred, smashing the physician's face into a bloody mess.

Joachim and Gervaise stood in shocked surprise. The prior was the first to recover, but Simon grabbed the pannier, knocked Gervaise aside with his crossbow and threw himself at Joachim, who hastily retreated. Simon hurtled through the door, leaping over the lower cloister wall, pannier in one hand, the crossbow in the other. He dropped this as he raced through the precincts, the cloister bell beginning to peal the tocsin. He had a clear idea of the lazar house buildings, fields and gardens. He knew he must cross the great meadow and reach the high curtain wall. He knocked aside figures who emerged out of the morning mist. Memories sparked in his mind of the running street fights of his youth and the sweaty, deadly struggles in French towns or lonely copses in Normandy. He might be captured, but there again, Argentine was dead.

At last he reached the great meadow. A pain in his side made him wince; the pannier slipped and slithered in his sweat-soaked hand. He glimpsed the wall through the mist and paused at the deep-throated barking that rang through the morning air. He whirled around. Torches flared and he caught the glint of steel. The murk shifted to reveal his pursuers, mastiffs straining on their leases, their masters bending to loosen the clasps. Simon hurried on. The barking grew louder. He drew closer to the wall, racing towards a buttress. When he reached it, he turned, cutting the air with his dagger just as the leading mastiff, lips curled back in a display of jagged teeth, leapt towards him. The dagger slashed the side of the hound's face, forcing it to veer away into the path of the other two dogs. These, confused by the spraying blood, stumbled in their charge. Simon climbed the buttress, threw the pannier over and jumped down into the narrow lane. He grabbed the pannier and hurried out on to the thoroughfare leading down to the city.

Despite the early hour, the crowds were already out, a colourful, noisy stream of people, carts, barrows and wagons. An execution party was returning from the great gibbet and the red-masked executioners were already drunk. Around the hangman's cart jostled the traders, fripperers, tinkers and relic sellers in their cowls, hoods and snoop caps, men and women who always attended execution morning for petty trading. Simon mingled with these. Some he recognised, though he kept his peace, concealing his face and head by pulling up the deep cowl.

He reached the great fleshing market outside Newgate, the salty tang of blood wafting everywhere, the cobbles underfoot slippery with scraps of offal. A relic seller stood on a cart, claiming how the box at his feet held the remains of one of the Holy Innocents. A short distance away, two choir clerks sang in unison the hymn 'Ave Verum'. They had to compete with a chanteur who claimed he had news from the east, where a great army of yellow-skinned, red-armoured warriors massed under silk banners of the deepest vermilion. Such attractions drew the crowd, and it was hard to push through.

Simon turned and glimpsed lay brothers from St Giles not far behind. It was too dangerous to continue, so he hastened up the steps into the guild church of St Nicholas of the Shambles. The Jesus mass had finished, but people still stood in the nave, bathed by the light pouring through the lancet windows. Streams of incense smoke curled and twisted. Simon squatted on a stool near the great baptismal font close to the front door. A rack of votive candles glowed and caught the colours of a wall painting above the font. The vigorously painted fresco executed in red, green and blue celebrated the story of St Nicholas of Myra, who frustrated the designs of an evil butcher who had slaughtered some children, cut them up and pickled their flesh in a salt barrel. The artist had wondrously depicted how, due to the blessing of the saint, all the meaty scraps had reassembled into living flesh and the children, glowing with health, were restored to their parents. Despite his own troubles, Simon grinned at the irony of the painting here at the centre of the fleshers' trade; his smile widened even further as a thought occurred to him. He rose, walked up the nave and entered the sacristy, where the altar boys were busy stowing the sacred vestments in the cope chest. As he stood in the sacristy door, cowl pulled over his head, he caught sight of his quarry: Fleabite, apprentice to Brancome the butcher, who supplied the Roseblood with some of its meat.

'Fleabite!' Simon hissed. The altar boy stared through the gloom. Simon beckoned him closer, a fresh coin glinting between his fingers. Fleabite, ignoring the muttered grumblings of the bell clerk, hurried across. Simon led him back into the nave and crouched, face close to the boy's. 'It's Master Roseblood.' He pulled back his hood.

'Sir, your head and face, your hair is—'

'I have been on a journey. Now listen. Get rid of your cassock and cotta. Take this coin and go as swiftly as you can to the Roseblood. Seek out Master Ignacio.'

'The silent one?'

'Yes, the silent one, together with Wormwood. Tell them to hasten here with clothing and weapons as swiftly as possible.'

'Master, what—'

'Another coin will be yours.' Simon pushed the one he held into the apprentice's hand. 'Don't worry, I will settle matters with Master Brancome. Now go.'

Fleabite needed no second bidding. His vestments were quickly discarded and the apprentice sped like the wind through the Devil's door, taking a route that would evade his sharp-eyed master manning a stall not so far away.

Simon returned to the baptismal enclave. He took out the ledger and, in the fluttering candlelight, carefully read Argentine's chronicle, or, as the dead physician pompously described it, his 'Mirror of Truth'. Argentine had made his entries in good Latin, beginning each clause with the word 'item', as if he was a lawyer drawing up an indictment. He presented as if it were the gospel truth all the malicious chatter and scandalous gossip from the courts of York and Lancaster. Depicting himself as the royal birthing physician, he cleverly insinuated that both Edwards – the son of King Henry as well as the offspring of Richard of York – were illegitimate. Full of righteousness and quoting verses from Scripture and canon law, he described how the royal prince Edward was in fact the son of Edmund Beaufort, Margaret of Anjou's alleged lover. He argued how King Henry, at the time of the child's conception, had been infected by a mental stupor that rendered him impotent in every way. Indeed, he declared, King Henry himself, once he recovered his wits, believed that his alleged son must be a second divine conception, because he had no knowledge of it.

Argentine was equally scathing about the birth of Edward of York, repeating rumour and gossip from the birthing chamber: how Richard of York, the supposed father, had been away from Rouen at the time of his son's conception, whilst his duchess had become deeply infatuated with a tall captain of archers in the English garrison. He spun his tale most subtly, quoting this person or that, or referring to particular incidents on a specific date at a certain place.

'You have crafted a clever illusion,' Simon whispered to the darkness. 'As skilled as any Cheapside minstrel.' Argentine, he reflected, had been a master of the masque, a creator of charades. Little wonder the lords of York and Lancaster were so keen to seize him and his manuscript. 'I did not want your blood on my hands,' Simon murmured, yet he conceded that the Beaufort lords would be very pleased. Argentine's prattling mouth was closed for ever, and Simon now owned his secret chronicle. York would pay handsomely for it, whilst the French court's interest in Argentine was obvious.

Simon stirred on his stool, watching the candle flame dance as if to some invisible music. He wondered about LeCorbeil. The French had certainly entered St Giles, but for what? To keep an eye on Argentine? To arrange his escape? Or had they come hunting poor Holand, or himself? He couldn't decide. He returned to the contents of his pannier, sifting through the indentures, letters, bills and memoranda; personal items, nothing extraordinary except for two intricately drawn maps. Simon recognised them both. The first was a carefully inscribed outline of the south Essex coast delineating Walton, the Naze and the river Orwell. An ideal place, he concluded, for a French carrack or galley to slip in and take someone off.

The second map was a finely etched description of the roads leading north from the Tower along the Mile End Road to Bow and across the Hackney marshes into that desolate area of south Essex with the dense sprawling greenery of Epping Forest and a line of isolated villages and hamlets stretching from Wodeforde to Chelmsford and Colchester. One such village in a heavily wooded area had been emphasised. Simon translated the abbreviation for Cottesloe and recalled from his smuggling days how Cottesloe was one of those villages annihilated by the Great Pestilence that had swept like the Devil's wind across the shire.

He tapped his fingers on the manuscript. LeCorbeil must have wanted Argentine. Were they going to smuggle him out of London through the wilds of Essex, perhaps sheltering at Cottesloe before moving on to the coast? They must have been waiting for the right occasion, perhaps hoping that when Lancaster and York clashed, they would seize their opportunity. LeCorbeil must have had an agent in St Giles, and Master Joachim had been in full connivance. They had become overconfident and been taken by surprise. Sevigny's visit would have alarmed them. Perhaps they were preparing to leave and decided to settle matters with Holand once and for all.

Simon stared down at the leather-bound ledger. What should he do with it? His allegiance to Beaufort was unwavering, yet, he reflected, he was feasting with wolves, smiling faces that concealed brutish, beastly hearts. When war came, the Beauforts and Queen Margaret would prove as ruthless as York, but he had no choice other than to hunt with them. He rose to his feet and, putting the ledger back in the pannier, walked to the main door, staring out at the fleshing stalls. Soon the Great Slaughter would begin, the strongholds would be stormed and all the furies of Hell would be unleashed. He gripped the pannier. He would keep Argentine's chronicle for himself, a sure defence against the coming storm.

Katherine Roseblood

London, May 1455

Katherine Roseblood sat deeper in the arbour, almost hidden by the riot of greenery that had sprouted over the years. She brushed leaves off her lap and stared at her fingers. 'I wish they were pale and long like those of the Lady of the Lake. You know, Melisaunde, on that tapestry in the Camelot Chamber.' She turned as if her mythical friend was really sitting next to her in that flower-shrouded part of the great garden. For as long as she could remember, Katherine had met her make-believe friend here; certainly long before Mother died. She blessed herself at the thought and, as her brother Gabriel had advised her, whispered the words of requiem for her dead mother's soul. 'Where are you?' She spoke her thoughts. 'I hope you are happy now.'

All her memories of her mother were bittersweet, especially the last years, her mother's pallid face betraying a sadness in her marriage her daughter could not comprehend. Katherine truly adored her father, yet there was something, a shadow that deeply tinged their relationship. Her father had enjoyed a rich past. Katherine had heard the whispers about his former life: a street fighter, a riffler, a soldier, a courtier, a spy, and, if some of the whispers were true, he had even considered becoming a Benedictine monk.

Ah well, that was the past. She rose to her feet. Father had returned the previous day. She had been shocked at his appearance, hair all shorn, his face deliberately pockmarked. He had kissed her before becoming closeted with Raphael, Ignacio, Wormwood and the rest of his inner cabal. The pot of politic was certainly bubbling furiously, and all sorts of things were rising to the top. The salacious gossip of the taproom and buttery was now heavily laced with a cloying fear, and this was not just over murdered streetwalkers. Another prostitute's corpse had been found, her remains crammed like a bundle of old rags into a steaming laystall on the corner of Ink Pot Lane. However, greater fears than this were now gathering.

The recent French attack on Queenhithe had sharpened the realisation of how the tide of war had savagely turned. The French were now bringing to the southern ports and London itself all the horrors heaped on their coastal towns by English privateers. There was no real shield or defence, no bulwark against the creeping terror. The King was weak, the Council divided, the warlords of York and Lancaster ready to sharpen their swords on each other rather than some foreign enemy. York would march and the King could not decide whether to treat with him or bring him to battle. If war did break out, London would erupt like some festering boil, with the gang leaders eager to settle scores. The Roseblood would be swept up in this. And Sevigny?

Katherine stepped out of the arbour. Soon the market bell would ring and she and Dorcas would have to leave. Mistress Eleanor had sent an urgent message begging to see her in All Hallows before Vespers. She did not say why, but according to Dorcas, the personable young man who had delivered the message spoke prettily about how urgent it was and how Katherine must not tell anybody. Yet despite all this, even now Katherine felt that presence in her soul that had brought her out to this secret bower.

Sevigny! Her thoughts returned to him constantly. She had heard all about his prowess in the battle against the French, his ruthless ferocity. Such stories only deepened her fascination with the enigmatic clerk. He was no longer Mordred lately come to Camelot, but one of those mysterious knights at Arthur's table. Nor had he deserted her. The gargoyles and the babewyns had glimpsed him in the nearby streets and alleyways. Dorcas maintained that she had even seen him in the old Roman ruin on the hill behind the tavern. Katherine had searched for him; she wanted to meet him again. She felt complete when he walked beside her, and they had talked so merrily, as if she had known him for ever. He was still a mystery, yet she wanted to be with him so much.

Katherine blushed and, despite being on her own, felt the embarrassment sweep through her body. She knew all about romance and dalliance. God knows, the tales of Arthur were rich enough, but when it came to kissing, embracing and coupling . . . She ran a hand down her full breasts on to her stomach. When she had helped bath her, Dorcas had remarked that Katherine was full, ripe and ready. How they had laughed at that! Katherine's courses had begun five years ago. She'd heard all the salacious stories in the taproom; the sly allusions, the bawdy insults as well as the tittle-tattle of the tavern women about the prowess of certain men. When she had hid in the stables during the cold weather, she had often heard the language and sounds of love-making. The tavern galleries echoed with the same, and Dorcas was forever teasing her with crude details about men's hungry cocks and greedy hands. Surely it would not be like that with Sevigny? And where would their lovemaking take place? In some lush, serene garden, or perhaps a broad four-poster bridal bed . . .

'Mistress Katherine!'

She patted her cheeks, which she was sure were flushed, and hastened out of the bower to where Dorcas was waiting. The tavern lay quiet: Simon, Raphael and the others had left for Smithfield, to barter as well as meet the leaders of the various gangs in the Bishop's Mitre, the sprawling hostelry that overlooked the great market. Toadflax had been left to guard her and would follow Dorcas and herself down to the church.

The plump, insolent-eyed maid handed Katherine her

cloak with its deep capuchon and they left by the wicket gate, hastening through the alleyways to All Hallows. Katherine glanced over her shoulder. Toadflax was shambling behind them. Dorcas, all breathless, recited the gossip of the kitchen and buttery whilst loudly praising the handsome messenger, as well as speculating on why Mistress Eleanor should send such urgent pleas.

Katherine ignored her, mind still brimming with thoughts of Sevigny. She peered out of her hood and, for the first time, wondered about the wisdom of what she was doing. The day was drawing to a close and the denizens of the mumpers' castles were emerging to watch, prey and hunt. Soldiers gathered outside tavern doors, bellies full of ale, hearts bubbling with resentments, mouths yelling strange oaths, fingers not far from sword hilt or dagger handle. Queenhithe was still trembling after the savagery of the French attack, and there was the prospect of more tumult. Mounted archers swung by on their horses, scattering groups, pushing past carts and barrows. A funeral procession emerged from the throng, growing increasingly raucous as the mourners, most of them drunk, staggered, juggling the corpse on their shoulders. Behind these, bagpipes wailed as streetwalkers tied to the tail of a cart were whipped down to the stocks. A baby shrieked, competing with the screeching of a dog crushed beneath the wheel of a barrow till someone cut its throat.

Katherine, Dorcas hurrying beside her, turned thankfully off through the lychgate and up the pavement that cut across God's Acre. The main door of All Hallows was locked. Surprised at this, she led Dorcas round to the corpse door. She pushed this open and stepped into the cold darkness of that mystical place. Spears of sunlight pierced the windows, sending the dust motes dancing, Eleanor had once told her that these were angels who could assume any size they wanted. Candle smoke teased their nostrils and Katherine felt the perpetual damp that seeped through the ancient flag-stones. She glanced over her shoulder again. Toadflax had not followed them in.

'Eleanor?' she called. 'Mistress Eleanor?' She walked across to the rood screen door and started as it opened abruptly and Father Roger staggered into the nave.

'What is it?' The priest stood swaying, voice slurred as he peered through the murk.

'He is sottish!' Dorcas giggled. 'Drunk as any ale taster!'

Father Roger stumbled closer, singing softly under his breath. He stepped into the dappled light, his cheeks and chin unshaven, eyes bleary, mouth slack.

'Father!' Katherine hissed. 'You are not well.'

'Too true, too true.'

Katherine heard a sound further down the nave and glimpsed a shadow move. She felt the cold chill of this ancient church wrap itself around her.

'Mistress Eleanor!' she called. 'Mistress Eleanor!'

'Fast asleep,' Father Roger murmured, swaying dangerously. 'As I should be!'

'Mistress Eleanor, it's Katherine.'

'Come!'

She followed the direction of the voice towards the darkness of the transept, beckoned on by the light glowing through the anchorhold squint. She reached the cell door, its hatch pulled back, and smiled at Eleanor. Shrouded by a starched white wimple and a dark blue woollen veil, her aunt's face was more beautiful than ever.

'Mistress Eleanor, you sent for me, an urgent message?'

'I did not, oh sweet Lord! I saw figures slip in here. I thought—'

Katherine whirled round. Dorcas screamed. Father Roger staggered over to a pillar, where he leaned, staring in disbelief at the figures who had slipped out of the shadowy recesses. They wore pointed hoods, cloaks fanning out like the wings of some malevolent bird. They moved soundlessly yet menacingly through the gloom. Father Roger tottered towards them, hands raised. Katherine could only stand in abject fear. A trap was being sprung and she could do nothing about it. The church was empty. These nightmare figures could do what they wished. The corpse door would certainly be guarded; if anyone entered, they would be cruelly dealt with.

'Who are you?' she blurted out.

'Bitter memories,' a voice called back. 'The past's dark dreams. Mistress Katherine, you are to come with us. Do not cry out. Toadflax is gone.'

Katherine started forward but was surrounded and roughly seized. A sack was thrown over her head, hands and feet tightly bound. From the cries and shouts around her, she gathered that Father Roger and Dorcas had also been seized, whilst a crack of splintering wood showed that the anchorhold was being forced and Eleanor dragged out. For a while the nave echoed with cries and shouts; then there was silence as gags were fastened and the sacking tightened around their heads.

Katherine tried to control the sheer panic seething within her. She strained to listen; her abductors were now whispering in French. She heard weapons being sheathed. She was lifted, the hands that grasped her paying little respect to modesty as they clutched and turned her body. She tried to struggle. Someone cruelly squeezed her breast; another hand went up her skirt and petticoats. She hung limp. A man laughed and the hand was withdrawn. She was carried roughly up through the church. She suspected they were going through the sanctuary and into the sacristy. Voices muttered; a door opened.

Katherine felt a gust of the cool evening breeze before she was dropped roughly into a cart. She could hear the others being thrust in alongside her, the clink of the tailboard, the snap of reins and the clop of hooves. The cart shook and rattled forward. Tightly bound and gagged, she could only close her eyes at the brutal jolting, which seemed to bruise every part of her body. Shooting pains coursed up her legs, her belly pitched and she fought against the nausea. She bit on the gag, then spluttered as her head banged against the cart's wooden floor. She struggled against the bonds, but it was useless. She realised that they had been taken out of the sacristy to where carts stood to unload supplies for the church. They would soon be out of the cemetery and in the tangle of narrow lanes around All Hallows. But where were they going?

A deep frustration swept through Katherine. Only a short distance away were men who would give their lives to free her, but there was nothing she could do. She heard the groans and stifled cries of her companions and wondered who her abductors were and where were they going. She summoned up memories of Sevigny walking alongside her. If only he were here! She calmed herself. She was being abducted for a reason. She had been summoned to All Hallows at a time when it would be deserted, between the blowing of the market horn and the Vespers bell. Her captors were certainly French. She recalled the stories about someone or something called LeCorbeil, rumours about some hideous massacre during the war in France. And weren't LeCorbeil connected with Uncle Edmund's mysterious death and the recent attack on the Roseblood? She must be their prisoner, for what, a ransom?

The iron wheels of the cart hit a rut and the boards bucked beneath her. Katherine jarred her head even as she caught a salty freshness in the air. Foreign voices shouted. The cart abruptly stopped; men clamoured in. She was released from her bonds and dragged out. Blinded by the light and stupefied by the sudden violence, she could not protest. She was hurried with the others up the gangplank of a large ship and thrust down narrow steps into the first underdeck, which reeked of horse dung, urine, straw and the pervasive stench of tar and pitch. They were left there, the trapdoor pulled shut above them.

Shouts and cries echoed. Footsteps pattered along the main deck. The ship creaked and swayed, sending all four of them staggering around the stinking hold. Father Roger crouched in a corner and began to sob. Eleanor hurried to comfort him. Dorcas clung to her mistress, her sheet-white face marked and bruised, her lower lip bloodied where she had bitten herself. They all nursed bruises and bumps, especially to the head, face and knees. Katherine embraced her maid, holding her close even as she realised that the pain in her leg had not appeared. The ship swayed again; still clutching Dorcas, Katherine crouched down. The vessel was under way, creaking and straining, voices shouting, ropes whining, sails clattering. It lurched clumsily, and Katherine heard the whinny of horses in the stable holds below. She stifled her despair. They must be leaving Queenhithe. Only a short distance away from them stood the Roseblood and everything she loved. Comforting the sobbing Dorcas, she wondered if Sevigny was there, sheltering in that old Roman lighthouse.

The trapdoor was abruptly opened, a rope ladder was lowered and a voice ordered them to climb. Katherine was first out on to the slippery, swaying deck. Her arrival provoked catcalls and jeers from the dark-skinned, black-bearded crew, who, half naked, clambered swift as squirrels, fighting to unfurl the main sail on the central mast. A voice crackling with temper ordered them to remain silent. Still blinded by the glow of the setting sun, the four prisoners, staggering and slipping, were led across to a canvas sheet spread out beneath the taffrail. They were ordered to sit, shown where they could relieve themselves and told to be silent.

Katherine leaned against the bulwark, shading her eyes. She stared around the broad deck, noting the three masts, the high stern, the prow castle and the jutting bowsprit, glancing up as the great scarlet banner of Venice with its four golden lions was unfurled to greet the evening breeze. She realised this was a Venetian carrack, *The Golden Horn*, from an inscription she could make out on the mainmast. The vessel was the latest of its kind, a fighting ship but also a merchantman capable of carrying stores, horses, armed men and all the impedimenta of war. She had seen and studied such ships before. It might sail under the banner of Venice, but, like many of its kind, it was a mercenary ship for hire to the highest bidder.

She forgot her pain and scrutinised the men milling about. There were two groups: the half-naked dark-skinned sailors; and others, about a dozen in all, fair- or olive-skinned, dressed alike in dark murrey sleeveless jerkins over white shirts, black hose pushed into boots, war belts strapped around their waists. Each jerkin bore the insignia of a crow in full flight clutching a dagger between its claws. These men kept to themselves near the cabin built beneath the sterncastle; they seemed to be in deep discussion, now and again turning to stare across at the prisoners. Katherine glanced away. The ship pitched. Gulls swooped and screamed. The carrack's mainsail billowed vigorously whilst the one on its mizzen mast also unfurled to catch the strong westerly breeze.

The ship raced forward, but bucked and twisted in the powerful currents that marked their course down to the estuary. Father Roger, followed by Dorcas, clambered to his feet to vomit over the taffrail, provoking fresh jeers from the crew. Katherine rose to help him. Dorcas was shivering with fright; Father Roger was no better. Eleanor, ivory-pale face all bruised down one side, came to assist. Once they had emptied their stomachs, she helped them sit down. Katherine remained standing, staring out across the river. They had left the city of Westminster, the distant northern shoreline being marked by fields, copses and the occasional solitary dwelling. They were approaching the estuary, the setting sun gleaming on the fast-running water. The sky was clear except for wispy white clouds, though the sun had a strange reddish glow, which, sailors had informed Katherine when they gossiped at the Roseblood, always presaged a storm.

'Sit down. Eat.' Katherine turned. One of LeCorbeil – she reckoned him to be their captain – had walked across. Beside him, one of his retinue carried a battered wooden tray with bowls of dried bread and fruit. 'Sit,' he repeated.

Katherine obeyed. A bowl was thrust into each of their hands and a small water skin was thrown down at their feet. The man then crouched, staring at

Katherine. In some ways he reminded her of Sevigny. He was olive-skinned, his raven-black hair tied in a queue behind him. A handsome clean-shaven face with a firm chin and full lips, though his grey eyes frightened her. They were dead, as if no soul lived behind their stare, a cold, calculating, empty gaze.

'My name is Bertrand LeCorbeil. These,' the man indicated with his head, 'are my companions. We all bear the same surname, bound together by the fire of revenge.'

'Against me?'

The steel-grey eyes did not flicker. 'Against you and your kind.' His English was precise and clear.

'Why?'

Bertrand gestured at Eleanor. 'Perhaps she can say; I will not. I am here to warn you.' He edged closer, remaining steady against the pitch and shudder as the carrack hit the swift-flowing currents of the estuary. 'If you try to escape,' he pointed to the other three, 'I will deny them a swift death. This is a Venetian ship. It does business with the Moors of North Africa. The two women will be raped and raped again before being sold to the slave markets of Tripoli and Alexandria. The priest will be castrated and offered as a eunuch. Believe me,' Bertrand smiled, but only with his lips, 'a living death that could last longer than a score of years.'

'I would die first.' Eleanor leaned forward, face full of fury. 'I know who you are,' she spat out. 'Five years ago you lured my husband to his death.' She lunged towards the Frenchman, but Katherine restrained her. Bertrand did not move a muscle.

'Your husband,' his voice was almost a drawl, 'paid for his crimes.'

'And me?' Katherine asked, swallowing hard against the fear in her belly; the sheer ferocity of the man's gaze was chilling.

'Enough of the past,' he snapped. 'Your father, the criminal, the felon Simon Roseblood, has something we need. We have left messages. Once we have it, you will be returned.'

'What is it?'

'Oh, don't worry.' Again that humourless smile. 'Master Roseblood knows full well.'

'I am a priest,' wailed Father Roger, edging along the bulwark, 'a cleric.'

Bertrand's hand flailed out, slapping the priest's face so hard that his head jerked back against the wood. 'I couldn't give a fig if you are the Pope of Rome. You, sir,' the Frenchman edged closer, 'are a Judas priest. My spies along the alleyways have kept me informed about your filthy doings.' He punched the cleric again, this time in the mouth, splitting his lip, enjoying his moans.

Something in Father Roger's pleas seemed to provoke Bertrand further. He sprang to his feet, kicking the priest, knocking Katherine and Eleanor aside as they tried to intervene, shouting orders at his men. One of these hurried across with a coil of tarred rope. Others joined him. Bertrand, white foam flecking his lips, pointed at Father Roger, screaming his orders. The priest, nose and mouth bubbling blood, was dragged to his feet. The ship rocked and swayed. The master on the sterncastle shouted a question; Bertrand replied in a tongue Katherine could not understand. The master shrugged and waved a hand, as if what was plotted had nothing to do with him.

Roger was seized, the rope lashed around his waist, a knot secured, then he was lifted and tossed overboard. Katherine stared in horror; this was a nightmare, the ship juddering, the gulls screaming like lost souls. Eleanor and Dorcas were sobbing with terror. LeCorbeil gathered closer, jeering and mocking. Katherine peered over the side. The priest had sunk beneath the swirling water. Bertrand shouted. The rope was pulled back and the priest emerged from the sea, hands flailing, mouth open in a silent scream.

'Again!' Bertrand yelled. The rope was loosed and the priest disappeared beneath the frothing water.

'Please!' Katherine pleaded.

'Please!' Bertrand mimicked with a lopsided grin, which quickly faded as Katherine hoisted herself up to lean dangerously over the side. She did not care. All she wanted was for this nightmare to end. She thrust out a hand as Bertrand took a step closer.

'I will!' She held that ice-cold stare. 'I am no use to you dead,' she jibed. 'No use at all!'

Bertrand nodded imperceptibly. He raised a hand; the rope was pulled back even as the captain began to curse, gesturing at the threatening sky. Father Roger was dragged up over the side, his face a mask of bloody bruises, and thrown down to the deck, a moaning, sodden bundle of cloth all slimed with green. Dorcas and Eleanor went to help him; the priest whimpered like a child, waving his hands before his face.

'Some clothes.' Katherine confronted Bertrand. 'He will die of cold. Some clothes, food, and I promise . . .'

'Promise what?' Bertrand frowned in puzzlement.

'I will say a prayer for you just after my father takes your head.'

Bertrand stared at her, then threw back his head and roared with laughter, slapping his thigh and sharing the joke with his companions. They grinned and, shaking their heads, turned away to help the crew.

Katherine leaned against the side and stared up at the sky. *The Golden Horn* was almost through the estuary. Darkness was falling. A mist now curled, hiding the tapering coastline, but the real threat was the dark, lowering mass of cloud coming in off the North Sea. Already the master was alarmed. He'd made his decision, brushing aside Bertrand's objections: they would turn, shelter in the estuary and ride out the storm.

Katherine and her companions were ordered down into the hold, cold and black as pitch, where they spent a miserable night as the carrack swung at anchor, buffeted by the waves. Dry clothes were brought for Father Roger, but he was almost out of his wits, teeth chattering against the cold, demanding that they fetch another priest to shrive him. Now and again the hatch would open and they were dragged from the stinking darkness on to the windswept deck to relieve themselves before being driven back to their dungeon. Fresh water was served, along with a cracked bowl of hard bread, dried salted meat and slices of unripe apple. They had little time or inclination to talk to each other; instead they huddled closer for warmth and waited for dawn.

By first light the storm had swept away and they were brought up on to the deck. A grey day with a shifting blanket of mist. They were herded on to the canvas sheet; Bertrand, grinning at Katherine, fetched a small fire urn stocked with fiery charcoal so that they could warm themselves. Bowls of steaming oatmeal were brought from the makeshift grill set up over another brazier, with a wine skin of the richest claret. Katherine ate and drank greedily, persuading the others to do the same. Eleanor was strangely quiet; not frightened, but lost in her own thoughts. Dorcas, shivering and moaning, just stared around, whilst Father Roger ate and drank, spluttering mouthfuls as he continued to insist that he be shriven. Once finished, they were allowed to stay on deck while *The Golden Horn* made ready for the open sea.

Eventually the mist lifted, a weak sun emerged and the carrack, so Katherine learned from the shouts and cries, turned north, with the Essex coast to port. She tried to draw Bertrand and those who served them food into conversation, but they remained coldly deaf to her questions. The sun strengthened, and the mild weather returned as the wind shifted, coming out of the south-west.

Katherine recalled all she'd learnt from the smugglers and contraband sailors who used these sea roads past the lonely inlets and deserted coves along the Essex coastline. Why were they sailing north? she wondered. She asked her companions, but it was futile. Father Roger had fallen fast asleep. Dorcas was no better, whilst Eleanor simply crouched, lips moving soundlessly. Katherine rose to her feet. She sensed a change. The ship's crew were extra vigilant. More braziers were brought up from between decks, their charcoal fired; next to these were small catapults and rounded bundles of rags tied tightly with twine and reeking of oil and tar. Lookouts took turns in the small cradle high on the mainmast. The master constantly watched both sea and sky.

A bell fixed just under the small forecastle marked the passing hours. It had just finished tolling what Katherine reckoned to be midday when the lookout cried a warning. For a few heartbeats, all activity ceased; there was a brooding silence except for the creak of the carrack as it rose and fell, breasting the swell. The master and his crew now thronged on the other side of the ship. Again the lookout shouted. Katherine staggered across the deck, clutching at ropes and whatever else kept her balance. No one objected, everyone answering the lookout's warning. Again the cry. Katherine peered across the running swell and, at the same time as the others, glimpsed two dark smudges against the bright horizon. The entire ship waited in silence, listening to the lookout chant like any monastic cantor singing the opening verses of Divine Office.

'Two cogs, hulks, closing fast!'

Curses greeted this, a chorus of alarm and threats.

'Two hulks, fighting ships, closing fast. I see fires lit!'

The lookout's description deepened the tension. The approaching warships intended to attack; their companies had already prepared fire balls for catapults and arrows.

'What banners?' the master called.

'Red crosses on a white field,' the lookout eventually chanted back. 'I see more: blue, gold and red, lions and lilies.'

This was greeted with roars of dismay from the Venetian crew. Bertrand and his comitatus remained grimly quiet.

'Yes, I see banners fully hoist,' the sharp-eyed lookout called. 'Royal cogs, probably out of Ipswich . . .'

The rest of his declaration was drowned by the master bellowing orders and the rush of feet that followed. Somewhere a tambour began to sound its heavy beat. The carrack swiftly transformed itself into a powerful ship of war. The small catapults were primed, missiles soaked in tar and oil moved closer to the braziers or large copper fire bowls. Sand was strewn across the deck. Great buckets and vats of seawater were hastily filled; bows and arrows, swords, maces and other weapons were collected from the war chest. The Venetians armed themselves as the carrack turned into the mist that curled between itself and the distant shore. Katherine and the rest were ignored. The crew was summoned to battle stations. Flames fed by bellows flared up in their baskets and bowls. Acrid smoke curled and shifted. LeCorbeil also prepared, putting on helmets, brigandines and coats of mail. Each man was armed with sword and dagger as well as a powerful Brabantine crossbow, leather quivers containing feathered barbed bolts strapped on to their war belts.

Katherine staggered back across the deck. The ship pitched. She slipped and blundered into sailors hurrying to their stations; these roughly pushed her aside. She reached the other prisoners, sheltering beneath the taff-rail. Father Roger still slept, Dorcas crouching close beside him. Eleanor was alert, lips moving in silent prayer.

'Rescue?' she asked. Despite the circumstances, Katherine laughed sharply.

'Father has influence, but not for this. It is too soon after our disappearance. These cogs are not from London. Raphael has told me about them: privateers with letters of marque. A Venetian carrack would be a splendid prize. They must be surprised at seeing one here in the northern seas rather than the Channel Narrows.' Katherine drew a deep breath, surprised at how calm she felt, pleased that she could recall the knowledge she had acquired from sailors and merchants along Queenhithe. She closed her eyes and, murmuring a prayer, rose to her feet. 'Now,' she mocked herself quietly, 'I am about to learn a little more.'

The two cogs were closing fast, their names recognised and spread amongst the company. They were ships of war well known in these waters, *The Kyrie* and *The Calix*, massive fighting craft with a central mast and high bows and stern; menacing and dark-shaped, they were using the shifting wind to close with the Venetian. Bertrand and two of his lieutenants came striding across, fearsome in their sallets, mail coifs and armour.

'You may go down into the hold.' Bertrand shrugged. 'However, if our ship is fired or breached, you will,' he grinned, 'either burn, drown or probably both. I advise you to stay on deck.' He bowed mockingly and turned away.

'He has left us to the terrors!' Eleanor remarked clambering to her feet. 'Either way we will experience all the horrors of battle. To think . . .' She paused, biting salt-caked lips. 'To think that I once trusted my life, my beloved, our future to such a man.' She lifted her face, all drawn. 'Now you know why I do penance, why—'

Eleanor's words were cut off by shouts, followed by the whoosh of flaming materials from the carrack's deck. *The Calix* and *The Kyrie* responded, scoring the greyish-blue sky with streaks of fire. The carrack's aim was more true, and the keen-eyed reported fires aboard *The Calix*. *The Kyrie*, however, closed, more flame-fed bundles whistling through the air. One hit a sailor, engulfing him in flames; he collapsed screaming to the deck, as comrades tried to smother the fire with vinegar-soaked cloths.

As the air became riven with fire, arrows and barbs, Katherine rose gingerly to her feet. Oil-soaked plumes of blackness hung over the carrack. *The Kyrie* was now almost on them, turning to take them on the port side whilst *The Calix* attacked the starboard side. For a brief, heart-chilling moment, all three ships became locked together. An ominous silence descended. The fog of war thinned to reveal Bertrand and his comitatus lined up in two rows facing *The Kyrie*, whose crew, eager to board, were throwing out nets, planks and hooked ropes. The Venetians resisted. LeCorbeil remained as a phalanx; the first rank knelt, the second stayed standing. The crew of *The Kyrie* were now massing ready to board.

'Loose!' Bertrand's voice thrilled. The kneeling crossbowmen released their barbs, each finding their victim. Bodies from *The Kyrie* toppled into the narrow gap between the two ships. LeCorbeil's second rank moved forward and knelt, even as the first prepared their crossbows. The enemy were caught unawares, thronging along the side of the ship armed only with hand weapons. Their archers could not loose, whilst LeCorbeil moved in a well-practised formation, their rain of squat barbed shafts devastating the enemy. Katherine reckoned they had received at least thirty bolts, each finding its mark.

The Kyrie's crew retreated, cutting ropes and nets in a desperate bid to escape. LeCorbeil turned, hurrying across the deck to inflict similar damage on *The Calix*, which hastily swung away. Now free of his adversaries, the master of *The Golden Horn* took advantage of the strong breezes. The carrack turned, aiming directly for the mist-shrouded coastline of Essex.

Katherine crouched down. Dorcas sat petrified, swaddled in a cloak. Eleanor had found her Ave beads and was threading them through her fingers. Father Roger knelt, face pressed against the bulwark, hands clasped in prayer. Katherine moved over and put an arm around his shoulder. He turned, eyes glaring madly in his bruised, unshaven face.

'They have come to take me,' he whispered. 'The ghosts. I am being punished, yet what I did was just. I saved their souls. I consigned their filthy, smelly bodies—' He broke off as Katherine withdrew her arm and stared in shock. She recalled what Bertrand had said about this priest.

'Who, Father?' she hissed, ignoring the tumult of battle. 'What are you saying?'

'I suspected as much.' Eleanor had drawn closer. 'I saw him once with Margot, one of the slaughtered whores. I have also seen him after he has locked and bolted the church. Dressed in a hair shirt, he prostrates himself. I have heard the whip slashing his back. I did wonder. I wanted to talk to your father, but . . .' She shrugged, wiping the spray from her face.

Katherine, despite everything that was going on around her, could only crouch and reflect on what she was seeing and hearing. Father Roger had blessed her as a child, shriven her at the mercy pew, given her the Eucharist, exchanged the singing bread; could he be the barbarous killer of those poor streetwalkers? Here was a man who had danced on her name day, who had sat at their family table and blessed the feasts they'd shared.

'Why? Why?' She turned back angrily, but Father Roger, eyes closed, was now banging his head against the bulwark, bloody lips chattering nonsense. Katherine comforted Dorcas and got up.

The battle was over. *The Golden Horn* had broken free, and was heading due west towards the treacherous Essex coastline. The two royal cogs, which had sustained dire punishment, were reluctant to follow. A sailor, elated by their escape and relieved to be alive, chattered amicably to Katherine in the lingua franca of the port, a mixture of English, French and doggerel Latin, until Bertrand intervened, grasping her shoulder and pushing her back towards the other prisoners.

'Mistress, the danger has passed. I will send you meat, bread and wine.' He gestured at her companions. 'They seem to need it. Both the crew and my men have remarked on your courage and fortitude.' He paused. 'Believe me, you will need both if your father does not respond.'

'To what?'

'To my demands. A blood feud exists between him and me. Simon Roseblood should be careful which path he chooses.'

'What is it you want?'

'Information.'

'About what?' Katherine steadied herself against the pitch of the deck.

'He will know.'

'And this blood feud?'

Bertrand gestured at Eleanor, who crouched watching, eyes large and black. 'Ask her. Now,' he pointed into the mist, 'we have escaped the hulks; soon we will be off the Colvasse peninsula and the Orwell estuary, where we will land and meet the rest of our company.'

'And then?'

Bertrand shrugged.

'What did you mean about our priest here?'

'Ask him yourself. He certainly can't judge us. We have kept Queenhithe under very close watch. Murder stalks its filthy streets. We were surprised to discover it wore a cowl and boasted a tonsure.'

Bertrand walked away. Katherine watched him go. She was pleased that he had recognised her courage; she would hate for a man like Bertrand to hold her in fear. But what did he want from her father? Was it connected with Simon's mysterious disappearance over the last few days, then his sudden return, his appearance all changed, just before she was abducted? She also resolved to question Eleanor about the so-called blood feud. As for Father Roger . . . Katherine repressed a shiver as she glanced at the now demented priest, still banging his head against the wood, mumbling incoherently to himself. She drew a deep breath, smiled at Dorcas and persuaded the maid to stand and walk with her, albeit stumbling and slipping, along the deck. Again she was surprised to find that the pain in her right leg had not appeared. Encouraged, she urged Dorcas not to be frightened, though the young woman seemed to be broken, clinging like a frightened bairn to its mother.

Over the next few days, Katherine strove to compose herself, and to impose some order on her little group.

She demanded and obtained better food and water, a brazier to drive off the chill and a more private place to relieve themselves, away from the catcalls of the watching men. Bertrand seemed amused by her forcefulness. Katherine, however, recognised that the man was very dangerous and would have no scruples about carrying out his threats. She also distracted herself by speculating about the carrack and its journey north.

The Golden Horn had come through the battle relatively unscathed, whatever damage it had sustained soon repaired. As the days passed, Katherine walked around the ship whenever she could. The weather remained dull and misty, the sea fast-running but relatively smooth. She realised that the carrack was not only a means to elude and mystify any pursuer; LeCorbeil had hired it for more sinister and secret reasons. Horses had been brought aboard, undoubtedly mounts for Bertrand and his company, whilst the massive holds were packed with purveyance. She had glimpsed some of the contents as she passed open trapdoors with ladders down to the cavernous storerooms. She also stood close to the ship's clerks with their indentures of goods and long lists of items spread out over the tops of barrels. The carrack was carrying everything a fighting force would need: weapons, dried meat, horse fodder and harness, armour and medical stores, vats of wine, barrels of gunpowder, two small cannon and a trebuchet. The clerks and crew talked easily amongst themselves, as if they were unaware of her presence or how knowledgeable she was about what was happening.

She also noticed that *The Golden Horn* was brought in as close as possible to the long black line of the Essex coast, whilst Bertrand and two of his henchmen closely studied the charts and maps the master spread out in front of them. The more Katherine watched, and the more she recalled her father's talk of war and the chatter of soldiers in the tavern taproom, the more certain she became that Bertrand had hired the carrack and planned this journey for other reasons apart from herself. LeCorbeil, mounted and armed, would prove to be excellent scouts; they were undoubtedly preparing for the day when York and Lancaster clashed. They were waiting for civil strife. If they sheltered in Essex, they would be free of the Beauforts in London and find it easy to ride north to join York. Katherine was certain that was the real reason for their journey. She had been abducted as an act of revenge but also as a bargaining counter, which was part of a greater strategy. She decided to keep her thoughts to herself and not even discuss her suspicions with Eleanor. She comforted herself that Bertrand had made a serious mistake. He thought she would be terrified, like Eleanor, Dorcas and Father Roger. She would resist, watch and wait for her opportunity.

The following day, late in the evening, *The Golden Horn* slipped into the lonely Orwell estuary. Katherine and her companions, legs shaking, faces and clothing coated in salty spray, were bundled ashore and taken to a prepared campsite, where they were given food and left to their own devices. Eleanor was now more alert, full of questions. Dorcas just relaxed and slept, quivering in her dreams, whilst Father Roger, once he was ashore, regained his wits and sat brooding, staring down at the ground. Now and again he would lift his head and gaze around. Katherine flinched at the sly malevolence of his gaze and realised that the priest's madness had turned into a chilling cunning. She decided to ignore him and instead watch the carrack being unloaded of stores and horses. After dark, a troop of horsemen dressed in LeCorbeil livery, crossbows hanging from their saddle horns, entered the camp. Katherine reckoned the entire force was now about fifty, well armed and amply provisioned.

They stayed in the campsite for two days and nights. Once the carrack had unloaded its cargo, it put back to sea, whilst LeCorbeil organised the transportation of stores to hidden places between Orwell and Walton. Katherine and her companions were largely ignored. She welcomed this, as she was growing more concerned. Father Roger kept to himself, constantly conversing with some invisible presence. Dorcas, her clothes dried and belly now full, whispered about escape, whilst Eleanor became increasingly lost in her prayers.

On the third day after disembarkation, they moved deeper into the Essex countryside, travelling south back towards London. That night, Katherine gathered her companions around the campfire, sharing out a rabbit that had been snared, skinned, gibbeted and roasted. Bertrand had sent them another wineskin; Katherine filled the battered pewter cups to the brim, and they celebrated their return to dry land, away from the dangers of the sea. Eleanor and Dorcas fell quiet as Father Roger began to chatter. His eyes were too bright, his gaunt whiskered face twitching as he blithely described his visit to Colchester to attend his mother's funeral. He chattered like a squirrel on a branch, clasping his cup close as he explained how he had discovered that his mother had been a courtesan, well known for conferring her favours on all who would buy them. During her life she had maintained the mask and disguise of a seamstress, but once dead, the truth had emerged.

Katherine sat growing more anxious as the priest, now in his shriving time, as he described it, launched into a filthy diatribe about whores, prostitutes and streetwalkers. She could only watch that tormented soul unburden itself of all its guilt and nightmares. A man, she concluded, who had done hideous wrong and now regarded his present troubles as punishment from God. Dorcas could only blink like an owl at the priest's stream of invective. Eleanor tried to intervene, but he ignored her, chanting out his litany of hate-filled obsessions. Katherine did not know what to do except let him rant. When at last he finished, his face coated with sweat, chest heaving, he sketched a cross in the air.

'I absolve myself!' he shouted, eyes gleaming, tongue wetting chapped lips. 'I absolve myself from all my sins!' He broke off his manic chant and rose to his knees. 'And for my penance,' he slurred, 'a visit to the latrine.'

He stumbled to his feet, cloak over one arm, and staggered into the darkness.

'He is mad, moonstruck,' Dorcas wailed. 'Mistress, he is a killer, he has become lunatic.' Katherine tried to comfort her, then squatted, heaping small handfuls of bracken on the fire, attempting to soothe her own panic. Dorcas was correct: their world was fractured. Eleanor seemed lost in her own dark memories. What was frustrating was that they were so close and yet so far from home.

Katherine stared around in the light of the dancing flames. The campfires of LeCorbeil surrounded them; beyond these were picket lines and sentries. There could be no escape, not from here. It would be impossible to steal horses, whilst on foot they would be caught within the hour. Moreover, Bertrand had warned them how the surrounding moorland thickets and copses concealed deep morasses, treacherous marshes that could drag both horse and rider down.

'No need to warn me,' Eleanor had retorted. 'My mother's people hailed from Walton.'

Katherine studied Eleanor's peaked face. Her aunt troubled her. This was the first time in years that Katherine had been in close company with her. She had noticed how Eleanor, when relieving or washing herself, made sure that Dorcas and Katherine were never close; at other times she would clutch her stomach, face strained with pain.

'They are hoarding supplies.' Eleanor spoke up, gesturing with her head. 'You know that, don't you,

Katherine? French galleys sailed up the Thames recently. I am sure that one day soon, a similar fleet will appear off Walton to land an invading force.'

'But they will be resisted.' Katherine's voice faltered.

'This is a wilderness,' Eleanor replied. 'The French have chosen well. Villages and hamlets disappeared during the Great Plague; there are derelict farms, houses and cottages where supplies and provisions can be secretly stored.

'You may not know the story, but many, many years ago, Isabella the She-Wolf, another French queen,' she laughed drily, 'landed at Walton with her lover Mortimer and a host of Hainaulters. She came to topple her husband, and so she did.' Eleanor gestured into the darkness. 'They say her ghost still haunts this place.' She threw more bracken on the flames. 'The French have not forgotten. They will watch and wait. When this kingdom slips into civil war, they will land here.' She took a deep breath. 'Then the concealed pits, the secret barbicans and the disguised storage holds will be opened. They will draw out weapons, harness, dried fodder and food. They will have maps of the coastline and the countryside. But you suspect that already, Katherine, don't you? Our abduction is only a small part of a greater plan.' She stretched across and gently caressed Katherine's cheek, then withdrew hastily to rub her own stomach. 'I saw you watching them.'

'They think we are stupid women,' Katherine replied, 'who do not realise what is happening.'

'Wrong!' Eleanor countered fiercely, 'Oh so wrong!

Watch them, Katherine; Bertrand is certainly studying you.' She paused. 'By the way, where is our priest? What is he doing?'

Dorcas, full of wine, simply snored. Katherine rose to her feet.

'Leave him,' Eleanor warned. 'Do not pursue him, even here in this armed camp.'

'Did you suspect?' Katherine asked, sitting down again.

'Yes, I did. But suspicion is one thing, belief another. Our curate always had an eye for the ladies. I heard the tale he just told. How he returned to Colchester for his mother's funeral only to be told that she, like her own son, had a secret life. She acted the courtesan, pandering to the greedy needs of certain burgesses.'

Eleanor blew out her cheeks and paused at the ominous cry of some night bird carrying through the brooding darkness. 'A harbinger,' she murmured. 'It will be cold tonight.' She pointed to the makeshift bothy LeCorbeil had built out of branches, heavy blankets and armfuls of bracken and gorse. 'At least we will have some comfort. Anyway, let me finish before our priest returns. Father Roger's wits were never the strongest. I have watched him and reflected. I believe he used to seek out whores for solace, then turned on them in unresolved fury against his mother. You have heard similar tales from streetwalkers, surely? Men who like to be violent in their swiving, to beat a girl, to mock her body; this gives them great pleasure. A few do not stop at that; murder is in their heart.'

Katherine nodded in agreement.

'Never mind him,' Eleanor continued in a hushed whisper. 'Do not be fooled. LeCorbeil knows you have been watching them, and for that reason alone, they will never let us live.'

Katherine's heart missed a beat, and she flinched as if an ice-cold wind had brushed her back and neck. She made to protest, but conceded to the steely look in her aunt's eyes.

'Katherine.' Eleanor stroked her hand; Katherine noticed how fine and long her aunt's fingers had become. 'Katherine, believe me. Bertrand and his company of devils have no intention of letting us live. Somehow they will use us to entice your father into a trap, as they did me and Edmund some five years ago. Listen well. Edmund's murder was LeCorbeil's doing. I do not know the full story, or exactly what was going on in my husband's mind after he came home from France. The emergence of the maid, Joan of Arc, was the beginning of England's defeat; however, Edmund, and certainly your father, had profited from the wars.'

She paused as Dorcas pitched dangerously forward, head towards the fire. She and Katherine made the maid comfortable on the ground, covering her with a cloak and a shabby blanket.

'Your father came home as he always did, a roaring boy, but Edmund had greatly changed. Secretly he told me how he had witnessed bloody slaughter in France, the climax being a savage massacre in the Norman town of LeCorbeil. No, they were not involved or responsible, but your father and Edmund certainly viewed the aftermath. Edmund was full of contrition at his part in the war. We married, planned to raise our own family, but his soul was still deeply stricken by what he had experienced. He took to visiting the Good Brothers, the Franciscans at Greyfriars. He would take your brother Gabriel.' She blinked away her tears.

'They became very close, more like father and son than kinsmen. Simon deeply resented all this, as he did my marriage to Edmund. He accepted it, but he has a will of steel. He knew something was wrong, but was frustrated at being unable to help. He and Edmund became estranged, especially when Edmund tried to keep clear of all the nefarious goings-on at the Roseblood. In truth, he dreamt of becoming a merchant, of breaking free of the past. He often wished he could make reparation.

'Then, about six years ago, Edmund confided in me how he had met young men from LeCorbeil. How he had explained to these emissaries that he was not to blame. He was most secretive about this. He told me how the survivors of the massacre were building a chantry in their parish church to honour the memory of the victims of the massacre; about how the local bishop wished to obtain the names of all those responsible.'

Eleanor paused as one of their captors passed the campfire, leading a sumpter pony.

'And he believed this nonsense?' Katherine asked.

'He was full of guilt, gullible, desperate to make

amends. We had no knowledge of the truth, not even a shred. Edmund believed the fairy tale being spun around him because he desperately wanted to. He never discussed it with Simon, only me. And I encouraged him wholeheartedly. I truly loved Edmund. I could see how he wanted to escape the pain, and so did I. God forgive us, we came to fiercely resent your father. We kept LeCorbeil hidden from him. We even ignored his warnings, allusions to LeCorbeil being the arrow point of French attacks on our southern coast.

'Five years ago, Cade proclaimed himself Captain of Kent and marched to London.' She paused, hands going out to the flames. 'It happened so quickly, Katherine. Edmund received an invitation to meet an emissary of LeCorbeil. He and I were so eager to escape the Roseblood. Cade's rebellion and the riots in London amply demonstrated the violence we had both grown to hate. Edmund went, and he was murdered.' Eleanor's voice broke. 'Decapitated, abused, a dead crow left beside his poled head. Of course we had been tricked. So sudden,' she murmured, 'so swift, like a summer swallow skimming over the grass. I could not believe it. We had been seduced, betrayed and shattered.' She grasped her niece's hand. Her fingers were as cold as ice. 'I urged Edmund along that path. My guilt, my sorrow, my mistake: that is why I am an anchorite. More importantly, now you will realise that LeCorbeil will never let us live!'

Eleanor paused as Dorcas struggled awake, moaning quietly and rubbing her stomach. 'I must go to the latrines.' The maid staggered to her feet and disappeared into the darkness.

'How do we escape?' Katherine urged. 'And even if we do, I have heard the chatter amongst LeCorbeil. We are journeying south to Cottesloe, a deserted woodland village. They talk about meeting their seigneur. They also gossip about how the armies are on the move. The King has issued his writs, his commissioners of array are moving through the shires trying to raise troops. They are even offering pardons to outlaws.' She closed her eyes, trying to recall the conversations she had overheard whilst they had been setting up camp. Indeed, that now frightened her, for it proved that Eleanor was correct: their captors had talked freely, confident that their prisoners would never—

Katherine opened her eyes and sprang to her feet at the heart-piercing scream echoing across the camp. 'Dorcas!' She grasped a brand from the flames and hurried through the darkness, the night air reeking of leather, burnt meat, horseflesh and human sweat. Others, also alarmed, were hastening towards the screaming; already two of LeCorbeil were flanking her. Katherine stumbled and slithered, her cloak catching briar and gorse. They reached the latrines, an ancient ditch behind a hedge of wild bramble; the stench was offensive. Dorcas stood on the lip of the ditch, gesturing wildly towards a clump of trees close to the picket lines. Peering through the gloom, Katherine could see that LeCorbeil were already there. She gingerly crossed the ditch. Dorcas stood still, pointing into the darkness.

'I went over there. I did not want the men to see. The priest . . .'

Katherine ignored her and hurried across the heathland. She threw the firebrand away as she joined the ring of torches. LeCorbeil were staring at Father Roger, hanging from the outstretched branch of an ancient oak. He had apparently ripped his cloak, fashioned a noose, clambered up the gnarled trunk, tied the other end securely and let himself drop. He hung feet down, hands by his sides, head strangely twisted; in the dancing torchlight, his liverish face looked truly grotesque, eyes popping, swollen tongue thrust out.

'The Judas priest.' Bertrand was now beside her. 'He spared the hangman.'

'Cut him down!' Katherine begged. 'Please.'

Bertrand agreed, but despite the tearful pleas of both women, he ordered the corpse to be thrown into the latrine pit. They had to watch it sink beneath the filthy mud before being escorted back to their bothy.

Eleanor had not moved. When Katherine told her what had happened, she just sat staring into the fire. 'I wondered,' she whispered, 'I truly did. I mean, how it would end. Oh God rest his miserable soul.' She helped Katherine to calm Dorcas, then all three women crawled into the bothy to sleep.

They were aroused at first light, given some bread and ale and mounted on horses. They left the camp and entered the dense woodland, threading their way along dark paths, the trees pressing in from either side. The company were well armed, each carrying an arbalest looped over their saddle horn. They moved purposefully, aware of the sounds of the forest: the flutter of birds, the various calls and all the other eerie noises. Simply by sharp observation, Katherine realised that their passage was being noticed by the forest people: charcoal burners, poachers, outlaws; all those who lived their hidden lives in the green darkness. No one dared approach them. LeCorbeil were professional soldiers journeying to join other men at war, and so were left well alone.

Katherine grew increasingly concerned about her two companions. Eleanor was in constant pain, clutching her stomach; Dorcas slumped in the saddle bemoaning her filthy clothes and the numerous pains and aches that vexed her. The maid's mind began to wander. She would call Katherine's name and ask how long it would be before they reached the Roseblood. This provoked jeers from those close to them. Katherine could only gaze pityingly back and pray quietly for help. Yet how could they escape from this green fastness, the sun and the wispy white sky blocked by the tangled canopy of branches? The bracken and closely packed trees thronging on every side were like the bars of a prison cage, and only God knew what other dangers lurked deeper in the forest.

They reached a clearing and paused to break their fast. Katherine helped Eleanor down from the saddle and offered her a wineskin. She heard cries and turned quickly. Dorcas had slipped from her mount and was running as fast as she could across the clearing, desperate to reach the far line of trees. Katherine screamed at her to stop, but Dorcas, head back, hair tossing in the breeze, ran on. Some of their escort mounted in pursuit but then paused. Dorcas had reached a stretch of greenness lighter than the rest and was floundering helplessly. Katherine stared in shock as her maid, stricken with terror, sank deeper into the treacherous forest marsh.

'Help her!' she shouted at the mounted men.

They reined in, quietening their horses, as Bertrand, one hand raised, rode slowly across the clearing, checking the ground around him. Dorcas, realising that she was trapped, tried to turn back, only to sink more deeply into the green morass. Katherine, lifting the hem of her dress, sped towards her. One of her escort shouted and Bertrand skilfully turned his horse, blocking her path.

'Don't follow.' He leaned down. 'There is nothing . . .'

Katherine was powerless to move; she could only watch in horror as Dorcas, head back, mouth open in a silent scream, disappeared beneath the shifting, moss-strewn marsh. She crumpled to the ground, sobbing bitterly. She could hear Eleanor crying as if from a long distance away, and was aware of Bertrand moving his horse, his strong hand grasping her by the hair. She was dragged to her feet and roughly pushed back to join the rest.

For a while, she could only crouch with Eleanor's arms around her. Eventually they were separated, pulled apart. A small manchet loaf was thrust into her hand. She was ordered to drink from the wineskin and then lifted back on to a horse.

'She was warned!'

Katherine gazed at Bertrand's cold, handsome face. 'One day,' she breathed, 'I hope to kill you.'

'One day,' Bertrand retorted, 'is here and now.' He walked away.

They continued on their journey. Darkness had fallen before they entered the derelict and deserted village of Cottesloe. Katherine felt she was entering the realm of ghosts. Houses stood either side of the weed-choked main trackway, gaping windows and open doors staring blindly out. The tavern's battered sign swung on a rusty chain, creaking as if it called the dead; the horse trough in front of it brimmed with water. The village well still had its red-brick wall beneath a well-maintained coping. Katherine glimpsed ovens beside what must have been the bakery. Stalls and benches stood in front of derelict shops and houses. Doors creaked open in the wind as if in ghastly welcome. Before them rose the ancient parish church with its great front door, narrow windows and soaring bell tower. A dismal silence brooded, as if just beyond the veil, the restless spirits of the dead, those cut down by the Great Plague, watched and seethed at this intrusion by the living.

Katherine glimpsed torch- and candlelight in some of the houses they passed. A small group of LeCorbeil were waiting for them just on the edge of the church enclosure, six in all, grouped around a grey-haired man who welcomed Bertrand and his companions warmly. He glanced at Katherine and Eleanor, then shrugged and turned away.

They were ordered to dismount and taken to a cottage close to the cemetery. Its windows were boarded up, but the walls of dried mud and wood were in good repair, as was the thatched roof, whilst the heavy door could be padlocked and secured both from within and without. Inside they had a small brazier to warm themselves, sacking for beds and a few sticks of furniture. Katherine, still shocked after Dorcas's death, simply threw herself down on the makeshift palliasse and promptly fell asleep.

She awoke cold and aching the following morning. Eleanor lay moaning in her sleep, but when Katherine turned her over, she simply shrugged her off. Katherine lay down again until the door was unlocked and guards brought in some charcoal and bracken, followed by bowls of oatmeal. Eleanor, looking pale and wan, rose and ate some of the porridge. She offered the rest to Katherine, assuring her she had taken enough. Katherine ate greedily with her fingers whilst her aunt hobbled outside. A short while later Eleanor returned, closed the door and squatted down on her bed.

'Don't worry,' she murmured. 'God will provide.' Katherine could only wonder how.

She felt exhausted, but as the morning wore on, she became more determined. She accepted that she had been given a rough awakening to the harsh realities of life. She had enjoyed the good things of her father's wealth, lost in girlish dreams about Camelot, but, she conceded ruefully, Camelot had been invaded and the golden glow had died. She recalled one of her father's favourite quotations from the Bible: 'There is a time and season for everything under Heaven. A time for reaping and a time for planting . . . a time for peace and a time for war.' This was war. The day of reckoning had arrived, but how was she to confront it? She recalled Dorcas sinking into that marsh. Father Roger swinging by his neck from a branch. She huddled deeper into her cloak, listening to the sounds from outside.

Abruptly the door was flung open, and one of LeCorbeil entered and threw a small oilskin at Eleanor's feet.

'You asked for it,' he declared. 'Said you needed it for cleaning.'

Once the man had left, Eleanor roused herself. She went to the door, opened it, stared out, then closed it and came to crouch close to Katherine.

'There is a faint mist,' she declared. 'Listen.' Katherine heard shouts and calls. 'They are practising at the butts with their arbalests; they are preparing for the coming war.'

'On whose side?'

'Oh, undoubtedly York's, but I suspect their real purpose is simply to deepen the darkness and spread the chaos. Now I understand that we will be allowed to wander, but we will be watched. Once twilight falls, we will be locked in here again and that's when you will escape. I have planned it. You will go but I will stay.'

'Eleanor!'

'Katherine, listen well,' Eleanor pleaded. 'I am dying.

For months I have had bleeding, a constantly cutting pain here.' She clutched her stomach. 'I also have a bubo, a swelling on my right breast.' She touched her throat. 'Sometimes I cannot swallow. Our abduction, I am sure, has hastened matters.'

Katherine gazed stricken at Eleanor's pale face, her sharp cheekbones, her eyes dark pools ringed by shadows. She clutched Eleanor's hands, holding them between hers. 'Surely it is just exhaustion,' she pleaded.

'No.' Eleanor shook her head. 'It's more than that. Please don't say I must come with you. I cannot. This is my last act of atonement for Edmund, God bless him, for Simon, but most importantly, for you. LeCorbeil have no souls, no compassion, no mercy. They fully intend to murder us. No,' she held up a hand, 'I will not come with you, but I can save you.' She pointed to the far side of the cottage, which faced the cemetery wall. 'Today we will dig through that, clear away the plaster and wood, create a gap big enough for you to crawl through. Once you have done that, you must hide in the cemetery and await the sign.'

'What sign?'

Eleanor smiled. 'You will recognise it when you see it. Now come, you must eat what they bring, then go out and wander around. Memorise the distance between this wretched cottage and the cemetery wall. Learn what you can. How to scale it in the dark and where to hide in God's Acre. When you see the sign, follow the path leading through the village; it will take you back to the trackway we turned off. Turn to the right, hide in the fringe of trees. That trackway must lead on to the ancient road, where you will find merchants and pilgrims making their way into London.' Eleanor spread her hands. 'It is the best I can do. I am too weak to go with you. If we stay as we are, we are no better than hogs in the slaughter pen.'

Katherine reluctantly conceded to her aunt's importunate pleas. Food and drink were brought. They broke their fast. Afterwards, using their fingers and shards of pottery, they began to clear the bottom of the cottage wall facing the cemetery. They worked furiously but quietly, digging and hacking. Eleanor warned Katherine to keep her bruised and bloodied fingers hidden beneath her cloak. Now and again they were visited. Bertrand wandered in, stared at them, smiled to himself and left. Scraps of food and watered ale were served as the morning wore on. Katherine, at Eleanor's whispered urgings, left the cottage. The mist had lifted, though the strengthening sun did little to dissipate the gloom of that deserted village, a place caught between life and death. LeCorbeil were busy practising with their weapons or tending to their horses. The smoky tang of the smithy and the ringing of hammer on anvil wafted through the air. They were apparently preparing to leave. Would they travel south, Katherine wondered, to meet her father, set their lure and spring the trap?

Bertrand was talking to the grey-haired, narrow-faced man who'd greeted them when they first arrived. He caught Katherine's eye and summoned her across. The stranger, dressed in a costly dark blue woollen robe spangled with streaks of gold, studied her with his soulless eyes, scratching at his close-clipped grey moustache and beard. A clever, cunning face, she thought, full of hateful menace. At last he nodded and flicked gloved fingers in dismissal.

Katherine walked back up towards the cemetery, a wilderness of overgrown yew trees and straggling bramble, briar and gorse that had wound around the crumbling headstones and decaying crosses. In the dark, she realised, this would be a tangle of traps. She studied and memorised the narrow winding paths that could lead her safely across, walking through the cemetery till she reached the enclosure that must have housed the poor man's lot. Once through this, she concluded, she would climb the crumbling wall and thread her way through the outlying copse on to the trackway leading out of the village.

As she stared at the wall, she grew distinctly uncomfortable. She was certain someone was watching her, though she could glimpse nothing untoward. She walked back to that part of the wall facing the cottage; thankfully it had plenty of cracks and crevices that would provide sure footholds in the dark. She glanced down and noticed how the plaster of the cottage wall was beginning to crack. She hoped that it would evade notice. She drew a deep breath, closed her eyes and prayed for herself and Eleanor.

She was tempted to resist her aunt's plan, but when she returned, Eleanor proved to be even more adamant. She had dug a great deal of the inner plaster away, creating a gap in the ancient latticed framework that would be broad enough for Katherine to squeeze through. They covered the loosened plaster with some of the bed sacking. Katherine could have wept at the bloody mess of her aunt's once elegant fingers and nails. Eleanor ignored this, urging Katherine to memorise what she had learnt in the cemetery. She asked about Katherine's leg and accepted her niece's assurances that the aches and pains had mysteriously disappeared. Katherine had wondered about this. She recalled a venerable physician whom her father had hired. He'd gently hinted that the source of the pain might be in the humours of her mind rather than her flesh. Her parents had dismissed this, but perhaps he had spoken the truth. Eleanor still studied her closely, asking if all else was well. She also checked Katherine's sandals, and showed her scraps of food she had hidden in a rag: pieces of dried meat and even harder bread.

'You must take this,' she urged.

'And the sign?' Katherine asked.

Eleanor just smiled and turned away.

For the rest of the day, Eleanor and Katherine prepared. Eleanor begged one of the guards to fetch a wineskin so that she could drink to dull the pain in her belly. The guard brought the coarsest wine Katherine had ever tasted. Eleanor went walking in the cemetery and brought back leaves from various plants that she insisted on grinding with a stone. Darkness fell. The guards ensured that the door was locked and bolted. Once they had left, Eleanor embraced Katherine, both women's cheeks wet with their tears. For a while they just held each other. When Katherine made to move away, Eleanor hugged her even tighter.

'Katherine, my beloved, even if I was safe and sound in my anchorite cell, I would be dead by autumn. God knows I might still escape, but it's vital that you do. Give Simon, Raphael, Gabriel and all those I hold dear my unending love. Now,' she pushed Katherine away, 'we must act.'

Pulling aside the sacking, she hacked again at the great gap she had gouged out. The cold night breeze swept through. Katherine lay down and crawled forward, then pushed herself back.

'It needs widening!' she gasped.

Once again they clawed and tore at the ancient plaster and wood, coughing on the dust, pausing now and again to listen for noises from outside. At last Katherine whispered that she was satisfied. Once again they embraced. Katherine made sure she had everything and crawled out into the dark.

The night air was thick with the heavy scent of vegetation and the odours of the camp. Voices called faintly, followed by snatches of song. Katherine scaled the cemetery wall and sheltered beneath a deep-shadowed yew tree. She stared back at the cottage, waiting for the mysterious promised signal. Night birds chattered, bats swooped swift and darting, black smudges against the fading light.

She smelled the smoke first, then caught her breath at the orange-yellow flames that burst up through the thatched roof of the cottage she had just left, a spurt of furious fire to greet the gathering night. As she stared in sheer anguish, a horn wailed its warning, followed by shouts of alarm. Katherine opened her mouth in a silent cry. She recalled the kindling, the oil, the wine. The inside of the cottage was bone dry; its wooden timbers and scraps of furniture would be kindling for a furnace. Eleanor must have collected herbs to induce sleep, mixing these with the wine to dull her senses so that she could go quietly into the eternal dark. Katherine fought to curb the sorrow piercing her heart.

The yelling voices drew closer, the flames now roaring up. LeCorbeil could do nothing. The cottage windows were sealed, whilst the locks and bolts on the door would be fiery hot. Any trace of Katherine's escape would be destroyed by the conflagration. Eleanor had sacrificed herself, and Katherine realised she must ensure it wasn't in vain.

She crept out of the shadows and almost stumbled into the figure that rose from behind a tombstone. A gloved hand stifled her screams. She struggled madly, but her assailant's steel-like grip did not slacken. Katherine was raging so much at being trapped, she ignored the hoarse whispers in her ear. Then she felt the prick of a dagger.

'Katherine, for pity's sake!' The voice was clearer; the grip over her mouth slackened. 'Peace, Katherine. It is Amadeus Sevigny. I am here to protect you.'

Katherine let herself go slack, leaning against Sevigny, sobbing quietly, her ears dinned by the flames now roaring like those of a furnace. She recalled crossing the cemetery earlier that day, the feeling of being watched . . .

'Come, Katherine, come.'

She turned; Sevigny's face was almost hidden by a deep cowl and muffler.

'Come!' he urged. 'We must put as much distance as we can between us and them. No, don't speak.'

Katherine was half dragged, half carried across the cemetery. She scraped her leg on a sharp stone and winced quietly. At last they left God's Acre, Sevigny pulling her deeper into the trees along an arrow-thin trackway. She was aware only of the cold, the darkness and his strong grip. They reached a clearing; Katherine heard the whinnying of a horse, and Sevigny called out whispered endearments to his destrier Leonardo. The great silky black warhorse was harnessed and ready. Sevigny unhobbled it, lifted Katherine into the high-horned saddle and swung himself up behind her. Then he gathered the reins, guiding the horse out of the trees on to a broader path.

Once they reached one of the pilgrim roads, Sevigny dug in his spurs and Leonardo burst into a gallop. Katherine could only nestle closer, conscious of Sevigny's arms around her and the sheer relief of his presence. They rode all night, galloping through sleepy villages and hamlets, past the campfires of other travellers, until they reached the London road. Just after daybreak, they entered the yard of the Cokayne, one of those majestic taverns that served the pilgrim trade. Sevigny hired a chamber and Katherine collapsed insensible on to the bed.

She did not wake until long after midday. Once she had washed and tidied herself, they sat in the tavern's rose garden, feeding their hunger on strips of spiced chicken, fresh bread and a pottage of crushed onion, carrot and leek. Katherine ate quickly; Sevigny laughed and told her to be careful.

'You came looking for me.' Katherine held the clerk's hard gaze and recalled Bertrand's cruel face.

'Your father,' Sevigny replied, 'was distraught. He established that you, Eleanor and the others had been abducted. What happened to them, by the way?'

'Just tell me,' Katherine replied harshly. 'My father?'

'He realised that your disappearance was a well-planned abduction. He sent Wormwood to me. He wondered if it was York or Malpas's doing. I went to the Roseblood and told him not to be offensive; that I would never harm you. I insisted that you had been taken by a highly organised coven; I suspected LeCorbeil. I was soon proved right. Toadflax's corpse was discovered in a laystall, whilst a cart had been seen leaving the church. I warned your father against sending pursuers out of the city. The fact that they had used a cart meant they were not travelling far. A short while later, we found out about the Venetian carrack at Queenhithe. When questioned, some of the wharfsmen told us that they had observed a group of foreigners hurrying people aboard.' Sevigny shrugged. 'War is imminent; every man keeps to his own business.'

'And later?'

'Oh, the carrack was seen sailing north.' Sevigny forced a smile. 'I know all about Cottesloe village, the secret hiding place of LeCorbeil. I persuaded your father to allow me to pursue them. It was relatively easy. I made camp in the woods and waited. I saw you arrive, but I was frustrated. LeCorbeil are professional mercenaries, master bowmen, well disciplined and amply provided for. Your wandering in the cemetery alerted me. I could see you were plotting something. Thank God you did. Once darkness fell, I hid near the church. I saw the first flames of a fire.' He crossed himself. 'God rest poor Eleanor. So,' he drank from his tankard, 'what actually happened?'

Katherine told him everything. From the moment they were abducted, to her escape. Sevigny heard her out before gathering the remains of the food on the platter and gently coaxing her to finish it.

'Eternal rest to them all,' he declared. 'But Eleanor was correct. LeCorbeil would have used you to trap your father – indeed, if they could, your entire family. None of you would have been spared. A blood feud, Katherine. LeCorbeil want your deaths and there is nothing that will dissuade them from it.' He saw the fear in her eyes and took her hand. 'But your father is resolute. He accepts the blood feud, and given the opportunity, he will strike and strike hard.'

He took a deep breath. 'There is more. Your father has something that both York and LeCorbeil want, a chronicle of scandalous secrets affecting the royal family as well as that of the good duke. It is the work of a former royal physician. I have heard the chatter. I suspect your father killed Argentine and seized his chronicle. If he has any sense, he will either destroy it or hide it away. LeCorbeil want to trade you for that document. They plotted to seize you, obtain the chronicle and still carry out their vengeance. Eleanor was very brave and cunning. It might take some time for your abductors to realise that the blackened ruins of that cottage contain the remains of only one corpse. So . . .' Sevigny made to stand.

'Amadeus?'

'Yes.'

'You are York's man. You—'

'Not any more, Katherine. A long story that I will tell you as we ride.' Sevigny rose. 'But we should not tarry. LeCorbeil might discover your secret and pursue us. If not, they will journey north to join York's forces. I will confront them there.'

'But why did you come looking for me?'

'Oh.' Sevigny leaned over the table and swiftly kissed her on the lips. 'Because I love you, Katherine Roseblood.'

Raphael Roseblood

London, May 1455

'They have poured out blood like water . . .' The swelling voices of the Franciscan choir echoed across to the guest chamber a short distance from the Good Brothers' enclosure. Raphael Roseblood, sitting on a wall bench, leaned forward, feet apart, and threaded his fur-lined cap through his hands. The verses of the psalm were appropriate; the season of the sword was fast approaching. He glanced at his father sitting beside him, his back against the wall, face down, eyes half closed. He was not sleeping but, as he always did in such situations, carefully plotting. Across the herb-strewn flagstone floor, Raphael's younger brother Gabriel, garbed in the earth-coloured sacking of his order, sandals on his feet, hair neatly tonsured, knelt on the prie-dieu beneath the cross of San Damiano. Father had informed Gabriel of the deaths of Eleanor, Dorcas and Father Roger, the attempted abduction of Katherine and her safe return due to the brave intervention of the Yorkist clerk.

Once again Raphael peered at his father. Simon looked wearied. He had been left distraught, almost to the point of madness, by the abductions, but this had turned to speechless joy at Katherine's safe return. Sevigny had been very astute, avoiding all drama. Katherine had appeared, cloaked and hooded, in the tavern porch, to be swept away by her father. Sevigny had only returned after dark, slipping into the tavern to join them in the Camelot Chamber. Simon's joy at Katherine's return had been tempered by the news of the deaths of the others. He had, for a short while, kept to his own chamber. When he re-emerged, his face, still not fully recovered from his furtive escapade in the lazar house, was drawn and tear-stained, his eyes dulled and red-rimmed.

Father Roger's suicide had remained confidential. Father Benedict had been summoned to join Simon's council, where Katherine had informed him about what she had heard, seen and felt. The old parish priest simply shook his head, threading his Ave beads as he listened. Once Katherine had finished, he sat for a while, head down. When he looked up, his craggy, lined face was twisted in sorrow.

'Roger was strange. I tried to treat him as a son,' he murmured. 'A man besotted with his own mother. After her funeral, I did detect a most subtle change. He was a priest who always found his celibacy a great cross, but a murderer . . . ?'

'I have seen the same.' Simon spoke up. 'As I am sure others have: men who hate women to the point of violence.'

'And I have heard similar stories in the shriving pew.' The old priest sighed. He got to his feet and nodded at Sevigny. 'My thanks, sir, for bringing home our little Roseblood. What I have seen and heard in this chamber I regard as sacred and secure, as under the seal of confession. Simon,' Father Benedict spread his gnarled hands, 'whatever Roger was, whatever he did, I cannot leave his body to rot in a latrine ditch. Dorcas too; her corpse should be brought home.'

'Katherine will give me precise details,' Simon replied. 'I will provide a cart and some of my men. As for the burial, Father, I will leave that to you.'

The priest thanked him and, lost in his own thoughts, walked slowly towards the door.

'Father?'

'Yes, Simon?'

'Eleanor . . .' The taverner fought to keep the tremble out of his voice. 'How much did she tell you?'

'My friend,' Father Benedict walked back, 'not a day passed that Eleanor did not mourn for your brother. She told me that he was her soul, her life.'

Simon swallowed hard, as if he had been struck. He closed his eyes, not wanting to meet the searching gaze of Raphael and Katherine.

'And her illness?' He opened his eyes, blinking furiously.

'She complained about pain but dismissed it as some petty ailment. Simon, Eleanor has gone. I will sing masses for her soul, but I wager she is more at peace now than she ever was.'

The priest left. Simon sat quietly for a while before abruptly asserting himself and summoning the mute, who stood guard on the door.

'Ignacio,' he spoke even as his fingers translated his words, 'the King has issued his writ. I must leave with men from this ward to join the royal marshals of array. You, however, take careful note of what I tell you. Find, if possible, the corpses of Roger and Dorcas. Take as many men as you can summon, all those who owe me favours, both here and beyond. Search out Cottesloe village. LeCorbeil will have left. Find the remains of Mistress Eleanor, preserve them in waxed linen sheets and bring them here for burial. Then,' he smiled dourly, 'burn that village and everything in it. Pollute the well and, before you leave the area, spread the word about those hidden pits. Tell the farmers and peasants that there is a veritable treasure of stores to be unearthed. Don't worry,' he laughed sharply, 'those moorlands by the sea might be deserted now, but when the news spreads, not for long. Order the fishermen to keep a sharp eye out for French ships.'

Satisfied, Simon brusquely turned to other business, listening again to Katherine and Sevigny's description of what had happened.

'And what will you do now, Master Clerk?' he demanded of Sevigny.

'Thanks to you,' Sevigny replied wryly, 'my visit to London was not as successful as it should have been, but,' he pulled a face, 'I will tell my master what I have seen and heard. After that . . .' He paused, as if choosing his words carefully. 'My lord and I have reached a parting of the ways. I will formally withdraw from his service, both pen and sword.'

'He will permit that?'

'Reluctantly, but he will know exactly what his loving wife tried to do; I've told you about Bardolph. York and I are finished.'

'And then?'

'Times are changing, Master Simon.' Sevigny smiled quizzically at Katherine. 'I shall certainly return.'

Raphael had glimpsed the deep blush in his sister's face, as had his father, who just nodded and casually told Sevigny he would always be welcome. Raphael knew then that Sevigny was the chosen suitor for Katherine's hand—

'Brother, Father. You wanted to see me?' Raphael broke from his reflection and glanced up sharply. Gabriel had finished reciting the De Profundis and was standing before them, hands in the sleeves of his robe.

'And you, my son, wanted to see us.' Simon stirred.

'Yes, yes.'

'Why did you do that?' Raphael asked. 'How did you do that?'

Gabriel stared back, blinking like an owl. You look like Uncle Edmund, Raphael thought; the same serene face, eyes ever watchful.

'Brother?' Gabriel asked.

Raphael got to his feet, seized his brother by the shoulders, drew him close and gave him the kiss of peace.

'What did you mean?' Gabriel demanded, stepping back. 'Why did I do that, how did I do that?'

'Look so pious,' Raphael teased. 'As if you are about to ascend into Heaven.'

Gabriel stared at his brother, then burst out laughing, a merry sound that filled the austere chamber and gave Gabriel that boyish, impish look that so attracted others. Their father, roused from his inertia, joined in.

'I am sorry,' Simon declared, 'to bring such doleful news, so it is good to laugh. I will leave silver for masses to be sung for our dead. Now, Gabriel, your brother and I have been summoned to a meeting of the royal Council at the Tower.'

'I heard that the militia is being raised and the King is to leave London, and so am I.' Gabriel smiled at his father's surprise. 'But let Prior Aelred explain. I believe he is waiting.' And without further ado, Gabriel hurried from the chamber. Raphael walked across to stare at a wall painting depicting St Francis embracing a leper.

'I could not do that,' Simon remarked drily. 'I have had enough of lepers to last me a lifetime . . .'

He broke off as Gabriel returned with Prior Aelred. The Franciscan clasped hands with both visitors and introduced Brother Wilfred, their recently appointed almoner, a round tub of a man with a jolly face. Raphael had to bite his lip: Wilfred looked exactly like the mummer who played Friar Tuck in the Robin Hood masque staged every spring in the Great Cloister at the Roseblood. Once the introductions were finished, Prior Aelred came swiftly to the point.

'Master Simon, you are on your way to the Tower to meet the royal Council, yes?' Simon agreed. 'We too,' the prior explained, 'have met the Council, at the request of our provincial and minister general. They wish us to mediate with the Duke of York and seek his admission into the King's peace. Brother Wilfred and your son Gabriel will join me. We intend to leave on the morrow.'

Raphael hid his astonishment. He glanced quickly at his younger brother, who smiled and shrugged. Raphael winked back, even as he felt the tug at his heart; that smile, the shrug, brought back sweet memories of Uncle Edmund, who had exerted such influence over Gabriel. Simon, however, just sat as if studying the cracks in the ancient paving stone.

'Why my brother?' Raphael asked. 'He is only a novice and has not yet taken solemn vows. Would you agree, Father?'

Simon did not reply. Raphael secretly wondered if his father's grief over Eleanor's death, as well as his rage at the insults heaped on his daughter, had blunted his wits. He remained sitting, head down.

'We want him to go,' Aelred declared. 'Gabriel is young, strong and a good companion. He knows about this city.' The prior's gaze quickly shifted to Simon. 'He is more than aware of, how can I put it, the complexities of our situation.'

'Yes, let him go.' Simon rose to his feet. 'Gabriel is not in vows, so he needs my permission. He can leave with you, Prior, on one condition: that my eldest son,' he winked swiftly at Raphael, 'also accompanies you.'

Gabriel clapped his hands. Raphael decided to remain silent, whilst the prior pulled a face and whispered to Wilfred, who just nodded.

'We agree.' Aelred held out his hand; Simon, then Raphael, clasped it.

'We will leave tomorrow morning,' the prior warned. 'Just before dawn.'

'And we will leave now.' Simon picked up his cloak from the bench. 'The Council expect us before the market horn sounds.' They confirmed the arrangements, Simon and Raphael had a few brief words with Gabriel, then they slipped out of Greyfriars along the narrow lanes leading down to the Tower.

The crowds were out; a throng of shifting colour jostling and shoving past the stalls heaped high with bales of coloured cloth, copper, bronze and pewter pots, lace from Liege, leather from Cordova, spices from Outremer. Traders and apprentices shouted their cries. Itinerant cooks with their mobile stoves on barrows pushed their way through. For a while Raphael and his father hurried on without speaking, knocking aside the wandering fingers of nips and foists. Both men pulled their cowls up so that they could slip unnoticed past the dung collectors, market beadles and street beggars.

At last they reached Dowgate, where they decided to hire a four-oared barge flying the livery of the city to take them along the Thames. The river was fast-flowing. They hurtled under the towering mass of London Bridge, the water crashing furiously against the starlings. Once through to the other side, Raphael could glimpse the severed heads of traitors stark against the light sky.

They disembarked at Tanners' Wharf, a little distant from their destination. York's spies, as well as those of Sheriff Malpas, kept a close eye on those who left and entered the Tower by barge. They fought their way through the crowd of porters, creelmen and other common carriers trundling barrows or dragging sledges heaped high with skins to the nearby tanning sheds. A filthy place, reeking of foul smells, where a miasma of red-flecked smoke ebbed and flowed. The laystalls were crammed high with refuse, which included the swelling corpses of horses, cats and dogs, a banqueting hall for teeming rats and flocks of scavenging kites. The ground underfoot was a foul muck of manure, mud and rotting entrails that wept filth like pus from an infected wound. The noise and din from the makeshift sheds and bothies was incessant. The apprentices who worked there, all smudged black by the smoke, pounded and flayed the skins under the vigilant eye of their masters, who bawled a stream of instructions. Only once did silence fall, when the funeral bell from a local parish church tolled to solicit the prayers of the faithful for the peaceful soul-flight of a member of the tanners' guild. Simon and Raphael could not converse and found they had to cling to each other to keep their balance as they crossed the slippery ground.

'My apologies,' Simon whispered. 'I had forgotten how bad this was.'

They left the tanners' concourse and headed down an arrow-thin alleyway reeking of rotting fruit and into a tavern that boasted the sign 'Three Turns of a Tide'. This macabre establishment was managed by the Thames hangman who executed river pirates on the line of gallows further down the bank, making sure his victims dangled until the tide had turned three times. The hangman-cum-taverner was keen to proclaim his trade. A long dark brown coffin in the centre of the taproom served as the common table. Dim light was provided by candles placed in the skulls of executed pirates mounted along the walls, whilst a hangman's noose dangled from the rafters above a rusting gibbet.

'Old Peterkin,' Simon murmured, 'enjoyed a macabre humour. He is now gone the way of all flesh and his heir does not know me.' He pushed Raphael into the shadows beneath the tavern's only window. A slattern brought their order, two stoups of strong London ale. Simon tasted it, smacked his lips and toasted Raphael. 'Go with the Good Brothers,' he declared. 'Be a member of their peace party. Raphael, war will break out. If Beaufort is triumphant, then we have nothing to fear. If Beaufort goes down, York will try to indict me. If I am still alive and escape, it's best if I flee abroad for a while. They will then try to sequester my property—'

'But if I can show I was with Holy Mother Church, pleading for peace?' Raphael broke in.

'Precisely,' Simon agreed. 'In this we safeguard the family. I may have to flee, but you and the rest will remain safe in the Roseblood. Now listen, Sevigny asked to speak to me alone. What I now know, so must you. Sevigny may well renounce his allegiance to York, but he has warned me about LeCorbeil. They know what I seized at St Giles. They fish in troubled waters and stir the mess for the sake of a stink; they are mercenaries and killers. Sevigny met their leader at Cottesloe. He boasted, albeit discreetly, how LeCorbeil were responsible for the death of the "greyhounds". That is the insignia of the Talbots of Shrewsbury, who were killed at Castillon. Now they hunt Beaufort.' He sipped again at his tankard. 'Beaufort must not underestimate, as I have, the sheer malevolence of LeCorbeil. They attack me and mine, they lead galleys up the Thames, they prepare for a French landing in Essex and now they intend to join York, eager to seize the opportunity to murder all on their list for vengeance.'

'But war could still be avoided?' Raphael asked.

'I doubt it. York will demand Somerset's arrest and trial, whilst the Beauforts will insist that York disband his forces, give assurances of loyalty and return to his post in Ireland.'

'So Beaufort will fight as well?'

'I have no doubt about that. It depends on the King, and our noble but very pious prince is loath to spill blood, so let us see.'

They left the tavern and made their way along the thoroughfare to the Tower. Soldiers, hobelars, men-at-arms and archers were also streaming either up to the great fortress or to the mustering grounds at Moorfields to the north. Warhorses, pack ponies and creaking carts created a deafening din. The air was heavy with smoke, sweat, leather and the acrid stench of gunpowder. Knights in half-armour, acting as banner men and standard-bearers, tried to impose order. All around flared the gorgeous colours of heraldic insignia and devices: the gules of Buckingham, the wyvern wings of Clifford, the crimson unicorn of Dorset as well as the golden lions rampant of the royal household. Simon and Raphael kept their faces hidden as they slipped through the Lion Gate. A clerk wearing the insignia of the Secret Seal was waiting for them in the courtyard beyond. When he pulled back his cowl, Raphael stared into the smiling face of Reginald Bray.

'Come.' He gestured. 'Master Simon, Their Graces the King and Queen will meet with you privately. My lord the Duke of Somerset will, of course, also be present.'

'Of course,' Simon agreed.

Bray glanced quizzically at the taverner and led them off along the cobbled, twisting battle runs that stretched beneath the soaring walls of the Tower. The great fortress, Raphael noticed, had truly become a house of war. Carts and wagons stood ready, stacked high with pieces of armour, helmets, brigandines, pole-axes, swords and spears. The smithies and armouries were busy, fire flashing against blackened walls as the smiths worked over their anvils. Horses were being led out, hooves and harnesses checked. The engines of war were being scrubbed and oiled. The squealing from the hog pens was chilling as the fleshers cut the pigs' throats, slashing their corpses, whilst others removed the entrails and tossed the hacked flesh into great vats of salted boiling water. Trumpets rang, horns brayed; messengers and scurriers, all booted and spurred, waited outside chambers ready to take messages from their lords closeted within.

Bray did not stop to comment, while the strident clamour and noise hampered any conversation. They reached the Garden Tower and turned into the great bailey that stretched around the soaring white keep, with its narrow windows and four lofty turrets. Knights of the royal household, resplendent in blue-gold livery, stood on guard. Bray had a word with these, showed their passes and they entered the White Tower, climbing the steep steps into the beautiful chapel of St John the Evangelist, an oval room with drum-like pillars down each side. At the far end stood a pure white ivory altar. Torches and beeswax candles clothed the chapel in a serene golden light. Frankincense, myrrh and sweet aloes perfumed the air. Just to the right of the altar sat the King, enthroned on a gilt-edged chair of state. Bray bowed and led Simon and Raphael towards him. Halfway up, he paused, gesturing at his companions to do likewise.

'Her Grace,' he whispered, 'will greet you first.'

On a quilted stool close to the King's right hand sat Queen Margaret, a veritable snow queen, Raphael thought as they approached, her lustrous blond hair not quite hidden by a beautiful gauze veil. An exquisite woman, with a rounded pale face, perfectly formed features and the most striking blue eyes, she was dressed in a high-necked gown of cloth of gold bedecked with dark red roses and deep green lozenges. Margaret of Anjou, already described as the She-Wolf, mother of the heir, the infant Prince Edward, looked what she was, a truly indomitable woman.

She rose swiftly to greet them; when Raphael and Simon genuflected at her feet, she softly stroked their heads, murmuring compliments in broken English. Raphael stared up into the beautiful face. She extended a hand, and he kissed the slender fingers glittering with rings encrusted with precious stones of every kind and colour.

'Please.' The Queen stepped back and gestured towards her husband.

Henry was a stark contrast to the vivid energy and exuberance of his wife. He was swathed in a thick blood-red cloak lined with ermine, slippers on his feet, a woollen cap pushed down on his head. He crossed himself, sighed deeply and straightened up, beckoning Simon and Raphael to kneel on the footstool before him. The King's long white face was lined with care, eyes dull, mouth twitching; now and again he would rub a rag across his mouth to remove the bubbling spittle. Simon and Raphael kissed his hands, then joined Bray sitting on a bench placed at an angle to the King's throne. Liveried servants, wearing soft buskin slippers, served cups of chilled white wine. The retainers moved soft as ghosts and Raphael recalled how the King could not tolerant harsh or strident sounds.

Whilst the wine and marzipan strips were served, the man who had been sitting quietly on the King's left rose, stepped off the dais and, having smilingly clasped hands, introduced himself to Raphael. Edmund Beaufort, second Duke of Somerset, was a strikingly good-looking man. His blond hair was cropped close like that of a priest, whilst his face reminded Raphael of a painting of an archangel he had seen in the castle chapel at Dover: strong features, piercing blue eyes, full red lips and a strong chin. His nose was slightly twisted from a blow in battle; his skin was a light tawny colour. He was clean-shaven, his face glistening with perfumed oil. A falcon of a man, Raphael concluded, sharp-witted, possibly imperious, but, as now, devastatingly charming. He had the long legs and arms of a born horseman and swordsman, yet he was dressed like any court fop in a tawny quilted jerkin with puffed sleeves and a high gold-encrusted collar, tight deep-blue hose pushed into soft boots of the same colour as his jerkin. He was armed: a war belt of the costliest leather, stitched with silver thread, circled his slim waist, and he carried a jewel-hilted dagger in a gold-plated sheath. This concession was a sign of the Queen's great confidence in him; very few were permitted to wear arms in the royal presence. Simon and Raphael had given their own war belts to the guards outside without a second thought, and even Master Bray had handed over his dagger.

Once the introductions were finished, Beaufort ordered

the chapel to be cleared. He spoke quickly in Norman French, snapping his fingers, gesturing at the servants and guards to leave and close the door behind them. Once they were gone, he sat down beside the King, who still stared, eyes narrowed, as if searching for something. Raphael noticed how Henry's hands were wreathed in Ave beads, and when his great cloak slipped, the mass of chains carrying miniature reliquaries slung around his neck could be clearly seen.

'Your Grace.' Margaret turned to grasp her husband's hand.

'I shall die here,' the King declared loudly.

'Nonsense, Your Grace.' Beaufort's voice was clipped; the duke stared despairingly across at his beloved Queen.

'My father,' the King continued, as if unaware of the interruption, 'died screaming in the marshes outside Meaux, his bowels turned to a sludge of putrid matter and blood. He must have seen the ghosts of the myriads he had slain both in France and here. They would have gathered around his bed, bodies all rent and split, blood-caked mouths open in protest.' He paused, 'My father shouted that he was not lost, how his soul was with the Lord Jesus. When I die here, I wish to breathe my last with a similar prayer.'

Beaufort made to speak, but Henry raised his hand, and for just a few heartbeats Raphael glimpsed the steel in this strange king's will. He recalled the stories of how Henry V, the King's father, had been a bloodthirsty warrior, whilst his mother, Katherine of Valois, was of tainted stock.

'Your Grace.' The Queen's voice thrilled with passion. 'You have many years to reign, more sons to raise, a kingdom to rule.'

'I will shed no man's blood,' snapped Henry, abruptly asserting himself. 'I will not have the blood of my beloved cousin York – or indeed of anyone – on my hands. I have peered into the darkness of the night and seen visions.' He rattled the rosary beads around his hands. 'Our earth is soaked with innocent blood; this gives voice to countless calls for vengeance, so loud, so strident that they even drown that of our father Abel, whom Cain slew with the jaw bone of an ass.'

'Your Grace,' Beaufort pleaded. 'We wish to live in peace too, but our spies and scouts have returned. York and his Neville allies are moving south with great force and banners raised.' The duke gestured at Simon and Raphael. 'Master Roseblood is no common taverner. He is a vintner and an alderman of the city; more importantly, he controls the streets and listens to the chatter of the marketplace. Sire, York's minions plot our downfall only a bowshot from here. He intends war.'

'Let him sit on the Council.' The King smiled as if the idea was original.

'Your Grace, York will not sit on the Council unless,' Margaret gestured at Beaufort, 'unless Edmund Beaufort, second Duke of Somerset, is surrendered into his care. Sweet husband,' she insisted, 'if Edmund is handed over, he will die, and whose hands will be stained with his blood?'

Henry closed his eyes and shook his head, unable to concentrate. Beaufort slipped to one knee from his stool.

'Sire, I beg you, unfurl the royal standard. Order the heralds of your household to proclaim the King's peace. Instruct all sheriffs and bailiffs that anyone, and I repeat, sire, anyone who then advances against your royal banner be regarded as a traitor guilty of high treason, so forfeiting life and goods.'

Beaufort's plea echoed like a funeral knell around that ghostly chapel. Queen Margaret clutched her husband's wrist, but he gently loosened her grip.

'I will die here,' he declared in a ringing voice. 'I, the lamb, will break the seal of God's vengeance and justice.' He struck his breast three times. '*Mea culpa, mea culpa, mea maxima culpa* – through my fault, through my fault, through my most grievous fault. My blood will atone for that of King Richard, foully slain by my grandfather at Pontefract Castle.' He raised his hands like a priest at mass. '*Ecce Agnus Dei, ecce qui tollit peccata mundi*,' he intoned. 'Behold the Lamb of God, behold him who takes away the sins of the world.' His sorrowful voice filled that ancient chapel. 'I shall atone for the rivers of blood created by my grandfather and sire, from the royal blood of Pontefract to that of the saintly Joan the Maid.' He paused, head down, then struck his breast again and mumbled the 'I confess' before falling silent.

An eerie hush descended. A draught from somewhere made the torchlight dance, and for a brief while, the candlelight seemed to turn a pale blue. Raphael shivered and recalled the ancient tale about how ghosts turned all flames blue. Some men said Henry was a saint, others a fool. Raphael could sense the King's obduracy as well as the sheer desperation of Beaufort. He glanced swiftly at Simon, but he sat, hands on knees, staring fixedly at the King. Was Henry really mad, Raphael wondered, or was he secretly pursuing vengeance against not York but Edmund Beaufort, second Duke of Somerset, alleged lover of the Queen and, as some evil tongues wagged, the true father of Margaret's only son? He reflected on the present danger: if the King would not move, Beaufort would fall and the consequences for the Rosebloods might be devastating.

'We shall go to meet Cousin York,' Henry murmured. 'I have already asked the Franciscan, Friar Aelred, to take messages of peace to Duke Richard.' For the first time the King seemed to notice Raphael and Simon. He glanced at them and smiled, which transformed his pallid, narrow face. 'I understand, Master Roseblood, that one of your sons will be part of that Franciscan delegation?'

'Indeed two, sire,' Raphael replied quickly. 'I have also been asked to join them in their quest for peace.'

'Good, good,' murmured the King. 'Tomorrow you will leave.'

'But sire,' Beaufort, who had been communicating with the Queen with his eyes, spoke up, 'the Rosebloods are here to advise you about York's great treachery, his alliance with enemies of this realm.' And before the King could object, he ordered Simon to give his news.

He did so, swift and succinct, describing York's meddling in the city, the presence of Sevigny, the duplicity of Sheriff Malpas, the attempt to rob the silver and above all, the presence of LeCorbeil and what they intended. Raphael watched the royal party and felt a sharp spurt of fear. Beaufort was truly whistling into the dark; the King still wanted peace. Despite Simon's stark description of the threat LeCorbeil posed, Henry was not moved.

'We will order the Sheriff of Essex,' he declared, 'to ensure the village of Cottesloe is cleared. We shall search for these hidden pits, and my lord of Beaufort will send a war cog to stand off the mouth of the Orwell.'

Simon pressed on. He described the scurrilous writing of Argentine. How he had closed that physician's filthy mouth once and for ever and destroyed his chronicle. Again the King was impassive. Once Simon had finished, Henry thanked him graciously and invited both father and son to kiss his hands. The meeting ended in an atmosphere of deep exasperation. Henry rose and wandered down the nave to stare at a wall painting depicting St John on the island of Patmos. Queen Margaret rose and collapsed quietly sobbing into the arms of Beaufort.

'*Nous sommes tous perdus*,' she whispered hoarsely. 'We are all lost.'

Beaufort tried to comfort her, then beckoned Bray, Simon and Raphael to join him in the aisle. Once assembled, the duke stood drumming his fingers against his dagger hilt, watching narrow-eyed as the

Queen went to join her husband at the far end of the chapel.

'We will march north,' he whispered. 'We have troops enough. Raphael, go with the Franciscans, let us know what happens.' He took a deep breath. 'Master Bray, you will stay with me. Before we leave London, destroy any document that may prove dangerous. Simon, summon your levies and march with us. I want you to organise a cohort of bowmen to protect me.' He gnawed the corner of his lip as he stared down the nave at the King and Queen. 'It has begun,' he whispered. 'Remember this day, this meeting; this is where it all began. The kingdom will be torn apart. Mark this well; look to yourselves also, for the very Devil is loose.'

Amadeus Sevigny

St Albans, 22 May 1455

Amadeus Sevigny crossed himself, unbuckled his war belt, laid it beside his gauntlets on the small table and knelt down on a flock-filled cushion before Richard, Duke of York. Sevigny was here for the diffidatio, the solemn refutation of allegiance to his seigneur. He stared into his lord's blood-flecked light green eyes, noting the grey in the once silver hair and freshly clipped moustache and beard, the deep furrows of care around the duke's eyes and down his cheeks.

They were alone in this strange six-sided exorcist's chamber built into the north wall, close to the Devil's door of St Swithin's church, which served the hamlet of Key Field, close to St Albans, where the royal forces had set up camp. Sevigny had arrived the night before, and in whispered conversations had informed York about Malpas, the situation in London and, above all, the alleged prophecies of Ravenspur. He had kept silent about Katherine Roseblood and his own secret meetings with her father and family.

York had been taciturn, distracted, more interested in Ravenspur's prophecies than anything else, asking Sevigny to repeat them time and again. Sevigny had decided to keep his own counsel. Soon York would no longer be his lord, and if the duke wished to dabble in sorcery, then he must pay the consequences. If he patronised LeCorbeil, that too would demand a price. Sevigny had informed York, without giving precise details, how LeCorbeil, although acting as mercenaries, were certainly in the pay of the French Crown and might even be planning to aid a landing by their countrymen along the deserted coast of Essex. York had been dismissive about that; he would, he claimed, use LeCorbeil to win his rightful place on the Council of the King and provide strong government. Only in this way could England be defended from outside attack. Sevigny had accepted this in silence. There was much left unsaid. Both he and York knew that the good duke and his family were intent not just on controlling the royal Council but on seizing the crown itself. Eventually York had dismissed him, but told him to meet him here in this eerie chamber just before dawn. Outside, in St Swithin's spacious graveyard, the duke's retainers were preparing for York to meet the Franciscan envoys.

'So, Amadeus, you have come to bid farewell.' York's voice was soft, and Sevigny, for all his mistrust, caught a genuine sadness in the duke's eyes.

'I have come,' Sevigny half smiled, 'to formally withdraw from your household and service.'

'My clerk has destroyed the indenture,' York agreed. 'And now,' he stretched out his hands, and Sevigny gripped them in the solemn clasp of farewell, 'I withdraw my protection from you, Amadeus Sevigny. You are no longer in my love, but I shall do nothing to hurt you.'

'Or to help me,' Sevigny broke in. 'Bardolph the bowman was no assistance.'

'I know, I know.' York glanced away; when he looked back, tears laced his eyes. 'I have always loved you, Amadeus. I saw you as a son, a skilled clerk, a true warrior, but above all, a man of good heart.' He paused. Sevigny guessed what he was going to say next; no wonder he had insisted that all his servants and henchmen leave the church. 'My wife Cecily, the duchess . . .' He glanced up. 'I love her, Amadeus.'

'And you need her kinsmen, the Nevilles?'

'Yes, yes, I do.' York balled his fingers into a fist and gently beat against Sevigny's shoulder. 'Amadeus, you heard Ravenspur's prophecies. Richard II was deposed by the House of Lancaster. The House of York has a better claim. The crown is our destiny, our right.'

'Ravenspur is a witch, a warlock, a traitor. He may help you,' Sevigny lifted one hand, as if taking an oath, 'but, I swear in this holy place, once he has inflicted vengeance on Beaufort, he will turn his fighting dogs on you. Moreover, if he had found Argentine's chronicle—'

'Well he didn't, and neither did you,' York snapped.

'You say Roseblood may have it.' He shrugged one shoulder. 'It doesn't matter now.' He added in a half-whisper, 'I am sure our French bitch-queen will think the same as me: at least Argentine is dead and his prattling tongue is silenced for ever.' He got to his feet. 'The diffidatio, this renunciation of homage, is completed. Strange,' he mused, gesturing around. 'This was once an exorcism chamber, a holy place to eject demons and drive them out through the north door. Today, Sevigny, I will exorcise mine—' He broke off abruptly and strode out of the chamber, calling over his shoulder that the rest of his household would be waiting to receive the Franciscan delegation.

Sevigny stood listening to his former lord stride away. He realised why York had stopped himself so sharply. The duke had been on the verge of conceding that whatever the Franciscans said or offered, he intended to attack immediately. Such suspicions had been pricked when Sevigny first arrived in the camp the night before. He had seen the preparations: phalanxes of spearmen being organised, archers waiting at arrow carts, war bows being strung, daggers and maces distributed. The King and Beaufort had moved north and were now lodged at St Albans, a few miles away. Today, 22 May, the Year of Our Lord 1455, would not pass unnoticed. King Henry could talk peace to the last trumpet, but York intended to seize the moment and settle matters once and for all.

Sevigny doubted whether any battle orders had been distributed to the royal levies. He recalled riding through

St Albans over a year ago, its narrow streets leading on to the main thoroughfare of St Peter's Lane. Those streets could be infiltrated by men-at-arms supported by archers. He thought of LeCorbeil creeping forward, arbalests primed, intent on one target and one alone: the total destruction of the Beaufort lords and their allies. He stared up at a stone carving of a crowned angel and suppressed a shiver. Was it just the Beaufort lords York wanted to destroy? What if the King was slain, even his lady wife? Their son was only a child, and York would not tolerate the prince living any longer than his parents. Others were also in St Albans, unaware of the trap closing around them, including Simon Roseblood and his Queenhithe company.

'Amadeus,' York's voice rang out, 'your last task.'

Sevigny joined the duke near the baptismal font. York clutched his arm as a sign of farewell, then strode forward and opened the great door of the church, going out on to the wide, sweeping steps to receive the acclamation of his massed troops. For a short while Sevigny was blinded by the rising sun, dazzled by shimmering steel and the myriad colours of heraldic devices that seemed to fill the church's great cemetery. He glimpsed the blue and murrey of York hoisted above the raven's sable, the ragged staffs and muzzled bears, the blue, yellow, scarlet, green and gold of fluttering pennants and standards. The hoarse voices of the thronging soldiery chanted greetings. Over all swept the smoke and stench of war. Destriers eager for the charge pawed the ground, metal shoes drawing sparks. Archers were stringing their bows, their boys mixing pots of fiery charcoal; nearby, war carts laden with barrels of pitch stood at the ready. Sevigny glanced at these and recalled the thatched roofs and wood and plaster walls of those houses in St Albans, where men might hide only to be burnt out.

He followed the duke to the edge of the steps and glanced to his right, where York's waiting lords, already dressed in half-armour, grouped around the mastiff-faced Richard Neville, Earl of Warwick, a man by his own public admission born to war and keen for the kill. For a while York just stood revelling in his power before raising his arms in salute, to be greeted by fresh roars of approval and the ominous clatter of swords against shields. This was a war host intent on battle, whatever courtly formalities might take place.

York moved across to whisper to Warwick. Sevigny swiftly surveyed the massed ranks and found what he was searching for: the dark blood-red livery with its black crow wings spread. LeCorbeil! They stood, about sixty in number, under the standard of a crow in full flight. They did not join in the general acclamation, but just watched silently, at their feet the arbalests with which they were so skilled. Sevigny used the excitement of the acclamation to study LeCorbeil more closely. He searched out their leader, Bertrand, a cloak half hiding his mailed shirt, standing slightly forward. 'A veritable hawk of a man,' he whispered to himself. 'Like me, a killer to the bone.' His hand fell to the hilt of his dagger. If battle came and God was good, he would seek out Bertrand and kill him.

York continued to revel in the salutation, until Warwick sidled up, whispering in his ear and pointing across the great cemetery. Sevigny followed his direction and glimpsed the Franciscans in their earth-coloured robes assembled under the massive lychgate. York signalled to his heralds, and the trumpeters blew shrill blasts, stilling the clamour. Once silence had fallen, the words of the 'Veni Creator Spiritus' wafted clear and strong as the Franciscans, led by Brother Gabriel carrying a cross, moved up the paved cemetery path to kneel on the bottom step to the church: Prior Aelred, Wilfred, Gabriel and, beside him, Raphael Roseblood, also garbed like a Franciscan in a simple brown robe. Raphael, still chanting the verses, glanced quickly at Sevigny, who just stared back.

Once the hymn was finished, Prior Aelred lifted his hands and in a clear, resounding voice declared the King's peace before moving on to the real content of his visit. York must disband his forces and withdraw to his post of Lord Lieutenant of Ireland; only then would the Council meet to discuss the resolution of his grievances. The prior laced his talk with allusions to Scripture and the classics. Finally he begged York to stay within the King's peace and enjoy his love. Then he fell silent.

York was brutal in his reply. Sevigny clearly saw the shock in the poor Franciscan's face.

'Henry Beaufort, Duke of Somerset,' bellowed Warwick on behalf of his master, 'must, for the sake of peace and the common good, surrender himself to His

Grace the Duke of York, without any qualification or quibbling, for judgement.'

'But my lord . . .' Aelred, still kneeling on the bottom step, clasped his hands in prayer. 'That will not happen.'

'Then we must,' Warwick shouted back, 'seize Beaufort as the traitor and felon he is and prepare him for judgement.'

'But the King—'

'The King is ill advised.' Warwick's powerful voice carried for all to hear. 'Beaufort must surrender himself within an hour of your return. Once Beaufort is removed, His Grace the King will be able to receive good counsel and guidance for the safety of his realm.'

'Go back to His Grace,' York called out. He gestured at Sevigny. 'My household clerk will accompany you and ensure your safety. Tell the King my terms.'

'Or else what?' Gabriel, kneeling beside his prior, spoke up.

'Or face war with fire and sword,' Warwick retorted.

'We are finished,' York declared, and spinning on his heel, he walked back into the church followed by Warwick and other of his captains.

Sevigny recalled Ravenspur's words. York would unleash his war dog Warwick. He hurried down the steps and, gesturing with his arms, swept the hapless Franciscans back along the path to the lychgate. Once there, he clasped their hands, teasing Gabriel that he recognised him immediately as his father's son. Then he indicated with his head.

'York's soldiers will not harm you, but LeCorbeil are

here. The King, and more importantly, your father, must be warned.'

'It is war!' Prior Aelred wailed. 'Our words meant nothing.'

'Good Father,' Amadeus retorted, 'not even an angel from heaven could change York's heart. Warwick is his war master; his host is well armed and prepared. As God is my witness, they hope to be in St Albans before the Angelus bell sounds. So hurry, we must go.'

He coaxed and bullied the Franciscans on to their sorry mounts, then harnessed Leonardo, collected his bulging pannier and checked his armour and harness on the sturdy sumpter pony. Nobody troubled them, though he glimpsed two of LeCorbeil watching intently. He ignored these, keeping up his haste. A short while later, he led the Franciscans and Raphael out of Key Field. Once they were in the countryside, he turned his destrier, going back to console Prior Aelred, who was almost in tears at his failure.

'Father,' he pleaded, 'you have done what you could. Remember the psalms: "Put not your trust in princes." York wants war sooner than you think; within the hour his troops will be on the move.'

He dug in his spurs and forced his escort to do likewise, galloping along the lanes and into the cobbled streets of St Albans. His heart sank at what he saw there. The blue and white standards of the royal household were everywhere, as well as the banners of the various Lancastrian lords. Troops were bivouacked in the town but were totally unprepared for any attack.

Streets and lanes were open; no carts or chains had been pulled across. Scouts and messengers galloped furiously south to where, Sevigny supposed, more royal forces were mustering, yet there were no defences to the north or east.

'In God's name!' he whispered. 'York could stroll in here and take what he wanted.'

A royal messenger gave him directions, and Sevigny led Prior Aelred's party up Cock Lane into the broad expanse of St Peter's Street. Only here had the danger been sensed. The busy main thoroughfare of the town was empty of its usual market stalls. Soldiers thronged about, but there seemed to be little preparation for an imminent attack. Sevigny and his party dismounted in the great tavern yard of the Castle Inn. Prior Aelred had urgent words with the knight bannerets of the royal chamber, and they were allowed into the spacious, sweet-smelling taproom.

The light was dim, the windows still shuttered, but the taverner had lit candles and lantern horns. A group of men and a woman, heavily swathed, sat around the great common table. A voice told the prior's party to approach. They stepped into a pool of light and genuflected. Sevigny recognised the warrior-faced Edmund Beaufort, Duke of Somerset, sitting at the centre of the table; on his right was the beautiful Margaret of Anjou, her halo of golden hair and lovely face shrouded in a dark blue ermine-lined hood. The rest of the men, like Beaufort, were in half-armour. They looked ill at ease, fingers dropping to the daggers on their belts or tapping at the platters and goblets on the table.

A member of the royal bodyguard standing in the shadows brought them tub stools to sit on. Beaufort pointed a finger at Sevigny.

'I recognise that face.'

'Amadeus Sevigny,' the clerk replied. 'Formerly of the secret chancery of His Grace the Duke of York.' His declaration provoked gasps and a few curses. 'I have left York's service.'

Beaufort nodded, eyes never leaving Sevigny.

'I can vouch for him.' A shadowy figure further down the table leaned forward. Sevigny recognised Simon Roseblood.

'As can I.' Reginald Bray stepped out of the shadows of a window seat behind the table.

'Then so do I,' Beaufort declared. 'Prior Aelred, what news do you bring?'

'War.' Sevigny spoke up. 'Battle within the hour. York is already marching on St Albans.'

'Impossible!' someone shouted. 'Our scouts—'

'My lord,' Sevigny insisted, 'I know York, or rather his master of war, Warwick. They assemble fully armed and will strike. They will not deploy, send heralds—'

Sevigny was interrupted by a scurrier, dusty face all sweat-strewn. He burst into the taproom and fell to his knees, pointing at the door and gabbling how the look-outs on the tower of St Peter's, where the King was attending the Jesus mass, had glimpsed the sheen of a moving body of armed men. The messenger paused to take a breath, and in answer to Sevigny's question confirmed that this was directly to the east of the town, adding that they were moving extremely swiftly.

Uproar ensued. The Lancastrian lords shouted for their retainers. Beaufort ordered the Queen to be escorted to the nearby abbey and dispatched household knights to St Peter's to seize the King.

'Drag him out if necessary,' he yelled, 'and bring him here. Master Simon!' He beckoned Roseblood out of the corner. 'See what you can discover and keep us informed.' As he spoke, he lifted his hands as a sign that his squires help him prepare for battle. 'Collect your company, small as it is,' he added wryly. 'Go to St Peter's, set up watch at the tower, send scurriers.' He flailed a hand in dismissal.

The taproom now became frenetically busy with knights and squires arming. Outside rose the clatter of steel, shouted orders and the neigh and clop of warhorses. Sevigny greeted Simon and clasped his hand. The taverner was already armed for war in a brigandine, a sallet in his hand, a war belt looped over his shoulder.

'Welcome, clerk.' Simon then embraced Gabriel and Raphael, warmly greeting Prior Aelred and Brother Wilfred. 'You had best stay with us,' he advised them. 'This is truly a day of wrath. Many good men are going to die.'

'You have the Roseblood company here?' Raphael asked.

'Some,' his father replied evasively. 'But come.'

They left for the chaotic stableyard, where Sevigny

collected Leonardo and his sumpter pony. Wilfred tried to soothe the agitated Aelred, whilst Gabriel fetched their mounts. Simon hurried away, then returned saying that his company was now outside. When they left to join them, Gabriel exclaimed at the small number: no more than twenty mounted archers wearing the livery of the vintners' company.

'Why so few?' Sevigny turned on Simon. 'For God's sake, man!'

'This battle,' Simon replied, 'was lost before it was ever fought. I realised that when we met the King at the Tower. I am more concerned about the second battle.'

'Which is?'

'LeCorbeil.'

Simon swung himself up into the saddle and led them off down St Peter's Street. Many of the town's citizens had fled. Soldiers were barricading the mouths of alleyways and streets. The royal standard had been set up on a war wagon being dragged into the centre of the marketplace. Beaufort's commanders were hastily deploying their forces, a long line stretching from St Peter's church in the north to the river Ver and the great abbey to the south, where many townspeople were now sheltering. Sevigny realised that the royalist forces were overextended; knowing York, he would seek a gap, a weakness, and dispatch a phalanx to smash their way through.

The noise in the streets heightened the sense of panic and fear. Citizens were shoving their way down to the abbey; women crying, children screaming, livestock wandering aimlessly adding to the confusion. Columns of archers and men-at-arms tried to push through. Horsemen gathered, attempting to form themselves into some sort of company, only to be broken up by the press of bodies, lowing cattle and heavy-wheeled carts. Fires had started, the flames leaping up against the blue sky, plumes of thick black smoke stinging eyes and throats.

Sevigny realised that Roseblood was correct: short of a miracle, this battle was already lost. He glimpsed through the shifting smoke haze a posse of royal knights, their pale-faced King at the centre, hurrying back down St Peter's Street to the Castle Inn, where Beaufort had set up his standard.

They entered St Peter's cemetery. Roseblood ordered his company to stay whilst he and Sevigny entered the dark, cold church. A priest tried to stop them, whining how he should secure the doors. Roseblood pushed him aside, shouting at Wormwood to follow them to act as their messenger. Sevigny led the way up the steep, winding staircase, its corners festooned with dust-laced cobwebs, the walls green with mould and damp. They reached the top, pushed back the trapdoor and, with the breeze buffeting them, stepped on to the shale-covered floor of the tower roof. Its crenellations were high and linked by rusting bars. The three men staggered across to lean against the ancient stonework, catching their breath.

Sevigny peered round, gazing out across the town, and his heart skipped a beat. The beautifully clear May morning, free of any haze or mist, revealed an awesome sight. The duke had moved swiftly. Two great battle divisions were advancing on St Albans. To the north, the blue and murrey standards of York could be clearly seen. To the south, the coloured banners of Salisbury. More terrifying, in the centre and even faster-moving, a column of archers, foot and mounted knights under the white ragged staff of Warwick was lunging like a spear directly at the town. Sevigny stared down at the King's forces, small, scurrying figures. A few of Beaufort's captains had recognised the danger. Some troops were moving up St Peter's Street to challenge York. Another force was moving fast downhill towards the river Ver and the precincts of the great abbey to check York's left flank under Salisbury. News of Warwick's imminent approach was also known. Many of the streets and alleyways to the east of the marketplace, were being hastily barricaded, archers and men-at-arms manning the defences.

'York intends to encircle the town,' Sevigny shouted against the stiff breeze. 'He will force an entry to both north and south, but it is Warwick . . .'

His voice trailed off at Simon's shouted curse. Behind Warwick's screed of archers came LeCorbeil in their dark blood-red livery and gleaming sallets, all grouped together in a phalanx under the crow banner. Warwick's division was advancing swiftly up Shropshire Lane, the central thoroughfare, outpacing the Yorkists to the north along Cock Lane, and Salisbury's force, which had reached Sopwell Street, leading to Holywell and up into the marketplace. Sevigny suspected that the three enemy commanders were competing to see who would seize the royal standard.

He looked again, drawn by the shouts, cries and clatter of weapons. Warwick's column was already trying to force the barricades. The archers manning these loosed volley after volley of arrows, swift showers of dark, deadly rain. Warwick's advance stumbled, broke and retreated. Sevigny watched the small figures scurrying back. The royalist centre column was holding its own, but Beaufort's captains had underestimated Warwick, and were too meagre to hold their defensive line between the Key and the Chequers, two ancient inns. Warwick's troops were peeling off under the banner of Sir Robert Ogle, his chief henchman, infiltrating the alleyways either side of the Lancastrians. Meanwhile his archers had inched forward. Again the arrow storm. Warwick's men replied with fire shafts against the barricades and the houses either side, whilst the dull thud and puffed smoke of cannons tainted the morning breeze.

The smoke shifted. Roseblood yelled, pointing down at the streets and alleyways either side of the royalist force battling Warwick. These runnels were now packed with soldiers wearing the white ragged staff, outflanking the barriers as well as racing towards the marketplace and the Castle Inn. Sevigny stared in horror. Roseblood screamed at Wormwood to warn Beaufort and the rest.

'We will go ourselves!' Sevigny shouted. 'We are no use here. Warwick, the cunning bastard, has broken through the wood and plaster walls of the houses either side. They will be in the marketplace soon, and LeCorbeil with them.'

They hurried, slipping and slithering, down the tower steps and into the cemetery. Warwick's surprise move was already deepening the confusion and chaos. Royalist troops were pouring out of the thoroughfares, terrified of being surrounded. They realised that York's forces were encircling the town and were fleeing to the only place of safety, the countryside to the west.

'We have to be careful,' Sevigny warned. He grasped Simon's arm. 'You are right, this battle is lost.'

They collected their company and entered St Peter's Street, riding as hard and fast as they could through the press of fleeing soldiery until they reached Beaufort's position at the Castle. The royalist commanders were totally unprepared. Taken by surprise at Warwick's unexpected manoeuvre, they had called in what meagre forces they could to fortify the tavern, but it was hopeless. The makeshift barricade across the stableyard gate was manned by a few archers and knight bannerets. Beaufort, Percy of Northumberland, Clifford, and Stafford of Buckingham were gathered in the courtyard; Sevigny and the Roseblood company were allowed in. One glance at Beaufort's panic-stricken face chilled Sevigny's heart.

'We cannot summon forces!' the duke declared. 'Our troops are moving,' he gestured wildly, 'either north or south. Warwick's men now control St Peter's Street.' He plucked at the delicately edged white collar of the cambric shirt beneath his dusty breastplate. 'We never thought,' he spoke as if to himself, 'we never thought they would advance so swiftly.' He turned away like a dream-walker to join Buckingham and the others.

The spacious tavern yard reflected the confusion and chaos of the royal forces. Horses whinnied and reared, panicked by the trailing plumes of smoke and the clamour of war cries beyond. Wounded men lay against the walls or on filthy straw beds in the stables and outhouses, gasping for water and screaming in pain at their wounds. More ominously, many of the able-bodied were beginning to desert. Archers, men-at-arms and even household knights slipped back into the tavern, hurrying along its stone-paved corridors to the great meadow at the rear, which stretched to thick copses of trees and the trackways leading to London: a welcome escape from what was fast becoming a bloody slaughter ground. Those who had horses led their mounts along the narrow paths between the tavern and its outbuildings, also intent on fleeing.

'Master Simon.' Sevigny and Roseblood turned. A dust-covered Reginald Bray, his face bruised and marked, beckoned them closer. 'We must leave.'

'But what about my lord?' Simon pointed at Beaufort. Bray handed him a small scroll. Simon, ignoring the growing clamour, unfurled it.

Beaufort and the other lords were now grouped around a distraught Henry. The King had emerged from the tavern and two of his retainers had brought a throne-like chair for him to sit on. He slouched, a forlorn figure, swaddled like a child in a blue robe, the gold circlet around his head slightly askew.

'My lord,' Bray hissed, 'insists that we flee, hide and wait for a better day. Simon, Master Sevigny, if we stay here we shall be slaughtered. York will try to annihilate Beaufort and all associated with him.'

'Flee?' Simon asked.

'Read the scroll,' Bray insisted.

The taverner did so, then closed his eyes, murmured a prayer and handed it to Sevigny. The message was terse. The Duke of Somerset thanked Simon Roseblood for his allegiance and loyalty, but begged him to take Master Bray and his company out of the battle should it go against them. He reminded Simon to be loyal to his kinswoman the Lady Margaret, and to render her the same service he had to her father and others of her name.

'We must do as he says,' Sevigny declared, even as the first crashing against the tavern gate and its barricade echoed across the courtyard. A shower of shafts, some of them fire arrows, forced them to retreat into the tavern porch. Beaufort and Buckingham were now screaming at the King to rise and move. Sevigny stared around. Within minutes the gate would be forced and the most hideous hand-to-hand fighting would break out. He knew York and Warwick. This was their day, and even if they faltered, LeCorbeil would certainly take up the struggle. There would be no chivalry; no surrender would be asked, no pardon offered, nothing but a fight to the death.

'Go!' he urged the Roseblood company. 'Go! Gabriel, Raphael, take Prior Aelred and Wilfred. We will join you.' Simon agreed, shouting to his sons to gather and wait at the far edge of the great meadow. Sevigny collected his mount and pushed Leonardo's reins into Raphael's hands. 'Take him and the sumpter pony—'

He broke off. Beaufort, Clifford and Buckingham were still shouting at the King, begging him to shelter in the tavern, but Henry was in shock. He sat gabbling to himself, his face white as snow. More arrows fell. Buckingham screamed, staggering away, an arrow deep in his right arm. Simon ran forward; smoke billowed and parted. Sevigny glimpsed figures garbed in dark red on ladders above the rim of the tavern wall. He shouted a warning, but a volley was loosed and a barbed bolt skimmed the King's face, a slicing cut. Henry crouched forward in pain, turning to Beaufort, who just stood staring speechlessly down at the crossbow bolt embedded in his own chest. Clifford staggered away, an arrow in his neck.

The red-garbed figures now swarmed like demons from Hell along the top of the tavern wall. A few archers and men-at-arms rushed to fend them off. Sevigny raced forward and grasped Simon's arm. 'It's over!' he shouted. 'There is nothing to be done.' Simon, his face white and tense, agreed and they left the tavern yard, hurrying along its passageways out into the garden. Raphael had assembled the company near the wicket gate leading to the great meadow. Sevigny noticed some empty saddles.

Wormwood, mouth all bloodied, told him that they had lost men in the retreat.

'Why so few?' Sevigny whispered. 'Such a small company?'

'Why bring so many to the slaughter?' Simon replied enigmatically, swinging himself up into the saddle. Sevigny did likewise and gazed across the bright greenness of the meadow. The royal army no longer existed. Men had doffed their livery and were fleeing for their lives.

'What now, Master Simon?' he asked.

The taverner just sat, head to one side, listening to the furious shouts of battle. 'Let us go,' he urged at last, and led them off through the gate into the meadow. They did not canter, but moved leisurely, a tightly formed company. Once they had reached the fringe of trees, Simon reined in and raised his hand. Around him milled two dozen or so of his company and the Franciscan envoys.

'What are you waiting for?' Sevigny asked.

Simon ordered Wormwood to unfurl the vintners' standard so that it could be clearly seen by the enemy, who had broken through the tavern and were now massing on the far side of the meadow. Sevigny mused aloud, 'I doubt whether York will follow in pursuit. The duke has got what he wants. He has captured the King and made sure that Beaufort and the others are dead. LeCorbeil are a different matter: they will pursue, yet you seemed eager to entice them on.'

'Master Sevigny,' Simon declared, 'I am tired of

LeCorbeil hunting me, threatening me and mine. I stood by the King and Beaufort. I have done my duty to my lord. Now I will do it for myself and my family. Rest assured, I have planned and I have plotted.' He stared, shielding his eyes against the noonday sun. 'You see them, Amadeus. The crows gather.' Sevigny followed his direction. LeCorbeil had now brought up their horses, mustering under their banner. 'They feasted well,' Simon murmured, 'and they are greedy to feast again, so let's help them.'

The taverner turned his horse, and Sevigny, glancing back over his shoulder, followed him through the copse of trees on to the great broad trackway leading south to London. Refugees from both the town and the battle now milled here. These would have little to fear. Beaufort's power was shattered and any pursuit by Yorkist forces might prove dangerous. Only LeCorbeil would sustain their feud to the death.

Amadeus and the rest rode for a while, a long line of horsemen galloping in a cloud of dust, forcing others to stand aside. Now and again they would pause, and Wormwood, who brought up the rear, assured them that LeCorbeil were in hot pursuit. Sevigny now realised that Roseblood was not as helpless as he pretended. The taverner intended a trap. They turned off the main trackway near the village of Isley and rode deep into the trees, Simon making sure that they were seen by others from the battle.

'They will tell LeCorbeil,' he confided to the clerk, 'who will think we are in a panic.'

'Until you spring the trap?'

'More a place of slaughter.' The taverner took off his sallet and wiped the sweaty dust from his face. 'Trust me, clerk, LeCorbeil are not the only ones who know about deserted villages. Cottesloe was one, Thorpensoke is another. You have heard of it, and its church, St Michael-in-the-Forest?' Sevigny shook his head. 'Well, the great Archangel will defend us on the day of battle.'

Simon broke off, summoning Wormwood and whispering in his ear, sending him off at a fast, furious gallop further along the trackway. The rest of them followed at a more leisurely pace, an eerie experience, the trees either side becoming more dense, the branches of ancient oaks stretching out to form a thick green canopy over the sun-dappled path. Now and again they disturbed a deer, which would swerve in a flicker of shifting colour deeper into the wooded darkness. Strange forest sounds trailed across; there were bursts of sunlight, then they rode even deeper into the shadowy silence of the trees. Simon ordered his men to deliberately drop pieces of armour or weapons. On one occasion he loosed those horses without riders back along the path, heightening the impression that his small company were fleeing in panic. Scraps of armour were left to glint beside water pannikins, cooking pots, the occasional broken spear shaft, the head of an axe, scabbards and parcels of dried meat and bread.

They pressed on. Eventually the trees gave way to a spacious glade, which led to the deserted village of Thorpensoke. They passed along the ancient high street, derelict houses, cottages and outbuildings ranged on either side. The great well, in what used to be the marketplace, was overgrown. They turned a corner; the high street widened, leading straight down to the grey, lichen-covered mass of St Michael-in-the-Forest, a magnificent building with a broad front, spacious steep steps and a heavy oaken door that had withstood the ravages of time. The company dismounted, their horses led away. Simon took out a hunting horn, blew three shrill blasts and waited. Sevigny, standing beside him, watched the trees behind the church. At first he thought his eyes were playing tricks, then he grinned at the scores of hooded men garbed in Lincoln green who emerged like silent ghosts.

Simon shouted for silence, ordering his own company to open the doors of the church and take the good brothers inside whilst he greeted the newcomers. Sevigny, counting quickly, reckoned there must be at least a hundred men, well armed with sword and dagger, each carrying a war bow with a quiver crammed with arrows slung across his back. The leading figure pulled back his hood, and Sevigny smiled at Roseblood's shadow, Ignacio. Hands were clasped, greetings exchanged, but from further back along the trackway came warning whistles. Simon urged Ignacio's company up the steps into the church, then followed them in. He and Sevigny pulled the ancient doors closed, lowering the great bar into its iron clasps.

'I had Ignacio prepare everything,' Simon gasped, leaning against the door. 'Look around you, clerk, see the trap that has been primed. The fowler's net is ready.'

Sevigny, quietly admiring Roseblood's cunning, turned and stared around the nave, which stretched, simple and stark, down to the chancel, sanctuary steps and ruined high altar. Narrow windows high in the wall afforded meagre sunlight. The nave was gloomy; even from where he stood, Sevigny found it difficult to distinguish the company making itself ready for battle.

'LeCorbeil will think we are trapped,' Simon murmured.

'They will force the doors,' Sevigny agreed, 'and will never expect what they find inside. When they do, it will be too late.'

He and Simon searched the church. Its one weakness was the number of side doors. These were boarded up and barred, though they could still provide entry. The north door, corpse door and sacristy door were vulnerable to attack. Sevigny ordered all three to be watched by small groups of bowmen and a few men-at-arms. The rest of the force were arranged in two long lines of archers, forty to each column, with a small reserve in the rear. As the hasty preparations were completed, Sevigny sensed the camaraderie amongst these men, all from Queenhithe, owing a deep allegiance to Simon and the rich life of his tavern. Most of them were former soldiers who had served in France.

Simon swiftly explained in hushed tones how, after his meeting in the Tower, he had realised that the royal army was marching to destruction. He pointed across to where Prior Aelred had taken sanctuary in the church's only side chapel.

'Beaufort could have sent all the angels of Heaven, but the King was reluctant to fight and York was determined to do so. I decided not to waste good men but to bide my time. I dispatched Ignacio and the greater part of my company to sweep the countryside round Walton and Orwell, burn Cottesloe and then assemble here in the forest. Many of these men have lived as outlaws or poachers. My only worry is whether LeCorbeil will walk into the trap.'

As if in answer, a horn wailed from outside and Fleabite, the butcher's apprentice who had somehow joined the Queenhithe company, stumbled through the door. He stood, hands on his knees, catching his breath, before straightening up and announcing that LeCorbeil had arrived. Again the horn wailed. Sevigny glanced around: they were ready. The two lines of bowmen spanned the nave, the reserve behind them on the sanctuary steps, with small groups guarding the postern doors. He nodded at Simon and they walked to the main door. Sevigny pulled this open, slightly dazzled by the sun pouring through, a possible weakness for the bowmen behind them. He shaded his eyes and stared across at the massed ranks of LeCorbeil, about sixty in number, all garbed in their blood-red livery, sallets hiding their faces, arbalests looped over the horns of their saddles, warhorses shaking their heads, blowing noisily or pawing the ground. He glimpsed the war cart pulled by four drays and caught his breath. LeCorbeil had brought a small culverin or cannon. They would use this against the main door and, once they gained entry, shatter any barricade or defence.

'*Pax et bonum!*' he called out. 'Peace and goodness. What troubles you? The battle is over. We still enjoy the King's peace and protection.'

'The battle is done,' a voice agreed, 'but not for all. It is Sevigny, is it not? Amadeus Sevigny, formerly chief clerk to the Duke of York? Come forward in peace, clerk. You are protected. No man will hurt you, at least not yet,' the voice added spitefully. 'Approach. Hear our terms.'

Sevigny ignored the whispered warnings from Simon standing just within the doorway. 'Prepare yourself,' he murmured. 'Perhaps I can learn something.'

He undid his war belt, placed it on the ground, extended his arms in a gesture of peace and walked forward. He could already see that some of LeCorbeil had dismounted and were threading their way through the tree-lined cemetery, searching for any weakness or opening in the church's defences. On the war wagon to one side, bowls of fire were in full flame and the culverin was being released from its cordage. He strode forward to greet LeCorbeil's leader, who nudged in his spurs and rode leisurely towards him. When they met, the Frenchman took off his helmet and Sevigny stared into the sallow, handsome face of the devil he knew to be Bertrand. He glimpsed hard eyes, a cruel mouth, and felt the sheer balefulness of a soul steeped in hate. Bertrand, however, acted all courteous, leaning down as he stroked his horse's neck.

'Master Sevigny, we have done business before. Our quarrel is not with you.' His voice rose dramatically. 'Or with many here. We demand the bodies of Simon Roseblood and his two sons.'

'Gabriel is a cleric, a Franciscan.'

'Roseblood and his two sons,' Bertrand repeated defiantly. 'If he surrenders the Argentine chronicle, his sons will live. If not . . .' He let the threat hang.

Sevigny stared round. Bertrand's company were already dismounting, arbalests at the ready. He realised that no mercy would be shown. These men were intent on battle, on killing and killing again.

'Go away, clerk!' Bertrand urged. 'Collect your warhorse and ride safely on. It is over. The King is taken, his snow queen caged, his great lords all dead, their bodies disfigured; only Buckingham survived. My lord of York is already marching on London.'

'You are Bertrand?' Sevigny squinted up. 'Yes? You abducted Katherine Roseblood?'

Bertrand sat back in his saddle, surprised. 'What do you—'

'I stole her from you.' Sevigny could feel his temper bubbling. 'Only one woman died in that hut. I rescued Katherine. She now shelters safely in London. I am not here to treat with you but to warn you: I will kill you.' Bertrand's hand fell to his sword hilt. 'Do not break the truce,' Sevigny warned. 'If you try, at least one of the bowmen who have arrows trained on you will kill both you and your mount.' He leaned up to cup the muzzle of Bertrand's horse. 'And that would be a tragedy.'

He waggled his fingers in farewell, turned, sauntered back, picked up his war belt and disappeared into the darkness of the church. Once inside, he leaned his sweat-soaked body against the cold stone.

'There are about sixty of them in all,' he murmured as Simon came alongside him. 'They are already breaking up, looking for the postern doors. The fire bowls are lighted, their culverin is fully primed.' He grasped Simon by the shoulder and gently pushed him up the nave.

They had hardly reached the line of bowmen when the assault began. The culverin loosed hot shot against the main door, while the posterns were battered with makeshift rams. All the defences held, though the main door, dry as tinder, not only bent, but caught fire. Under the incessant rain of shots from the culverin, assisted by LeCorbeil piling bundles of dry bracken against the wood, the flames roared up. Pouches of gunpowder were thrown into the blaze and the wood began to crack and shatter under the intense heat. The defenders within remained silent. Only a few arrows were loosed through the widening rents in the main door.

Sevigny was concerned that the posterns would break first and LeCorbeil would discover that the force within was much greater than they had thought. Bertrand, however, had made a fatal mistake. He truly believed that only a few panic-stricken defenders sheltered in this trap they had fashioned for themselves. Above all, he was impatient. The war wagon, on which a sharpened stake had been placed, was pushed up a makeshift ramp to batter what was left of the main door, which was flung back to hang askew on its thick leather hinges. LeCorbeil, now using the wagon as a shield, surged into the church. Over and around the wagon swarmed red-garbed bowmen, arbalests at the ready. They had burst in so abruptly, moving from sunlight to the gloomy nave, that they remained unaware of any danger until Simon screamed, 'Loose!' and a cloud of yard-long shafts whipped through the air.

The war wagon and the very speed of LeCorbeil dented Roseblood's surprise, yet the effect was still devastating. Many of the attackers, caught so close to their assailants, were flung back by the grey-feathered shafts that hissed continuously towards them. Corpses littered the wagon and the entrance to the church. The wounded jerked screaming, arms and legs flailing.

Once they realised what was happening, LeCorbeil hastily retreated, pulling their wounded out of the church. They then renewed the attack using the wagon thrust across the threshold as a barricade. They moved slowly, their arbalests taking a deadly toll on the massed English archers. Sevigny shouted at these to retreat deeper up the nave. The corpse door abruptly buckled and was flung back, and LeCorbeil crept into the church, using the shadowy transept pillars as a defence. Sevigny ordered a further retreat towards the ruined high altar, whispering to Simon to draw the enemy even deeper into the nave. The French company were now much depleted yet still determined. Sevigny quietly issued fresh orders, organising a small phalanx of bowmen reinforced by men-at-arms led by himself.

'Now!' he shouted. The phalanx moved out of the shadowy gloom, the bowmen loosing shafts as fast as they could before Sevigny and his men-at-arms charged through the ranks. Some fell, struck by the whirling bolts, but the speed of the charge caught LeCorbeil by surprise. They were preparing a second volley when Sevigny and his company crashed into them, sword and dagger thrusting in a frenzied, bloody hand-to-hand struggle. The nave rang with the clash of battle, groups and individuals locked in whirling arcs of steel. Simon had also committed his forces, and LeCorbeil became surrounded.

Sevigny felt the savage surge of conflict, the frenzied joy of combat, an eagerness to close and slaughter. The tension within him erupted. Screaming with sheer elation, he cut his way through, unaware of others around him as the red mist descended. He whirled his powerful razor-edged sword two-handed as both flail and scythe. Faces floated before him, but he smashed them out of the way, feet scrabbling for a hold on the blood-wet paving stones. He was back on that fateful dark night at his parents' manor house, but this time he could see Katherine standing beneath that tree, arms outstretched, waiting for him. He would not stop; those before him collapsed or staggered away with hideously gaping, blood-gushing wounds.

He was nearly there when Bertrand confronted him. Sevigny screamed defiance and closed. The Frenchman was experienced, yet he was no match. Sevigny danced, swerved, thrust and hacked. He summoned up all his skill, using every trick to confuse and confound the opponent. Then . . . nothing. He turned, whirling his sword, angry at the silent emptiness around him. Someone was calling his name. He lowered the sword, blinked and drew a deep breath. More shouts and cries. Figures moved about him; someone poked his shoulder. Sevigny stepped back, lifting his blade.

'Amadeus, it is I, Simon. It is over.'

Sevigny could feel his sweat cooling; his arms and legs ached. He lowered his sword and stared at Bertrand, flung back against a pillar, an ugly red gash splitting the side of his head and most of his face. He was dying, eyelids fluttering, lips twitching; then he jerked and lay still. Sevigny turned and gazed round the church. The fighting was over. The Roseblood company were looking after their own and cutting the throats of the enemy wounded.

'Some of them escaped,' Simon declared, pointing to the corpse door. 'Bertrand is dead, but their leader, Ravenspur, has fled back to York. We should not tarry long here.'

Sevigny shouldered by him and went and crouched next to Bertrand. The Frenchman's face was a mask of blood. The clerk became increasingly aware of what was happening around him. Simon grasped him by the elbow and led him into the nave of the church, where Master Bray, Raphael and Gabriel together with Wormwood and Ignacio were waiting. The corpses had been removed and their wounded were being tended in the ruined chancel at the far end of the church.

Sevigny squatted down with the rest and gratefully accepted the battered pewter cup of wine thrust into his hands. He drank deeply, nibbled at some salted meat and stared round. Roseblood and his companions looked worn and tired. Though elated by their victory against LeCorbeil, they realised that the royal cause had sustained a hideous defeat. York now probably held both King and Queen, and he would spare little mercy for Somerset and the others. No pardon, no amnesty would be given.

'What would you advise, Sevigny?' Simon asked. 'The battle is done, the day is dying and we must be gone.'

Sevigny took another gulp of wine; he could feel the warmth return. He narrowed his eyes, watching the dust motes dance in the fading rays of sunlight. He glanced back up the church and listened to the sounds of men outside preparing to leave.

'York has won the day,' he began. 'He and his Neville allies will show no mercy. He's probably dispatched Warwick to hunt down any leading royalists who've escaped. He will collect his forces, let them rest, then march on London. He will enter in glory, the conquering hero; his faction within the city will welcome him with open arms. The bells will ring, the incense clouds gust back and forward as hymns of thanksgiving are chanted in the churches. York will separate King and Queen and keep them under comfortable but secure arrest. Oh, he will act the part, the loyal servant of the King trying to protect the crown and the royal dignity, but in fact he'll be plotting furiously. He'll gain control of the

Tower and have himself appointed leader of the Council, which of course he'll pack with his own retainers. All appointments, both church and state, will have to be approved by him. Wouldn't you agree, Master Bray?'

Beaufort's man seemed numb with shock at the growing realisation that the family he had served so loyally faced catastrophe.

'Master Bray?' Sevigny repeated, 'Would you agree with what I have said?'

'Yes, yes, I would. The Lancastrian lords will retreat to their castles and fortified manor houses. York will not have it all his own way, but it will take months for the opposition to gather.'

'And London?' Simon asked.

'York will be prudent,' Sevigny replied slowly. 'Oh, he'd love to purge the city council, arrest those who oppose him and lop their heads off, but London harbours the mob. York doesn't want to stir this up. I suspect he will only target those who actually fought against him. Now,' he pointed at Raphael and Gabriel, 'like me, you are protected by both the Crown and Holy Mother Church as sacrosanct envoys; that's our reason for being here. Master Simon, I strongly suggest that your sons look after the Roseblood; you will definitely be a wanted man, having fought against York at St Albans. It's exile for you, at least for a while.' He paused, listening to the sounds outside. 'The sooner you go, the better,' he insisted. 'We must hurry you to the nearest port.'

Simon came over and crouched close to Sevigny, clasping his hand.

'And you, my friend,' the taverner whispered, 'must go to London. My sons will hold the Roseblood. I charge you with protecting Katherine.'

'I swear.' Sevigny gripped Simon's hand tighter. 'Katherine is my life, and she always will be.'